Series By Michele L. Coffman

The Alpha Evolution Series

The Battle for Liberty Series

The Universal Guardian Series

THE PURIFICATION

BOOK ONE
THE ALPHA EVOLUTION SERIES

MICHELE L. COFFMAN

Launch Point Press
Portland, Oregon

Copyright © 2021 Michele L. Coffman

ISBN: 978-1-63304-227-8
Ebook: 978-1-63304-036-6

First Printing: 2021

Editing: Kay Grey, Jane Cuthbertson, and Rob Bignell
Formatting: Patty Schramm
Cover and Book Design: Lorelei

Launch Point Press
Portland, Oregon
www.LaunchPointPress.com

THE PURIFICATION CAST OF CHARACTERS

Surface Survivors of the Apocalypse

- Christina Burgos- Young woman born and raised at CDC in Fort Collins
- Dr. James Burgos- Virologist, Christina's father
- Eva - Dr. James Burgos's wife, Christina's mother
- Jennifer - five-year-old orphaned girl
- Christina's friends from school: Stephanie, Adam, Gabe, and Brian

Bunker Survivors of the Apocalypse

- Trish Webber – Julie Webber's daughter, conceived and raised in NORAD bunker
- Dr. Julie Webber - Trish's mom, scientist who specialized in Biochemistry and Molecular Genetics
- Dr. Frank Webber - Trish's father, virologist
- Colonel Aralyn Williams – Head of bunker security, Trish's godmother who was Julie's "best friend"
- Captain/Major Rebecca Thomas - Aralyn's Second in Command
- Sergeant Jason Givens - Weapons specialist
- Lieutenant Carlen Strong - Specializes in electronics and programming
- Lieutenant Susan Travis - Specializes in medicine

- Staff Sergeant Stan Phillips – Specializes in maintenance and explosives
- Corporal Eric Leonard - In charge of Supply, youngest team member
- First Sergeant Todd Stevens - Weapons specialist

Additional Characters

- General Princeton - Director of Military Forces for the government
- Major Steven Porter - American astronaut working for the government
- Amy Daniels - Reporter for WDC9
- Major Reilly – John Reilly's dad, in charge of security on the bunker fifth-level, section B
- John Reilly - Major Reilly's son
- Dr. Jenkins - Trish's Genetics instructor
- Staff Sergeant Young - Medic
- Corporal Davis - Major Rebecca Thomas's team
- Lieutenant O'Brian - Major Rebecca Thomas's team
- Staff Sergeant Perez - Major Rebecca Thomas's team

To my daughter Ashley and my son Phillip

for filling my life with meaning, my heart

with love, and for always having faith in me.

And to my granddaughter, Michele, whose

extraordinary personality engulfs my heart.

PROLOGUE
APRIL 15, 2070

Lieutenant Colonel Aralyn Williams climbed down from the bus and glared past the swarm of confused and frightened others exiting a parade of buses pulling into an open field. She wanted to locate any landmarks which would reveal their location. Spotting a colorful insignia affixed to a three-foot stone monument and an inscription plastered on the outside of the closest building, she knew at once they were still in Colorado. They had been brought to the infamous NORAD bunker. She'd never been here before, but she knew enough to understand a troubling dilemma. The moment the fabled blast doors sealed, there would be no leaving until those high up in the government deemed it safe to do so. Probably years, and how many, Aralyn had no idea.

She removed her cell to try Julie Webber's number for the fifteenth time, since she'd been ordered onto the bus by soldiers with lesser rank than hers. Still no service. Aralyn couldn't head inside the bunker without Julie. She'd rather suffer through the nuclear aftermath than be safely locked away to never see her dearest friend again. The thought of living a life without Julie was too painful.

Only ten of her soldiers had been transported on the same bus along with a dozen or so strangers, none of whom were employees from the CDC where her unit was assigned. Doctor Julie Webber, Doctor James Burgos, and the other scientists were nowhere in sight. Aralyn had seen additional buses driving around Fort Collins before they left, surely others she knew would arrive before the drawn-out evening came to a close.

April 15, 2070. This was a day she would never forget.

If the global threat were at the disastrous scale the personnel who collected her had said, then it made no sense for the government to save her and those guarding the scientists at the CDC and not save the actual medical geniuses. Following a nuclear war, the researchers, scientists, and doctors were who would be needed to oversee post-apocalyptic cleanup once the bunker finally opened.

"Colonel Williams, they're waving us over," said Captain Rebecca Thomas, her second in command and dear friend. They'd met five years earlier during their yearlong deployments to North Korea, in a never-ending nightmare she knew she'd never forget. Aralyn was a Major then, and Rebecca a bright and shiny butter bar. During that bloodstained conflict, Aralyn secured the promotion to lieutenant colonel despite her young age.

Aralyn tossed her rucksack over her shoulder, her gaze sweeping through the thousands gathered, searching for anyone who resembled Julie. Temporary fencing encircled the multiple rows of parking lots and connecting fields, enclosing an area the size of two football stadiums sitting parallel to one another. The enclosure was split down the middle by an additional chain-link barrier, easily ten feet in height. The half to the right held red signs marking out fourth-level, and dark-blue postings labeled the left side with fifth-level.

Those masses inside each enclosure wore similarly colored armbands identical to the section to which they were assigned. Throughout both segregated areas, clusters were huddled by temporary drink stations or waiting to enter one of many restroom trailers while others picked at ration trays under canopies as massive as traveling circuses from years ago. But most were standing aimlessly about, eyeing the armed guards keeping everyone in line or too overwhelmed to do much but stare off into the commotion.

Before proceeding to the edge of a lengthy stretch of tables where many intake workers sat, Aralyn spotted several of her soldiers waving. She watched their movements from the fifth-level side of the fenced-in complex. Her excitement rose. Like them, maybe Julie was already here.

Aralyn stepped up to the table, and an emotionless woman gestured for her to place a hand on the portable tablet. The device beeped. Aralyn was a bit taken aback as her name and photo appeared along with a flashing *fifth-level commander* in black lettering. What exactly did that mean?

At once, the woman's humdrum attitude disappeared. "They've been expecting you." The woman waved over a guard standing behind the table. "Please take Colonel Williams up to the bunker for processing."

A man sitting in the next chair over passed Rebecca a dark-blue armband before directing her to the left-side fenced in area. Aralyn and Rebecca shared an uncertain glance.

Aralyn shifted her concern to the woman checking her in. "What about my troops?"

"They will follow you up, Colonel, just as soon as the fourth-level has finished housing their occupants. Shouldn't take too long. Three hours tops."

As if on cue, a trolly, pulling five sections of empty seating, emerged from the tunnels entrance, and headed down the road toward them. The guards in the fourth-level enclosure directed groups of families and individuals to meet the ride. Everyone else in the area nervously surveyed their departure.

Aralyn's focus shot to the woman sitting behind the table. "Has a Julie Webber checked in?"

The woman stared at her evenly. "Even if I had that information, which I don't, I wouldn't be permitted to tell you one way or the other."

Aralyn leaned forward, her eyes stern. "Then let me talk to someone who has the authority to answer simple questions."

The woman raised her chin and narrowed her eyes. "I beg your pardon."

"Colonel Williams!"

Aralyn spun to the sound of Rebecca's shouting, surprised when she saw the Captain was already inside the fenced-in area with the rest of their unit, at least with those of her unit who'd been brought here. Aralyn ignored a protest from the woman at the check-in table for holding up the line. She cupped a hand behind her ear to signal to Rebecca that she was listening.

"Private Jason Givens saw Julie and her husband Frank enter the bunker over thirty minutes ago," Rebecca called out. "She's here, Colonel. Did you hear me? Julie's inside."

Breathing an enormous sigh of relief, Aralyn gave a curt nod to the agitated woman at the table. She heard the woman grunt and mumble something under her breath, which was clearly meant to be insulting. Aralyn didn't care. Let the woman vent if she needed. Julie was safe, nothing else mattered.

CHAPTER ONE
MAY 4, 2070

The sun had set for the seventh time since Major Steven Porter had awakened at midnight. In less than forty-five minutes another sunrise would be popping up through the darkened horizon, shining light on the Earth below. Major Porter lowered his headset and pressed the button for the intercom. "Hustle up, people. Ten minutes to showtime."

After unfastening his lap belt, he slowly floated from the main console. His thumb brushed against the sheath under his jacket for the third time. Steven knew the blade was there, but still, the contact brought him comfort. He wasn't planning on using the weapon. The outcome could prove to be too messy. Yet, having the fallback was nice.

Steering his body through the abundance of rations and hygiene supplies affixed to the wall of the module, Porter drifted out into the additional section the space program added a few months previously. For the last ten years, top governments around the world had contributed generously to this ever-growing space station. The additional legroom was welcoming and so were the extra recreational amenities. Unfortunately, the stockpile of supplies and frivolous comforts meant the people calling the shots were preparing on leaving him and his skeletal crew up here longer than they had originally said.

He had been involved with the space program since January of 2059. In less than seven months, he was planning for a deserved, early retirement from a twenty-year life of military service. It wasn't until his higher-ups approached him two months ago that he understood his retirement would be on hold, indefinitely. They had, theoretically, given him a choice of turning down the assignment. But he knew with the gravity of the task laid out before him, if he had said no, they would have killed him. A design of this importance was far too fragile for loose ends.

Cosmonaut Alek Sidorov was waiting at the hatch for docking-station-six when Porter arrived. "You vatch game yet?"

Porter returned Sidorov's wave. Even with the thick Russian accent, Steven recognized a vast improvement in the commander's English since first meeting him five years ago. "Not yet," Porter replied, drifting closer to peer out the porthole.

The shuttle was less than ten feet from docking and would be attached in a few minutes. He glided his body away from the porthole. "Where's the rest of the crew?"

"Zey are on vay." The cosmonaut's eyes widened, and so did his grin. "Ah, speak of devils and zey shows."

Porter silently observed the other American astronaut, Rodriguez, Cosmonaut Faddel, and the Canadian astronaut Volkov as they maneuvered their way into the area.

His muscles relaxed. He moved aside to give Captain Rodriguez, the newer recruit, a front row view of the shuttle's attachment while Commander Sidorov manned the door. Porter momentarily locked eyes with Captain Rodriguez before drifting to the supply box. He undid the clip and pulled the injector gun from the container. "I want everything unloaded in record time," Porter called out over his shoulder.

Porter heard the metallic click from the hatch and turned the moment Commander Sidorov opened the first of two metal doors and stepped into the connecting section. When he opened the second hatch, an injector shot out from inside the shuttle and jabbed Commander Sidorov dead center in his throat. Captain Rodriguez was on Commander Sidorov before the cosmonaut had time to react.

Porter swooped forward and pressed the injector into Faddel's esophagus and pulled the trigger. The cosmonaut made a *humph* sound before going limp.

Doing a quick survey of the scene, Porter glanced at his watch. A Japanese astronaut exited the shuttle with a hard-plastic trunk labeled

Explosives and floated toward Porter, the crew's new commander. He lowered his head slightly before passing the secured, red container to Commander Porter.

Porter turned to Rodrigues and Volkov and said, "I want the rest of the virus unloaded and Faddel's and Sidorov's body disposed of within the next sixty minutes. People, we have less than two and a half hours until this station is in position. I don't need to stress to everyone how the survival of our governments, let alone the fate of the world, rests on our shoulders. We need to work fast, or else we'll miss our window."

Reporter Amy Daniels watched the display on the screen count down from ten. She shook her arms out at her sides seconds before the numbers reached *one*. She felt the surge of adrenaline as her heart raced. An uproar was going on all round her, but she did not worry about being heard above the crowd. The voice-activated mic was programmed for her vocals alone, while leaving a moderation of background noise for effect.

When the beep in her ear sounded, her smile broadened, and her customary greeting followed. "Good afternoon, Washington, this is Amy Daniels coming to you live on WDC9. I'm standing on the grassy strip of the National Mall, and as you see behind me, the dome of the Capital Building is shrouded with flags of the United World Task Force. The United States government, like everyone else on the planet, is using today to demonstrate their gratitude for the manpower and sacrifice the UWTF has contributed to humanity.

"With our world population just under eleven billion, resources are running low, and pollution has hit an all-time high. We, as a species, were heading swiftly to the brink of disaster. For the last ten years, funding for global advancements came to a halt when the frightened masses turned to their governments for help. After ten years of working tirelessly, the UWTF has solved our planet's food, fresh water, and pollution crises."

She inhaled deeply and touched her hand to her stomach. She wanted to cry, and laugh, and run with the groups of kids chanting their cute musical jingles to honor the UWTF. To stretch her arms out and twirl with the teenage girls, and drink, and eat, and kick off her shoes to feel the grass beneath her feet, whether the greenery was fake or not.

Struggling with her building excitement, she continued to direct her energy to the camera. "Businesses and schools all around the world have closed today. Volunteers are passing out free beverages and containers of food, and they promise, even with the thousands upon thousands here, there will be more than enough to go around, and you don't need a ration card to enjoy it. From what I'm told, it's the same all over the world."

From the studio, her co-anchor and husband Michael Daniels said, "Amy, our producers offered you several choices to air from. I'm interested in why you picked this specific one. Is there a significance to your location, or did you hear this was where the free adult drinks would be?"

Michael's lighthearted question echoed from her earpiece. His upbeat attitude wasn't surprising because this day would not only change Amy's and their unborn child's lives, but also ensure the survival of all of humanity. "I wanted to be here surrounded by the monuments our ancestors erected on the day the Nations of the UWTF chose to celebrate the end of our worldwide crisis."

"Amy, we have less than five minutes to go," Michael said, his voice sounding as excited as she felt. "We're displaying the countdown on the screen behind you now."

Was he thinking about the future of their unborn son? Even though she was still in her first trimester, and Michael wasn't ready to tell anyone, she knew he was happy.

Amy stepped to the side so she could glance away from the camera to the backwards rolling clock and keep track of time. "Thank you, Michael. WDC9 has been given permission to share with the viewers a video on how the firework pods operate."

The video played out on Amy's small monitor. She read the teleprompter beside it. "With the capsules needing to travel from space to Earth, engineers had to come up with a casing able to withstand the friction upon entry, which causes a heat of roughly three thousand degrees Fahrenheit. The pods will open and ignite the fireworks when they are five hundred feet from the ground."

Michael said, "What if one enters above a structure like the Empire State Building or the Eiffel Tower? Would it hit these obstacles before going off?"

Amy's grin widened. "Good question, Michael. No, the pods are designed to sense all types of obstructions, including earthly terrain like a mountain, and open five hundred feet above whatever surface the sensors detect. From what I'm told, the patent is still pending, so NASA couldn't go into too much detail." She caught sight of groups of jumping children behind her who were trying to secure their brief moment of fame on the news. She giggled and turned to the camera. "Although it's not dark out, the UWTF has assured us, even in the daylight, the exhibition will be visible. They're launching the capsules from the space station as it passes, so everyone around the world can celebrate the mark of a new world era within minutes of each other."

She shifted to face the camera squarely. "Now let's go to Commander Sidorov on the International Space Station. Commander, I'm told the ISS completes a full orbit around the world in ninety minutes. How are you and your crew timing the pods to be released within a twenty-minute window?"

The silence trickled, then the voice from her news producer followed. "Amy, our technicians are having an issue with ISS comms."

Amy did not lose her cheerful composure despite the update in her ear. In her line of work, she was used to switching gears on the spot. "It appears the ISS crew is loading the capsules now, but we'll follow up with them later. Me, personally, I would be interested to see footage of the capsules being released in space and sent to Earth. If they film their work, I'll make sure WDC9 airs it later tonight."

The commotion around her grew with the echo of voices shouting "*thirty*," then "*twenty-nine*, twenty-eight . . ."

Amy pivoted to the clock. "This is it. We are near the moment humanity celebrates taking back control from our failing Mother Earth."

The pale sky filled with a plethora of glowing light. A few seconds later, a faint crackling noise was heard. As the objects drew closer, Amy counted down from ten along with the excited crowd packed into the area. The moment the gathering hit "One," eruptions rang out overhead, and colorful displays showered down above them.

Groupings of red, orange, and purple exploded into pictures of planets, and the crowd *oohed,* and *aahed.* Red, white, and blue star shapes filled the sky, and the pandemonium was magnificent. When the five-minute grand finale of dazzling shades painted the sky, Amy's tears of happiness flowed, and those around her cheered.

Once the last of the pods ignited and the final fireworks trailed away, Amy beamed wide-eyed to the camera. "I can feel it. It's like a watery mist of life on my skin." She rubbed the droplets in and gladly accepted a jumping hug from a teenage girl beside her. "It's amazing. I wish you all were here to enjoy it. Now, I'm going to go eat, drink, and be merry with everyone else. This is Amy Daniels, signing off."

CHAPTER TWO
AUGUST 4, 2070

Doctor James Burgos replaced the slide on his microscope and rubbed his irritated eyes. He bent forward, refocused the magnification to a different setting, and inspected the image. The specimen was the same as the last fifty or so he studied earlier today. He jotted down a few notes and peered into the eyepiece. The long work hours and catnaps had taken their toll. He felt ten years older since the day the contaminated pods exploded three months earlier, leading to the cruel deaths of over six billion people.

Several of the virologists James worked with throughout the CDC went missing days prior to the capsules being released. Others died from the virus contained inside those capsules. He and a handful of colleagues were left to determine what the virus was and where it came from. Within the first few weeks, they discovered the virus had been genetically engineered from Ebola, Marburg, and some unknown RNA strand which appeared to be synthetic. Whoever designed the complex bug knew what they were doing and must have been working with unlimited resources.

The virus had a one-hundred-percent fatality rate within days of initial exposure, then spread through direct physical contact to others through bodily fluids of the living or the dead. The virus died out after the first month for two reasons. First, the pathogen was only able to survive for a few days in the virion stage outside the living host. Second, unlike the unmanipulated Ebola or Marburg strands, this virus was neither zoonotic nor vector-borne. James's published theory stated that whoever invented this monstrosity made it extremely lethal, but because of this, the virus was also weak when it came to its own survival.

"James, I brought you some dinner."

Spinning around in his seat, James stood. "Eva, you shouldn't be in here. It's not safe, especially in your condition."

"Our baby is fine, James. I'm more worried about you. You haven't eaten all day."

"I'm good. I'll eat when I'm done with this group." Even though he verbally protested, James removed his gloves and mask and allowed his wife to lead him from the lab, out to the seclusion of the hallway.

"I thought you said the virus is no longer active. If it's dangerous, shouldn't you be wearing your little yellow suit?"

Tickled by his wife's comment, James took the plate from his wife and kissed her on the lips. It amused him when his wife referred to his bulky protective gear as the *little yellow suit*. She made it sound insubstantial, like one of his scarves or hats.

"The virus is no longer active, but this doesn't mean I want you or my son anywhere near it."

Eva laughed. "Your son? Have you received a vision from God telling you the sex of our unborn child, or are you performing ultrasounds on my belly when I sleep?"

"No, I guarantee you, neither has occurred." James's voice held a layer of amusement. "But I have noticed, how all the names you've asked me to choose from have been for a boy." He bent and kissed her belly. "I assumed, since you were carrying this miracle, you knew something I didn't."

"That's because I've already decided on a name if we have a daughter, and I don't want to hear your arguments on the matter." She snatched the fork off his plate and skewered a bite of ham. "Now eat."

James's eyes widened, and he tilted his head. "If I promise not to add my two cents, will you tell me what the name is?"

Her paternal glow brightened. She shoved the meat in his mouth and waited until he chewed and swallowed. "I've decided on Christina for a girl, after my grandmother." She retrieved another morsel of meat and fed him again.

He tossed the fork on the plate and discarded his meal on a nearby cart. Before she could protest, he pulled her close and kissed her fully on the lips. Her body melted under his embrace, as it always had. Oh, how he loved this woman. When he broke the connection, his eyes locked with hers. "I believe Christina is a beautiful name. If we are blessed with a girl, it's certainly fitting she be named after the woman who raised such an amazing creature as you."

"Creature?" Her tone was soft, her eyes glistening with her love. She playfully slapped his cheek then curled herself into his arms. "I want our child healthy and strong, whatever sex it may be."

"I agree, but I cannot lie. I pray every night it's a boy."

When she jerked back, her frown changed with his laughter. "You're incorrigible."

A lab technician sprinted down the hall, heading straight for them. "Doctor Burgos, they're launching the pods again!"

Fear gripped James and his mind raced, trying to understand what was happening. Who could do this to humanity a second time? "Quick, sound the alarm. Then gear up. We need to go up top and collect samples."

The young man turned on the spot and raced away.

"No, James, I forbid it!"

James met his wife's frightened gaze. "Eva, you must lock yourself in with the others. If we're going to fight this, we need to dissect an active sample. I'll be in quarantine for the next two weeks, but know I'll be safe. I need to know you and our child are safe, too."

He kissed her on the lips and touched her stomach. "I promise not to take any unnecessary risks. I know what I'm doing, and I'll be extra careful, for you and our child. Be strong Eva, and please, do as I ask."

CHAPTER THREE
JUNE 1, 2075

The display on the door's monitor blinked *locked*, and Julie Webber wasted no time. She sat her daughter on the chair close by before removing her one keepsake from her past and lowering her bag on the ground next to her daughter's chair. Julie twisted the gear at the base of her grandmother's wooden jewelry box and opened the lid for her four-year-old to listen to.

"Can you hear the music, Trish?"

"Yes, Mommy."

"Good. You sit here like a big girl and I'll be right back. When I'm done, I'll take you to see the trees like I promised. Would you like that?"

Trish's eyes glistened with delight. "Real green trees? Will I be able to touch them?"

"Of course. We might climb one, but only if you're a good girl. Okay?"

The little girl's excitement grew. She focused solely on her mother's music box, as if showing her mother she could be good.

Satisfied, Julie rushed across the room to the wall safe and punched in her code. Even though nobody else knew the combination, not even her husband Frank, she was certain they would find a way to penetrate the locking mechanism. When the metallic *click* sounded and the door sprang free, she removed the stack of notebooks, ledgers, and computer drives. She ran to the closest lab table, deposited them onto the metal surface, then hurried to the hidden compartment behind her main desk. After saying the voice-activated code, the clasp unlocked. She pulled on the vacuum-sealed door, and when it opened, a chilliness touched her. She removed a loaded serum injector and a handful of vials containing the blue liquid representing her life's work.

The monitor to her lab *beeped* and fear froze her in place.

"Hey," a voice called out, "her lab's locked, I think she's in here. Doctor Webber, open the door please."

Forced on by her own personal crusade to destroy her cherished research, Julie went to the lab table and added the vials and injector to the pile of notebooks and drives. Hands trembling, she pulled open a side drawer. Shifting a few things around, she located a tiny hand drill and rushed to the lab's reinforced door. When the screws on the plate didn't turn, she inspected the drill. Cursing quietly, she rotated the tip from flathead to Phillips. After working all four screws free, she pulled the faceplate off and let it dangle by the multiple-colored wires.

Outside the door, a male voice said, "Doctor Webber, I believe your wife has locked herself in her lab."

Julie paused and stared at the door. This code her husband did know. She pulled the folded knife from her pocket and focused on which wires to cut. Damn, there were so many. Not wasting any time, she sliced through them all, and received a sting of a *jolt* from her impatience. She waited.

She heard multiple *beeps* on the other side and knew Frank was punching in the code. Thankfully, a *buzz* followed and not a *click*.

"Damn, she's locked me out. You, call up maintenance! We need this door opened."

Julie knew what was at stake, and because of this, she had to hurry. If they got their hands on her research, all hope for humanity would be lost. Without waiting any longer, she rushed to the table and grabbed up the pile of books and computer drives. She took them over to the dispenser by the sink and opened the top to the drum. She was careful when she lowered the items into the liquid, not wanting any of the acid to splash at her. She hustled back and collected the handful of vials and added them into the discoloring fluid as carefully as she could.

Julie rushed to her desk and waved a hand to activate the screen. She had insisted on a computer not connected to the network. This secrecy was the reason she agreed to continue her research when they'd arrived inside the bunker, five years earlier. They couldn't say no. Genetics bridging was her baby. She was the closest scientist they had to unlocking the potential for a marvelous human advancement. She hadn't realized until a few days ago what they had planned to do with it or how immoral this organization was.

Once the computer powered up, she wiped everything from the system. When she was finished, she focused on the cable behind her desk. Thinking she'd rather be safe, she knelt and unplugged the main drive and went to the tub of acid to dispose of the metal box. She waited until the liquid blackened as the device slowly melted.

Going through everything in her mind, she tilted her head to the side. She remembered placing the vials in the fluid, not the serum injector. She crossed the room to inspect her desk. She then checked all around the lab table, even in the drawer where she'd retrieved the drill. She was sure she pulled the injector from the hidden cooler with the vials, but maybe in her haste she forgot. Making her way over, she searched inside the cold box. Nothing. She must have already thrown the contraption in.

Only one last thing left to do. Julie removed a tiny drive from her pocket and studied the area, searching for an ideal hiding place. If she could come up with an excuse believable enough to spare her life, then possibly, after she faced the wrath from destroying her work, she could come back for the drive or send Aralyn after the hidden proof later. Others needed to know before more people died.

Her body grew cold. "Trish?" Where was her daughter? She rushed forward and peered behind the chair. "Patricia, answer me!"

"Mommy, it hurts."

Julie's gaze darted to the corner, and panic filled her chest. Even as she skidded over in front of her daughter, she could tell by the absence of blue in the clear window of the injector lying on the floor: she was too late. She scooped up Trish and removed her tiny hands from clasping the thigh of her right leg.

"It's okay, honey, Mommy's got you." She lifted the pantleg to see a red bump surrounding the prick of blood from the injection site. She pulled Trish close and her eyes watered. Not wanting to worry her child, she fought against her tears.

"Are we going to see the trees now?"

Julie breathed slowly, struggling with the urge to be sick. What would the serum do to Trish? Would the concoction kill her? Change her? She had used her own lipids for research, so maybe when Trish's body rejected the infusion, it wouldn't be as violent as what the other test subjects experienced. She thought of each of the mice, and she shuddered.

She heard sounds on the other side of the door and realized they would be entering soon. She needed to leave her daughter in God's hands and finish what she came here to do. After returning her daughter to the chair, she fiddled with the jewelry box. She flipped the heirloom over and worked at opening the bottom panel enough to place the chip inside. Once the panel was secure and the jewelry box was stowed in the bag, she ran for the injector.

When the door *beeped*, Julie spoke firmly to her daughter. "You cannot tell anyone about your leg. Do you understand? Not even daddy."

Trish nodded as the door slid open.

Clutching the injector, Julie rushed for the acid container.

"Julie, stop or I'll shoot."

She raised the injector. Two impossibly loud shots rang in her ears. Each one struck painfully into the middle of her spine. She tossed the injector even as she lost her balance and fell, striking the hard floor. The sound from the splashing of liquid was followed by a calming sense of cold and intense pain. She sensed movement all around her, but as the pain drifted away, so did her hearing. Her daughter's crying face appeared in her vision, and Julie gave her tears a weak smile.

"Hush my sweet girl, can you hear the music?"

Julie's chest constricted as someone removed Trish from her sight. She believed the someone was her husband, but her vision was blurring. She hoped for her daughter's sake Aralyn would find the proof, expose Frank for the monster he was, and take Trish safely away to care for her like she was her own.

Julie's eyes remained open as she took her last breath.

CHAPTER FOUR
JUNE 1, 2088

The fist struck hard, dead center of her chest, and Trish stumbled a few steps backwards. Not wanting to be caught off-guard a second time, she repositioned herself before the next series of attacks commenced. She dove under a leg and jabbed but was too slow to hit her mark. She spun in time to avoid rapid punches and pivoted to swing her leg up for a kick of her own. Her movement was less than a fraction off, and a fist shot outward, striking her again.

Aralyn gestured for a break. She ran her hands through her damp hair. "What's up with you today, Trish? Your entire form is off. You're not focusing and you're making carless choices which leave you vulnerable. Do we need to return to the basics? Let me know. I can pull out the boxing gloves if you want."

Trish frowned. She clenched her jaw and glared. "I had a long night finishing my homework assignments and I'm tired. I don't feel like training today." She moved off the mat and slouched her way into the locker-room, ignoring her name being called out from behind.

Today was June 1, 2088. Thirteen years earlier, on this very day, her mother had been killed in her lab. Being around people today, even Aralyn, was not what Trish wanted.

Trish sat on a long bench and stared down at her bare feet. She wished she were in the privacy of her room, curled up under the security of her blankets. She heard footsteps approach and braced herself for the verbal lecture she was about to receive. When none came, Trish glanced sheepishly to Aralyn.

Aralyn stood, examining her. She eventually lowered herself onto the bench. "I know what today means for you, Trish. I hoped the training would keep your mind off the memory of it, at least for a short time."

Trish gave a long sigh. She unwrapped the tape from her knuckles. "I can't picture her face anymore, Aralyn. I'm not even sure if the few memories I have of her are real."

Aralyn sat for a moment, then stood and went to her locker. Trish watched her retrieve something from the pants pocket on her neatly pressed uniform, but she couldn't tell what the item was. When Aralyn returned to retake her seat, she passed Trish a tiny box, which fit in the palm of her hand. "I know your birthday isn't until next week, but seeing as how you're becoming a young woman, I've decided to give you your gifts early this year."

Trish grunted when she fiddled with the green ribbon wrapped around the present. "I don't think seventeen brands me as a woman. If we were living before the worldwide attack eighteen years ago, I wouldn't be able to vote until next year, or drink until I was twenty-one." Not that either of these mattered inside the bunker. Alcohol was forbidden, and the government had switched from democracy to dictatorship overnight. The day the nuclear bombs of the Global Annihilation fell, their society became ruled by a committee of eight, comprised of key members inside the Presidential Administration.

"Trish, you're not like other seventeen-year-olds. You're advanced in so many ways, maturity certainly being one."

"I wouldn't know."

Aralyn shook her head. "Enough with the pity-party, now open your present before you hurt my feelings."

Trish's hands worked off the ribbon and removed the lid from its base. Inside was a golden chain with a matching locket. "It's beautiful. Thank you." She worked hard at keeping her voice an octave higher than her downcast mood.

"It opens, the real gift is inside."

Trish used what little thumbnails she had at her disposal to separate the clasp. When the locket opened, she knew instantly, the beautiful woman smiling back was her mother. "Where did you get this? I thought all her photos were destroyed?"

"I kept it hidden until you were older. No child deserves to have her mother erased from her life."

Biting her bottom lip, Trish wiped her eyes with the palm of her hand. "Best gift ever," she whispered.

"I'm glad you like it."

Trish cleared her throat, trying to remove the shakiness in her words. "Aralyn, do you believe my mother was a traitor?"

Aralyn waited for a moment before answering. When she finally spoke, she bent in closer and kept her voice low. "Julie Webber was one of the finest people I knew and a dear friend. She always put the welfare of others before herself. No, your mother was anything but a traitor. Like I've said before, you must never mention her name to anyone, especially your father, do you understand?"

Trish's mother had been Aralyn's closest friend, even before the Global Apocalypse, when Aralyn was stationed at the CDC in Fort Collins to oversee defense. She was the only link Trish had to her mother. When Trish agreed to stay silent, Aralyn rose. "Good, now no more despairing talks. Get cleaned up and we'll go see your other presents."

"My other presents?"

Trish's question was met with a wink.

She watched Aralyn snatch her shower bag from her locker and towels off the stocked shelf and head toward the secluded section in the back. Trish blinked several times and gently touched the picture. She wished she could remember the feel of being wrapped in her mother's arms. Even though her memory was virtually absent, one thing she was sure of, her mother had loved her. Any time she tried picturing her, or even recalling the tiniest of details from their past together, Trish always experienced a warming sense of calm and affection.

With her father, the relationship was not loving or tender, if any relationship existed at all. He was hardly in her life, and his brief appearances always revolved around discipline with the belt he left hanging by the bathroom door as a warning, or an addition to the rules which kept his daughter confined. Trish eventually developed the understanding that her father showed himself solely out of obligation for a daughter he regretted having. He wouldn't allow her to attend classes with the others her own age, since she would have to leave this section of the fifth-level to do it. Instead, he assigned her a tutor who was as cold as her father was himself.

She did have most of section A to explore when she wasn't studying or doing homework. She knew her limited level of freedom was due to Aralyn, who had always served as her godmother, was the closest person Trish had to an actual parent. When Trish was eight, her father had loosened his restrictive grip and allowed Aralyn to train her. Aralyn had insisted Trish's body needed a chance to build muscle and burn off energy. Aralyn had also argued how keeping a developing child too secluded was mentally cruel, even for Frank. Aralyn was the head of security throughout the entire fifth-level and had a knack for getting what she wanted.

Hearing the water turn on in the showers, Trish closed the locket and retrieved her own bag from her designated locker. Section A on this level had the least number of occupants and the largest quarters. Even though there were two gyms in this segment, which housed fewer than a thousand people, many of the residents were older and worked in labs like her father. They had no time for the gym or the individuals who frequented them who were usually Aralyn's security staff and a few of the lab and medical technicians. Countless times when she and Aralyn trained, the place was empty.

Trish showered and changed into her dark-blue utility pants and matching T-shirt. She laced up her sneakers and threw on her jacket. The bunker maintained a constant temperature of sixty-five degrees Fahrenheit. The thermostats in the individual quarters could be adjusted a few degrees up or down, but no more. Many people regularly wore their uniform jackets because of this. For Trish the cooler temperature was never an issue. She wore it for the additional pocket-space it offered.

Her father claimed the uniforms were to make life easier for everyone while they lived inside the bunker for the twenty years Earth needed to repair itself from the twenty-year winter. Aralyn had told her the different colors were a way for those in charge to verify people were where they were supposed to be. The higher-ups, like her father, dressed in business suits. Security was issued black-and-green camouflage uniforms, medical had red or black scrubs, and the rest wore outfits like Trish's, but in a different color for each level, except for maintenance and janitorial staff who wore a drab brown color no matter where they were assigned.

She inspected the photo one last time before placing the locket in her pocket and making her way to Aralyn who waited for her in the corridor. They marched in stride with one another, passing the chlorine stench from the pool, the laundry section, which always carried an odor of soap bubbles and bleach, and the scentless clatter of the canteen. Most of the meals were heated in their prepackaged containers and opened by each individual after leaving the grab-and-go line. On Christmas, and the fourth day in May marking the world's new Thanksgiving, the stoves fired up and a succulent wave of all-out cooking aromas filled the pale-gray hallways.

When they came upon the tinted, bulletproof walls of security, Aralyn stopped at the entrance and swiped her hand over the panel. Registering her handprint, the door slid open, and they hastened inside. Trish heard the rapid fire coming from the range down the hall and silently wished today was Tuesday, the single day out of the week her godmother assigned her to a security rotation to train with handguns. She doubted her father knew, and she sure wasn't going to tell him.

"Colonel Williams, I was getting ready to page you."

"What is it, Sergeant?" Aralyn asked, taking the clipboard Sergeant Jason Givens held out to her.

Trish grinned at Givens's wave and hurried behind the partition he was assigned to give him a hug. She'd spent most of her life, since her mother died, with the security personnel in this section under Aralyn's command. They were her only friends, and some, like the older weapons specialist returning her embrace, considered her the child they helped raise.

"When did you intercept this?" Aralyn asked.

Givens spun all his attention on his commander. "Last night, on the same secured line. Colonel, does this mean what I think it does?"

Aralyn scanned the pages once more. She handed the clipboard to Givens. "Sergeant, we'll discuss your findings later with the others." Her somber demeanor shifted. "Can you grab Trish's present from my office?"

His eyes widened as he scanned both women. He frowned. "Her birthday party isn't until next week."

"You're throwing me a party?" Trish said.

Aralyn scowled at Givens. At once, the man moved through the door behind the desk.

"The celebration was supposed to be a surprise," Aralyn said, shaking her head at Trish.

Trish clapped her hands together. Other than the exchange of gifts, people didn't have parties in the bunker. They weren't forbidden, but personal social gatherings were frowned upon. "I'll act surprised."

"*Humph.* I knew someone was bound to ruin all our planning. I figured it would've been Lieutenant Strong or Lieutenant Travis. I guess my faith in Sergeant Givens's tight lips was misplaced."

Stretching, Trish threw her arms around her godmother. "Even though your secret is out and I still have to wait a week, thank you."

Aralyn shifted her weight. She patted Trish awkwardly on the back. "Okay, enough. Your display of affection will weaken the fear I've instilled in my soldiers.

Trish knew the soldiers felt no fear of their commander, but instead, respect. At six-foot-two, Aralyn often referred to herself as the dark-skinned Amazon, but those who took orders from her secretly dubbed her their Warrior Queen. She was a force to be reckoned with and stood her ground to defend her staff whenever needed. Trish knew Aralyn's soldiers would charge into Hell if she asked. Trish would, too, the more she thought about it.

Trish released her grip but held her glow of admiration. "You're too badass for that."

"Language!"

Trish rolled her eyes. "I'm a young woman now, remember?"

"Being a woman doesn't mean you can talk like a drunken sailor."

Trish raised her brow in question.

Aralyn sighed. "Never mind."

Givens bustled through the door. "Ma'am I wasn't sure if you wanted me to bring up everyone's gifts or not, so I collected yours and mine and left the rest."

When Trish pivoted to the approaching Givens, her excitement grew. "You're giving me my own crossbow?"

Givens held the weapon out to her. "Several of us had a hand in the construction, but the initial designed came from the colonel herself."

Accepting the tactical bow, Trish marveled at the lack of weight. Black, like the ones she'd fired on the range numerous times, but the body was thicker in shape.

Givens pointed out a few of the retrofitted features. "The colonel had me construct the body to double the automatic reload from three bolts to five, but you feed them in the same way. This here is a safety switch, yes, so push . . . okay, you've got it. You can store five more bolts on either of the side mounts, and even though the bolts are an inch shorter, and the crossbow feels lighter, I guarantee the firepower is as fast and deadly as the ones in the armory." He pointed to the notch beside the safety switch. "Same with the others, if you run out of nitrous, here's where you attach the handle to hand crank tension into the string."

Trish flipped it over and saw her name carved into the bottom compartment where the nitrous capsules and handle were normally stored. She gave Aralyn another hug. "It's beautiful."

"Hey," Givens said, "I helped."

Trish laughed and awarded him with an embrace of his own.

"Here's the extra quiver and sling. I've finished thirty bolts so far, but I'll make more before your party." Givens pulled out a black pouch, the same carrier their security staff used on the utility belts, and handed it to her. "I also crafted you your own throwing knives. Now, you can stop practicing with mine."

"Wow," Trish said. Before she could thank him, the exterior door beeped and opened, and Lieutenant Carlen Strong strolled into the room.

"Have you heard anything new?" Lieutenant Strong stopped and smiled inquisitively at Trish. "Why aren't you with your tutor?"

Trish glanced at her watch. "Oh, I've got to go before I'm late."

Aralyn said, "Trish, hide those gifts in your quarters first."

Trish hurried toward the exit, throwing a rushed goodbye to those in the room. If she made it to class late again, she knew her evening would be filled with a great deal of additional homework.

Relaxing her body, Trish floated for a few seconds before slowly sinking into the clear chlorinated water. No matter how hard she tried, her muscular body refused to keep her above the watery surface. Swimming had been her Achilles heel since her lessons began at the age of five. She and Aralyn had spent extended hours in the pool for Trish to learn how not to drown. She had to rely on her muscles to maneuver through deep water, and when she went under, the strength in her limbs was what brought her up to the surface. If she wanted to relax and float like others, she needed something to assist her. Today, she used the edge of the pool.

She stretched out her limbs, closed her eyes, and focused. Once again, her brain reminded her of the piles of homework waiting in her room. She tried blinking it away, but as her legs and lower body submerged, the image of her tutor's scowl pressed her farther under. She allowed her entire body to retreat into the pool's depths. When her feet contacted the bottom, she kicked off hard and shot upward.

She reached the top with minimal effort and grasped onto the ledge. Pulling her upper body out of the pool, she rested her chest on the concrete floor while her legs dangled in the coolness of the water. She relaxed her arms and laid her cheek down into the pooling puddle and closed her eyes.

She had never understood why Mr. Sourpuss disliked her, but their relationship had been a difficult alliance since day one. When she was six, and he realized she had a photographic memory, able to read and comprehend five thousand words a minute, his assignments more than tripled. By thirteen she'd finished the required classes of prewar high school, something every student in the bunker was compelled to do. She went on to specialize in Biochemistry and Molecular Genetics like her mother. Her father had protested her decision of not following him in the field of Virology, but on this aspect of her life, she held her ground.

Her tutor worked with other scientists in the complex to devise the proper ways to teach her. On occasion, the unpleasant man allowed her to work in labs with the same scientists who were eager to educate a hungry, youthful mind such as hers.

An older geneticist, Doctor Jenkins, who she usually shadowed, had once told her the bitterness of the man responsible for her education came from his lack of intelligence compared to her own. She had laughed off this belief at first, but by the time she was fifteen, she realized her advanced intelligence had, in fact, intimidated the man. When she tried to approach this subject to ease the tension between them, the failed attempt made matters worse. Her mounds of homework and extra schooltime both increased, and he rarely took time out of his lectures to answer her questions. She kept her head down and did as she was told with the knowledge these extensive work hours would make her mentally stronger in the long run.

She wiped away the droplets on her watch and realized she had been in the pool longer than her tight schedule allowed. Plopping the upper half of her body into water, she kicked off from the wall and swam toward the far side of the pool. The moment her hand touched the ladder, the door to the pool room opened and she heard hushed giggling.

A woman's voice said, "Seriously, you two need to keep it down. If they catch us, we'll get into trouble." Her voice was young, a teenager maybe.

"Stop worrying and live a little. No one's going to find out. The snobs in this section never go swimming." This voice was deeper, masculine.

"Exactly how many times have you snuck in here?" asked the woman.

Trish peered over the ledge at a teenager. He shrugged. He was close to her own age with a scruff of a beard on his square chin. The other boy looked older, his chin covered in a dark beard.

Scruffy-beard said, "Four or five times, and anyone I pass has never given me a second glance. So long as we act like we belong, we'll be fine."

Trish lowered her head and sank a few inches into the water, weighing her options. The two guys and the girl all wore the same dark-blue uniforms assigned to the fifth-level, so they had to be from a different section, but why were they here?

"Oh wow, the pool is bigger than ours," said the girl. "The cushions on the chairs, elegant murals on every wall. I can't believe how well they live. My god, even the trees in the planters are real. Come feel this. How do they keep them alive? I don't see any UV lights, do you?"

"See, I told you. The water's warmer, too."

"Is that alcohol? Where did you get it?" The other male voice was deeper than the first.

"I have my connections," she said, "and now let's enjoy the pool while we can."

When Trish heard rustling from above, she realized they were all undressing. She had to make a move now, before naked bodies plunged into the water behind her. Taking a breath to steady herself, Trish climbed the ladder to the sight of the woman, already in her T-shirt and undies. Scruffy-beard was about to remove his briefs, and their third companion, with no shirt on, was chugging a mouthful of drink from a red plastic container, clearly the alcohol they'd mentioned.

The guy guzzling choked on the beverage when he saw her, and the other two froze in place. Ignoring their surprised expressions and exchanges of worried frowns, Trish casually meandered over, and retrieved her towel. "The water's a tad cool today, but still refreshing," she said, drying herself off.

She slipped into her shoes and was about to head to the locker-room when Scruffy-beard recomposed himself. "Who are you? I've never seen you in class before. With a body like yours, I would've remembered."

The young woman punched his arm.

"What?" he said in a peeved tone. "Do you know who she is? It's not like we have a large section of classrooms. Everyone knows who goes to the fifth-level school, and she doesn't." He whirled toward Trish and moved a foot closer. "Do you even live on the fifth-level?"

"John." The other guy reached out and seized his friend's arm, but John shook the hand off and said, "No. Our parents earned the right for us to be on this level, so upper-level scum shouldn't be here. If she lived on five, we would know her. I bet she comes from level four."

"John, look at her face. Who does she remind you of?"

"My God, you're right," said the woman. "What was her name? Webber? You remember, John, the traitor. We studied her in sixth grade."

John frowned at his friend, then squinted at Trish. Trish clenched her fist and tightened her jaw muscles. They *teach* about her mother in school? She pictured rows of faces laughing as malicious images of her mother were displayed on wall screens.

A grin spread across John's lips. "Wow, your mom's famous. How does it feel having a traitorous bitch for a mother?"

The man beside him sniggered. He took a long drink from the container and tossed the alcohol to the woman. "Careful, John, I think you're making her mad."

The girl giggled, and the high-pitched vocals played on Trish's anger. She wanted to rush in and defend her mother's honor, to strike out for the pain her heart was feeling at their loose words and ill-mannered attitudes. She knew she couldn't. She had promised Aralyn a long time ago never to reveal her full strength or to lose control while she remained inside the bunker. Aralyn had told Trish she was different, special, and if her father found out, her limited freedom would be gone. Because of this, Trish always cantered away from even the mildest of conflicts. She restrained herself during training and never lifted heavy weights inside the gym when she worked out in the presence of others.

Pressing her lips together, Trish headed toward the locker-room, but stopped when John moved over, blocking her way. She stared at him for a moment, then sidestepped to go around. When he shifted his position to block her again, the other two snickered. This fueled him on. He made a fake jump, like he was getting ready to move aside, but changed his mind.

"Okay, John. Let her pass. I want to go swimming." The woman's sigh resembled a long, drawn-out moan.

Trish spoke through clenched teeth. "Yes, John. Move aside. She wants to go swimming."

Slowly, John tilted his head, but his eyes remained fixed on hers. "I don't believe I like your attitude. Do you know who my father is? Major Reilly. He's in charge of security on the fifth-level, section B."

Trish glanced lazily upward, then to John. She snapped her fingers together. "Is he the short, baldheaded guy who has a constant bead of sweat on his upper lip? Yes, I've met him several times. He works under my godmother, Colonel Williams. Do you know who *she* is?"

John's cocky facade twisted into a blend of uncertainty and concern.

"John, we should go," said his companion, and the woman instantly agreed. John took a few moments to decide, but eventually, he moved out of Trish's way.

She started for the locker-room. Without warning, John hooked his foot around hers, taking her off guard. She stumbled forward and fell, striking her head hard on one of the stone planters a tree was housed in. The impact shot instant pain throughout her head and down to her jaws.

"Hey, what are you kids doing?" Trish heard the voice but didn't recognize it.

She detected multiple sets of running feet behind her and knew the three were fleeing the area. When her eyelids parted, she was on her back, and a warm wetness obscured her right eye. She moved to sit up, but a figure beside her held her in place.

Coarse material was pressed onto her forehead, and the throbbing pain became even more intense than before.

"Don't move, Trish, you took a severe blow to your head."

Trish brought her hand up and used a piece of the cloth to wipe her eye. "Doctor Jenkins, what are you doing here?" She moved her hand and applied pressure on the towel with his guidance.

"I swim on the evenings when I'm not working in the lab, which isn't often. Usually, everyone else is gone from the pool area by then." His concentration flashed from the door the teenagers had dashed through to her. "Trish, do you know who those kids were?"

"I've never seen them before."

Using a balled-up towel, he elevated her head. "All right, I'll let security handle it. You stay here. I'm calling to have the hospital send someone to get you."

Her breath caught, and she sat up straight. "No need. I'm okay. It's only a scratch."

"Trish, you have a gash which will need stitches and a possible concussion. You're going to the hospital whether you want to or not. Or I can call your father. Which would you prefer?"

Trish tried to think of a way out of either of those choices. Aralyn had stressed, under no circumstances, was Trish to have her blood drawn or any test run, unless by Doctor Harris, but he had been moved to a different section last month, and she wasn't sure where. "Can you get Colonel Williams instead?"

He shook his head. "I saw her head to the sixth-level for their weekly meeting. She'll be unreachable for most of the evening." He eyed her curiously. "Is there any reason you don't want to go?"

Trish wiped the red smear of blood covering her hand on her bathing suit. "I don't like having my blood drawn. It makes me queasy."

He laughed. "You work around bodily fluids all the time when you're in my lab. Is having your own blood drawn the issue?"

She nodded.

"My baby sister was the same way. Like you, she could get a cut and be fine, but if a needle went in her veins, vomiting or unconsciousness always seemed to follow. Don't worry, they'll give you something to deaden the area for the stitches, but they shouldn't need to take any blood. Can I call them now?"

When she nodded again, he gave her an empathetic pat on the knee, and went to use the area phone.

Trish was wheeled into a hospital wing where the reek of disinfectant blending with the odor of sweet sickness stained the air. Instinctively, Trish brought her hand up to cover her nose. Feeling rude, she lowered her hand to her lap and tried breathing through her mouth. She had been here a few times with Aralyn to see Doctor Harris when she was younger. Even though years had passed, she didn't remember the air smelling so foul.

The white tile floor matched the hallway along the main corridor of the bunker. Trish tried focusing on the tiny gray lines separating one tile from the next to distract her mind from the stench.

She wanted to leave, to jump up from the wheelchair and run from the room, but she couldn't. Doctor Jenkins remained by her side, and she knew he would notify her father if she did. Not because he was a bad man who wished to see her punished. Truth be told, he didn't know how unpleasant her relationship was with her father. How could he? No, her Genetics instructor was genuinely concerned for her wellbeing.

When two members of the medical team rushed by, the wheelchair stopped, and Trish lifted her eyes to see they were both in black scrubs, gloves, and masks, and were running with arms filled with various medical supplies. Once they passed the reception desk, they paused long enough to use the hand scanner to open the door. The instant the door slid to the side, a scream was heard, and then another, followed by a nauseating stench.

Wide-eyed, Trish leaned forward, but she couldn't see anyone injured. The scene was blocked by a cluster of people wearing scrubs or surgical gowns and a few in business suits. As the two carrying the provisions rushed inside, the sea of people parted to give them room.

Trish's eyes widened and her body turned numb. She made a move to stand, but the woman pushing the wheelchair pressed her down. "Not yet honey, we're almost there."

She lowered herself in her seat, trying to make her form as insignificant as possible, but when the sharp-blue eyes of her father locked onto hers, she knew her prospects of concealment had come and gone. The door heading to the adjacent area shut, blocking out the screams and commotion. Trish held her breath and waited. When the wheelchair started rolling again, Trish released the air from her lungs, but her eyes remained fixed on the door. It didn't open. He clearly saw her, but he must be too busy to come check on her. Whoever that horrible-smelling screaming wraith was, was more important to him than Trish was.

Thankfully, the woman wheeled her in the opposite direction, through a different set of doors and into a private exam room. The space was floor-to-ceiling white, which made the lights appear much brighter, and furnished with an exam table, an ugly, brown chair, a sink surrounded by a few cabinets, and the standard medical devices one would expect to see in an exam room. The woman locked the wheels on the chair, and she and Doctor Jenkins each secured an arm to assist Trish onto the bed.

"You know, I'm feeling so much better. I can always come get checked out later if you guys are busy."

The woman folded up the wheelchair and placed it off to the side. "Nonsense. You have a nasty head injury. I'm the physician's assistant, and I'm not letting you out of my sight. Whatever's going on in the east wing, we have more than enough staff to handle it."

Doctor Jenkins cleared his throat, and the PA veered a probing frown toward him.

"She gets ill when she has her blood drawn," he said, throwing Trish a wink.

The PA lifted the stethoscope from around her neck and listened to Trish's chest and back. "Don't worry, I'll order a CT and give you a few stitches. You won't need any blood work done." She inspected the temporary dressing on Trish's forehead. "Let me replace the gauze, you've soaked through this dressing already."

"What is this?" a loud, deep voice hollered.

Both Trish and the PA jumped at the unexpected shout. The PA pivoted smartly around. "Oh! Doctor Webber, you gave me such a fright."

Trish's heart sank when her father entered the room. His piercing-blue eyes paled with his displeasure. "Why is my daughter here?"

Doctor Jenkins stepped forward. "Frank, your daughter was attacked in the pool area by a group of teenagers, but I managed to scare them off. I informed security and they believe the deviants were from another section. They're searching for them now."

Doctor Jenkins patted Trish on the arm. "Since your father's here, I'll take my leave. If you need to reschedule our lab training on Thursday, I'll understand."

Her father stared at the PA briefly, at Trish's head, and then glared at Doctor Jenkins. "Have my daughter escorted to her room when you're finished. I'll follow up with security later."

Doctor Jenkins opened his mouth to speak but then hesitated and closed it.

"Yes, sir," said the PA.

Trish felt the woman remove the tape off the dressing, yet her gaze didn't leave her father. Her anxiety lessened drastically when he turned to leave.

Of course, he would leave. His time was too valuable to be wasted on a teenager, especially his own daughter. She knew he had made an appearance solely for the benefit of others. He wouldn't want people thinking he failed as a parent. The truth could tarnish his pristine reputation.

"Oh my, I don't understand."

Trish glanced to the PA holding the blood-covered dressing. Doctor Jenkins did too. His mouth parted, and Trish studied the confused expression on Doctor Jenkins face. He bent in closer and touched her forehead. "That's impossible."

Trish's concern shot quickly between him and the PA. The injury must have worsened. Her hand moved directly to her forehead. When her fingers found the site where her forehead had impacted the concrete, she felt nothing but skin. No swelling was present, nor was there an open wound for blood to seep from. A crusty line ran lengthways an inch or two, but was so minute, she wasn't even sure if the blemish was a wound or dried blood. She pressed her fingers in, poking, prodding, and no feeling of discomfort emerged. She pushed in harder, and still she experienced no level of pain.

"How bad was the injury?"

Her heart raced. She hadn't noticed her father reenter the room, or move a few feet beside her, but there he stood, glaring directly at her.

Doctor Jenkins frowned. "She had an opened gash deep enough I could see bone."

"It's true," the PA said. "I showed up not long after he called us, and I physically saw it."

Trish felt her body grow colder. She watched her father pull his communicator from his inside suit pocket and punch in something on the screen. When he was done, he replaced the hand-held and casually waved them to the door.

"Thank you for your help. My staff and I will take over her care."

CHAPTER FIVE

"I said, *no more*." Trish sent the tray flying across her father's lab.

A stocky man holding an unused syringe jumped to the side. Before the tray, the empty vials, and medical equipment smashed onto the gray epoxy-coated floor, Trish was off the bed and standing on slightly shaky legs. She removed a medical band from her wrist and threw it to the ground.

"Listen, you little turd," the nurse said, "your father personally told me to draw your blood every three hours and take mouth swabs. This is his call, not mine."

"You go tell my father, this is *my* body, not his, and I said no."

The heavyset man glared. He slithered around the bed, snatched the tray off the floor, and went to the cabinet to remove several more vials. "I don't care if it's Saint Peter's body, I'm doing my job even if I have to physically restrain you to do it."

He shuffled forward. She backed up and centered her footing. When she raised her arms to defend herself, the nurse stopped advancing and slid the vials and syringe in his scrub pocket. He was a few inches taller than her five-ten build, and from the bulges under his overstretched outfit, by her guess, he never used the gym. He grabbed for her arm, but she exploded to the side and shifted backwards.

"I've let you poke me with your needles for—for, I don't even know how many days! And you still haven't told me *anything*. So, for the last time, I said no."

He examined her in silence, then raised his hands in surrender. "Fine. You're right, you deserve—"

He broke off and rushed at her. Trish spun away, and his arms came up empty. She pushed over a wheeled medical cart which landed with a shattering *bang* on the unyielding floor. The neatly folded towels and packaged medical supplies scattered all around. She swiftly lengthened the gap between them. He scurried across the mess and toward her. When she pivoted out of the way a second time, she pulled a blood pressure machine down in front of him, and he stumbled over it.

He was still half in a lunge and didn't stop his body's momentum in time. He crashed face first into the far cabinets and tumbled to the ground. A moan escaped as he struggled to his feet. He reeled to her, a splotchy-red hand covering his bloody nose. His eyebrows pulled together to make a bushy streak of hair. Through red and watery eyes, he shot her a piercing glare of hatred but didn't say a word.

She squared her shoulders and smirked. He made his way to the line of counters by the bed and removed a set of keys from his pocket. With a shaking hand, he unlocked a wall cabinet, removed a single-dose vial containing a cloudy liquid, and pulled an injector gun from a drawer.

He's going to try to drug me, Trish thought as she watched him insert the vial into the gun. Before she could decide what to do, a *click* echoed from the door behind her, and she whirled to see her father in his well-pressed suit. He lingered in the entryway, eyeing his daughter's defensive stance. She was prepared to react but remained motionless as his glance drifted over the muddled mess around her and the nurse with a face streaked with blood.

Frank locked eyes with his daughter. "Are you quite finished?"

"I want out of here. I'm done being your lab rat."

Frank moved to his workstation and deposited his notebook and medical folders in the top drawer. "You have your mother to blame for this."

Trish clenched her fist tight, and the sliver of her nails cut into her flesh. "Unlike you, my mother loved me," she murmured, trying hard to contain her rising temper.

She felt the pinch on her neck and brought her elbow back hard, striking the nurse dead center of his nose with a *crunch*. Wide-eyed, she spun around. The nurse screeched out in pain. With the additional flow of blood, he dropped the injector gun and stumbled backwards.

Her stomach churned. Had the dose been given? She couldn't tell. The injector was rotating in her vision, picking up speed. She blinked several times and refocused. The injector gun wasn't twirling—the floor was. Frightened, Trish swayed forward, trying hard to steady her balance. Her peripheral vison became blurred, and she staggered toward the door. Before she could raise her hand to the scanner, her vision went black, her body went limp, and she fell into a cloudy sea of darkness.

As a shaving of light slowly penetrated her slightly parted eyelids, a muffled noise intensified until Trish recognized the sound to be words. She tried to swallow but couldn't. She felt paralyzed from head to toe; even her mind stood sluggish. Her hearing seemed to be the lone body part working. Without any comprehension, that part was useless. She concentrated on separating the tones of the voices, trying to jumpstart the neurons in her brain so her mind would function. The effort was exhausting, and she had to fight the urge to drift off to sleep.

"Can you see the resemblance? Look at the edges."

The unique pitch wasn't her father's voice, even though she was positive she had heard his guttural tone before, but from where? Was the sound coming from behind her? No, but something was. She'd heard a *beep* a moment ago, she was sure of it. There it was again.

Someone else was talking, and Trish steered her attention to what the person was saying. "I see it, but it's not the same as the original virus. It's different."

Was it a woman speaking? *Beep.* Or a man with a tone gentler than Trish was accustomed to hearing?

"Maybe it's the same virus, but it evolved."

Beep. The voice definitely came from a woman. *Beep.* The rhythmic beeping behind Trish grew irritating, and she tried to drown it out. The more she tried, the more focused she became, and her eyelids widened a little farther. Again, she fought to swallow, but couldn't.

THE PURIFICATION | 39

The man's response was matter-of-fact. "Whatever pathogen this is, we know our vaccines are useless against it." Trish finally pictured the man connected with this voice. He was a scientist who worked under her father's supervision, but she couldn't remember his name. She'd stopped going into her father's lab when she was around five or six.

"I know," the woman said. "We'll need to work on a new vaccine as soon as possible. We have two years left until the rest of us go topside, which should give us plenty of time."

"Doctor Webber doesn't want us to start on one yet. He's intent on reconstructing his wife's serum from his daughter's DNA."

Her DNA, Trish wondered? They were running tests on her because of her DNA. Why? She understood then why she was there. Her father was keeping her anesthetized so they could perform their experiments. But why would her DNA be the key to her mother's serum? Was it inside her, housed in her cells? Had her mother used her as a lab rat as well? Trish tried to swallow again. For a moment, she thought she might gag.

The woman said, "What about the teams we've already sent up top? Are they coming back?"

"No. Doctor Webber said if they don't continue their pre-scheduled workload, we'll have to remain down here longer, and nobody wants that."

"What about those creatures?"

"The teams will be fine. They're sending up more troops for security, and they have bigger weapons. Don't worry."

"They better have. I'm told our patient shot the creature six times with his revolver before he was attacked and infected, and still, someone else had to kill it."

"I don't doubt it," said the man. "Our specimen has been infected for fourteen days now, and already his bone density and muscle mass are increasing. Not as strong as Doctor Webber's daughter, but pretty dang close. And his body's still developing."

Trish opened her eyes wider, and she was able to make out the image of the two individuals in gloves, gowns, and masks. They were sitting at a wall-to-wall counter on the other side of the room mulling over images on separate microscopes. She was still in her father's lab, but she wasn't the only occupant. Another bed paralleled hers an arm-length away. A man in a ripped and raggedy security uniform lay on top. Trish focused harder on the unconscious man, and when her eyes adjusted, her panic increased. So did the beeping behind her. The thing lying on the bed wasn't a man at all—or maybe it once had been, but not anymore.

The woman scientist swiveled in her chair, and Trish swiftly closed her eyes. She heard the rubbing of leather and knew the woman was now standing. "I think she's waking. I'll give her another injection."

"I gave her one thirty minutes ago. She's probably having a bad dream."

Trish wrestled with her building anxiety. As time ticked by, the noise coming from her vitals machine steadily decreased.

"Hey," the woman said, "have you noticed the pustules on this guy's neck?"

Wheels were rolling, and Trish heard more stretching of leather. The male scientist must have stood. "Oh, that's new. Get a sample and we'll run some tests."

Before either could move, the door opened and someone shouted, "On the ground! Both of you, get on the ground now!"

"Colonel," called out a soldier in a combat bodysuit, "Trish is here."

Trish opened her eyes as far as she could. Three of her godmother's soldiers were zip-tying the scientists' hands behind their backs. When Aralyn entered the room, Trish wanted to cry out her relief, but she choked instead.

Aralyn, armed with a handgun, scanned the room, then rushed to Trish's side. "Lieutenant Travis," she barked out, "I need you over here."

Trish's eyes gyrated upward toward Susan Travis's gentle reflection. Susan performed a quick inspection, then stroked Trish's hair. "I'm going to give you something to help bring your body fully out of sedation before I remove the tube. You'll gag for a bit, but I promise, you'll be fine."

A tube? So that was it. She was intubated. No wonder she felt so helpless.

"Hurry up, Lieutenant," Aralyn said. "We need to move."

"Okay, here we go." Susan pressed an injector into her neck. Trish, acutely aware of the tube in her throat, began to choke.

"Patience," Susan said. "Just breathe . . ."

The tube came out, and Trish coughed a few times and took in gulps of air.

"Well done, Trish. Now let's get those arms and legs moving."

"My DNA," Trish croaked out. "My mom's serum is in my body." She took a breath and coughed violently before continuing. "They have samples."

Aralyn touched her arm. "We know. We're destroying everything now. Work with Lieutenant Travis. We need you up and able to go in the next five minutes. Everything's ready, even your bags are packed. We're leaving the bunker."

"My mom's jewelry box and—"

"Trish, don't worry. I have all your things."

By the time Trish was sitting up, flexing her fingers and toes and drinking an energy shake, Susan was able to help her into a combat bodysuit the soldiers had set aside for her. She slipped into the boots and Susan laced them. When she stood, Susan gave her another shake and said, "I want you to drink this as we move. Stay right beside me and try to lose the nervous expression on your face. The rest of level one and two is leaving the bunker tonight to go topside, and we're blending in with them. We'll meet the rest of our group at the vehicles. Understand?"

Trish nodded. She was a little wobbly, but by the time they exited the lab, she felt considerably stronger, though her throat still hurt, and she had a hard time speaking clearly.

They moved down the hall and stopped in front of the double-wide elevator, waiting for the others. She was startled when a wall of flames flickered into the hallway from her father's lab. Then her godmother and three of her soldiers emerged and headed toward them. The lab door slid shut and the wisps of smoke and fire disappeared.

Safely inside the elevator, Trish downed the drink and tossed the package in the corner. The soldier beside her offered her a full rucksack. "Here," he said in a deep voice, "all the soldiers are issued these. Carrying them is mandatory and you need to blend in. Is it too heavy?"

Trish held it by the straps. "No, the weight isn't bad at all."

"Good. Now here's your utility belt and helmet. When we get out in the open, I want you to lower the visor until you're in the vehicle. By the way I'm Staff Sergeant Stan Phillips, the colonel's go-to soldier on the fifth-level section D." He spoke to the soldiers on either side. "Who's got her R19?"

A soldier in the corner muttered, "Here," and passed it to him.

Phillips held up the weapon. "The others tell me you know how to use this."

"Yes, the rifle part. I haven't yet fired the grenades on the range." She fastened the supplied utility belt around her waist then wiggled into the rucksack.

He snorted. "The restrictions on the range sucked, didn't they?" Bringing the rifle closer, he showed her the switch on the side. "You flip this for grenades. It's loaded to max capacity of ten. But don't use it."

Trish gave a slight nod. "I won't, I promise."

"Keep your rifle with you at all times and leave the switch on safety unless told otherwise. I'm serious. Even if you use the bathroom, you take your firearm with you. Your gear is top-of-the-line, and it will help keep you alive and well, but you need to respect it." He handed her the weapon and pointed to her helmet as the elevator doors opened. "Put that on."

She did as she was told, then remained beside Susan when their group moved through the hallway. The corridor was narrower than the one on fifth-level, and as they passed many of the empty rooms, Trish noticed how the doors swung inward, unlike her level where the doors slid open and required a handprint pass. The bays inside held numerous bunkbeds and rows of lockers. The setup was the same throughout each section on this level.

They came to a stop behind a group of more than a hundred soldiers and personnel, all waiting in front of a metal door that stood over ten feet in length and width. Ideal protection from the Global Annihilation years ago, she thought. When it opened, Trish saw how the barrier was several feet thick, and a matching door stood on the other side, less than fifteen feet from the first. A rudimentary sally port. A group of around thirty shuffled through the entrance, and the door closed with the sound of a metallic *click*.

She looked around and saw Susan fidgeting with the pouch on her utility belt. Staff Sergeant Phillips redistributed his weight from one leg to the other. Someone close by kept clearing their throat, as a handful of others whispered soft-spoken prayers to the ground or ceiling. She wondered if the bulk of the masses gathered were as worried about what awaited them on the other side of the door as she was. What was left of surface life after a twenty-year winter? And since only eighteen years had passed, was the planet even safe to roam upon?

Other than pictures or videos, Trish had never experienced the beauty of the planet like most of those gathered here. Being conceived and birthed behind walls of concrete, her knowledge of mother nature's splendor had been nothing more than photos on a page or recordings on a screen. But even those had offered her imagination countless hours of wonderful daydreams and a chance to mentally escape when her own life pressed her down. Would all her hopes and dreams be shattered once she stepped outside?

Close to five minutes later, the door reopened, and another group entered. The corridor behind Trish filled with additional personnel, all quiet and edgy about leaving the seclusion of the bunker.

Finally, Trish and Aralyn's group stepped through the doorway and waited for the metal structure to seal itself and the next one to open. When they passed through the second door, they came out onto a dome-shaped cavern with white, freshly painted walls and a solid black foundation. The clean black and white contrast gave the wide tunnel a crisp appearance. To the right was an opening to a huge cavern where multiple vehicles were lined up, uninhabited, and to the left, the tunnel snaked around a bend, trailing from sight. Numerous pipes ran overhead, and several groups of personnel in orange vests were passing out plump packages to everyone exiting.

"Bless you for your contribution," said a middle-aged woman who held out a flimsy nylon pull-string backpack. Trish thanked the woman and accepted the bag. She lowered her visor and followed Susan and the others to an awaiting tram.

After taking a seat next to Susan, she spotted a colorful sign above the entrance they had come through: *Cheyenne Mountain Complex, Colorado.* Right below the red, arched lettering was a larger word in blue: *NORAD.* She wanted to lean over and ask Susan what the letters stood for, but she remained in a robotic state, not wanting to catch anyone's attention. She sat silently and stared forward like Susan and those around her.

Once the next group of people exited the bunker and boarded the sectional vehicle, a driver climbed in and the trolly moved. The ride was slow, and Trish did her best to keep her inquisitive eyes from roaming. As they approached the end of the cave, a gust of wind blew under her visor, and Trish's pulse raced. She closed her eyes and breathed in the different odors filling her nose. *Freedom, this wonderful aroma is what natural air smells like.* The odor of dirt, like what filled the planters in the pool area, was so overwhelming, she wanted to raise her visor, jump up from the trolly, and go explore. To see actual trees and run her hands across their texture. Learn all the earthy fragrances the planet offered above the confines of their concrete and steel prison. *This was it. They were finally leaving the bunker.*

When the trolly came to a stop, everyone but the driver climbed off. The trolly drove past the guard shack and swung around in a wide circle before heading inside the cavern. A guard saluted Aralyn, took the paperwork she handed him, and performed an in-depth inspection of each page. He returned the papers to Aralyn and waved her group through.

The moment Trish cleared the opening, she froze in place. Her entire body shivered with delight as the vast night sky twinkled down at her. So many stars glittered through the shroud of overhead darkness that the sight was mesmerizing.

Susan nudged her forward and whispered in her ear, "I promise, once we're away and safe, you'll have time to drink in the beauty of this planet."

"I thought, because of the twenty-year winter the sky wouldn't be so dazzling or smell so fresh."

"We'll go over that later. Now we need to follow Colonel Williams to our ride outta here."

They proceeded to a far cluster of ten jet-black, armor-plated vehicles, each with an intimidating weapon mounted on top and a pulley system attached to the front. They were semi-boxy in shape and impressive in both length and width. She wondered if she'd need a step-stool to get in. By the luxurious design and overbearing firepower, their ride looked as if the military couldn't decide whether they were building a state-of-the-art tank or a souped-up SUV.

Trish spotted Sergeant Givens climb from the driver's seat of the lead vehicle, open the passenger door behind him, and wave her over. Susan muttered her consent and Trish happily obeyed. She pulled off her rucksack and clambered in. A whiff of fresh leather and lemon greeted her.

The interior was spacious with two rows, three seats per row, located directly behind Givens and Aralyn who were seat belting themselves into the driver and front passenger seat. A generously stocked storage area was located in the very back, which was packed from floor-to-ceiling with black duffel bags. Trish figured if they folded the seats inward and emptied out the storage area, four grown men could stretch out comfortably for the night.

She checked the safety on her rifle and held on to the smaller pack, wondering what was in it. Squeezing the bulk of the bag, she felt what she assumed was water bottles and heard the rustling of plastic. She placed it on the ground between her feet.

Through the tinted windows, Trish watched Susan make her way around to the other side. Trish leaned over the empty seat and grabbed

Susan's rifle, then stretched out a hand to help pull her in. Not that Susan was out of shape. She was five-foot-five with an athletic build, and like all the soldiers under Aralyn's command, she kept herself fit for duty. But their equipment was awkward, and the undercarriage of their ride stood a good two feet off the ground.

"Thanks," Susan said as she stripped off her rucksack and dumped it on the seat between them.

Nobody jumped into the seats behind them. Givens turned on the headlights and started up the engine. Filling the front console, green and blue lights of various shapes and designs haloed in the darkness, and a twelve-by-twelve-inch monitor dropped from the ceiling between Trish and Susan. Mimicking Susan, Trish attached her weapon to the quick-release mount next to her, used the power button to recline her seat to the maximum setting, surprised by how comfortable the leather seating was. She fastened her seatbelt but seeing the guards standing by the final opening in the wraparound chain length fence, she left on her helmet. She didn't think they could see in, but she played it safe, just in case.

She remained motionless until their convoy approached the last security gate. As soon as the guard gestured them through, Trish removed her helmet and bent closer to Susan. "What does NORAD stand for?"

Susan lowered her window with her nose raised, taking in the scent drifting in as the vehicle picked up speed. "North American Aerospace Defense Command. The base was used by the United States and Canada for aerospace defense and warnings. In 2060 they closed the base for expansion of the facility."

The faint sounds of sirens blared behind them. Twisting in her seat, Trish saw numerous flashing lights rotating on fifty-foot-high poles surrounding the complex. The gate their convoy had just exited closed, preventing anyone else from leaving. She spun to the front, uncertain of what to do. Should she ready her weapon, throw her helmet on, what?

From the front seat, Aralyn angled her head around, and offered Trish a reassuring smile.

CHAPTER SIX

Trish awoke to a hand massaging her arm. "Trish, we're here."

With heavy eyes, she scooted up in her seat and yawned. Her throat still felt scratchy, and her tongue's texture was a thin film of plastic against the roof of her mouth and tasted bitter. She removed a flexible canteen from her utility belt and took a drink. "Did we pack any toiletries? I need to brush my teeth."

"Yes, and I do too." Susan unfastened her seatbelt when the vehicle stopped. Let's get inside, and we'll shower and change. I doubt you had one during all the time you were in your father's lab."

"Exactly how long was I sedated?"

Susan took a deep breath. "It's June eighteenth. You've been out for two weeks."

"Two weeks?" Her own words sounded as hollow as her chest felt.

Aralyn peered over the seatback, her expression sour. Was she sad or tired? Trish couldn't tell. "I'm afraid Lieutenant Strong's right. We couldn't free you until they sent another group out. We wouldn't have made it past security." Aralyn turned to Givens. "Sergeant Givens, spread the word. We're taking the remainder of the night to rest and collect ourselves. We'll have a meeting at zero-six hundred tomorrow." Aralyn opened her door. "Trish, you're with me."

Trish exited the vehicle. Despite having slept for a while, her body felt heavy and slow to respond to her brain's orders. Whatever she'd been sedated with, some of it must still be in her system. For two weeks? She was under for two weeks?

She threw on her rucksack, grabbed her helmet and the other pack off the seat, and slung the rifle over her shoulder. She knew she felt estranged from her father, and when it came to his daughter, he had never seemed to care much. Yet, to leave her unconscious and dependent on machines for half a month—how could he! She was still his flesh and blood. Didn't this bear even the slightest bit of pull on the strings attached to his blackened heart?

Resentment pierced her. She slammed the door, tightened her fist, and bowed her head against the black metal. "I'm done with you," she whispered, more mentally than verbally. "I hope I never see you again."

She kept her head low as she followed Aralyn. Trish didn't glance up until they were almost at the structure. She heard a *clanking* behind her, and her eyes explored the commotion. Two of the soldiers were closing a gate, separating their group from the rest of the world.

In the spill of light from vehicle headlamps, she noticed an abundance of overgrown weeds poking their heads up through the driveway of gravel she trod upon. The ungraded, stony path stretched from the fence all the way to a metal door embedded in the hillside. From what she could see in the darkness, the area on the other side of the twelve-foot chain-link fence, with concertina wire rolling along the top, was filled with clusters of trees and open fields. Her heart ached when she pictured herself touching a tree. She wished her mother were here to see the way the wind stirred the leaves on the swaying branches.

Shifting her gaze from what little landscape she saw, Trish maneuvered around a few of the lead vehicles crammed into the area.

Aralyn was at the door gazing down at her left wrist. A holographic screen hovered directly over her black and silver wristband. Curious, Trish drew closer and eyed the contraption. An inch above Aralyn's wrist, a picture of a map hovered, bright-blue and semi-transparent like the computers in NORAD. The display was roughly the size of the pieces of bread they consumed on Christmas. Yet the device Aralyn wore was no more than two-inches wide and about half-an-inch thick and fit the wrist like a carefully formed glove.

Aralyn used her thumb and index finger to enlarge the map on the phantasmal screen.

"What is that?" Trish finally asked.

Aralyn tapped on a yellow glowing dot twice, then scrolled through a list of commands. "Our way into the supply bunker," Aralyn said, and at once, the door *clanked* three times, then slowly swung toward them to reveal dim light inside.

The door was shorter and not as thick compared to the bunker entry they'd left, but still, Trish felt a sickness building in her stomach. The last place she wanted to be was inside a concrete, windowless fortress, which lay covered under a mound of earth, sealed behind a steel, reinforced door. The bunker might not be as drastic as NORAD, but the idea of it still felt like an airless prison.

She stepped off the path to take a breath of clean, fresh air.

When the gathering of soldiers followed her godmother in, Trish backed up even farther to give them more space. The air around her grew thicker with every breath. She squeezed the bodysuit covering her hands against the growing dampness forming on her palms.

"Hey, would you mind giving us a hand?"

Trish's body jerked, as if awoken from an interrupted dream-state. She whirled, facing the soldier who had spoken to her in the elevator. Like most of the troops who followed Aralyn, he was in his early-to-mid-forties and matched Trish in height, with a slight peppering of grey along the sides of his hair directly above the ears. Similar to the seasoned soldiers Trish was raised with, he carried himself as if he were constantly observing his surroundings, preparing for and anticipating the worst.

He held up his hands and laughed. "Easy, I come in peace."

"Oh, hi, Stan . . . I mean Sergeant Phillips." Her shoulders relaxed and her cheeks grew warm. "Sorry, I guess I'm not excited about being locked away again."

He lowered his arms, his tone sympathetic. "Several of us feel the same, so we volunteered to take first watch." He gestured to the opening of the underground fortress. "These bunkers were constructed to hold a company of thirty guards comfortably, where we have forty-two in our group. It'll be a tight squeeze in there. Might as well wait until everyone gets settled and claims their floor-space."

Trish remained silent until more than half of the soldiers had disappeared inside the mouth of the cavern made of stone and steel. "Does NORAD know about this place?"

"Unfortunately, they do. We discovered the government built and stocked bunkers like this all over the United States, to help sustain society when they reclaimed the land."

"What about my father? Those in NORAD? Won't they come after us?"

Phillips grinned wide, as if proud. "That Lieutenant Strong—I believe her name is Carlen—she did several clever system hacks before we left NORAD, including planting false data inside their network to send them on a wild goose chase. This should give us some time to get ourselves settled and a plan hashed out before they catch on. To be honest, with our group, I almost feel sorry for whoever they send."

Trish observed the last two soldiers enter the bunker. No, she wasn't looking forward to going inside in the slightest. "What do you need me to do?"

"First, go drop your gear in the vehicle you were assigned to, but keep your rifle and helmet out. You'll need them. I'll have someone run in and tell the colonel where you are."

Doing as he said, Trish went to the armor-plated vehicle and opened the rear hatch. Every inch of storage was utilized with the black duffel bags, and each was labeled with either a name or category of contents. About to close the hatch, she spotted her own name on a duffel sitting between a bag marked *rations*, and another branded *medical supplies*. She stretched her arm out and rubbed her hand across her name. Her jewelry box and locket were probably inside.

Fighting the urge to pull the duffel bag from the organized pile and search through the contents to reassure herself her cherished items were packed, Trish closed the hatch and went around to her seat. She tossed both her rucksack and the extra nylon bag on the floorboard. Slinging her weapon higher on her shoulder, Trish clutched the helmet and shut the door.

Aralyn was talking to Sergeant Phillips when Trish rounded the next to last vehicle. By the scowl on her godmother's face, she wasn't happy. Trish stopped and waited. She didn't want to go into the bunker. Whether the tartness of her mouth repulsed her or her body screamed out "wash me," she wasn't ready to leave the earth beneath her feet nor the open space surrounding her.

Once Aralyn reentered the bunker, Trish made her way over to Phillips, who was rubbing the back of his neck.

"I'm really sorry," she said. "Did I get you into trouble?"

He let out a long sigh. "No, not really. The colonel's upset because she's worried about you. I think she feels guilty for not getting to you sooner. You understand, she didn't have a choice."

Concerned, Trish studied the bunker. "I know she didn't. She's been a mother to me for most of my life, so I'm sure she came to get me as soon as she could. The last thing she should feel is guilt." Trish shifted uncomfortably. "Maybe I should go inside and talk to her."

"The colonel is a grown woman. She'll be fine. I told her you needed some more time outdoors before venturing in, plus, guard duty is a great opportunity for training. You know how she is—a stickler on being prepared."

"Training? On what?"

He flicked his head for her to follow and they strolled their way toward the fence. "Young one, you have so much to learn, and I'm not talking about the crap they teach you in school. You need to know how to survive and live in a world none of us are truly prepared for." He stopped at the fence. "What did you notice about the soldier strapped to the bed in your father's lab?"

"Nothing about his skin was normal," she said, thinking back with a shudder. "The texture was tough, scaly even." Her stomach churned as she recalled the image. "On parts of his head he was missing clumpy patches of hair." Lowering her voice, she glanced out at the darkness before continuing. "His mouth and hands were what frightened me, though. His fingers were long and curved into claws. I couldn't see his nails, but I had a feeling they were long, too. And his mouth . . ." She shivered. "His mouth was too small for his teeth. Like they weren't even his, but if he was once a normal guy, I don't understand how his body could change so fast."

"Something happened eighteen years ago which, we believe, wiped out the world's population, and not a nuclear attack like we've been told. Whatever occurred, there are things out there that are extremely dangerous, especially since we don't fully know what they are, or how they evolved. Also, the leadership in the various bunkers like the one we left have not merely lied to the population inside, but probably had something to do with the creatures out there."

"Bunkers, as in plural? There are more?"

"Yes. The device the colonel and a few of the others are wearing not only shows where over two hundred supply bunkers are located in the United States alone, but it lists the location of twenty colonized bunkers throughout North, Central, and South America that the United States occupies. We're sure the other countries of the task force have them as well."

"The task force?"

Phillips eyed her carefully, clearly surprised by the question. "Yes, the UWTF. In 2060, the United World Task Force was appointed from the leading nations trusted by most everyone on the planet. Did they not go over any of this in school?"

Trish shrugged. "I didn't attend the normal classes, but my tutor talked about the rising pollution. He said the world's food and fresh water supplies were struggling to sustain the overpopulation on the planet. That several governments had band together to resolve the problems, but then the terrorist attacks happened. I watched videos from social media showing the panic before the bombs fell, then some of the devastation after, before everything topside went dark."

"When we came to NORAD, we were shown similar videos. Fake propaganda is what they were." Phillips sighed. "This task force was meant to put an end to our worldwide crises, like the pollution and supporting the population you mentioned. For ten years they told the world they were working on a solution. Then, two weeks before the first of May 2070, they started filling bunkers.

"Soldiers were ordered to go. Others—doctors, scientists, engineers, people who had no idea what was happening—were scared into vehicles with threats of a worldwide nuclear attack. I heard some were forced onto buses at gunpoint without their families. Those they deemed worthy anyway. The rest, the billions left . . . they're gone. Purified from the earth is my belief. Slaughtered by those who were supposed to save them."

He picked a flower and pulled off the petals, one right after the other. "I was stationed at Fort Carson at the time, working on testing prototypes for the Army. Next thing I know, I receive a call from my commander telling me to report to the motor pool. A bunch of us from the base were loaded onto buses and taken to NORAD. I was engaged to a woman who had two beautiful little girls." He threw the stem at the fence and recomposed himself. "I'm not sure why they picked me, all I know is most of us had no idea what was happening. No warnings, nothing. We believe the UWTF is the reason those left topside are gone, vanished. I don't know, maybe some have survived, probably hiding, but almost eleven billion people? And no contact. Where is everyone? Maybe the creatures got them."

Trish couldn't believe what she was hearing. She squinted out into the darkness on the other side of the fence and wondered if the creatures were watching them now. Were they dangerous? Maybe they'd been provoked. When something appears foul, it doesn't necessarily mean it is. Were all the people who lived outside the bunkers dead, or were they turned into creatures like the one who infected the soldier from the lab? Could there be survivors?

Phillips let out a tense laugh and slapped her on the back. "Look here, I've gone and frightened us both. Whatever happened, we can't change the past, but we can ready ourselves for the future. You need training, and I—Staff Sergeant Stan Phillips—am just the person to teach you."

"I don't mean to come off as being rude, but I'm not a soldier, and using ranks with last names feels impersonal to me. Would you mind if I called you Phillips?"

His grin was genuine. Trish understood why he was among the troops Aralyn brought with her.

"Phillips at your service. I specialize in maintenance and explosives. You might say I'm a Jack-of-all-trades, yet master of two. The Colonel put me in charge of your training."

Trish returned his smile and shook the hand he offered her. "Civilian recruit, Patricia Webber reporting for duty."

He spent the next hour going over how the bulletproof suits worked, as well as the helmet's functions. He explained the bodysuits were constructed during the ten years the bunkers were being built, and he was one of the volunteers who had tested them. When he first pressed the button that sucked her helmet in and sealed the wearer against unwanted contaminates, she was caught off-guard and began to hyperventilate. He had to reassure her the suit allowed her to breathe with no undue restrictions. When the night vision on the helmet engaged, she was able to see the second fence line surrounding them, more than three hundred yards away.

"You can wear the suit underwater and it does provide oxygen if you're not more than seven feet down, but let me tell you, it sucks. It feels like running a five-k while plugging your nose and breathing through a single straw. I wouldn't recommend staying under for more than five minutes or dropping lower than seven feet if you don't have the attachment on. I believe we have a few of those with us. I can show you later how the oxygenized pack works once we're settled."

The idea of being able to breath underwater, to remain under without fear of drowning, to explore the aquatic life in a river or ocean . . . The concept for Trish was awe-inspiring.

"Now, this suit keeps you semi-warm and toasty down to twenty-two degrees Fahrenheit, and they say it'll keep you cool in temperatures over a hundred and five, but by the time the temp hits ninety-eight, most of us are sweating."

"Do I need to clean it?"

He laughed. "I ask politely, as someone who doesn't want to smell month-old body sweat coming from the person standing beside him, please do. I make a spray that works well, but wiping it down with soap and warm water is as good. I've packed you two others suits, another set of boots, and a second helmet. The supply bunkers may have more, I'm not sure yet."

"Wow, really? I've never seen my godmother or any of the soldiers wear anything like this until tonight. They're probably not hanging in everyone's locker. Are you sure you can spare three?"

"Of course. We have plenty. Even though this one should last you until you're old and gray, I took every suit the fifth- and fourth-level armories had. Why should we leave them in the bunkers for soldiers who take their orders from people who were probably responsible for mass genocide?"

"You have a point there."

"When we're settled and have time to do the fun training, I'll go through the weak spots in the suit, so you'll know where to shoot to drop someone. Unless you want to keep firing at the chest or head until you destroy the armor. I feel that tactic is a waste of bullets, and I'm told you're an amazing shot. Now, let's patrol the fence line, and we'll go over the hand commands we use in combat."

Since they were no longer connected to NORAD's signal and unable to utilize their handheld cellphones, Phillips showed Trish how they communicated with short-range radios, at least until Lieutenant Strong could come up with something better. He said the wrist processors were for long-range signal, but not everyone had one, and the processors on the vehicles were having issues without first connecting to a wrist processor. They had many issues like these to iron out once they found a good spot to call home.

After another hour of Phillips demonstrating to Trish how to activate and use the vehicle's computer console, Captain Thomas came out of the bunker. She informed Phillips that Lieutenant Strong had picked up movement on the motion cameras they'd planted outside of

NORAD. Even though NORAD had mobilized a recovery force faster than Aralyn had hoped, they had taken the bait and headed south.

The meeting to discuss the group's plans was still set for zero-six hundred, but they would be leaving the area shortly after.

Before Captain Thomas headed into the supply bunker, she let Trish know she was assigned to be her bunkmate for the night. Since Trish was younger and more agile, she would take the top bunk. Captain Thomas also warned Trish to wear her earplugs to bed. If not, Trish should prepare herself to be lulled to sleep by multiple instances of heavy snoring.

Trish entered a familiar living space filled with matching bookshelves and furniture, which appeared both comfortable and practical. Even though decorative frames held pictures full of laughter and love, the stillness in the air frightened her. Visually, she was alone, but spiritually, someone or something else was present. She shuffled forward, toward the center of the room, and lay down on the softness of the area rug. She began to cry.

The scene around her instantly changed. She propped herself up on her elbows and visually scanned the shadows of a room she hadn't stepped foot in since she was four. The cold hard floor of her mother's lab sent a shiver down her spine. The air was unnaturally chilled. Even though she couldn't see it, she knew a black shadow was slithering its way to her, ready to devour. When she blinked, her mother's unmoving form appeared, lying on the floor beside her.

Her mother smiled. "Hush, my sweet girl, can you hear the music?"

Trish jolted upright. She heard no music, only the sound of her own rapid breathing. Both the T-shirt and shorts she wore were soaked through with sweat. The dream felt so real, unlike any she had experienced before.

In the darkness, she tossed off the blanket and swung her legs over the side of the top bunk. Wiping the sleep from her eyes, Trish scooted her butt to the edge and jumped off. Her right foot landed on something hard, and pain shot through her heel. She bit down on her bottom lip, trying not to wake anybody else. She felt around for the footlocker between the bunkbeds where she'd stored her stuff before turning in. She collected her bulletproof bodysuit, the fresh undergarments, her utility belt, the bulky helmet, and lastly, she positioned her boots on both sides of the headgear until she had a manageable grip. Remembering what Phillips had told her in the elevator, she bent and grabbed her rifle and maneuvered it to the top of the pile. She had to shift the items around in her arms to hold everything steady.

Moving slowly, using one foot as a guide, she inched her way through the overcrowded sleeping bay until she spotted a slit of light on the ground to the left. Taking longer strides, she made her way over and fumbled with the doorknob. When it opened, her rifle muzzle tapped the edge of the doorframe. It slipped from the stack in her hands and tumbled straight to the floor. The echoing *clatter* was loud, breaking the silence around her. She held her breath and waited. When nobody called out and no movement came, she rolled her eyes and pushed her foot against the door. She used her other foot to nudge the rifle into the community bathroom. Once the door closed, she moved over to a bench and emptied her hands, then retrieved the rifle. She inspected it for damage and finding none, she leaned it against the wall by the bench before using the restroom.

By the time she was standing in the shower, she was relieved to find the water was warmer than the first cold experience she had before bed. Unfortunately, it didn't last. Within two minutes the showerhead sputtered out a wet chill, and her flesh was covered in goosebumps. Cursing silently, Trish washed the soap from her hair, and pressed the button to shut off the water. She used one of the few remaining towels from the shelf and dried off.

She changed into her uniform, fastened her utility belt, and went to the cabinet by the sink, where several disposable kits remained, to brush her teeth and apply deodorant. Avoiding the puffy eyes staring back at her from the mirror, Trish ran a miniature comb through her long, thick, wet hair. Once the tangles were out, she threw it in a simple ponytail, cleaned up her mess, and snatched her helmet and rifle.

Trish peeked out of the shower room door and ventured into the dark sleeping bay. The key would be not to trip over anyone snoozing on the ground like she did when she first entered the bunker after midnight. Susan was still awake then and had helped her maneuver around with a flashlight.

Since the supply bunker had more than enough provisions to sustain a small city for over a year, their duffel bags remained packed on Aralyn's orders, in case they needed to leave at a moment's notice. So while Trish showered, Susan fetched her the ugly green undergarments and sleeping outfit from storage. But now, Trish was on her own. Suddenly, it struck her. The utility-belt. She reentered the lit bathroom and studied the pouches around her waistline. Trish opened one on the side, resembling the shape of what she was looking for. When her fingers pulled out the black canister, she squinted and read the tiny, yellow lettering. *Danger: do not use around open flames.* That certainly wasn't it. Replacing the item, she pulled out an object from the row of pouches on her other side. Bingo, a flashlight.

She pivoted and crossed into the darkness as her fingers searched for a button. Damn, she should have done this in the shower room. She stuck her helmet under her arm and tried twisting the flashlight, but still, it didn't work. Did it have batteries? She shook it close to her ear and listened. At once, the light came on, but the glow was dim. It must work by friction. She shook it longer, and the beam brightened. Too bright. Quickly, she covered the light with her free hand. Sighing, Trish gave the device another twist, and the light radiating around the black fingers of her bodysuit gloves vanished.

Switching it to the lowest level she directed the beam a foot in front of her boots. She shuffled her way through the room, staying as quiet as she could. When the light moved over a sleeping bag, she was relieved to discover it empty. She continued forward, trying to stay as close to the center of the room as possible. Again, a second sleeping bag was on the ground, but was rolled into a ball, apparently left by whomever had used it. She came to a halt, and cast the beam upward, toward the closest bunkbed. Both mattresses were empty. The light worked its way over to another set of bunkbeds, and no occupants remained. For the first time, she realized the sporadic snoring she heard throughout the bay when she entered earlier was now completely gone. Absent in the darkness. She shook the light again and with a brighter glow, she noticed that none of the beds or bags around her were inhabited.

Seeing the light switch on the wall she rushed across the room and pressed it. The place was deserted. Instinctively, Trish glanced down to her watch, but the item wasn't there. Remembering she removed the timepiece when she took the bodysuit off a few hours earlier, Trish ran to her bunk, dropped her helmet and rifle on the bottom mattress, and searched the top bed. When she didn't find it, she rummaged around the footlocker. She located her watch between the wall and footlocker and flipped it over. Six-forty-eight in the morning. She was late for the meeting. Why didn't they wake her? Did they think she wouldn't be interested in what was going on, or did they believe she was too young to be involved with any of the plans?

She put on the watch, switched off the flashlight, and returned it to its pouch. Slinging her rifle, she grabbed up her helmet. Rolling her eyes, she realized she could have used the night vision on her helmet and avoided wasting precious time. At least now she knew where her flashlight was and how it worked.

She hastened from the cluttered bay, passed the various turnoffs from the main tunnel, and out through the open, reinforced door. The sky was turning a pale blue and the clouds in the distance held a reddish orange blend, but instead of marveling at dawn's great beauty, Trish focused on moving through the abundance of winks, smiles, and nods with which she was greeted. Many of the soldiers were sitting inside the vehicles with the doors propped opened or on the ground resting beside them. Ignoring their amusement, she fixed her gaze along the fence line where she saw patches of colorful wildflowers, purple, red, and yellow swaying in the slight breeze. Were they still in Colorado?

She spotted Givens and Susan settled sideways on the seats of the open-doored vehicle, and she increased her pace. They were watching a handful of personnel mulling over something on the surface of a desk, which must have been removed from the bunker and positioned out to the center of the group. Aralyn was hunched over the desk, talking and pointing to a map of some kind.

"What are they doing?" she asked Givens, who was swallowing a mouthful of food.

"Memorizing the map. Working out the tiny details before we leave here. How'd you sleep?" He shoved the rest of a black cake into his mouth and removed the other from a two-pack.

Trish watched him suck down a long swig from a bubbly caramel-colored drink before taking his next bite. Her stomach growled. "Where did you get that? From the bunker?"

When he crammed the entire cake in his mouth, he gave her a bulging grin. Her mouth watered, and she smacked her lips and swallowed.

Susan laughed. "It's our care packages. They filled the bags with prewar goodies. I don't know who or how they made these, but they taste as fresh and wonderful as ever. Here, pop a squat and enjoy."

Susan reached for Trish's pull-string backpack from the floorboard and passed it to her. She handed Susan her weapon and helmet before sitting down on the gravel surface and opening the bag. It felt like Christmas in June, and her eyes marveled at the items inside. She pulled out an assortment of ten packaged pastries and several clear plastic bottles of different-colored liquids, all with tiny bubbles inside.

Susan poked her on the shoulder. "Be careful about flaunting your tasty haul with this lot. Soldiers have been known to kill each other for less."

Trish double-checked to make sure the bag was indeed empty. "I can see why. This care package is amazing."

Trish's training soldier, Staff Sergeant Phillips, strolled toward them. "Hey Trish," Phillips said, "I'll trade you these two packs, for that chocolate one there."

Phillips held up a package of yellow cakes and a package of white ones with a red jelly smeared on the bottom. He rubbed his stomach with heightened exaggeration. "C'mon, two for the price of one."

"Don't do it, Trish," Susan said. "The chocolate cakes are the best. They have a creamy filling inside that's so sweet and fluffy."

Trish grinned, met Phillips's gaze, and gave a shake of her head. He frowned, acted mock-mad, and picked up a piece of gravel and loft it at her. It smacked one of her boots and bounced to the ground.

"Hey, keep it civil," Givens bellowed.

Susan said, "Shhh, Sergeant Givens."

Trish peeked up and saw her godmother and a few of the other officers standing around the desk looking straight at them. She lowered her eyes, selected the clear drink beside her, and opened the lid. Once the seal cracked, the beverage inside fizzed unexpectedly. Before it could overflow, she twisted it shut.

Susan wiggled her fingers toward the bottle. "Here, hand it over."

Trish gave her the container and watched Susan open and close the lid several times until finally the liquid inside settled. Susan replaced the lid and handed it back. Trish rotated the bottle to read the bizarre list of ingredients. The more she read, the more the drink's unusual fizzing effect made sense. She removed the lid and lifted it toward her nose. The drink smelled good and she was excited to explore the mysterious flavor the beverage offered. Before the round opening made contact with her lips, she spotted a sparkling fleck floating toward the bottom then disappeared from sight.

Curious, she brought the bottle closer and inspected the clear fluid. It wasn't until she gave the bottle a shake that something inside sparkled again.

Givens's voice rumbled from the driver's seat. "You know, strangely enough, most people drink it."

Ignoring Givens's sarcastic comment, Trish dug at the gravel beside her and cleared an opening down to the packed dirt below. Slowly, she upended the bottle until the miniscule object floated out. She heard someone say her name in protest, possibly Phillips, but she didn't glance up to confirm it. She was too busy examining the silver object lying against the dampened earth. She reached down and seized the item. Hard, shiny metal, no bigger than a few microns. She didn't think this was a component a beverage typically offered.

Angling her head to ask Susan what the mysterious artifact was, she saw Susan's bottle moving up toward her mouth. She grabbed at the bottle, spilling a little in the process.

Susan shouted, "Jesus, Trish!" then her gaze shot over to the grouping of officers. Cheeks reddening, she waved to Aralyn. "Sorry, Colonel, we had a bit of an accident. It won't happen again."

Susan wiped off the droplets from her bodysuit. Somewhat irritated, she said, "What the hell were you doing?"

Trish poured out the rest of Susan's bottle and found another metal object. She held both of the tiny items in her palm and squinted to figure out what they were.

When she looked up, Aralyn and two of the officers were watching her. Beyond their gawking expressions, Captain Thomas was opening the lid to a caramel-colored beverage.

Trish jumped to her feet and ran forward. "No!" She smacked the beverage out of the captain's hand.

"What the hell," Captain Thomas yelled, but Trish snatched up the bottle from the ground. She swiped the map off the desk as those around her protested and dumped the liquid onto the surface. Before the bottle was completely empty, a miniature device flowed out. Trish placed the two she already had next to it and gestured to Aralyn, who stepped closer.

Trish said, "I don't know what these are, but I'm guessing they're not supposed to be in our bottles."

Aralyn shouted, "Everyone! Stop eating and drinking the items from your care packages. They laced the contents with tracking devices."

Susan ran the scanner over Trish's body just in case. Even though she hadn't consumed anything from the care-package, Aralyn insisted *everybody* was to be scanned. Unfortunately, whatever was left from the bags had to be burned, and Trish's stomach was still growling.

Susan had explained that the trackers were used by the military before everyone went into the bunkers. They activated when mixed with stomach acid, and once the devices opened, they imbedded themselves into the lining of the stomach. To destroy them, the scanner mimicked a miniature EMP, an electro-magnetic pulse. It was safe to use on human tissue and created solely for this purpose. After the scanner disabled the tracker, they dislodged, to be excreted with the body's waste.

Trish observed the long line of soldiers still waiting to be scanned. Some fidgeted nervously with their gear, many holding hushed conversations. "Why would the military use trackers?" Trish asked, thinking of the civil rights which had once existed.

Susan pressed a button on the side of the scanner and the screen flashed to the main menu. "They were given to special forces during dangerous or covert missions. If their command lost communications with any team member, or if troops were taken prisoner, they had a constant fix on their location."

Trish's stomach quivered. "Then NORAD knows where we are?"

Susan squeezed a comforting hand on her shoulder. "At a minimum, it takes twenty-four hours for the trackers to open, fully imbed themselves, and go online." Susan motioned for her to step aside for the next soldier. "You're all done. Do me a favor, go find Aralyn and let her know it'll be a good twenty minutes until I'm finished here."

Once the issue had been dealt with, Aralyn reformed the meeting. This time, the plan was ready to share with the rest of the group. They had devised a surveillance mission to send a team of two vehicles and nine personnel to spots along the Canadian border, a matching number to locations along the Mexico border. Two vehicles and eight soldiers were to go to California, and a similar number would head to Virginia. They were to observe, run tests, and send reports to Aralyn's group daily.

The officer in each vehicle wore the wrist processor, which showed the locations of supply bunkers where they could regroup and restock, as well as the colonized bunkers, which they were to observe for movement or for work performed topside.

The teams carried radiation sensors and were to take samples along the way of water, air, and vegetation to see if any fallout or contaminants were present. They were also instructed to look for the decayed bodies and bones or mass burial sites of the multitudes whom they assumed had died.

The routes were mapped out to the letter, so if anything went amiss or a team was in danger, the others would know where to go to provide support.

Aralyn's group, consisting of the last two vehicles and a team of eight, were to find and secure someplace far enough away from NORAD to serve as a home base. In the future they would conduct observation of the work NORAD was doing in Colorado Springs. As of now, NORAD appeared to be building a wall around the city and removing waste and rubble to a nearby reclamation center.

Their primary mission was to find and collect data to show those who had been sent to the bunkers that they had been lied to. No nuclear attack or twenty-year winter had existed. They were to gather information about what had happened topside for the past eighteen years. If it were a virus, and those in charge had released it intentionally as Aralyn and the others believed, any information or proof they could obtain to expose this would aide in bringing down those responsible for billions of deaths.

Before the meeting came to a close, Aralyn stressed for everyone to remain safe and to keep an eye out, not only for survivors in need, but for the creatures who had attacked the team NORAD sent to do a simple recon of Denver a few weeks earlier. Once she ended the meeting, the commotion in the area grew. People added supplies from the bunker to their vehicles, stenciled numbers onto the bumpers, and double-checked their gear one last time.

Trish found a nice quiet spot out of the way by the fence where she broke open a prepackaged meal to eat. Susan assured her several times that the ration packs, which were genetically modified food, scientific-cally processed, and with no expiration date, wouldn't be laced with trackers. "It wouldn't be cost effective, plus the trackers would need to be scanned and linked into an assigned monitoring program prior to ingestion."

Resting against the fence surrounded by flowers, Trish wished she had a book to read. The idea of moving through the plethora of people to head inside the bunker and find a book wasn't a task she had the patience to take on. Her body was still fatigued, and she hadn't gotten enough sleep, so she ate and rested.

She stopped eating when she spotted movement in the far distance. She stood and stared at four deer running through the overgrowth of grass and weeds. The two in the lead stopped to graze. When the third drew closer, it bounced around the others. The four took off, staying along the horizon. They were playing, Trish thought, and felt blessed to witness such a peaceful sight.

"What do you see?"

She didn't need to turn. She knew the voice now and the question came from Phillips. "Four does off to the right."

"What else?"

This time she glanced to Phillips, then focused to the deer. "There's a buck in the distance, less than a hundred yards behind them."

Phillips came up beside her, squinted, and let out a long whistle. "You have picture-perfect eyesight, but no, that's not what I'm referring to. It has something to do with the deer. Think of the need for survival and pay attention to their actions."

Frowning, Trish peered closer. The deer were leaping about, eating grass, and enjoying one another's company. Trish inhaled sharply. "They're playing. They're not afraid, so no danger is over there."

"Exactly. Always observe your surroundings and follow your instincts. Don't survey the world in black and white, Trish. Like the tracker in the bottle, you need to take in the colors. Hone in on every detail, and let your mind discover the answers."

In awe at the simplicity of how Phillips explained such a vital bit of information, Trish's excitement rose. "I'm glad we're on the same team, Sarge. I like the way you take the time to teach me, and I love learning."

"Young one, you make me blush," he said. "Enough lessons for now. The Colonel needs us inside. The rest are about to leave, and she wants us to clean the area before we start packing."

CHAPTER SEVEN

Taking mental notes, Trish silently observed Givens demonstrate a routine vehicle inspection. After his checklist was finished, he bent forward, put his mouth close to a port along the side base, and pressed his finger down on a tiny nozzle. Hissing like a snake, pressurized gas released. He breathed in deeply, filling his lungs.

She said, "I'm guessing this huffing isn't a normal part of our daily walkaround."

Straightening, Givens offered a sly smirk. "Hi, nice to meet you." His voice was high and mousy. "My name is Jason, I'm a man who laughs like a child. Bahahaha."

Trish couldn't help but chuckle. "Is that helium? Let me try."

He pushed the tiny valve, releasing more gas. She leaned forward and breathed in the clear vapor. He did the same. "Hello Jason, I'm Trish." She giggled at the way she sounded. His absurd, high-pitched cackling fueled on her squeaking laughter.

Out of nowhere, Aralyn was at his side. "Sergeant, I take it the vehicles are ready to go?"

Givens cleared his throat before speaking, then cleared it again as if to be sure. "Yes ma'am. I was showing young Trish here where the ultra-dense deuterium is stored." He pointed to the side of the fusion chamber.

Aralyn used her wrist device to close and latch the door on the bunker while Eric Leonard and Todd Stevens, from the second vehicle, planted motion sensors around the compound. Leonard was the corporal in charge of supply. At twenty-three, he was the youngest

Aralyn had under her command from the fifth-level. Stevens on the other hand was the oldest, and like with Sergeant Givens, he was a weapons specialist. He was also the group's First Sergeant and probably the deadliest man left alive.

Trish returned Lieutenant Strong's wave before removing her weapon and climbing into the rear seat in the vehicle. She fastened her seatbelt and continued to watch the movement of those around her. As Aralyn had told Trish before they left the supply bunker, these seven were now her family. She needed to learn from them and trust they would protect her with their lives. Trish felt a sense of satisfaction from that.

Givens climbed behind the wheel, Susan claimed the seat across from her, and Aralyn opened the front passenger door, situated herself, then passed Trish a chilled bottle of water. Other than Phillips, she had known this entire team since birth, and Phillips's personality fit right in with the rest of them. If the decision were left up to her to pick, this family tree was the one she would have chosen.

During the drive from the supply bunker, a few miles outside Fort Collins, Colorado, to Scottsbluff, Nebraska, Trish observed all she could. From the abandoned past luxuries of Arrowhead, Colorado, to the unkept homes of Waterglen, the view was as heartbreaking as it was captivating. So many people had once lived in the homes now covered in vines and lawns littered with overgrown vegetation. The vanished populous had worked in the crumbling structures aged from weather and lack of repair. Vacationed in resorts catering to those who could afford their services, which now held a ghostly ambiance of a civilization quickly forgotten. The various colors of this outside world mixing together was welcoming compared to the confines of NORAD, yet Trish was pained at knowing the vastness of human existence once covering the planet had ceased almost two decades ago.

The ride was a little bumpy, but the main roads were still drivable. The few vehicles she spotted from the Interstate had been left abandoned off to the side or in driveways and parking lots and covered with dirt and cluttered personal belongings.

When Trish asked why there were so few vehicles, Susan explained how, a handful of years before going into the bunkers, the levels of fuel reserve left on the planet had hit a critical point, so companies implemented conversion of vehicles to solar and fusion power. Since many people couldn't afford them, public transportation became the main way folks got around.

Susan said the military vehicles like the one they were in were called Gladiators and were prototypes using both fusion and solar power. The Gladiators' reinforced armor and weaponry were advanced, but unfortunately, there had not been much time for testing before everyone headed to the bunkers. The vehicle was also designed to drive through deep water, but this, too, hadn't been fully tested.

Trish said, "In other words, we're not sure how reliable these Gladiators are?"

The right side of Susan's lips curved upward. "If it makes you feel better, the tires come with a lifetime warranty."

For a split second, Trish sat there speechless. Susan's tiny stab at humor, Givens's helium stunt, the elation Trish had felt since escaping the strict NORAD setting was also shared by the others, her chosen family. "You have to admit, it's a start." Ogling a few deer in the distance, a thought from earlier struck her. "Susan, don't the people in charge have a way of tracking these vehicles?"

"No, we've deactivated that feature. Same with the wrist processors and these bodysuits we're wearing. The supply bunkers were monitored as well, but Lieutenant Strong disabled the detectors before we left NORAD." Her eyes brightened. "She also installed her own personal cyber-virus before we left. Most of their security programs, as well as the surveillance satellites, were completely wiped. You've really got to admire Lieutenant Strong's programming skills. That woman is a genius."

"We're here," Aralyn said from the front seat. "Once we run our tests, we'll head to the supply bunker along the border of South Dakota for the night."

Trish waited for Susan to reach into the row of seating behind them to remove two separate, handheld cases from the top of the pile. Trish offered to carry one, but Susan told her no. "I need you to stand guard with Stevens and Leonard, while the Colonel, Lieutenant Strong, and I take the samples. Givens and Phillips will stay with our ride."

The Gladiator with the number TWO stenciled onto the rear bumper pulled in beside them, under the shade of a hearty oak tree, and everyone exited. The drivers, Givens and Phillips, remained with their weapons by the vehicles. They were both on alert, surveying the area. Trish unslung her rifle, too, and visually explored the terrain.

A sweet, floral perfume filled the air, mingling with a fishy, earthy tang from the river. Trish inhaled deeply; her entire airway tingling with delight. Trudging behind Susan, her curiosity vanished the moment she realized she'd left her helmet on the floorboard by her seat. The veins in her neck throbbed cold, sending a chill down her arms and legs. Everyone else had theirs on. She felt a dampness form on her hands, yet the temperature was moderate. Should she go and get it?

Susan gave Aralyn one of the cases. "I'll head to the river and test the water. Lieutenant Strong only knows how to take air samples, so you're left with soil and vegetation, Colonel."

"Lieutenant Travis, get your air samples close to the Gladiators," Aralyn directed. "The drivers can keep an eye out until you're finished. First Sergeant Stevens, remain with Susan. Trish, go back and get your helmet, then I want you positioned over by the picnic area so you can watch both groups. Corporal Leonard, you're with me." Aralyn slung the strap of her weapon over her head like a sash and clutched the handle on the brown sample case.

Trish's clammy, gloved hands gripped tighter around her rifle. Blushing, she rushed to the Gladiator marked ONE, snatched up her headgear, and threw it on. She double-timed her way through the weeds to stand beside the weathered benches and tables her godmother had pointed to. With her visor raised, she searched the overgrown brush on the other side of the river. Her senses told her those around her were watching, judging her, or to be more exact, concerned by her adolescent blunder.

She visually swept the area across from Susan and First Sergeant Stevens, then scanned for foes along both sides of the Gladiators. Phillips was staring at her. When they locked eyes, he tapped his helmet and tilted his head as if asking what the hell she was thinking, going off and forgetting such a valuable piece of equipment. She shrugged and glanced away. Additional shame washed over her, and she knew somehow, her physique had shrunk two inches.

She continued circling her gaze to the far row of vine-covered trees. Other than squirrels flicking their tails from low-hanging branches and a congregation of brown and white birds leaving the trees and flying overhead, Trish saw no movement. Normally, she would have marveled at the experience of seeing these animals for the first time. Even the wild growth of plant-life surrounding her was spectacular. But now, all she could think about was returning to her seat in the vehicle and away from the belief that everyone around her was gawking judgmentally at the stupid mistake she'd made.

She spotted Aralyn and Corporal Leonard over by a grouping of trees near the river. She examined the terrain on either side. When her godmother finished taking a sample of something on the ground, Aralyn closed her case and stood. She spoke to Corporal Leonard, looked over to Trish, then made her way to the gathering of trees where the squirrels had frolicked.

The squirrels, Trish thought. Where were the birds? She pivoted her body to the line of trees, flipped up the scope and raised her rifle. She counted a total of three formerly active squirrels, now stationary high above in an oak tree, whipping their tails about wildly. She remembered reading how squirrels flicked their tails as a way of signaling danger.

She scanned the brush line below. A barbed wire fence poked out in various places. Past a gap of vines, a field of tall, tangled grass grew on the other side of the fence. Even though she couldn't see any movement, the entire area was swarming with places to hide. Something in the overgrowth was threatening enough to send the squirrels into a frenzy and drive the birds away.

Knowing her scope narrowed her vision too tightly at this close of a range, she spun the scope to the side and rotated the rifle's selector switch from safe to single fire. Carefully, she advanced toward the location. The air around her shifted. A putrid whiff filled her nostrils, strong enough that she had to fight off the urge to gag. Scrunching up her nose, she stalked on, observing brush and shrubbery for subtle alterations. Realizing Aralyn and Corporal Leonard would reach the overgrown area before her, she quickened her pace and hollered for them to stop.

The shrubs around the trees exploded with activity. A filthy man covered in dirt, mud, and raggedy clothes leapt from concealment. He ran toward Aralyn and Leonard on all fours. His head was hairless, his eye color was a golden-orange. Face distorted with rage, he bellowed out a hideous cry.

He's infected, she realized. She was aiming her rifle when Corporal Leonard fired at the creature, a hundred feet away. The bullet struck its chest and jerked him backwards, but he didn't fall. An initial stunned expression switched to fury. Pouncing forward on all fours the creature rushed Leonard.

Leonard's bullets went wild, kicking up dirt around the swerving attacker. Matching her weapon sight with the creature's speed, Trish steadied her breathing. Using the brightness of its eyes as a target, she exhaled, squeezed slightly on the trigger, then fired.

The creature's head snapped to the side. Its body fell, skidding sideways into the dirt.

She rushed forward, her heart beating so fast she thought she'd faint.

The creature's arm flinched, but Leonard was on it. He shoved his rifle in its mouth and pulled the trigger three more times.

A high-pitched scream rang out. Trish spun her rifle to see two more monsters emerging from the growth beneath the trees. One was male, the other, with wider hips and narrower shoulders, appeared female.

Trish squeezed off a round into the female's eye-socket, then tagged her again in the throat before she fell.

Leonard and Aralyn had their weapons raised and fired at the male until it dropped.

Trish didn't turn when she heard the tires of approaching vehicles crunch against the gritty earth. Instead, she continued ahead, scanning the tree line.

Phillips rushed forward and stopped beside her. He held his arm up to block her path. "Be still. Be ready," he said.

He shot several rounds into random locations in the undergrowth. No sound or movement came.

Trish did a full 360, with the realization she no longer felt as if others were watching her.

Once Phillips signaled to Aralyn that the coast was clear, Trish made her way over to Susan who was examining a body. The odor around the corpse was dreadful, reminding Trish of the time the sewer in the fifth-level bunker had backed up. She noticed how the hands and bare feet were longer and more powerful than that of a human, with claws stretching out of every digit. Was it their eyes she had felt watching her? If so, how was she able to sense them? Did it have to do with her mother's serum, or was it an intuition brought on by something else?

"We should get samples," Susan announced.

Without waiting for an order or for someone to volunteer, Trish went to the Gladiator to collect the supplies Susan would need.

Handing Phillips her bodysuit a third time, Trish rolled her eyes and waited. Over two hours earlier, they had set up camp in the supply bunker on the edge of Hot Springs, South Dakota, secured the area, and locked up the security fence to the outside world. As others went inside to shower and tuck in for the evening, Phillips gave Trish the chore of thoroughly washing both Gladiators before entering the bunker. After her shower, he then nitpicked the cleanliness of her bodysuit, his form of punishment for Trish forgetting her headgear. He scanned over the uniform, and on this cleaning inspection spent more time searching along the gloves and foot section than before.

Emitting an exasperated sigh, Trish sat on the chair across from him.

"Do you have somewhere you need to be?" His voice was casual, not raising his gaze with his question.

"I want to go outside and read while there's still daylight."

"Have you restocked the meals in your rucksack?"

"Seriously? There's so many duffel bags full of rations in the Gladiators, we could eat for a year."

"Which are for when we get settled." He passed her the suit. "Until then, we need to continue to live off what's in our rucksacks. It'll take about twenty minutes for your suit to finish air-drying, plenty of time for you to go shopping."

She was about to ask him why she couldn't wear her T-shirt and shorts outside, since the area was secure and the sensors were in place, but she didn't want to listen to any more lecturing today. She took the suit and hung it on her bunk to dry. Seizing her rucksack, she went into a supply room in the back stocked full of large boxes, plastic totes, and pallets piled high with provisions. Thankfully, everything was labeled.

She went to a ration pallet and grabbed from a box someone else had already opened. She knew she was moody, but she was tired and had a headache. She thought she had handled herself well during the attack, but she'd received three separate lectures. One sermon came from Phillips, who threatened to glue her helmet to her head if she ever forgot it again.

The next stern discourse was from her godmother, who scolded her for being too impetuous to advance on creatures they had no knowledge of. She told Trish she should have been more cautious and let her and the others handle the bulk of the danger until Trish had the proper training.

The third, more gentle reprimand was from Susan, who had pulled her aside and reaffirmed what her godmother had already said.

Scarcely skimming over the meal selection, she selected two breakfast meals and a dinner and shoved them in her bag. She pulled out another breakfast meal for tonight, then read through the tags in the room. She opened a box labeled *Disposable Toiletries,* and tossed two kits in her bag. A section along the far wall contained snacks. She resisted the urge to fill the rest of her bag space with the colorful packages. Instead, she selected four and stuck them inside. Searching through the feminine hygiene items she found the right size and snatched a box of ten for her womanly cycle, less than a week away. She seized a roll of toilet paper, but with limited bag space, she replaced it with a handful of the smaller packages designed for individual use.

After loading up on flavored drinks and bottled water, she decided she had put in enough time "shopping." She closed her rucksack and headed from the room, put the bulging bag by her bunk, and took her bodysuit with her to the shower room to change. When she finished, she found Susan.

"Where are the books located?"

Susan stared at her blankly.

"Phillips said the bunkers had actual books. I need something to read."

"Oh, okay. They're in the room across from the commander's quarters." She pointed toward the direction of the entrance.

Trish thanked her, went to her bunk, and put on her boots and utility belt. She slung her rifle and stuffed her meal and a bottled water inside the helmet. When she passed Phillips, she held up her helmet and smiled, with no sense of humor in her effort.

Across from her godmother's private quarters was a door labeled "community room." Trish went inside and greeted Strong, First Sergeant, and Givens sitting around a table playing cards. She strolled over to the first of two packed bookshelves, and at once, her happy anticipation plummeted. The first bookcase was crammed with military training manuals, and the second was chock-full of military specialized courses and survival guides.

"Are these the only books in the bunker?"

The door opened. Phillips traipsed into the room, heading to the first bookshelf.

"I'm afraid so," Lieutenant Strong said.

Phillips pulled a book off the shelf and held it out to her. "I recommend you start with this one, *FM 3-21.75.*"

"Ah," First Sergeant said, "*The Warrior Ethos and Soldier Combat Skills.* Good choice, Phillips. Do you know in 2067, the idiots talked about rewriting that book?"

"Shameful," Phillips replied, beaming at Trish.

Feeling her temperature rise, Trish seized the book, placed it on top of the items in her helmet, and shuffled around him. As the door was closing, she heard the hearty laughter flow from the community room.

Spooning out the last bite of ham and eggs, Trish set the ration tray on the ground beside her and continued reading. She had to force herself to skim through the material as slowly as she could, or else she would have to read it a third time. Or go inside to get a different book from the bunker. Neither idea appealed to her. She tried watching the scenery, but it had been so long since she read, her brain felt dehydrated.

Opening the sealed package marked *pancakes*, Trish added water to the dotted line, retrieved the butter flavored tablet, and dropped it in. Folding over the top, she shook the container to her desired temperature, and reopened it. Instead of placing the newly fattened, hot pancakes on the disposable tray, she opened the syrup and dumped it in. Reusing the plastic fork, she tore-off a piece and ate it.

In the distance, Corporal Leonard robotically marched from one end of the gate, spun, and retraced his steps. She could go relieve him from guard duty when she finished eating. He had to be tired. The idea of leaving the seclusion of the cluster of elm trees wasn't high on her list. Unfortunately, the sun was rapidly dropping, and she knew those inside wouldn't let her stay this far from the entrance once the sun had set. Having an extended family sounded nice at first—until she realized they would all act like parents.

Trish glanced down at her half-eaten meal, appetite lost, set it aside and closed the book.

The area of green trees and chirping birds at this corner of the compound was stunning. She squinted down to the old, abandoned, two-story hotel across the street covered in thick, creeping foliage and surrounded by a forest littered with life. The drop off was around seventy feet beneath the bottom of the chain-link fence encompassing their compound. She bet she would find several abandoned books just asking to be read over there, past the shaded street. The idea of climbing the fence and scaling the rock wall beneath it crossed her mind.

She stood slowly, not taking her eyes off the building. What if I'm quick? Her eyes drifted to the entrance area of the compound, then to the fence. She made her way over and grasped the twisted metal. Her pulse did a somersault and settled. She wasn't a prisoner after all. She was seventeen. She should be allowed to come and go if she wanted. Yeah, right, she thought, rolling her eyes. If she genuinely considered herself so independent, she would leave through the gate, and not cower while going over the fence.

She lowered her shoulders, struggling with a plague of guilt. Her entire life had been nothing more than strict rules and concrete barriers. She had felt more loathing than love. Yet, those who she was with now had been her closest family since childhood. Did they deserve to be subjected to her sudden jolt of rebellion?

She kicked at a twig and grunted. If she left the compound, she would be at risk, but in this wild world they were living in, full of monsters and the unknown, death could easily find her tomorrow, or next week. She had always played by the rules of others. This she wanted, no, she *needed* to do for herself. After all, what good was living in a world with a presumably shorter life expectancy without some excitement before she died?

She went for her rifle and helmet, slung her weapon, and put on her helmet. She raised the visor. She took hold of the fence and pulled up. She tried using her feet, but her boots were too big for the woven links of the barrier. She let go and dropped to the ground. Scowling, she backed up, dashed forward, kicked off from the clinking wall, and jumped. Her hands shot upward and clutched at the links. Using only her upper body, she pulled herself up the last several feet with little effort. She scaled the horizontal pole at the top and yanked her body up and over. The climb down the fence was even easier. She let her feet dangle while she used her arm muscles, until her feet contacted the rock ledge. The slight burn from the exertion in her arms was invigorating.

Twisting her head, Trish located the best plausible area to descend from. Keeping a tight hold as she moved, she slid along the ledge three of four feet before lowering her right foot onto a three-inch-wide bulge protruding from the wall of rock. With the shadows growing thicker down below, she knew she needed to hurry to make it back before dark. She clutched at a lower area of fence, dropped her other foot, and braced it inside a crack in the rock. She continued working her way down, until both hands were holding onto the ledge.

To her left, she heard a bang and froze. The sound of high-pitched squealing followed, and she spotted a sizeable bus swerving to a stop below her. The bus door opened, and four men exited with firearms. They were actual people, not the infected she'd seen earlier. They wore jeans and shirts, not uniforms, even though their movements suggested they had some form of tactical training. Her heart raced. She watched how each took a position of defense around the tinted windowed vehicle.

One soldier signaled toward the front windshield, and another man with aged-graying hair exited. Breathing deeper, Trish watched the man place his hands on his hips and stare at the deflated front tire. He then headed toward the rear of the bus and disappeared.

Pondering, she glanced up to the fence. She didn't know if they were friendly or if they would consider strangers, such as herself, a threat. She needed to tell the others before this group left. Let her compadres decide the proper introductions.

She focused her attention on the bus again. The last man who had exited was now rolling a tire toward the front. The guard beside him spoke to someone else inside the disabled vehicle. He forcefully shook his head. The man with the tire said something to the guard, who threw up his arms as if annoyingly defeated. Using short, direct movements he waved over the person inside the bus. A young woman with long, black hair pulled into a ponytail exited the bus with a child in her arms. Her complexion was honey-beige and Trish guessed she was in her late teens, to early twenties. The young woman turned around and motioned to someone inside the bus. Three more kids rushed out, and once the woman spoke, they all held hands. She moved the kids to the edge of the hotel entrance and the guard followed. One of the girls squatted in the corner, but Trish's eye was drawn to the man who propped a replacement tire against the front of the bus before returning to the rear of their vehicle.

Suddenly, the tiny hairs at the nape of her neck felt like a cobweb had been drawn over them. They tingled like they did when her group had collected the samples earlier that day. She felt alone, exposed, and she needed to hurry. Trish stretched her arm out and locked onto the metal links of the fence, her muscles solid. Who was watching? Her head spun from side to side so fast she almost lost her footing.

The woman and children were still huddled by the hotel. The guards were monitoring the vicinity. The man fixing the tire was carrying a gadget toward the wheel.

Alarmed, Trish scanned the area as the prickling sense of being watched grew stronger. She thought about shouting, but what if the threat she was sensing hadn't spotted this group? Her words of warning could direct a threat their way and place them all in danger, but the idea of a pack of creatures going after the kids was unthinkable.

She needed to get closer first.

Trish lowered herself as rapidly as possible while maintaining good footholds. The climb would have been faster if she stopped peeking over her shoulder at the group, but she couldn't help herself.

She was halfway down when she saw the guards clearing additional children from the bus. Her stomach tightened. She scurried faster. Twice she lost her footing, but both times her hand strength kept her from falling.

She heard a hollow cry and swiveled toward the commotion. The guards around the bus darted about, their weapons ready, searching for the vocal creature. The repairman dropped a tool and removed a pistol from behind his waistband. He hurried even more children off the bus, and pointed to the young woman in the front, then to the hotel door.

Trish gauged the distance. She still had more than twenty feet of air between her and the ground. She continued her descent.

Scattered gunfire broke out, and she clutched the rocky handholds in alarm. She heard a deep howl, looked around, and saw the repair man face up on the ground covered in blood. A creature leaned over him, gnawing into his throat.

Near the hotel entrance, an older woman and the younger one with the frightened kids screamed in unison. The younger woman frantically opened one of the hotel doors and rushed the hysterical woman and the children inside. Two of the guards went in with them.

Shots rang out and three more infected emerged into the open. The first creature, chewing on the repair man, finally took a bullet and fell. Another advancing beast lunged into a guard loading his weapon. The man cried out against the powerful slashing claws, then stopped moving when a second beast jumped forward and ripped deeply into his face and chest. The speed at which the creatures moved was terrifying.

Trish calculated the distance to the ground. Ten feet, maybe fifteen. Relaxing her tightened muscles, she released her grip and kicked off, letting herself fall. When her feet touched, she bent her knees and rolled to the side.

The last guard left outside sprayed bullets all around. Horrified, he backed up against the half-brick wall. Trish stood, wide-eyed, as a creature attacked him. He lifted the flailing man easily overhead and threw him forcefully against a pillar several feet away. The creature's sheer strength was shocking. All three dove in and attacked the flailing man until his limbs stopped moving.

The first creature rose and retreated from the slaughter, face saturated in human blood. He loped to the door and went inside the hotel. She heard rapid gunfire. A front door window shattered.

A second creature raced inside. Trish unslung her weapon and ran like hell for the door. The last creature was about to enter, but it froze. Tilting its head upward, Trish saw the filthy face of something that was once a woman. Now it scowled with red-stained teeth toward the bus. On all fours, it lumbered away from the hotel. Trish skidded to a halt, brought her weapon up and aimed. Before she fired, it moved out of sight toward the door of the bus.

Trish sprinted to the vehicle. As she reached the body of the dead repair guy, she heard a child scream from inside the bus. A low, throaty growl followed, and Trish smelled the horrible rank stench that trailed the creature. She lowered her visor, hopped over the body, and darted through the door to the stairs. Pressing the button to seal her helmet, the smell of rotten waste disappeared.

The child's sound vanished before she reached the top step leaving an eerie silence. She was too late. Her tightening stomach turned nauseous. She raised her rifle toward the creature in the last row with its bloody claw poised high and motionless in the air. Trish squeezed off three rounds into the center of the hairless beast. It jerked, then dropped.

Fearful of what she would find, Trish charged down the aisle, reached the creature and fired three more times to be sure.

When she peered over the seat, a tiny brown-haired girl, perhaps four or five years old, covered her eyes and whimpered.

Trish bent and picked her up. "Are you all right?" The words came out muffled.

The girl looked at her, eyes wide, and screamed a piercing, curdling shriek that hurt Trish's ears. She raised her visor. The girl stopped screeching and stared, mouth open.

"I need to go inside and help the others. Can you stay here until I return?"

Eyes wide, the girl shook her head. Trish spotted a half-open door with a sealed-off toilet inside. She tried to sound reassuring, but her words came out desperate, pleading. "What if I put you in the bathroom and you lock yourself in?"

Again, the head movement was a no. This time, the girl wrapped her arms around Trish's helmet and held on tight.

Securing her grip on the child on one hip, Trish shut her visor, raised her weapon, and exited the bus. She stopped outside the hotel entrance and listened. The gunshots halted. She heard someone scream out, "Run!"

Trembling, the girl hid her face in Trish's shoulder. At least the kid was light. She wore scuffed red tennis shoes, jeans, and an over-sized black t-shirt with a picture of a roaring lion on front, some sort of college mascot.

Tightening her grip, Trish sucked in a breath and crept inside. A contorted creature lay face down on the bloodstained carpet on the other side of the semi-lit entryway. Its body was skewed over a mound of opened luggage, with long-forgotten clothing and toiletries scattered into various piles.

Rifle in a ready position, Trish tiptoed through an area marked, *First Floor Lobby*. Her gaze passed over dusty, discarded outfits on the floor or draped over furniture. Socks protruded from footwear, jeans or slacks, and personal accessories, like watches, rings, and handbags were left scattered to the sides of each one. The ghostly scene was as if the fabled, religious rapture had struck the building years earlier, taking only the bodies and leaving everything else behind.

Trish cringed when she spotted a guard from the bus lying motionless on the murky stairs. His broken body folded backwards in an unnatural way. Whatever happened to those who were infected, it gave the creatures enough strength to toss a stout man through the air, and snap another's spine in half, folding the entire human body completely backwards so the heels of the feet actually touched the skull.

Trish whispered, "Close your eyes tight and keep them shut, okay?"

The girl nodded and clutched on more tightly.

Flipping the night vision to auto, Trish bypassed the dead man and ran up the stairs to the second floor. She heard a resounding crash down the right hallway, and a wave of tiny screams bounced around the darkness. She lowered the child into a chair in the far corner and told her to keep still. Ignoring the child's protests, Trish pivoted and sprinted off toward the commotion. As she neared the last room on the left, the shouting and growling grew louder. She hurried through a smashed-in door and raised her weapon at a creature clawing wildly, shredding a mattress someone was holding between it and the cries of multiple children.

Unable to fire, for fear of hitting someone on the other side, Trish pulled her weapon back and smashed the butt into its skull. The creature's body fell against the mattress with the impact, but it didn't go down. Before it could regain its balance, she struck it again. Still, it refused to drop. Natural light was coming in from somewhere farther in the room, but with the mattress in the way, the murky halo wasn't enough for her night vision to disengage. How well could the creatures see in the dark?

She needed to get the beast out of the room and away from the kids. With any luck, her night vision would give her the advantage. When it righted itself and came at her with that remarkable speed, she didn't have time to turn the gun around to shoot it. She drew back, preparing for a harder strike with her weapon. Before the hardened plastic made contact, the creature swung out of the way and bellowed a cry of hatred. Trish stopped her momentum, but her balance was off. She stumbled forward.

The creature raised a powerful arm and struck her with a blow that made her ears ring. She smacked hard into the wall. The creature advanced as she hit the floor.

Arms up like a silverback gorilla preparing to pound on its enemy, the beast slugged her with its massive paw. She looked for her rifle. Couldn't see it anywhere.

She was trapped. Every time she tried to get up, the foul-smelling brute hit her again. She got a look at the expression on the beast's face, and she swore it looked triumphant—almost human—as if it were grinning with glee. Was he toying with her?

She tried to launch herself around the beast, but another blow knocked her against the wall. Her head spun. She raised her arms and closed her eyes against the thrashing.

The reality of her life coming to an end due to her own carelessness struck her. But the image of the creature tearing apart the defenseless girl from the bus once he was finished with those in this room made her temper flare. She pressed her right hand and foot against the wall and pushed as hard as she could, diving for the demon's mid-section. She wrapped her arms around the creature's waist and flipped it over her body to the ground. She landed on top and pressed her knees in, pinning its shoulders. Her entire left side felt like one massive, throbbing bruise, but she pushed the pain away. She tightened her fists, clenched her jaw, and punched with all the strength she could muster.

With a look of surprise, the creature sliced its claws at her, but with its shoulders pushed to the floor, it couldn't make contact. It shrieked and roared, snapping its bloody jaws in the air between her thighs. She shifted slightly to avoid its teeth. It broke an arm free, swung wide, and hit her hard on the right side of her helmet. Even with the protection her head-cover offered, she reeled from the blow, landing on the ground beside the creature's thrashing legs.

With her night vision flickering off and on, she struggled to her feet. The creature lunged at her, knocking them both out into the hallway. She staggered to her side and slammed her fist against its jaw twice. It growled in pain, reeled an arm outward, and threw its force against her helmet. The strike and its momentum landed them both on the floor. The creature was still for a moment, panting from exertion.

Exhausted and in pain, she rolled over to stand. The creature rose first, a gleam of satisfaction on its disgusting face. Its arm was raised, ready to make the killing blow. She scrambled, trying to rise and avoid the final punishment.

A barrage of blasts exploded from the room. The beast met her eyes, an expression of pain on its face. Slumping to the ground, his gaze never left hers.

Trish wobbled to her feet using the wall for support and drifted unsteadily to the creature. Before she could check to see if it was dead, the young woman emerged, shot the infected several more times in the face, then muttered something in Spanish. She eyeballed Trish and spoke in perfect English, "That ought to do it." Behind her, the older woman and a group of small figures stood not making a single sound.

Catching her breath, Trish peered at her rescuer. "Are you all right?" Trish's voice sounded even more muffled in the helmet than normal.

The young woman nodded, giving Trish an uncertain, "Yes."

Trish could tell her presence made both women uneasy.

"How were you able to fight the Gramite by hand? Does the suit make you stronger?"

"What?" Trish eyeballed the dead creature. "No, the suit's only bulletproof. Thanks for your help by the way. Can I have my weapon now?"

The older woman told her not to hand it over. "We don't know who he is," she whispered. "He could be dangerous."

Trish's vision kept going from light to dark. *He?* Seriously, they thought she was a guy.

Trish smacked her helmet, hoping the strobing would stop. The pounding made her head hurt, but she was struggling to see clearly between the flickers. She wasn't taking it off until she had possession of her rifle and was once again outside.

She reached out a hand. "My rifle please."

The younger woman didn't move, and again her companion protested.

"Look, ladies, I didn't have to come in here to help you." She gestured to the dead creature. "If I wanted to hurt you I would have let that thing finish you off."

Trish couldn't make out the expressions on their faces, just the outlines in the gloomy light. She wasn't sure if they were seriously feeling threatened, or if they were getting ready to shoot her. After a few moments of staring, the one with her weapon finally handed over the rifle.

"Thank you." Trish slung her weapon over her shoulder. She spun and tramped over the clutter lining the hallway.

"We have kids—small children—and we could really use some help," the young woman called out after her.

Trish went to the chair by the stairs, scooped up the little girl and situated her on her hip. When she returned to the end of the hall the women were no longer there.

She heard the older woman let out a bleating sound from inside the room, then whined, "What are we going to do? We won't make it alone."

Trish edged around the kids in the doorway and entered the room with the partially shredded mattress. From the view of the open window, she saw the sun was almost gone.

The young woman said, "Hush, Mrs. Johnson, you're frightening the children." She turned, saw who Trish was carrying, and emitted a sort of crying laughter at seeing the child. She stretched out her arms, but the girl refused to let go of Trish.

"Did all the kids make it?" Trish asked, praying for good news.

The young woman brushed her hand over the child's hair. "Yes. Jennifer here makes fourteen."

Trish examined both adults, working through her thoughts silently. Would taking these unknowns to her group be dangerous? It wasn't like Trish and her team were planning on staying at the supply bunker. They were passing through. Plus, neither woman gave off a threatening vibe. Just the opposite. They were scared, and so were the children.

"I'm Trish. What's your name?"

"Christina Burgos. And this here is—"

"Mrs. Johnson. I heard." She directed her next question to Christina. "Why are you out here with these kids?"

They briefly stared at one another. Mrs. Johnson shook her head slightly, until Christina finally gave her an answer. "The community where they were living had too many orphans to care for. We—where I'm from—let's just say we were helping them out by taking the children in. Mrs. Johnson is in charge of our orphanage and asked me along to help her with the transport. I'm sorry, really sorry, but I can't give you any more information than that."

Trish saw the honesty and regret in her eyes and heard the apprehension in her voice. She understood why they didn't want to divulge much to a complete stranger. Trish respected her for her reserve and was equally grateful for the limited trust. "If you want, I can carry her while you round up the others. My camp is not far, but I'd like to make it there before the sun is completely gone."

"You have a camp?"

Trish noticed the diminishing light on the other side of the window. They were wasting time. "It's more of a compound."

Trish turned to exit the room. When she realized nobody was following, she stopped. "I swear, it's safe." She waited. When neither moved, she continued, "You know it's too dangerous staying out here in the open, especially with all these kids. I do appreciate the risk you probably feel you'll be taking by coming with me, but please understand, I'm also taking a risk by bringing you to my group."

Trish shifted the girl higher on her hip. Christina and Mrs. Johnson were having some sort of silent communication.

Eventually, Christina let out a huff. "We don't have much of a choice," she said, motioning the kids to follow her. "Thank you by the way, for helping us."

"You're welcome. And listen, when you take them downstairs, have the children close their eyes if you can. The view isn't pleasant."

Before they left the hallway, a door on the right opened and Trish raised her rifle preparing to fire. A guard poked his head out from a janitor's closet.

Trish relaxed her trigger finger but kept her weapon pointed just in case. "I thought everyone else had been killed."

Mrs. Johnson's face stiffened. "Brian, you locked the door and left us to defend the children alone. How could you?"

The young man opened his mouth to speak, but he lowered his head instead.

Christina said, "Mrs. Johnson, this man's right. We'll deal with Brian later. Right now, we need to go."

Frowning, Trish cursed under her breath about their inability to tell she wasn't male. She wasn't sure why it bothered her. Wincing from her bruises and sore limbs, she slung her weapon and headed down the hallway. When she was outside and far enough away so Jennifer couldn't see the dead bodies, she pressed the button on her flickering helmet and removed it.

Smiling, the girl said, "You're pretty."

Trish laughed. "Not as pretty as you. Your name's Jennifer?"

With reddening cheeks, the girl's smile broadened before she buried her face in Trish's neck. The way the child held her, as if knowing her tiny life was safe in Trish's arms, sent a warmth, maybe a maternal instinct, through her. She paused and returned the embrace. That was when she noticed how the suit hid her natural curves. She understood then how they had mistaken her for a man. Several times. The suit was not flattering to the female body.

As the adults led the kids from the hotel, Trish waved them over to the bus. She continued to scan the area, concerned about everyone's safety. Where there were three creatures, surely there could be more. The tire still needed to be replaced, and the sun was nothing more than a fading haze of dusk off in the distance. The main gate to the supply bunker wasn't too far away. She reasoned with herself that it was better to embark on a quarter or half-mile hike with the kids, then wrestle with changing the tire in the dark and risking another attack.

The last of the guards, Brian, kept his head down and busied himself with collecting the weapons left on the ground.

She spotted the surprised glances and unspoken words between both women when they got a look at her face. Trish harrumphed. Did they not think a woman was capable enough to handle herself? Wait until they saw the other females from her group in action, especially Aralyn. Their gender-stereotyping arrogance would be shattered. They'd be in awe of any one of the capable women on Trish's team.

She shifted Jennifer onto her other hip and tried her best to block out the reek of blood and entrails drifting up from the dead. She was ready to be free of this place. Wearily she remembered she still had to deal with those at the supply bunker, and at this point, all she wanted to do was sleep. Fat chance of that happening any time soon.

CHAPTER EIGHT

Breathing a sigh of relief, Trish exited the seclusion of the trees and came out by the fence, not far from the compound's gate. The trip around the bunker took longer than she thought it would, and while trampling through the woods in the dark, she was afraid they'd passed the compound altogether.

She spotted the lights of both Gladiators moving down the gravel strip, and her heart sank. They had realized she was gone. She lengthened her strides and waved her helmet in the air. Not until the second Gladiator drove through the gate did the lead one came to a crunching halt.

Every door opened, almost simultaneously, and her teammates alighted with expressions of either worry or irritation. Once they took notice of the child in Trish's arms, every feature softened—except for Aralyn's. Her emotionless mask remained fixed in place. Trish couldn't tell if her godmother was pissed or scared. She had never before seen Aralyn show either reaction. Her disciplined persona didn't allow her to become overly emotional—or at least she made sure not to reveal it to others.

Aralyn spoke in a curt monotone. "Get in the vehicle, Trish. We'll discuss this in the bunker."

Susan stepped forward. "Wait, Aralyn, the tree line."

Spinning, Trish saw Christina and Mrs. Johnson had corralled the kids into a tight circle underneath the last of the low-hanging branches. Their rigid movements were uneasy, to say the least. Trish waved to them, and she heard Aralyn tell the others to sling their weapons. Neither of the women moved.

Trish wandered over. "I promise, you have nothing to fear from these people."

Mrs. Johnson eyed her suspiciously. "Where did your group come from? Those vehicles, your outfits and weapons, we've never seen them before."

Trish's head ached. She wanted to get inside, take a shower, and sleep. Her body felt spent and ached unrelentingly. "We're from a bunker called NORAD. We came out yesterday even—"

At the sound of a gun cocking, Trish stopped talking. The noise resembled an antique shotgun Givens had, one belonging to his father. He'd let her fire it once, but this weapon wasn't pointing downrange to a plastic target but aiming straight at her from somewhere behind the children. She was sure of it.

"Trish, slowly walk toward me," Aralyn insisted.

Trish saw the level of alert growing from those surrounding Aralyn. She took a step closer to the children, knowing she had to do something before the tense scene escalated into something more. Over her shoulder she said, "It's okay, guys. Everyone relax and we'll talk this out."

Mrs. Johnson pulled two of the children to her. "Brian, I think you've put the children in enough danger for today? Don't you? We're outmanned and outgunned. Don't be an idiot. Drop your weapon."

Christina moved to within an arm's reach of Trish. She was several inches shorter, with eyes shining green in the moonlight. Her gaze drifted to the others, then locked onto Trish. "I don't care what happens to us, but please, swear to me no harm will come to the children."

Trish was touched to see how much this woman cared for the little ones. "I promise, you're all safe here. This group, they're good people."

Christina eyed her a bit longer, then turned. "Brian, please drop the weapons on the ground by your feet. Carefully! And come out from the shadows so they can see you're unarmed."

Brian lumbered out from the trees with his arms raised.

Mrs. Johnson muttered under her breath, something about him not being so conscientious when they were actually under attack.

Brian's eyes remained lowered and he waited. No one rushed forward to detain him or search him for weapons. Susan and Givens approached, each giving a warm greeting. Phillips moved along the fence, visually searching through the trees, while also keeping an eye on Brian.

Susan held out her hand to the dark-haired woman beside Trish. "I'm Lieutenant Susan Travis, and this is Sergeant Jason Givens. It's a pleasure to meet you."

Reluctantly, the woman accepted the handshake. "My name is Christina, and this is Evelin Johnson. Oh, and you've met Brian," she said, as if an afterthought.

Brian's chin dropped to his chest. Even though he had acted cowardly earlier, Trish felt sorry for him. Those creatures, their brute strength and apparent thirst for a kill, would terrify anyone. Yet, if her life, or the lives of those she loved hung in the balance, she wouldn't want to have to rely on him for protection. He shouldn't have been out here in the first place.

She glanced over to the multiple tiny figures standing huddled together, frightened. None of them should be. Why did the children not have parents? How big was their camp, and how safe was it from the creatures?

Susan spoke to the women, and Givens made weird babyfaces at the kids. Trish tried to pass Jennifer to Christina, but again, her effort was hopeless because Jennifer wouldn't let go. With the girl in her arms, she strode over to the guard. "Brian, I need you to be honest with me. Are you unarmed?"

He nodded.

"I don't want to leave your firearms out here, but because of what happened, I don't believe they'll let you carry them. Would you mind if I have someone come and collect the weapons to hold for you?"

"Yes, please." The tone of his voice was soft, defeated.

Trish waved Givens over, and Brian showed him where the weapons were. When they emerged from the shadows of the trees, Trish was surprised to see Givens had Brian lugging a few. She thought this tactic probably eased the women's defenses considerably despite the fact that she knew Givens very well; he would have removed all the ammo before he let the young man near the guns.

Trish's team directed the group to the others who waited by the Gladiators. Other than the two drivers, Phillips and Givens, the rest of the soldiers remained outside while Christina and Mrs. Johnson loaded in the children. After securing the kids in the armored vehicles, each woman climbed into a passenger seat.

The girl refused to leave Trish's arms and sit with the other kids so Trish was stuck carrying her.

The Gladiators drove in a wide circle in the weeds and headed inside the compound as the remaining soldiers traipsed behind. This time, Aralyn posted a guard at the gate, and another to monitor the fence line.

When Trish headed toward the patch of elm trees where she'd been reading earlier, Phillips said, "Don't bother. I already grabbed your trash and the book when I came looking for you."

Trish heard the disappointment in his tone. Before she could respond, he headed off to help the others with the children.

Her mind felt weak, her body sore and tired, and she was more than ready to find someone else to take the Jennifer. She needed some time alone.

As she entered the sleeping bay, she saw the weary, yet happy faces of the kids. They were parading in from the supply room, clutching containers of food and drinks in their tiny hands. The oldest child couldn't have been more than five, maybe six, years of age. Givens, Strong, Phillips, and even First Sergeant was helping, several kids each, get the children settled into small, sitting circles along the floor to have their meals heated. The view was as unbelievable as it was touching. Seeing trained killers act like enthusiastic babysitters was uncanny.

When she skirted around a little boy and entered the supply room where a couple kids were still selecting what they wanted to eat, Jennifer all but jumped from her arms. Trish carefully lowered her. She was about to turn and escape to the showers, but she spotted Susan waving her over from the front of the shortening line.

"Aralyn wants to see you. She's in her room."

Trish inhaled deeply and groaned.

Susan shook her head. "You scared the crap out of all of us tonight. When Phillips burst in and told us you were gone and that there were bodies down on the street, we were all terrified you had been hurt or even killed. Listen, Trish. No matter what she says, you need to keep your mouth shut and take it. She's already been through enough this evening, so let her vent."

Trish sensed the probing eyes of Christina and Mrs. Johnson from all the way across the room. Feeling humiliated, she hurried off. The events of the day were so overwhelming, a pressure built inside her like a volcano in her chest was going to explode.

She went toward the shower bay to hide in a bathroom stall and collect herself. Before she even opened the door, she heard running water and did an about-face. She pushed through the sleeping bay with the knowledge that her breathing and pulse had both increased to what felt like dangerous levels. Instead of veering right toward Aralyn's quarters, she continued straight ahead, to find someplace to hide.

She stepped through the entrance to the bunker. The cool air touched her face, and she felt a tremor in her stomach. Running to the left, weaving around the bumper of the first Gladiator, she hunched over and heaved. Nothing came up, only the burning taste of bile at the back of her throat. Not wanting her stomach to convulse a second time, she stood, leaned her head backwards, and breathed slowly, deeply.

She heard footsteps approach. Before she could move away, Sergeant Givens was standing next to her. Her eyes blurred and she shook her head no. The second the first tear touched her cheek, he wrapped her in his arms, and she began to cry. She wasn't sure how long they stood there, but when she was able to compose herself, she released him and backed up.

He gave her a look and she nodded. He stared at her briefly, returned her nod, then bowed, and continued on his patrol of the area. Her eyes followed him for a moment, until finally, she felt ready for the Lecture of all Lectures.

After a short rap on the door, Trish waited until Aralyn hollered for her to enter. She moved inside the spacious bedroom, which had a sitting area to the right and an office area in the center.

Aralyn tossed a thick folder in a drawer, rose from the desk chair, and motioned for Trish to follow her. Aralyn didn't speak until they were both settled on the leather couch, with newly polished end tables lining both sides.

In a calm, measured voice, Aralyn said, "When you were younger, we promised we'd be truthful with one another, no matter what."

Remembering the day in her room, right after her father had told her she was now free to train with Aralyn and move around section A of the fifth-level, Trish bowed her head in disgrace. If it hadn't been for the love Aralyn had for her, she would still be a hostage under her father's rules.

"It pains me to say, I've broken our promise."

Trish's head snapped up. She was unsure if she had heard her godmother right.

"At first, you were too young to confide in." Aralyn's tone was softer than normal, bordering on the side of sad. "Then later, as you grew older, I became too protective of the young woman I'd raised and loved as my own daughter." Aralyn's gaze fell to her lap.

Trish was beside herself with surprise. Aralyn was opening up, exposing her feelings. She wanted to reach out and tell her godmother not to worry; she too regarded Aralyn as a mother. Would this make Aralyn uncomfortable? This emotional candidness from her godmother was new territory, and she wasn't sure which direction to take, so she sat passively, waiting.

Aralyn straightened her shoulders with a degree of determination etched on her face. "A few days before your mother was killed, she told me she overheard a conversation between your father and a committee member from the sixth-level. What they were discussing led her to believe no nuclear annihilation or twenty-year winter had happened topside. Instead, a deadly virus had been intentionally released onto the ten billion people throughout the world. She planned to sneak into your father's lab and snoop around the next time he was called to a meeting.

"I told her not to. I said I could investigate through different channels. If she was right, I stressed the sleuthing was too dangerous for her to take on." Aralyn drew in a deep breath and her eyes moistened. "I should've known she wouldn't listen. Like yourself, she was stubborn."

For the first time, Trish understood. Her godmother didn't *love* her mother, she was *in love* with her. Had her mother known? Was their relationship more than friendship? She considered these questions to be private and wasn't going to ask unless Aralyn brought it up.

"A few days later she contacted me. She said she had found the proof, and the corruption was worse than she ever imagined. She needed me to take her—and you—topside. She said those living in the bunkers were in danger, and she needed to make things right. She insisted she had to destroy her research before we left. I gathered those I could trust and was on my way to meet her in the lab when I heard gunfire. By the time I rushed inside, I was too late. She was gone. Even though I can't prove it, I'm positive your father shot her."

With parted lips, Trish's mouth grew drier with every breath. Her father killed her mother. Why?

To keep her arms from shaking, Trish death-gripped her knees to the point of bruising. Her mind raced as she tried to relive that day in her youth, but all was blank. Her nightmares came to mind, but she wasn't even sure if they were real or not. All she could think of was a memory of her father callously pointing a pistol and killing her mother. The darkness in her life snuffing out the light.

"He was like a madman, searching through your mother's lab, by the time I arrived. I grabbed you up and took you from the room, then when I noticed the injection mark and inflammation on your leg, I rushed you straight to Doctor Harris. I don't know why or how, but you were injected with your mother's serum. Doctor Harris ran tests and monitored your condition over the next several years to make sure your body didn't go through any adverse complications. Unfortunately, he didn't have the knowledge to figure out what the serum was. Your strength and intelligence rocketed within the first few months, and your body developed an immune system unlike any he had ever seen. Later, he realized your cell healing and regeneration rates were also off the charts."

Trish's body was numb, her head pounded, and the bomb ticking in her veins was on the verge of exploding. She jumped up, shambled forward, and pivoted to face Aralyn. "How could you let him get away with it? My mother's death, the virus, any of it?"

Aralyn stood, wide-eyed. "Trish, there was nothing I could do. I had no proof, and security throughout the bunker tightened after her death. Your father had personnel assigned to him around the clock from then on. I didn't know who-all was involved. All I could do was work under the radar, recruit others, and wait for the right moment. Then this year, as they sent teams topside, we not only found our way out, but we also learned things affirming your mother's suspicions. We—this team— decided since we had no access down below, we would come up here and gather evidence through test samples as well as try to find survivors."

Releasing a deadly virus, murdering her mother—her father was nothing more than a cold-blooded killer. Strangely, the reality of this news didn't come as a surprise, but it did make the truth of what her father was capable of harder to bear. Trish attempted to calm herself, but she couldn't stop her entire body from shaking. "He can't get away with this, Aralyn."

Aralyn rushed forward and held her.

Trish wept. "He needs to be stopped."

Her heartbroken state took some time and coaxing from Aralyn to lift, but eventually, Trish's emotions were under control. She sat in a chair by the desk, and Aralyn lowered herself to the chair beside her.

"I want to help, Aralyn. I don't want my mother's death to be in vain. My father—and anyone who had anything to do with these creatures or releasing a virus to kill so many innocents—they must be held accountable for their crimes. Let me help, Aralyn. Whatever your plans are, I want in."

"Trish, you *are* your mother's legacy. I'm not merely talking about the serum inside you. You're a part of her. If you died, I'd not only lose you, but also the last piece of her I have left."

Trish's lips parted. Before she had a chance to speak, Aralyn hurried on. "I'm not saying no, but you owe it to your mother, me, and those here who love you not to be so reckless going forward. *Think* Trish. Use that incredible brain your mother gave you and learn everything you can. Train. Be a better badass than anyone or anything else, like those creatures out there. Be fiercer than even me."

Trish stared at Aralyn briefly then nodded. "I promise to learn and train, but you have to promise to keep me informed with the plans."

"If I want to keep you safe from yourself, it doesn't sound like I have much of a choice. Now, go get cleaned up and get some sleep. You've turned the bunker into a daycare. Tomorrow, we'll need to figure out what to do about that."

Trish's eyelashes parted, her eyes slightly burning. At once, a pressure on her chest vacated with scurrying movement on the bed and giggling around her. She wiped the lack-of-sleep sting from her eyes and spotted Jennifer and two other children poking their heads up from below the mattress. Raising an outstretched arm, Trish roared at the kids. With high-pitched cackles, the two girls and a boy scattered. She shook her head in disbelief at how quickly they pulled together to whisper their next move of attack. Their amplified chatter was her cue to rise.

When her foot found the floor, she spotted emerald eyes staring directly at her. Christina stood next to a bunk on the other side of the sleeping bay, talking to Susan. The deep shade of green was so intense, the sight almost took Trish's breath away. Her eye color matched the leaves of the summer trees or the ripple of color swaying through the oceans of grassy fields they passed on their drive to the bunker. Trish found it hard not to stare.

Christina's smile widened, and the redness in her cheeks darkened before she averted her gaze. She wore the same black T-shirt and shorts outfit as Trish, supplied from the bunker, which showed off her shapely legs. She had a damp towel draped over her shoulder and Trish marveled at how Christina's hair became even blacker after a morning shower. When she noticed the smirk on Susan's face, Trish immediately stood, feeling a heightened level of awkwardness, and headed to the footlocker for her things.

"Nope, leave your suit. I have these for you instead." Phillips made his way over and handed her a folded up black and green camouflaged uniform, the same outfit their security personnel wore in NORAD.

"We're staying another day," he said. "A team will repair the bus, so we can transport the kids once we find out where they come from." He slapped her shoulder. "You and I have a full day of low-crawling around in the dirt together." He lobbed a helmet into her footlocker. "I located some gear in storage and switched this out with the one you had. I'm not sure how you did it, but your helmet was damaged nearly beyond repair. Please, be careful with this one."

He fastened a wrist processor to her left wrist. "We found extras in this bunker's armory." He briefly showed her how to use it. "This device links to your helmet. Once your helmet is sealed, it works off voice command, and the display appears on your visor. This will let you communicate with others who have theirs activated. Now, next time you wander off, we can find you before you get yourself killed."

He turned to walk away. "Don't bother to shower," he called out over his shoulder. "You'll be sweaty soon enough. Grab a meal, and I'll meet you outside in ten minutes."

Placing the last loop over a downed tree branch, Trish tied the ends together along the side. Not wanting to use her dirty hands, she shook her head to remove loose strands of hair from her eyes. She was ready to go inside and eat, even though Phillips told her she had to read the field manuals once dinner was over.

"I don't mean to interrupt," Christina said, "but what are you doing?"

The instant her head came up, Trish glanced away. At lunch she realized if she didn't stare into Christina's captivating eyes, she was fine and less self-conscious of her newfound clumsiness. She pointed to the branch. "I have to wrap the abdominal dressing around my patient five more times before I call it quits."

The laugh drifting downward was light. Trish's heart skipped a beat.

"Is there a reason for your madness, or did your friend run out of ridiculous things for you to do?"

Trish couldn't help but grin. "Phillips said my abdominal dressings needed work. He gave me the option of either doing this or digging out another muddy foxhole. I chose this."

"He's had you out here all day, even during the downpour of rain. I was hoping after lunch, once you changed and ran around the fence ten times, he would've let you go."

Trish's stomach fluttered. Christina had been watching her all day long, closely enough to even count the number of laps she ran. She busied herself with unwrapping the dressing and starting over, careful not to let the ends drop into the mud puddle. That's when she noticed how covered she was in brown, murky filth. Her cheeks flushed.

"How large is this compound?" Christina asked.

"Phillips told me from the gate all the way around is just over a mile."

Christina whistled. "Ten miles of running. A little excessive, don't you think?"

Trish snorted. "I believe, because of the rain, he was actually taking it easy on me. I do kinda deserve it after scaring everyone yesterday. That reminds me, when I passed the area of fence where I saw your bus, I noticed the bodies of the people in your group who didn't make it were gone."

Rubbing her hands together, Christina's dapper mood faded into grief.

"I'm sorry, I didn't mean to seem callous. I wasn't sure if they had been taken or became . . . infected when they died."

Lips now parted, Christina stood there in silence, and Trish had a strange feeling Christina was doing her best not to laugh.

"What, like zombies?" she finally asked.

"Something to that effect. I once read folklore from African text, and, well, I guess it does sound—never mind."

Christina knelt on the other side of the log, and Trish's lungs slowed, close to the point of stopping.

"No, the Gramites are not dead. They hunt to kill for food or to infect and turn others to build up their numbers. Yesterday, the slaughtering was for food. With the kids, they probably would have infected them instead of killing them. My father has done some research on these things. You should ask him."

"So, you've decided to let us take you home?"

Christina smiled and lightly batted her eyelashes. "Mrs. Johnson is still talking with your commander, but I don't see why we shouldn't. You have some dirt on your cheek."

Bringing a hand up, Trish ran her fingers over both cheeks. "I guess I need a shower," she said, as brown clumps broke off.

"You missed some." Christina gently touched Trish's face.

Trish took in vigorous, deep breaths, sure her breathing was heard all the way in NORAD.

Christina made several slow swipes, cleaning off more dirt. "That's better," she murmured.

Pulse thundering, Trish fidgeted with the dressing as her mind raced. Numerous questions flooded in, but Trish kept them to herself. She had read a romance novel she once found abandoned by the swimming pool in the bunker. Trish thought of the way the woman had seduced the man, with light touches to his arm or by batting her eyelashes. She wondered if Christina had not only read the same book, but personally written it and left it in the pool area for her to find.

Trish swallowed hard and stood. "It smells like the deer's done. You should probably get some food before these guys begin loading their plates."

Christina let out a tiny chuckle then bit on her bottom lip and stifled the rest. She stood and stepped over the log. When she gently touched Trish on the arm, Trish felt on the verge of hyperventilating.

"I came over to say thank you again for saving us. We wouldn't be alive if you hadn't helped. I'm sorry if you're in hot water because if it."

The tingling ache forming in her midsection was unexpected and grew rapidly to the point of becoming uncomfortable. Trish kept her eyes focused on her practice abdominal dressing, now absorbing liquid from the mud puddle it was lying in. "It really was nothing, but you're welcome. Now, I need to get this done before Phillips decides to keep me out here all night."

"I'll leave you and your patient alone. If you'd like to talk later, you know where to find me."

Trish watched her leave, then looked to the branch lying on the wet ground. She may not have experienced a relationship before, but she wasn't uneducated. She knew her elevated pulse and the stirring excitement between her thighs was a natural reaction to her body's release of hormones and neurotransmitters. She and Christina were both healthy and at a good reproductive age, so naturally, Christina would flirt, and Trish's body would react. She felt uneasy at how well this woman was able to seduce her emotions. Christina seemed well-practiced at seduction, too skilled at offering herself to someone, and this unnerved Trish. If she were to allow her body to act on impulse, it would be with someone less . . . experienced.

Trish bent down, wrung out muddy water from the bandage, and started to re-wrap the branch. She had rarely been in the company of those her own age. The two kids who had lived in her area and attended class in section B were several years younger and kept to themselves. So, she had never felt this drive of sexual attraction before. The more she met other survivors, she was sure these feelings would continue to emerge. Sexual response was, after all, part of life.

She glimpsed up at Corporal Leonard, who stood at the firepit cutting meat off the deer. He was an attractive young man, so why hadn't she felt anything for him? She stared at him closely, trying to picture their lips touching. Nothing sparked. Picturing herself kissing this tree branch had the same non-level reaction. When her mind turned to Christina's lips, she felt an unusual throbbing sensation, and she shuddered.

Okay, so she could be homosexual. Still natural, but that minimized her ability to have a child of her own, if she ever made it to, say, twenty-five-ish. Did she even want kids? Could she have kids with her mother's serum inside her? What would it do to them? Was she willing to take the chance of finding out? No. If she *were* a lesbian, her partner could carry a child, but still, a third party would need to be involved. A male donor.

Feeling flustered, Trish unwrapped the dressing and wrapped the decomposing patient again. She glanced to Leonard, to see if she could try harder to ignite an attraction. The idea of him taking off his clothes made her stomach a bit queasy. Since she saw him more as a brother, using him as a visual test subject wasn't a fair assessment of her heterosexual versus homosexual sex drive.

She jumped when someone spoke close to her ear.

"Would you like me to get his number for you? You could call him in a month or two, that is, once you've finished applying your dressing correctly."

Mortified at seeing Phillips watching her, she fumbled with the saturated material in her hands. Thinking of a way to justify her probing eyes, she said, "The deer smells wonderful. I'm so hungry, I could eat the whole thing."

Skeptically, Phillips pointed to the hunk of wood. "Stop killing my patient and go get yourself something to eat. Once you've cleaned up, I want you reading in the community room."

Trish closed the last book in the stack and viewed her watch. She still had thirty minutes left to read. Could time go any slower? She wanted to go help Givens and Phillips give the bus a good going-over before they left tomorrow. Even though none of the three adults had given Aralyn the location of their camp, she knew they eventually would. Trish's group was big-hearted. They surely could see this, especially with the way the soldiers doted over the kids.

She picked up the books as the door opened and Christina entered. When their eyes connected, Trish's stomach did a complete set of cartwheels. She looked away, rose, and returned the books to the shelf. As she reached for the next two in line, Christina moved around her to read the book spines in a soft tone. Their elbows touched.

Trish closed her eyes to the aroma of coconut shampoo and honeysuckle. A book slipped from her fingers and fell to the floor. Trish bent to reach for it, but Christina grabbed it first. When Trish stood, her hand brushed against Christina's left breast.

Christina's tan complexion reddened, and from the neck up, Trish's own temperature felt like a furnace.

"Here's your book." Christina smiled, lightly biting her bottom lip.

Trish again pictured herself kissing those lips. Frazzled, she averted her gaze. She thanked Christina and moved around the table to her seat, opened the book, and scanned over the words. She flipped the page. At the sound of a tongue clicking, Trish tried to ignore Christina and focused her mind on the book. She flipped the page.

Finger tapping and more clicking followed as Christina searched through the reading material on each bookshelf. Before Trish flipped the page again, she lost her concentration and had to skim over the last paragraph three times. Did Christina *have* to make so much noise?

"You guys have an interesting selection of reading material," Christina said, moving around and taking the open seat beside Trish.

Keeping her eyes on track, Trish grunted and flipped the page. The delightful fragrance from Christina was distracting. Trish brought her arm up and rested her head in her hand, with her elbow on the table and her finger blocking her nostrils. She flipped another page.

"I thought you were supposed to read that?"

"I am," Trish said, trying not to lose her place. She flipped to the next page.

Christina giggled and touched Trish on the forearm. "There's no way you can read that fast."

This time Trish released a sigh. "Look, I understand what's going on here, and even though it's a normal part of life, frankly, I'm not sure if I'm ready—or homosexual for that matter."

Christina stared directly at her. "Excuse me?"

Trish nudged her head suggestively toward Christina. "You know, our bodies' natural instincts to connect, the physical attraction, intimacy. I'm not judging you for being so presumptuous, I'm only saying I'm not ready."

Christina's eyes widened. "Did you just call me a slut?"

Hesitating, Trish wasn't sure what to say. Maybe she was too forward, or too honest. She closed her book. Before she could explain further, Christina stood and marched from the room, slamming the door behind her.

With her mouth partially open, Trish stared vacantly at the door. What did she say that would have caused such a heated reaction?

She headed from the room to rectify her apparent misuse of words. Passing Susan, she saw her confused expression.

Susan asked, "Hey, do you know why Christina's so upset?"

"What do you mean? Where did she go?"

"She ran right by me and headed out of the bunker. I couldn't tell if she wanted to cry or destroy something."

Trish's jaw dropped.

"What did you do?" Susan asked, meticulously inspecting the befuddled expression on her face.

"I'm not sure. I might have caused it. Crap, I don't know how, but I need to fix this."

Susan took hold of her hand and escorted Trish into the conference room. "No, you'll probably make it worse. You were raised by Aralyn after all, so there's no telling what you'll say."

"What's *that* supposed to mean?"

"First tell me what you talked about, and I'll tell you how your lack of social skills almost certainly hurt that young woman's feelings."

Trish blew out her cheeks then forcefully released the air. "I talked about the connection between us. You know, our bodies' pheromones, our desire to sexually reproduce, how the sensations are strong. Well, I thought I was clear with her anyway. All the signs were there, her flirting and my body's responses to those actions. I don't know, maybe I was too blunt."

Susan rubbed her temples. "Damn Trish, you sound like you've been reading too many textbooks. Sit down and tell me everything."

Trish told Susan about the feelings she was having and about the flirting from Christina since lunch, and how her body had responded positively to all that seductive body language. She then related what happened in the room before Christina stormed out.

"I'm not really sure what I did wrong. From everything I've ever read, the need for honesty is stressed over and over. Truthfully, I'm not sure if I'm even ready to be intimate with someone, definitely not with a woman who expresses herself so, um, freely."

Susan punched Trish's arm. "Okay, you idiot, I can see now, over the critical years of your young life, we may have missed some much-needed conversations. All that stuff you just told me—"

Trish rubbed out the sting on her arm. "Yup, it was good, right?"

"No, no, Trish, it's all wrong. This may be the body's scientific responses, but they are a way to see if *you* like someone, and if the feelings are reciprocated. It doesn't mean you—or they—want to have sex, but that the possibilities of more than a friendship could be there. The flirting and the body's reactions should never be spoken of out loud, and *not* in a conversation with anyone you've just met. Oh, and you never assume a woman is a Jezebel until you've taken the time to get to know her first. Be respectful of others' feelings."

Trish stared at her, puzzled and alarmed.

"So, sit back and listen. I'll tell you about the birds and the bees, the honey and the heart, and the dos and the don'ts of both. Then, once I'm done, you can explain to me how everything you did tonight was so very wrong."

CHAPTER NINE

Trish climbed into Gladiator One next to Susan and waited for the inevitable questions.

"Did you talk to her?" Susan whispered.

"I tried, twice." Trish dropped her helmet on the floorboard. "The first time, before I even got a word out, she called me narcissistic and said she'd never been so insulted."

"Damn! And the second?"

"She actually approached me the second time. Before I could tell her I was sorry, she asked if I got off on slut-slamming."

"Crap, what'd you say?"

"I didn't. I froze."

"Trish! That wasn't the right time to be speechless!"

Trish lowered her head. "I know, but I wasn't expecting it, and it confused me even more." Trish ran her fingers through her hair. "I'm done Susan. I'm better off not being around people my own age."

"Trish, it's a learning experience. Next time, you'll know."

"What will I know?"

Susan grinned. "When it comes to women, it's best to let us do most of the talking."

Trish sat up, irritated. "Hey, I'm a woman."

"Yes, but like your godmother, you think like a man."

Through the remainder of the fifty-five-mile drive to Rapid City, South Dakota, Trish kept quiet. Every time her mind drifted, another flashback sent her to re-experience the outpouring she'd shared with Christina. She sighed loudly, releasing built-up emotions, and fidgeted in her seat, unable to think of anything else, before reliving the dreadful experience over again.

"My God, child, what is it?" Aralyn finally asked from the front seat.

"What do you mean?"

Aralyn threw up her hands. "All that huffing and puffing and sighing. You sound like a steam train."

Mortified, Trish glanced at Susan. She hadn't realized she was making any noise. The last thing she wanted was to have to explain her dilemma to anyone else, especially her godmother.

"She needs to use the restroom," Susan said, offering a believable explanation.

Aralyn pivoted around. "We left the bunker less than . . . oh, never mind. You need to hold it."

"That's an impressive beast," Givens interjected from the driver's seat.

Trish peered out the front windshield. In the distance stood Rapid City, with a mammoth sectional wall Givens had called the "beast," circling the outside. The wall stood at least two stories high, with five to eight feet of chain-link fence secured on top and barbed wire feeding through the links.

Givens's voice was filled with admiration. "They wrapped their wall around the entire city, and then some. Take a look over there. They're building another section to enclose the stretch of crops along the valley."

Aralyn said, "That's the same wall NORAD is building around Colorado Springs. See those machines carrying the wall panels? They unload the slabs, position them, then drive anchors down into the bedrock, or into the first hard layer it detects deeper than ten feet. Then an attachment on the machine bolts the sections together to make one solid structure. A machine can lay several miles of panels in a single day. I wonder if this equipment came from Colorado Springs?"

Her companions continued to discuss wall construction while Trish's temporarily impressed mood shifted once again to the memory of yesterday evening. She sat back suffering and closed her eyes for the remainder of the drive. When the vehicle finally slowed, she gawked upward in amazement to see a solid gate, easily fifteen feet in height and split into two sections, each at least ten feet wide. Robust two-story concrete towers with a window in each stood on either side of the gate. High above, between the towers, a concrete walkway stretched from one to the other. This walkway had sheets of metal fixed to the front for added protection.

Their convoy maneuvered around steel barricades, which were located sporadically along the road. The barricades were perfectly positioned to prevent vehicles from crashing into the wall slabs or assault the gate at high speeds.

When Gladiator Two stopped, the bus and Gladiator One followed suit. Mrs. Johnson exited the lead vehicle and talked to a guard leaning out of a tower window. The moment he vanished, Trish overheard a brief alarm sound from above, and Mrs. Johnson signaled to Aralyn.

"I want everyone to remain in the vehicle, unless I call for you," Aralyn said, casting around her famous scowl designed to suppress any desire to argue. Satisfied at their nods, she exited the vehicle without her weapon. As she moved away, all three lowered their windows to hear.

Time passed before a deep male voice shouted out, "Colonel Aralyn Williams, I'm not surprised you're still alive. After the virus was released, I realized then, those of you who'd disappeared were a part of it. Looks like you've been promoted to full bird since I last saw you. I guess congratulations are in order."

"Doctor Burgos, I can assure you, none of us had any idea what happened. We were told a global war was imminent."

"Spare me your lies, Colonel. Where's my daughter, and the others who went missing? Are they alive?"

After a pause, the door on the bus opened and Christina leaned the top half of her body out. "Father, I'm safe, and so are the children. Brian is also on the bus. If it weren't for this group, we wouldn't have made it."

"Colonel Williams, what are you proposing? Are you needing supplies, food? What could we possibly have left for you to take?"

"Doctor Burgos, we didn't bring them here to barter with. We only need information, but if you don't feel comfortable with us being here, my soldiers and I will leave."

"And what will happen to my daughter and the others?"

"Father," Christina called out, "these are good people—"

"Be quiet and let me handle this. You don't understand who we're dealing with."

Behind Aralyn, the lead vehicle maneuvered carefully around the metal structures, trying to change course while avoiding hitting anything. Aralyn motioned for their vehicle to back up. The bus moved forward, to give the lead vehicle some room to drive around a barricade along the side.

"Doctor Burgos, we'll move away from the gate so your people can come in. My troops and I will set up camp out here tonight. If you change your mind and are willing to talk, signal us. If by tomorrow morning we haven't heard from you, we'll leave, and you'll never see us again."

Christina stomped off the bus. "Father, listen to me. You know it's not safe out here at night. These people didn't know about the virus. They're—"

"Christina, get on the bus. We'll discuss this once you're inside."

Aralyn offered Christina a passing nod as she made her way to Gladiator One, where Trish, Givens, and Susan were silently watching.

"Christina! Listen. Damnit, Christina!" The doctor called out his daughter's name repeatedly.

Ignoring her father, Christina ran to Aralyn who stopped next to the Gladiator's hood.

"Christina, please, return to your father. If something happened to you, I would never forgive myself. Besides, your father would blame me for it."

"I know my father. When he has his mind set, it's difficult to change it. Me staying with you is the best way for him to hear you out."

Trish watched Aralyn study the wall, then Christina. After some unspoken deliberation she motioned with her head toward the vehicle.

Christina grinned and sauntered to Susan's door. Instead of sliding over, Susan got out and motioned the young woman inside.

As Christina climbed in, she locked eyes with Trish and froze.

Christina flailed her way backwards out of the backseat and retreated to Susan who motioned again. Christina hesitated, even gave a little stamp of her foot, then wheeled around and climbed in. Over her head, Susan tossed Trish a covert wink.

Trish mumbled under her breath.

"Excuse me?" Christina asked, her head raising in defiance.

Something in Christina's tone struck a chord deep inside. Without saying a word, Trish grabbed her helmet and rifle, and opened her door. Yes, she screwed up, but she was done being an emotional target for this stranger to direct her irritable missiles at. Christina didn't know her, nor was she giving Trish a chance to rectify her mistake. This hot and cold performance was tiring. Trish waved over the other vehicle before it passed.

"Julie Webber," someone called out from the gate.

Confused, Trish peered up to the walkway between the towers. A man with salt-and-pepper hair squinted down from above.

"Did you say Julie Webber?"

"Yes."

Trish shaded her eyes and moved closer to look at the man. "That was my mother's name. "I'm Patricia, her daughter, but everyone calls me Trish."

"Her daughter . . ." He gaped at her. "You look just like your mother. Which vehicle is she in?"

Although her mother's death had been thirteen years past, the pain still gripped her chest. "I'm sorry, my mother's not here. She died when I was four."

From where she stood, Trish watched his shoulders drop. "I'm sorry to hear this. Your mother worked with me at the CDC in Fort Collins. She was a dear friend to both me and my wife. If you don't mind me asking, how did she die?"

Trish felt her already preheated temper rise. "My mother found out what had actually happened here, and she was killed for it. My father was the one who shot her. Were you friends with him as well?"

His hand gripped the edge of the walkway, and his eyes grew dark with either anger or pain. Maybe both. He disappeared from sight. She stared for a moment, then veered toward the second Gladiator. When she was about to open the door, the ample gate split at the center and one half swung outward. The man who'd spoken to her exited the city at a brisk pace. He was both alone and unarmed and went straight to Trish, which caused Aralyn to move protectively closer.

Trish was not sure if she should hold out her hand in greeting or wait for him to talk. She decided to let him dictate the exchange. He wrapped his arms around her in a heartfelt embrace, as if she were an old friend he had known for years.

Shocked, her body went rigid at his unexpected hug.

He drew back, his hands still light on her shoulders. "I'm so deeply sorry, Trish. You mother was a kind, brilliant woman who deserved to live a long, happy life."

Composing herself, Trish struggled to relax. Unsure what to do, she patted him awkwardly on his forearm. He released her, and she saw his sorrow was sincere. He spoke to Aralyn but did not take his eyes off Trish. "Julie went into the bunker with you?"

"Yes. It all happened so fast. We didn't know what was going on, only that a large-scale nuclear attack was projected. They loaded us onto buses with barely any warning. I thought everyone was being evacuated from the area. When we got to NORAD, I searched but didn't find Julie until I was already inside the bunker. We were on lockdown for the first few weeks. We assumed you and the others were taken to a different section or level. Over a month later, we discovered not everyone at the CDC had been evacuated."

His eyes met Aralyn's. "I knew when the government added the secured wing to the building and doubled your staff, something didn't feel right. I told you this, and you did nothing. When they brought their own virologist in to run the place, I warned you something bad was in the works, but you didn't listen. Instead, you allowed that man into Julie's life."

"Doctor Burgos, enough. I told Julie I didn't trust him, but she was a grown woman, and you know as well as I, Julie always did what she wanted." Aralyn's voice rose. "How can you stand there and blame me for what happened? You had no proof of what Frank was doing, and even if I gained access, I'm not a scientist. I didn't have the slightest clue where to look or what to search for. You were a virologist overseeing the Arboviral Diseases Branch. You had as much clearance as I did." She pinched her lips together. "We're not even sure if the virus *was* manufactured from our CDC."

By this point, all of the children on the bus were observing them from the windows, and both Gladiators had emptied out. Susan came over and touched Aralyn's arm.

Aralyn cast Doctor Burgos a displeased glare, did a swift one-eighty, and moved a few feet away.

Burgos stood, arms folded over his chest. "You're right, Aralyn. I should have done something. I think of that every morning, when I pray my wife or daughter are not taken from me. I've been luckier than most, and I know I probably don't deserve it."

"Doctor Burgos, you couldn't have stopped this. If you had attempted to, you would've been killed like Julie was. You can't change the past, but you *can* help us by removing whoever was responsible. They must not remain to govern humanity's future. I don't believe those of us who are left will be safe until we do."

"There's nothing left to govern, Aralyn. The society we once knew, it's but scattered clusters of humans and the Gramites."

"You're wrong. The United States constructed over twenty colonized bunkers. At a minimum, that's over a million people waiting to reclaim this continent in May of 2090. That's in less than two years. Do you believe those responsible will want survivors roaming around telling citizens what really happened? It won't be the creatures who kill off your *human clusters* but thousands upon thousands of troops with bigger weapons than ours. But like us, none of them know the truth about what happened either. Work with us in stopping this, before there's unnecessary bloodshed."

Burgos glared at Aralyn evenly. Deliberating. Trish felt like she and everyone else waited while holding their breath.

He shook himself as if out of a daydream and waved his hand in the air toward the gate. Both sections opened.

"We can discuss this over dinner."

Christina unpackaged the last pillow and placed it on the bed. "Now if you need anything, Jennifer, you let Mrs. Johnson or one of the staff know and they'll get it for you."

"Why can't you stay with me?"

Christina picked up the little girl and gently threw her on the newly made bed. Before the bed stopped bouncing, she tickled the giggling child. "I told you, I have to be somewhere tonight. But, I *might* swing by in the morning before my shift starts."

"Do you think Trish will come see me later?"

Christina rolled her eyes at the name. "I'm not sure. They're getting settled, and she has a dinner to go to in a few hours." Yeah, at my house with my family, Christina thought. She needed to find some way to get out of it if she could. The idea of sitting in a room with such a horrible person was not on her, 'must do,' list. Maybe she could speak with her mother.

"Why do you like her so much?" Christina asked.

The girl sat upright. "Because she's nice, and she's pretty like my mom was. Plus, I feel safe in her arms. Like when my father used to hold me."

"Okay, you go play with the other kids. I need to head home."

"Oh, and she smells good. She smells like pancakes and strawberry soap." The girl laughed.

Before Jennifer could make any more demands, Christina left the room. She didn't care how the woman smelled, or how strong she may be. On the inside, Trish was as sour as her mother's huckleberry pie. Trish's tall, athletic build no longer held a flicker to her candle, and those eyes, surely, were a frosty-blue due to the ice surrounding her frigid heart.

Christina went to the fire station garage where Brian had parked the bus. She spotted her backpack lying on top of a workbench. First she made sure the rest of the gear had been unloaded, then she snatched up her bag and went out into the warmth of the sun. She needed to hurry and find her mother before her father made it home. He would think it rude if she wasn't at dinner, especially since this group saved her life, but she simply could not go for fear of saying to Trish something unbecoming of a lady.

Picturing the way Trish had stormed out of the vehicle earlier made Christina fume with resentment. How could she say such hateful things, then afterwards, act like *she* was the victim? The recurring memory added more salt to Christina's reopening wound.

"Hey, Christina. Do you have a moment to talk?"

Christina spun to find Susan smiling at her. Now, *this* woman was both kind and outgoing. Too bad Trish hadn't been raised by her. She might have been better off for it. "Yes, if you're quick. I need to get ready for dinner." Not a complete lie. As of right now, she still had to attend. She hoped soon that wouldn't be the case.

"Could we step inside for some privacy?"

"Sure." She tossed her backpack strap over her shoulder, and they moved side by side toward the entryway. Now Christina was both worried and curious. "Is everything all right?"

"Yes, and no. If Trish found out I was here, though, she wouldn't be happy."

At hearing the name, Christina came to a halt. "Look, I understand she's your friend and all—and for that I'm terribly sorry—but I don't have time to hear you make excuses for her."

Susan sighed. "Christina, when we first met, I could tell you're an amazing woman who's both strong-minded and good-hearted. So I'm giving you the benefit of the doubt, and I want to clarify something. Trish is more than a friend. She's like my child, and as one of her mothers, please select your words carefully."

Christina frowned. She shrugged into her backpack. "I really need to go."

"I'm not here on her behalf, but for you. If you choose to sever all connection with Trish, that's fine, but you'll be making the biggest mistake of your life."

"Excuse me?"

"I would like to explain, but I'll only do so if you drop the defensive attitude. It's been a long couple of days, and I'm growing tired of youthful defiance."

Christina remained unmoving until finally, she nodded.

"Good," Susan said. She pointed to a bench under a long, dirt-stained window. Once they were seated, Susan asked, "Do you have many friends?"

Christina nodded.

"What sort of education and school-life have you had?"

Christina exhaled, unsure how this related. She felt an intense need to get home. "My mother taught me until I was around four. By then our numbers had expanded to the point the CDC group decided to establish a few classrooms. When we outgrew the complex, they built walls up around this city, after they cleared out the Gramites. We relocated here when I was ten. Several of the neighboring strongholds combined with ours, and since we had over forty kids falling within various age groups, we used a school in the center of town. Now our community is over five thousand strong with several hundred kids."

Susan whistled.

"I know. Last year my graduating class had twenty-two. Yet, if you think about the fact that this city alone had housed over a hundred thousand people, it's not such a great feat after all. And if you combine the population of the other towns and cities throughout this one state, you'd see there had once been just over a million people living in South Dakota. Five thousand compared to a million, it's sad when you realize our society may never recover."

"No, I believe we will, as long as everyone sticks together." Susan studied her for a moment, no doubt choosing her words carefully. "Trish doesn't have your experience with relationships. When her body reacted in a way she wasn't used to, she tried to rationalize it."

Christina dug deep, fighting to contain her temper. Why did people in this group assume she was some easy woman with loose morals? "Not that it's anyone's business, but I've never had sex. I was raised to believe waiting until you found the right person makes the entire experience so much stronger."

"Oh, Christina, I'm not talking about sex. I mean *any* relationship. Family, friends, yes, even lovers. Trish is extremely intelligent, but unsocialized. What I'm going to tell you about Trish is private. Do you promise not to repeat what I say, not to anyone?"

Christina paused. Even if she didn't like Trish, she wasn't one to gossip about her enemies. She was raised better than that. "I do," she replied honestly.

Susan smiled. "Thank you. First, you need to understand life in the bunker is quite different from what you have here. The first year was the hardest with so many deaths. Surrounded by concrete, unable to go topside and see the sun, people felt depression, claustrophobia, and fear. Suicide ran rampant throughout the underground fortress. Fights broke out daily, mainly on the upper levels, and mandatory pregnancy tests became our way of life. With strict rules and limited space, everyone's freedoms came to a crashing halt overnight."

"Mandatory pregnancy tests? Why? Didn't people want to have kids?"

"We had to survive underground for twenty years, supporting fifty thousand inhabitants. One would need a permit to have a child, and the number of births they allowed each year was based off the population count. Those on the first two levels were nicknamed the 'expendables'— soldiers, laborers—and for them, having a child was forbidden. They wanted the doctors, scientists, engineers—the people with the higher degree of intelligence on levels three to six—to produce the offspring. The soldiers, like myself and this group, who lived on these levels but worked on the security detail were also forbidden to reproduce. The women had to have pregnancy tests every other month, and if positive, they were given a pill to induce a miscarriage."

Christina didn't know what to say. She thought it sounded rather draconian . . . and cruel.

"When Trish was four, her mother was shot and killed in front of her by her own father. They said her mother was a spy, sent to the bunker by those responsible for the Global Annihilation. She was branded a traitor, and everything Trish had of her mother, pictures and all, her father personally destroyed. She wasn't allowed to even say her mother's name for fear of what her father would do. Aralyn was able to hide a few items for Trish, but they were nothing more than knickknacks."

Christina wasn't sure when she had clutched at her chest. The image of her own father killing her mother and of not having any pictures to remember her mother by was both terrifying and heartbreaking tied together in one big knot.

"Trish wasn't allowed to have friends or to attend classes with the other kids. Aralyn says it's because Trish's father was downright evil. I believe Frank's abusive restrictions had to do with the notion that his daughter might recall and say something about what happened the night her mother died. Information he didn't want others to know. She was most likely too young to remember, but he still treated her like a prisoner for so many years."

Christina had no words to express what she was feeling. She could only shake her head slowly in amazement.

"He offered her no love, only solitude. In a place void of the sounds of birds or the view of the sky, life was hard enough without further stressors. Her limited social experiences came from what she studied by herself off the academic workstations or from Aralyn and a handful of us soldiers under Aralyn's command. Trish can shoot and kill as well as the rest of us. Yet, put her in a room full of others her own age, and she would be miles outside of her element."

"How could he have been allowed to treat his own daughter like this? Why didn't anyone put a stop to it?"

Christina saw a flash of guilt on Susan's face. "You need to understand, civil rights were gone, the chain-of-command made the laws, and when an individual broke the law, punishment was swift and severe. Trish's father was far up the power chain, so nobody dared cross him. Occasionally, Aralyn went toe-to-toe with the man for Trish's sake. As soon as we were able, we got her out of there. Unfortunately, I worry the years raised in solitude will make it hard for her to thrive in a community like this."

"I see." And Christina *was* beginning to understand.

"Trish is the type of person to run into a burning building to save a complete stranger, with no fear for her own life. Yet because of how she reacted to you yesterday, she feels mortified, and she's not handling it well."

Christina felt a pang of guilt work its way in. "I'm such an idiot."

Susan shook her head. "No, this impasse is definitely not on you."

"Part of it is. I'd never met anyone quite like Trish before. She was strong, attractive, good with the kids. I was both scared and excited by how much I was immediately drawn to her. I wanted to get to know her. See what her personality was like." Christina felt the heat of embarrassment wash over her cheeks. "To be honest, when I realized how being around me made her nervous, I assumed she felt the same way. I utilized every technique my friends use, trying to get her attention. I guess I went too far and really screwed this up."

"You couldn't have known."

Christina sat up straighter and squared her shoulders. "What can I do to help?"

"Talk to her, try to forgive her, and if you feel a friendship could be salvaged from this, help her with learning to blend in with others her own age. She's too young to give up on making friends or finding lovers, but she will require guidance in doing this. And above all, she will need to know you're okay because this guilt will continue to eat at her until she does."

After removing some homemade bread from the oven, Christina placed it on a counter to cool. She took off her apron, gave her mother a peck on the cheek, and hurried from the room. Thinking of her conversation with Susan a few hours earlier, she hastened back. Her mother was by the sink, tossing newly chopped vegetables in a salad bowl. Christina gave her a big hug.

"What's gotten into you?"

"What do you mean?" Christina asked, plopping a cherry tomato into her mouth.

Slightly closing her eyelids, her mother gave her the *you know what I mean* glare she most often used on Christina's father. "You're acting very, shall we say, bubbly tonight."

"Come on mom, I'm always cheerful."

"Not when I make you help me in the kitchen. Speaking of which, you volunteered to assist with the cooking, which is also out of character."

Stealing another tomato, Christina laughed at her mother's investigative probing. "Dad's right, you're watching too many criminal-drama reruns. Adam has every *Disney* movie in his collection. I should copy some for you."

"Oh, I forgot to tell you. When you were taking a shower, Adam stopped by to see how you were doing. Best friend or not, I think he still has feelings for you. And stop eating those. They go in the salad."

Still laughing, Christina gave her mother another lengthy hug. She stuck a tomato between her teeth, revealing her defiance to her mother, and jumped out of the way before the end of a dish towel struck her hip.

"This hugging is also rare. Tell me what you're hiding?"

Christina placed her hands on her hips. "We always hug." She spotted the time on the stove clock. "I've gotta go wait on the porch, Mom. Love you."

"Because I'm the one who instigates it," her mother called out as Christina skedaddled.

She had a good fifteen minutes until dinner, but Christina wanted to be ready. Her goal was to pull Trish aside and talk with her on the porch before she came into the house. She did a swift visual inspection of her jeans and blouse, fluffed her hair one last time, flipped on the porch light, and opened the security door. Surprised by Aralyn and Susan approaching the steps, she pushed on the screen door with a friendly greeting. They were both in black and green camouflaged outfits. She wondered if their group had any normal clothes.

Aralyn was the first to reach her. "Sorry if we're early. Susan wanted to walk here, and I didn't realize you lived so close."

Christina waved. "Not at all. Please come in. Mom's in the kitchen and Dad should be home any minute."

The peculiar way in which Aralyn was looking at her when she passed worried Christina slightly. When Susan stepped forward, she pointed. "You have something on your nose. Looks like flour."

Embarrassed, Christina wiped at her face. "Where's Trish? Is she coming?"

Susan turned and Christina spotted Trish across the street sniffing the air. Curious, she was about to ask Susan what Trish was doing, until Susan called her over. Trish's hands were deep in her pockets, and her eyes were downcast. Susan went inside.

A deep sense of remorse filled Christina. As Trish came up the stairs, Christina said, "Trish, can we talk?"

Trish stared at her closely before finally agreeing. Christina moved over to the porch swing, and Trish followed. Taking a seat, Christina motioned to the other side of the swing, but Trish shook her head and instead leaned against the railing encircling the porch. Easing this tension wasn't going to be easy, Christina thought. She tried to recall all the ways she had planned on starting this conversation, but as she sat there, scarcely rocking, her mind went blank. *For the love of God, just say something,* her inner voice screamed, but still, Christina couldn't form any words.

"Do you mind if I go first?"

Relieved, Christina said, "Sure."

"I'm really sorry for last night. I didn't mean to insult you. I'm not sure how to explain it, but I didn't handle any of it well." Trish picked at a small spot on the railing where the paint was chipped. "You made me nervous and several unfamiliar sensations emerged. I tried to translate my feelings in a way to understand what I was experiencing, but evidently, I complicated the situation." Trish blushed. "You're a beautiful woman, and I'm not merely talking about your looks. The way you protected those kids with your own life, how you are when you're around others, you appear to be a wonderful human being, Christina. You appear smart—"

"Let me stop you there." Christina stood, trying to conceal her rising amusement. "When you're talking to others, especially in a positive way, don't use the word *appear*. Just tell them they *are* smart, or wonderful, or funny. If you don't think they are, it's best to compliment specific features, or even what they're wearing."

"I do think you're smart." Trish sounded newly flustered.

Christina laughed. "Well, thank you. I'm talking about those you haven't met yet. I thought on it some, and I figured, maybe—you're probably not used to life here outside the bunker." She pointed toward the house. "I mean, most of your friends are around my parents' age, and they speak an entirely different vocabulary than our own generation."

Trish studied her. "Did Susan talk to you?"

Before she could answer, her father came around the corner of the house, huffing and puffing as though he'd been running. "Ah, hey kids, am I late? Sorry, I was in the lab and lost track of time."

Christina grinned, pleased by her father's sudden appearance. "Nope, they arrived a few minutes ago. The others are inside."

He opened the screen door. "Are you coming?"

Christina nudged her head toward the door, her way of letting her father know she needed a moment. "We'll be right in."

When the door shut, she held out her hand. "Friends?"

Trish glanced from Christina's eyes to her hand, then tentatively shook it. "Friends. But you still haven't answered my question."

"We better go, Mom will be upset if she has to reheat the dishes. With planning a meal, timing is everything."

As they entered the house, the aroma of homemade bread, seasoned roast, and her mother's famous broccoli-and-cheese casserole grew stronger. Standing by the bar making drinks, her father asked Trish what her poison was. When she asked for water, Christina moved closer. "You know, you can have alcohol if you want. When we finish school, we're added to the rotation to do runs outside the city. Because of this, we're allowed to drink."

Trish leaned forward. "Our bodies are at a critical growth period. Consuming alcohol at our age can damage brain function, especially related to memory, motor skills, and coordination."

Christina hid her smile. "You read a lot, don't you? Are you telling me you've never had a sip of alcohol?"

Trish shook her head.

"Not even a drop?"

Trish chuckled. "Nope, and I'd rather not. I like being in control of my own mental state, and yes, I do read a lot."

Her father said, "Christina, the main course tonight is beef. Do you want red or white?"

Fascinated and still amused by Trish's response, Christina bit her bottom lip. "None for me, dad. I'll have water."

Trish said, "You know, you can have wine. I swear, I won't judge you for it. I restrict myself because I'm wanting to learn more to try to figure out my mother's work. I need every brain cell at my disposal."

"I'm fine. I don't drink often as it is, except with my parents during dinner." Christina took the glasses from her father and passed one to Trish. "What type of work was your mother doing?"

"She worked in genetics." Trish looked toward the front door. "Do you not smell that?"

"Oh yes, isn't it wonderful?"

"Not really, it reeks of raw sewage."

"Trish!" Aralyn scolded from her seat on the couch.

Susan sat beside Aralyn, shaking her head.

"You know, it's not polite to refer to the aroma of someone's cooking as *sewage*." Christina grinned at Trish, who was glancing wide-eyed around the room.

Christina's father laughed, and Trish held up a hand. "Wait, wait. I wasn't referring to your wife's cooking, but the smell coming from outside."

"Thank God. My wife will be relieved. I'm pretty sure she has never fed us sewage. Seriously though, the sewer line down the road does plug up on occasion, but you would have to have an extraordinary sense of smell if this were it. Your brain is probably tapping into a memory of an odor. Happens more often than we realize."

Eva entered the dining room and announced, "Dinner's ready." She placed a platter of roasted meat on the table, and Christina's father choked down his amusement as he moved into the dining room.

Noticing Trish's defeated expression, Christina touched her arm. "Stop beating yourself up. Your only fault is you're brutally honest, which is actually an amazing trait to have. You need to learn certain things are best left unsaid, or else clarify your thoughts to fit with what's happening around you."

Trish nodded but didn't meet her eyes.

Christina pulled Trish toward the table. Socializing Trish was going to be hard work—yet, Susan was right. The more she saw who Trish truly was, the more Christina wanted to help.

CHAPTER TEN

Trish pushed potatoes around on her plate. The constant glances from both Susan and Christina were growing tiresome. She was certain Susan had talked with Christina since their own conversation this morning, and told her what exactly? Every time her eyes flashed to either of them, she felt like a clumsy toddler in a social gathering she hardly understood.

Eva said, "I'm sorry, Trish. Is the seasoning on the potatoes not to your liking? I probably added too much salt."

Trish's lips parted, but Susan answered. "The potatoes, the entire meal, everything tastes wonderful. Thank you, Eva, for preparing such a superb dinner."

Trish shoved a bite into her month and wondered if they expected her to be writing their responses down for later use.

Doctor Burgos continued to expound about the virus. "The virus didn't cause the Gramites, not completely anyway. You see, once the space station released the second round of the virus, those left who were capable of trying to construct a vaccination came out with three untested serums. We later discovered that when Doctor Erin Gramite's vaccine combined with the virus, the fusion produced these creatures. They had made enough to supply the serum to less than ten percent of the two billion souls left around the world. The third and last round of the virus was released three months later. When those with Doctor Gramite's serum were infected with the virus, they turned into those horrible creatures within a matter of days. Those who didn't receive the serum either perished from the virus or remained hidden like us. As far as I'm aware, the other two flimflam remedies didn't work. The limited communications we had ceased less than a week after the final release, so we weren't able to construct a census of how many people were still alive."

Trish was fascinated to learn these facts from Doctor Burgos. What happened to the outside world was now becoming clear.

"After the third viral release, most everyone outdoors died from the virus, the Gramites, or were infected and turned into Gramites, and the rest of us struggled to keep going. We were too afraid to go outdoors for long. Mass graves were left open, bodies lined the streets, piled up at the hospitals, or remained untouched inside houses. Getting supplies was a nightmare. The smell, the creatures, a constant check of the sky for any signs of further aerial attacks. Frankly, I'm surprised any of us made it."

"Why didn't those left destroy the space station?" Trish asked.

"They tried. Right after the initial viral release, all communication and control of the space station from the planet ceased. From what I understand by listening to you guys, NORAD probably took it over. During the expansion of the space station, before the virus, the facility had become weaponized. Those on the space station destroyed damn near every satellite and repelled any missiles shot at it. We heard a rumor it ended up losing orbit two years later, and whatever was left after reentry ended up in the ocean."

Trish was about to take another bite of the meat, but the smell drifting in from outside was nauseating and growing stronger through the course of the meal. She wanted to reach back and close the window but being as she was a guest and was already under heavy surveillance from prying eyes, she took shallow breaths through her mouth instead. She stabbed the meat, removed it from her fork, then stabbed it again. When she glimpsed upward, Christina's green, mesmerizing eyes were watching her.

Eva said, "Trish, would you like me to make you something else? I have some leftover hamburgers I can heat up. Won't take but a few minutes."

Doctor Burgos sat up straighter in his chair. "If you're adding the fried onion and peppers like last time, I'll take one."

"James, finish your plate," Eva ordered, as she rose from the table.

Before Trish had a chance to politely decline the offer, Christina cut in. "Mom, I'm sure she doesn't want to trouble you."

Trish stood and dropped her napkin beside her plate. "Actually Mrs. Burgos, I'm sorry, but I need to go. Thank you for having me over."

When she opened the front door, Christina was calling her name, and she heard Mrs. Burgos scold both women for treating Trish like a child during dinner. Aralyn strongly agreed.

Crossing the shadows of the yard into the glow of the streetlight, Trish noticed the stench became stronger. This horrid stink was not her brain remembering a smell from her past. Even though, as she continued forward searching the air with her nose, the smell became increasingly familiar. She peered into the distance. Beyond the shine from the last light along the street, all was dark and moonless from the building clouds overhead.

"Trish, what are you doing?"

When Trish pivoted, the person advancing wasn't Susan or Christina parading up to point out her social shortcomings, but Christina's mother, Eva.

"Mrs. Burgos, how far is the wall from here?"

Looking surprised, Eva said, "Well, if you go five blocks east, by the former hotel where you're staying, you'll run into the main gate. The north side of the wall is two blocks straight ahead. The west edge of the wall is over fifty miles to my left, and the south is thirty plus miles behind me. They enclosed the entire city and some of the suburban districts, and there's still talk of expansion. It's more than we need if you ask me."

"Thank you."

Eva's eyes opened wider. "Wait a minute, though, you can't leave. It's too dangerous."

"I'm not leaving, just assimilating my bearings."

Eva looked like she wanted to say something but instead she pressed her lips together.

Trish plodded away from her hostess, growing closer to the smell with every step. When she reached the final light, the scent was so overpowering, even her mouth held a rancid aftertaste. Her sense of danger flared. She moved on until she was two hundred feet from the wall. Maybe the creatures roamed beside the structure at night, close enough for her to detect the stench and trigger the stabs of warning.

"Trish, I spoke with my daughter and Susan. I'm not sure what's going on, but Aralyn and I gave them a good talking to. Please come with me to the house. I made apple pie for dessert. My mother's recipe."

Trish was surprised to see Eva had followed. "Can you not smell that?"

"Do you mean the rain? Yes, it'll probably start any minute now."

At the end of the street Trish spotted the shadowed outline of the massive wall. The concrete beneath her feet shifted to grass about twenty feet from the barrier. Taking careful steps, she pressed on until the smell was losing potency. Her stomach tightened. She shifted the few feet to where the smell was the strongest, then headed east. The odor weakened before she reached a vacant house. She returned to the original spot and continued west, and again the unpleasant scent weakened. Her heart raced.

This time, she found where the putrid scent was most overpowering, and Eva was still standing right there.

"You know," Eva said, "I *can* smell something. It's a faint sewer odor, probably from this area not being lived in for so long. The pipes need a good flushing."

Trish got down on her hands and knees and inhaled deeply. She gagged as rot-tainted air filled her lungs. She straightened, still on her knees, her heart beating wildly. They'd tunneled into Rapid City. How deep were they? Why hadn't they dug upward yet?

"Eva, can you please go get Aralyn for me? Tell her to come at once. It's an emergency. The creatures have burrowed under the city wall. Have Susan get the others. They need to be armed and bring the vehicles with them. Ask her to grab my suit and rifle."

Once Eva left, Trish studied the area. She scanned the grass, unsure why they hadn't surfaced, but her night vision barely pierced the blackness. She wasn't about to continue traipsing over soft ground she couldn't see simply to plunge into a sinkhole full of the infected.

A storm drain was located along the curb about ten feet away. She rushed over to inspect inside the slanted opening, but the deep cavity was too dark to see beyond a few feet. If they dug a straight line from the wall, the creatures would soon hit the concrete storm box.

When she saw Aralyn and a few others heading her way, she relaxed a bit, until she realized the entire dinner group, including Susan, was with her. Trish's muscles tensed. The second Aralyn was within earshot, Trish said, "I take it no one went to get the others, or the weapons."

Eva's voice was tense. "I told them what you said, but they didn't want to make a commotion until they were sure your concern was an actual emergency."

Trish grunted.

"What's going on?" Aralyn asked.

Trish shot her godmother a glower that mimicked her mounting irritation, a pointed glare that Trish had never used before, and it was clear Aralyn wasn't sure how to react.

"Aralyn, they've burrowed under the wall."

Susan stepped closer. "Who has?"

"Santa Claus and his elves," Trish snapped. "Who do you think?".

"Trish!" Aralyn's look of disbelief hardened.

"No, I stressed we had an emergency, yet here everyone stands gauging whether I've lost my mind. No backup, no weapons." Trish forcefully pointed to the area the smell was strongest. "I don't know how, possibly because of my mother's serum, but I can sense the creatures. I can also smell them and *they're right below us.*"

"Whoa, whoa, wait a minute!" Doctor Burgos shouted. "Your mother completed her compound and it's *in* you?"

Trish didn't bother to respond. It was all she could do not to roll her eyes.

Doctor Burgos focused on his wife. "She actually did it, Eva." He turned to Trish. "How do you sense them? Is it a gut feeling, goosebumps, a tingle, what?"

Trish shrugged. "Besides the smell, it's hard to explain. Maybe a tingle. It's like when the hairs on the nape of your neck stand on end when you detect an unnatural presence. Except it happens inside me, all throughout my body, an eerie feeling of being watched by something dark, dangerous. Their rot smells putrid, like sewage turned even more sour."

Doctor Burgos and Eva shared a look of concern. "Eva, please go let the Governors know we have a breach and to notify city security."

"James," Aralyn stepped closer and motioned for Eva to wait. "Are you sure you want to frighten your people before we've had a chance to poke around? Maybe this isn't as dire as Trish thinks."

"Aralyn, I knew what Trish's mother was working on, and I also knew she had the talent and determination to succeed. If it's inside her daughter, Trish's ability to detect danger would indeed increase in intensity, compared to you or me. Including her sense of smell. At this point, I'm the one who's frightened. If your group could assist, we would be ever grateful."

Aralyn measured Doctor Burgos and Eva's looks of urgency, then she examined Trish. "Susan, I want everyone armed and here in thirty minutes or less.

The doctor said, "Eva, also have Bill bring some spotlights."

Susan and Eva both took off running.

James tried talking his daughter into going home to wait, but Christina refused. He managed to get her to stand under the streetlight by giving her the task of keeping unarmed onlookers away from Trish's indicated area of danger.

Trish was burning up because of Aralyn's lack of faith in her, but also oddly comforted about Christina's dad's opinion. Calmly she said, "I don't understand. We're what—twenty feet from the wall?"

Doctor Burgos nodded as they moved away from Aralyn.

"Why are they digging so far in? That's a lot of extra work—kind of stupid, actually." Trish tried to think like a predator, hunting for its prey, but it made no sense to her. "I was starting to believe these creatures were somewhat intelligent."

"You can keep on believing it. I've tried studying them. A colleague and I even set out on an expedition to track a small group for research. The more you know about your adversary, the easier it is to defend against them. By the second week we discovered we were the ones being tracked. He didn't make it, and I gave up my crusade as soon as I got the hell to safety."

"I'm sorry about your colleague."

He gestured with an insouciant flick of a hand. "His death happened a long time ago, but I can assure you, they're perfect killing machines. They've devolved from civilized human beings into instinctual predators. The virus overtakes every part of its host and alters the framework. Stronger muscles, denser skeletal structure, and the desperate necessity to survive. They feed when they need to and infect others when their food demands are met. They have newly formed secretion glands along their gumline and on the tips of their fingers. When they bite or scratch through flesh, their victim is instantly infected. This virus wants to endure, and it can only do so in a human host."

"Are they still human? If we killed the virus, what would be left?"

He shrugged. "Not sure. Our own survival has been our highest priority. My guess is the brain, or anything resembling who the person once was, is long since gone. Replaced by the virus."

"If they're as intelligent as you say, why didn't they come up once they cleared the wall? Why burrow this far inside the city?"

He motioned for her to follow him to the wall. When they were roughly ten feet from the structure, James stopped. "Because of this road," he said, tapping a foot in front of him.

Trish knelt and rubbed her hand over the black, coarse texture of the road.

"They probably tried to come up sooner, but we poured a ten-foot strip of pavement around the inside of the wall for our vehicles to drive over. Easier to monitor the structure for damage, or to gain access to each of the exit's doors."

"That makes sense then." She spotted the section of wall directly in front with its reinforced steel door. Crossing the black roadway, she saw the door was securely latched and a locking mechanism secured the thick metal bars.

"Can we unlock this?" she called out to him.

"We best not go outside the wall until morning. Those creatures hide in the shadows."

Bright lights flipped on behind them, and Trish nearly jumped.

A burly man, undeniably perturbed for being taken away from whatever he'd been doing, said, "As you can see, I brought the lights. So, what's with all the urgency?"

"Bill, thanks for coming. Trish says the creatures have tunneled under the wall to that point over there." Doctor Burgos pointed to the patch of grass.

"Oh, she has X-ray vision, does she?"

"Bill, I believe her."

"I told you I thought you were a fool, now this confirms it." He gestured toward the base of the wall as he crossed the asphalt. "We added extra anchors, like you said. They wouldn't be able burrow underneath. I'm telling you, unless they dig to China before tunneling up, it's not happening."

Not liking the way this man spoke to Doctor Burgos, Trish followed the trail of steel rods poking several inches up from the ground. "What about this section with the door? They're secured to the other panels, but I don't see any anchors."

The man sighed. "The three doors are the only locations without them. The chance of the Gramites inadvertently digging right where these five-foot sections are, as opposed to the almost two hundred miles of wall encircling this city, is impossible."

Doctor Burgos said, "Unless they were watching us when the wall went up, or they can see the difference in the texture."

The man rubbed his forehead. "We're debating this subject matter again, James? Like I and the others have told you before, brainless creatures who can't even wipe their own ass are not as intelligent as you think they are."

"You're way off base, mister." Trish spotted both their Gladiators arriving. "What exactly is your profession?"

Bill stared at her.

"If you have more intelligence then a virologist, I'd really like to know. In case you're not sure, a virologist is a medical doctor who oversees the diagnosis, management, and prevention of infection. In Doctor Burgos's case, his furthered education took him to a scientific level where he does research on various viruses and the diseases that cause them. Can you beat that? If so, I'm all ears."

Bill's stare became a frown. "Are you giving me lip?"

"I'm taking that as a no," Trish said.

Startled, Doctor Burgos changed his cackle into a cough. Before Bill could shoot out a retort, Trish strode off toward Aralyn who was having the vehicles positioned on either side of the grassy area. People began to show not long after, some armed, and those not carrying a weapon were shepherded away by Eva or Christina.

Trish opened Gladiator One and glanced around. "Where's my gear?" she asked Phillips as he wandered over.

"Nobody told me to pack it. Here, when we unloaded, I left two sets in each vehicle."

"Did anyone bother to grab my rifle?"

"Not that I'm aware of. Climb in and change. I'll keep watch."

Frustrated, Trish got in and switched her outfit. Why didn't anyone care if she was properly outfitted? And why was believing in a seventeen-year-old such a difficult concept for those who knew her? She'd always known her facts, she'd never lied, never given anyone reason to doubt her, so why? Yes, she snuck out once. Even with that one mistake, did she not prove her abilities to handle herself? She put on her helmet, fastened her boots, and exited the vehicle.

Trish spotted First Sergeant Stevens on the verge of wrestling with Bill, who was waving his hands about, while pounding his foot on the ground. They were both standing where the air was most foul. A surge of unexplained desperation took over and she ran straight for them.

". . . because I *said* to stay off the grass. I was given an order, and I aim to follow it. So back off, buddy."

"Get your hands off me! I'm not one of your soldiers. I'm an American. I have rights."

"An American? Are you serious?"

When she was but five feet away, the ground around the men shifted. They both let out strangled yelps, then disappeared, swallowed inside a newly formed hole in the ground.

In one fluid motion Trish pressed the button on her helmet, hit the night vision beside it, pushed off on her last step, and dove feet-first into a pool of darkness.

She dropped no more than seven feet down. Shifting her body in the air, her shoulder impacted a creature hard along its spine as it bent over the bodies of Bill and Stevens.

She was quick finding her footing and seized the creature's head. She twisted hard, attempting to snap its neck, waiting to hear breaking bones. The creature roared and flailed, trying to get away. Stevens's hand shot out clenching a knife. He jabbed it upward and stabbed the monster's chest and throat as he got to his knees. When the body fell limp, Stevens dove away, and Trish let the ogre drop onto a mound of dirt and clumps of grass.

A scream sounded in the tunnel, from the direction of the wall. No forms emerged. Stevens tried to rise, but fell over, dropped his knife, and reached for his ankle.

"First Sergeant, are you okay?" she asked, assisting the struggling Bill away from the dead monstrosity.

"I think my leg is broken. Otherwise, I'm all right. I'm plenty ready to get out of this hole."

"Okay, Bill and I will lift you out."

"Bullshit we will. You two are the trained soldiers, I'm a civilian."

"He's injured!" she demanded.

"Trish, it's fine," Stevens said. "Let's just get it done."

He reached a hand up, and she went to take it. Above them came the clamor of voices shouting and Aralyn's calm monotone issuing orders.

As Trish got First Sergeant Stevens to his feet, Bill suddenly jerked backwards. He shrieked out in terrified pain. As a creature bit into his shoulder, another dug its elongated nails into the flesh on his chest, firmly grabbing the kicking man. They pulled him away, snaking down the confines of the tunnel, where others were sure to be waiting.

Heart beating like a drum, Trish picked up Stevens's knife. "You need to have them pull you out so I'll have a clear opening when I return."

"Dammit, Trish, absolutely not! I'll go, you get out."

"You can't even walk!"

She spun and darted down the dirt channel, ignoring the colorful swear words pouring out from Stevens's mouth. Several feet ahead, a creature snarled at her. Golden-orange eyes glowed against her night vision, and she struggled to decrease the gap before they reached the end. The one not biting onto Bill shrieked every time its head spun her way. She noticed how his eyes darted about, as if frantically searching. She thought maybe his night vision wasn't as strong in this pitch-black cavern. Using this to her advantage would still be tricky in this tight of a space, but she needed to try.

Bill yelled and continued to struggle, but his cries were growing more feeble. His movements were slowing. When she had advanced to an arm's length from Bill's trailing foot, she lunged forward, clutching onto Bill's leg. The lead creature continued to pull, as the other released its jaw grip and came at her. Still holding Bill's leg, Trish gripped the knife's handle tight, waited for her opportunity, and struck the Gramite in the eye. She yanked the blade from the socket and jabbed it into its jugular.

The bleeding Gramite let out a gurgling moan, fell, and flopped wildly against Bill's twitching form. The lead infected released its grip, spun toward the dark tunnel, and screamed, high-pitched and frantic, like a woman about to be attacked. Other high-pitched screams responded from farther down the tunnel. Trish yanked hard and pulled Bill to her, while kicking the dead Gramite away.

"Move as fast as you can, Bill. I'll be right behind you."

Bill didn't need to be told twice. He twisted and crawled around her, toward a flashlight beam pouring in from the opening they had dropped through. Trish heard movement from behind her, but not close enough to look. Keeping the blade ready, she shuffled ahead on Bill's heels.

"Faster, Bill! Move your ass."

A hand emerged from the opening above. Bill lurched forward, fiercely taking the arm.

Trish's leg was yanked backwards. She landed on her stomach on the packed dirt. She felt heavy pressure on her legs and claws ripped wildly at the back of her suit. She kicked, got free, then was seized, and dragged several feet into the tunnel. When the claws finally breached her armor, painful stings raked along her spine, as strips of her flesh tore away.

Searching for inner strength, she breathed deep, twisted, and sunk the blade in the creature's chest. The tip went in about an inch before hitting hardened bone. She yanked it out, then sent it into the base of the creature's skull with all the force she could manage. The knife went all the way in. Golden-orange eyes flashed fiercely wild, then dulled. The creature fell flat. She yanked on the knife handle, but the way the creature had landed gave her no room to wrench the blade out.

Seeing the next set of eyes closing in, she released the knife and crawled backward toward the opening. She knew she wouldn't make it. A Gramite lunged forward and bit on her leg, but its teeth didn't penetrate the armor. It clawed violently. She wiggled and fought, seeing more pairs of eyes coming from behind it. She kicked out wildly. Her boot missed completely, and she wound up to kick again.

A gun fired, and a bullet stuck the creature dead center of its nose. The creature swayed, received a cheek-full of her heel, and fell in a heap.

"Trish, hurry!" The voice was right next to her ear.

Phillips! She felt his hands on her, pulling at her suit. She slid backwards on her butt. With her injured body leaning against his legs, she choked in short breaths of pain and terror.

Phillips raised his rifle and spewed the tunnel with the remaining sixty rounds. He dropped the extended clip and reloaded. "Hurry, stand up, the guys will pull you out."

Shaky and a little dizzy, she rose. Several hands grabbed her and whisked her upward. Once she was clear, someone dragged her backwards, away from the sound of more gunfire, leaving her panting on the ground.

They pulled Phillips up, gun still at the ready, and he spun with the others to spray the opening with ammo. A soldier tossed something sideways into the hole. A grenade exploded and rained dirt around her. She heard a voice holler for the cement truck, and another screeched, "Kill him, he's changing."

Aghast, she thought *Phillips?* But when she looked up at the big burly figure of Bill, he was growling at her and his eyes were turning yellow.

Despite cries of protest, one of the people from the city pulled the trigger on a pistol and sent a bullet into the Bill's forehead.

Trish sagged, her head thudding in her helmet. She bit her lip to the growing pain. Even though her body was surging with heat, a cold shiver coursed through her. I'm changing into one of them, she thought, feeling cool sweat form under her helmet. She needed to get it off, to take as many breaths of the night air as she could, while she was still herself. Before they had to put a bullet in her forehead, too.

She tried to rise but couldn't. Through blurring eyes she saw Christina and Eva huddled close by, crying. Susan held Trish's covered head in her lap, and those from the team circled around with weapons raised. They pointed their rifles toward a mob of angry faces. Christina's father stood between the mob and the soldiers, a hand raised to each group, while he talked feverishly to the crowd.

Trish brought a weak hand toward her helmet, and Susan pressed the button before removing it. "My back, I'm infected."

Susan wiped Trish's damp brow. "Hush, we don't know what'll happen. But either way, child, we've got you."

Susan's sorrowful voice was the last thing Trish heard before the burning darkness took her.

CHAPTER ELEVEN

Frank finished sending his final report to the sixth-level, reclined in his office chair, and stared at the ceiling. His entire week had been nothing more than incompetent staff, a sanctuary full of traitors, and a rebellious daughter with no obedience or gratitude toward the man who gave her life. He could have ended both mother and child on the same night all those years ago, but he had standards, and those on level six would have come down on him twice as hard. What he should have done was trust his gut and kept Trish confined with no contact from anyone, especially the traitorous dyke, Aralyn.

He locked his computer display, rose, and headed from the room. They'd had three more deaths due to another attack from the infected topside, and even though he provided proof to the committee that these beasts were not of his making, they were still treating him as if *he* were responsible. They didn't come right out and place blame, but the demanding way in which they ordered him to find a vaccine for this contagion all but affirmed it.

Walking into his lab, he scrunched his nose against the fresh smell of paint. A few more days and maintenance would have his work area presentable again. He nodded toward the specialist standing near the sink as he donned the basic protective equipment, gloves, gown, and a mask. He paused beside a table where the most recent captured victim lay unconscious. With the enormous strength of these creatures, heavy sedation and reinforced metal restraints had to be used.

The committee had first insisted he destroy the monsters before doing his research. He argued that if they wanted an antidote, he needed a live specimen to find one. Not completely accurate.

What he wanted most was to study how a creature who appeared so basic, so primal, could be so advanced both in strength and cunning.

"Did you finish analyzing the last batch of tests?" Frank asked the specialist, who was washing her hands vigorously at the sink.

"Yes, Doctor Webber. You were right. The vaccine we received before coming into the bunker, the one against the original virus, was ineffective. When this man was bit, the virus strand from the creature somehow mutated with the antibodies."

She sounded anxious, fearful. A normal response from those who worked for him. "I knew it. How long did it take him to transform?"

"They said about ten minutes. Like the others, his eyes changed colors, then a few minutes later, he was violent."

Ten minutes, he thought to himself. His eyes raked over the crusted pustules forming on the scaly flesh. "These abscesses, they're only produced from this mutated strand, correct?"

"Yes, Doctor Webber," she tossed over her shoulder as she continued to scrub.

His wrist processor flashed. "Good God, woman. You're clean enough. Stop washing and go tell security to have my vehicle out front and my team ready to go. I'll be heading to the city for a few days."

Due to this recent breach in security, most of the bunker had been moved to Colorado Springs ahead of schedule to work at making the city more secure and to recycle the rubble and trash within. Thanks to his construction of the virus, they didn't have to worry about tripping over substantial volumes of decomposing bodies. This had been the biggest selling point for his virus. Bones and all, the added component inside the virus sped the decomposition rate of those it infected to fifteen years.

He waited until she left the lab before removing his gloves and mask and activating the holographic display on the desk nearby.

"What is it Captain?"

"Sir, the convoy we've been tracking led us to a supply bunker outside San Francisco. They stole two of the supply vehicles and cleaned out the armory and most of the storage, including every bodysuit and wrist processor listed in inventory. We think they headed north this morning. The way it looks, we're not far behind. Do you want us to engage, or keep following?"

"Damn man, engage. I want my daughter alive. Send word the moment you have her."

Frank flipped off the hologram. They needed to find his daughter, yet, if his men couldn't apprehend her, or if she had already met an untimely death, then maybe he could use splices from this creature's DNA for his own phenomenal serum. What he had already acquired from his late wife's compound had helped form the exterior of the immunization for the original virus. Perhaps this repulsive creature had the structure inside to push him on a successful course to creating an effective serum.

This time, he wouldn't tell the committee once the serum existed, like he had with Julie's compound. He would use it for himself. No superhuman government to rise above the other nations that remained inside their bunkers. Instead, a faster, stronger, vastly intelligent man to tower over everyone world-wide. Once they saw his new form, marveled at his godlike abilities, they would have no choice but to place him at the head of a new world order. How could they not?

He might pass down his serum in the future to any deserving children he would have. This time, though, he would choose his own wife, not one forced upon him by his superiors because of research they wanted for themselves. After all, he would be their King Henry the Eighth, and he would rule them with both compassion, and fury.

His head came up to the sound of a man shouting from outside the room. Frowning, he waited. A minute later he heard a scream. A troubling idea struck him, and he moved over to the sink and inspected the area. His eyes widened, then he scowled. "The bitch," he breathed, seeing the discarded torn glove on the counter. Along the edges of the jagged latex were traces of blood. The fool infected herself.

He raced from the room, mixing in with those scattered few others running through the corridor. Inside his primary office, he powered up the display. Not wasting any time, he uploaded the drive to his wrist processor. When finished, he hurriedly packed a few necessary items and dashed from the room.

Relieved to see the elevator open and empty, he ignored the growing commotion down the hall and rushed inside. Ripping off the gown, he tossed it aside and fought to compose himself as the elevator rose. Once the doors parted and he was striding through the stillness of the first-level, he let himself relax.

His false sense of comfort vanished when he heard a beep from the elevator. Without affirming his fears, he set out running. He reached the first security door, scanned his wrist processor, and spun. Two people were rushing forward, not in a frenzy, but frightened. From where he stood, he saw they had yellowing eyes.

His heart raced. He squeezed through the tight opening, then shouted to the guard behind the panel to seal the door. When the door stopped opening, then began to close, Frank heard frantic shouting. A metallic click echoed, drowning out their desperate pleas and cries. He pointed at the other door and waited for it to open.

"Guard, until further notice, this bunker is to remain sealed."

"Yes, sir!"

Clenching his bag, he stepped through the second exit, and climbed into the vehicle waiting for him.

Trish clutched her leg, trying hard not to cry against the pain. The door beeped, sending fear into her mother's eyes, frightening her.

"You cannot tell anyone about your leg. Do you understand? Not even daddy."

Trish nodded. She watched her mother hasten toward the back of the room. She wanted to run after her, but when her father rushed in, she froze. Her heart sank and she knew they wouldn't get to see the trees.

"Julie, stop or I'll shoot."

Her father raised his hand, and two loud eruptions rang in her ears. Her mother stumbled forward, eyes widened in horror, before slumping to the floor. Trish jumped from the seat and ran toward her mother, but her daddy passed her and knocked her out of his way.

Instead of helping her mother, he headed to the sink, where her mother had thrown the terrible device that bit Trish's leg. By the time Trish reached her mother, her eyes were overflowing with tears. She knew the red liquid seeping out from her mother's shirt was blood, and blood outside the body was bad. Her mother's smile was weak, and when Trish touched her cheek, it felt unfamiliarly cool.

"Hush my sweet girl, can you hear the music?"

Hands gripped Trish's shoulders, and pulled her upward, holding her tight, forcing her from the room. Seconds before her nightmare ended, she stretched her arms out and screamed, "Mommy . . ."

Trish jolted upward, her own scream ringing in her ears.

"Trish, you're okay, you're safe," a deep voice rumbled.

Frantic, her eyes darted to the man beside her. His hands gripped her shoulders tightly. She flailed, struggling against the embrace.

"Trish, stop, you're safe." A woman rushed to her side.

When Trish spotted bright-green eyes, she recalled the woman's name. "Christina?" She twisted to the man trying to restrain her. "Doctor Burgos?" Collapsing onto the pillow, she cranked her head from side-to-side to try to see them both. "I'm sorry Doctor Burgos. I must've had a bad dream."

"Dream?" said a man behind Christina. "Hell, kiddo! That was a nightmare."

When Phillips stepped closer, her body softened even more.

Trish noticed how the older man massaged the joint along his right shoulder. "Did I hurt you, Doctor Burgos?"

Burgos rubbed his muscles, down to his elbow. "No, I'll be fine. You're a strong individual, which is why you're still alive."

Trish frowned. "What do you mean?" A memory flashed into her mind of a creature slashing away at her exposed flesh. Shuddering, she closed her eyes. "I was injured by one of those—those things. Am I turning?"

"No, your body's immune system is remarkably strong, and your cell regeneration rate is phenomenal. By day two, your body had completely killed the virus, and your wounds . . . well, you'll have a few scars, but scarcely noticeable."

"How long have I been out?"

"A week," Phillips said, squeezing Trish's foot. "Good news is you should be able to leave here tomorrow. Doc says at the rate you're going, you'll be fully healed by then."

Trish's eyes widened. "A week? What day is it?"

"June twenty-fifth," said Doctor Burgos.

She remembered the soldiers pointing their weapons at the crowd of angry people. She held her breath. "Besides Bill, was anyone else hurt?"

Phillips said, "First Sergeant Stevens has a broken ankle, but other than his moody disposition, he's fine. Not a guy you want to be around right now. He's not handling being confined to the hotel." Phillips rolled his eyes upward, displaying the sincerity of his words.

"What happened with the crowd?" Trish asked.

"As far as the townsfolks go," Doctor Burgos hesitated, and glanced to the other two, "we waited for a good hour before moving you to my lab, once I convinced them you weren't going to change. I told them you had a rare blood type, which was immune to the Gramites' disease. They've fixed the issues at each of the exit panels along the wall and left you some baked goods, which those in your group ate for you."

She watched his gaze avert to Christina and Phillips. When no one said another word, she finally asked, "What is it?"

"Many see you as an immortal badass, sent here to lead them into the light. You're the new Superhero." Phillips laughed, and Christina elbowed him in the ribs.

Doctor Burgos patted the air. "No, not exactly. However, they did want me to utilize your, shall we call it, uniqueness for a vaccine. Or to see if you would consider using your antibodies in case someone was bit. Now, I've told them your blood type isn't acceptable. To be truthful, I've never seen anything like it, but I know your antigens wouldn't work with anyone . . . human. If I had the right equipment, though, I might find a way around this."

"What about my mother's serum? Can't you extract it to use on others?"

He shook his head. "Trish, your mother's serum went in and did its job. It's not floating around in your blood or hiding out behind your cells for someone to find. From what limited amount your mother told me about her work, she was looking for a way to construct a compound which would cut segments of the host DNA and insert animal DNA to make a new genetic sequence, rDNA. Once she broke the barrier of in-depth bridging of the DNA from different species, her plan was to use segments of strands from multiple animals and remove whichever ones didn't combine."

"She physically altered my DNA?"

"Yes, she completely changed parts of it, which improved you in ways I don't fully understand. She had talents beyond anyone I've ever met and had a way of reading the codes in a genetic sequence, even without using any decoders."

"So, you can't reconstruct her compound?"

"No, the serum was her fingerprint in research. I doubt I could even get close."

"Doctor Burgos, once you have the machines, I hope you can make whatever you need to try to protect others."

Doctor Burgos squeezed her hand. "I've had many conversations with Aralyn while you've been out, Trish, and I must stress, I agree with her position about your unique situation. You can't tell *anyone* about your mother's serum. Everyone here who knows is sworn to secrecy. Like your father, there may be others who will try to use this to their advantage, with little to no thought for your wellbeing." He paused for a moment, then continued. "I would like to study you, Trish, see what your body can do and push you to your limits. Since you've had to keep the injection hidden in the bunker, your abilities have never reached their full potential."

Trish pictured a debilitated life full of needles and lab tests and experiences she hoped she had left in NORAD. "I'm tired of being a lab rat. If it's all the same to you, I'd rather not."

"I'm sure you are tired. But, I'm not talking about what I may discover in a Petri dish or under a microscope. I want to work you physically and mentally to your breaking point. Weight-endurance, speed, hearing, intelligence, the works. You've had a gift locked in a cage, and I want to help you open the door to see what brilliances emerge. After all, haven't you ever wondered what you're capable of?"

Trish thought for a bit, knowing this would bring her closer to seeing what exactly her mother had done. Yet, what if they toyed around with the concoction inside, and let out a creature of their own? One that couldn't be contained.

She shifted her attention to Phillips. "How long until we leave?"

"Colonel talked with Doc and the others in charge of the town. She wants us to stay, and the city was happy to oblige. Due to what we've learned about these creatures, she's already called the other teams in, and we're reconstructing the old hotel into our garrison. We've reinforced the entire basement for an armory and supply. We're now emptying supply bunkers and bringing everything here. Once the others show, and we've cleared out the bunkers in South Dakota and the surrounding states, and rigged motion sensors at each one, we'll take over the gate and city security."

"So you see," Doctor Burgos said, we can keep you working successfully in both worlds, at least for the time being."

Trish stared at him evenly. "Okay I'm in, on one condition."

"Name it," he said, thrilled by her decision.

"If at any time these tests bring out something dark—or dangerous in any way—we stop this study immediately."

Doctor Burgos grinned. "Trish, I don't believe that will happen. If it makes you feel better to hear me say it, then fine, I agree."

Phillips broke in. "Wait a minute, she's still training with me, per the colonel's request. I'll need her for at least four hours in the morning to cover physical and combat training." He held up the portable tablet. "I also downloaded every book and field manual you have left to read."

"Hmmm," Burgos said, "let me think about this for a moment."

Trish met Phillips's eyes. Phillips looked weary, dark circles under both. Her gaze shifted to Christina who also looked tired, but there was a spark of excitement to her. Her eyes were bright, and quite simply, she looked beautiful. She wished she could reach out, take her hand, pull Christina to her—

Burgos interrupted Trish's wayward thought. "Okay, that actually works. Since my lab is next door to my home, when she's finished with you in the mornings, Phillips, she can eat lunch with us, then go directly into the lab for a pre-checkup before we start. Then I can do the post-checkup and feed her dinner. On the days she's scheduled to do runs for the city, we can do something light after dinner." Doctor Burgos clapped his hands together in excitement. "This will free her for a couple hours of down time every evening for the reading."

Tilting his head to the side, Phillips's lips turned upward into a smirk. "You know what? That works. I'll give the colonel her schedule."

Christina let out a huff. "Why not shoot her up with caffeine, so she can work longer hours?"

Trish detected the layer of sarcasm in Christina's tone and fought against the urge to grin.

Phillips stared at Doctor Burgos. "I don't know, is that safe?"

"Are you both serious?" Christina raised her voice. "In case you forgot, she's an *adult*. Maybe she should have a say in her schedule, especially considering she just saved everyone in this city."

The way Christina stood up for her caused Trish to experience a swift emotional warmth. She again bit back her grin and kept her eyes on the string her fingers were twirling, attached to the blanket covering her. Christina had fire in her, an inner strength Trish knew she herself lacked.

Doctor Burgos said, "Christina—"

"No, Father, she can do four hours a day with each, and this includes reading time. None of this having her wrap a bandage around a damn tree or listening to long stories about how you and Mom first met. She works, you keep her productive so she learns, then she's done."

Trish remained quiet while Christina ranted. Her fingers pulled the string free then searched for another. Phillips exhaled loudly, but she noticed how neither he nor Doctor Burgos said a word.

"Oh, and her weekends are free," Christina said. "Just like the rest of us.

In unison, both men complained. Their voices interrupting the other, each rising and falling with half-voiced protests.

"No, stop squabbling," Christina cut in. "Don't forget she still has to do runs for the city. If she wants to put in extra time, then it should be her choice and not a requirement."

Phillips handed Christina Trish's tablet. "Fine, but you can be the one to talk to the colonel if she doesn't like the schedule." He gave Trish a quick pat on the leg then departed.

Doctor Burgos said, "I should go see if Eva finished lunch. Trish is probably starving."

Once Doctor Burgos walked out, Trish pulled herself up on her elbows. "That was quite impressive."

Christina flashed her a mischievous grin and set the tablet on the table by the bed. "That, my dear Trish, is how you work the older generation. Now, since tomorrow's Saturday, if Father and Susan lets you out of here, let's go shopping for some less militarized clothes."

"This is it, the largest shopping center in this city." Christina jumped from her father's truck, and Trish reluctantly followed.

The area was at least a mile around, consisting of long rows of buildings encircling an open courtyard. The expanded shops were connected by a barrier on the backside, with one entrance for deliveries and another for the shoppers. Christina said the city had two additional shopping areas, but neither held a candle to this complex. One could purchase virtually anything here if they had the right connections.

The idea of shuffling through all these people sucked the energy right out of Trish. "Like I said before, the clothes I have are fine. Save this for the families who need it."

"Trish, civilization provided for eleven billion people before the virus, give or take a few hundred million. As I've told you, we have more than we know what to do with, other than ammo, but your group is making more for the city as well as providing us with safety. Take this as a kind of thank you for everything you guys have done, or are planning to do. Plus, we're all on the same team now, and I'm not about to let my peeps look a hot mess."

Trish examined her black military-issued T-shirt and shorts and shrugged. "You would've hated the outfits they had us wear inside NORAD."

"If what you're sporting now is an improvement, then most definitely. Now, these buildings are supplied with the majority of the items we bring in from our runs. All these people in those colorful vests, they organize the boxes and resupply the shelves or bins when they run low. If you're wanting something specific, let one of them know, and they'll either direct you to the location of the item or put your request on the list for a later supply run."

"Recycling is important," Christina said as she all but pulled Trish through the entrance. "Like the rundown buildings, outdated vehicles, and crap from the landfills, which are broken down and used for the walls and other construction projects, we're working to recycle everything, including all the stuff here. If it doesn't get used, it gets reprocessed, so technically, you're rescuing whatever you purchase."

Trish dug in her pocket and pulled out a black card. "So, when I'm done, I give this to someone wearing a vest to pay for it. Will five thousand credits be enough?"

"More than enough, but right now I need to borrow that." Christina took the card. "Once they have your handprint registered in the city system, you'll no longer need this. They'll scan your hand." Christina directed Trish to a man standing off to the side. "Excuse me sir, my friend here needs some help. Can you show her the location for summer clothing?"

"I'll be happy to," the man said. Trish noticed how his gaze focused solely on the curves under Christina's shirt. Trish scrunched her forehead with a sudden unsettling of her morning breakfast. The man was twice Christina's age, if not more.

Christina put the card in her pocket. "Trish, he'll show you where the clothing shops are. Meanwhile, I need to run an errand. Pick out three outfits you like, and when I return, I'll figure out your taste. We'll find you an entire wardrobe based off what appeals to you."

"How will I pay for it if you have my card?"

"I won't be long. Don't worry. I've got your back." With a skip to her step, Christina took off in the opposite direction. "I'm your best friend, remember?" she called out as she passed a building advertising the sale of household appliances.

Not too thrilled about being left alone in such a strange and boisterous place, Trish silently watched Christina cross the courtyard. She went by two food venders, one selling homemade cinnamon rolls and the other shaved ice with ten fruity flavors to choose from. She zigzagged between a stone fountain and a seating area filled with picnic tables and floral arrangements, then vanished from sight.

Trish followed the strange little man to the far end of the outlet mall, through clusters of individuals working or exploring to buy. He told her the cost of the items were listed at each store, and when she was done shopping, she would go to the entrance and pay for her items there. After pointing out the row of buildings which housed the clothes, his creepy gaze bid her breasts farewell, and thankfully, he left.

It felt like hours had drifted by in the first store before she located a pair of comfortable jeans and two shirts. By the time she entered the second store, her brain became drowsy, as if she had been in the most boring class all day. She selected two colorful shorts, which also appeared comfortable, and another shirt. She snatched a pair of black sneakers right before exiting, just to show Christina she'd put forth the effort.

Outside, Trish had to squint against the sun's potency pouring down from directly overhead. She found a bench covered with shade from a few evergreen trees planted on either side where she'd be able to rest her aching feet. Before taking a seat, she spotted a display sitting up against the brick building. Wooden, windup jewelry boxes in various colors and sizes sat on the top shelf. When she lifted a box near the last row, her excitement brought forth a new wave of energy.

"I've been gone for less than thirty minutes and you're already done?"

Trish held her arms out to show Christina her outfits. Christina's nose wrinkled, and she gave Trish a look that plainly said, you are a hopeless case with no sense of style at all.

Trish knew her day was far from over. "Seriously," Trish grumbled, lowering her arms.

"Seriously? The shirts are all black and these shorts? Guys go swimming in them." Christina took a long, deep breath. "Okay, did you not like any of the feminine clothes?"

"Not in the slightest."

Christina nodded. "I didn't think you would. Let's get a cart and you can put everything back. We'll start over. The only thing that's adorable is the jewelry box. Don't look at me that way. I won't make you wear anything you don't like. But Trish, even athletic women, such as yourself, can have more care in how they dress."

Trish followed Christina into the first store. "I'm not needing to impress anyone. If they don't like me because of what I'm wearing, then—"

"I'm not talking about impressing others." Christina grabbed a cart. She snatched the jewelry box and placed it in the upper rack. "Who cares what others think. I'm talking about *you*. You've lived in a world where you couldn't find out your identity and express yourself. From here on out, this will change. What we wear, the music we like, the books we read, everything has its own way of entertaining and letting loose the unique parts inside, which makes us who we are. When we feed it, we fuel it, and we become happier individuals because of it."

"I wasn't allowed to watch any movies or listen to anything but classical music. I'm not sure what my tastes are."

Christina grew excited. "I have just the store to go to when we're done with your wardrobe. Now, let's get this done. Also, I spent fifteen hundred credits off your card. I guarantee, everything I bought is all for you. The last few days I've been helping your friends with cleaning the hotel. Unfortunately, the officers took all the third-floor suites, but everyone else was issued two rooms each, which they're converting into makeshift apartments. I ordered you some things yesterday I believe you'll love, but if you don't, Sam said we can return the items tomorrow and he'll replace the credits."

"Is thirty-five hundred enough for us to shop with?"

"More than enough. Everyone gets paid fifty credits for each day they work to support the city. Whether you do runs, work the crop machines, or are on staff in the hospital or stores or wherever, you receive credits. You can buy food, clothes, anything the city makes or brings in, except ammunition. This may change though once our shelves are restocked."

"A doctor's wage is the same as someone who produces the food?"

"The pay was decided by the Governors when the city first opened. Two of the eight, like my father, *are* doctors. They can't treat patients if they starve to death, and many of their patients work either the supply runs or security, to keep the city safe and provided for. Every year you work for the city, your pay increases by ten credits per day. It's all one big wheel that spins because everyone contributes. This may change as the city continues to grow, but it probably won't be in our lifetime."

Trish held onto the jewelry box and stopped her examination of it long enough to give a confused stare. "Why was I paid so much when I haven't done anything?"

Christina replaced the jeans on a shelf and threw the shoes into a re-stock basket. "If even one of those Gramites had snuck inside the city, this society we've created would've ended. This gift is the people's way of saying thank you. Please put your stubbornness aside and enjoy it." She pointed to the swim trunks and shirts laying in the cart. "You can wear those at the pool or to sleep in. If I catch you in them any other time, I'll personally rip them off your body."

Stimulated by a vivid visual, Trish blushed, turning her eyes away. "And you call me stubborn."

CHAPTER TWELVE

While waiting with Phillips for Doctor Burgos to unlock a security chain, Trish wiped the dampness from her face and neck that her body produced on her twenty-mile run. Doctor Burgos flung open the metal door and spread his arms out wide. "This is it, your new training site. What do you think, Trish?"

She inspected the piles of concrete, gravel, and weed-infested sand scattered throughout the old construction site. The place smelled of aged rubble. She saw limited patches of grass, but mostly, the packed earth was covered by either gravel or weeds, and in several spots with both. Off to one side, two abandoned trailers sat surrounded by weathered steel containers that looked like they belonged stored on a train or pulled by a semi-truck. The focus of the site was a central building not fully erected to which Burgos led her and Phillips.

A fading sign affixed to the metal wall at the entrance indicated the unfinished structure was to be a three-story office building scheduled to open in June of 2070. Eighteen years too late, apparently.

"It's filthy," Phillips said, stepping inside.

"It's got real potential." Doctor Burgos beamed. "We'll clean it up more, of course. Change a few things here and there." He waved to the mounds of material. "All that can be tossed."

"Nope, you're not throwing any of it away. It's perfect." Phillips slapped Doctor Burgos on the back. Trish could tell the manly impact was too hard from how the older man recoiled and he stopped beaming.

Phillips said, "We couldn't ask for a better training area. Sure, we'll clean it up a bit, but not too much. Most of this we can use to stage a few combat programs for Trish and for future training."

Doctor Burgos appeared pleased with himself. "I have an amazing builder. He'll be meeting us here shortly. Let him know what you need, and he'll construct it for you."

Trish strode a bit farther into the space and noticed a pile of brittle boards with rusty nails protruding from numerous directions. She silently wondered if they should all get tetanus shots before venturing the rest of the way in. She followed Doctor Burgos and stopped when he pointed to a steel mechanism that appeared newly fashioned.

"Since the seven hundred-pound weights in the gym are too light, I had my builder rig this for Trish. He said it should hold up to four thousand pounds, and if we need it to go higher, he can weld extra supports."

Trish didn't like how Doctor Burgos used the words *rig* and *should*. Apparently, Phillips didn't mind.

"Let's have her give it a go before your man gets here," Phillips said, taking off his jacket as if *he* was getting ready to do the heavy lifting.

"Good idea." Burgos fiddled with the machine. "We can change the settings and attachments to work different muscle groups, including legs, but right now let's just see how much she can lift. Here, I have it set for seven hundred pounds already. Trish, you stand here and grab the loops."

She moved a few steps forward, eyeballing the metal structure and the base the unorthodox contraption sat on. Inside the dumpster-sized bin the pulley system was attached to, Trish spotted slabs of concrete and strips of metal beams stacked on the bottom. She wondered how long it would take her to die once the weighty setup toppled down, crushing her. "Should I stretch out first?"

Debating, Doctor Burgos stared at Phillips. Phillips shook his head but looked to be contemplating at the same time. "Since you did some light stretching before you ran, you should be fine. I merely want to see if you can lift it. Don't go crazy. Just give us a set of ten."

Trish rolled her eyes and moved under the pulley. With these two running her training, she would be lucky if she made it to see her first snowfall, much less her next birthday. She widened her stance and pulled. She was surprised by her ease at moving the bin upward. Before the builder showed up, her unorthodox trainers had added more weights to the container, and she did set after set until her muscles burned.

"I heard you have the PX480 gaming system in your room," a girl named Stephanie said to Trish, flipping her hair dramatically and eying Christina. Extreme flirting seemed to be the custom throughout the city with Christina's generation.

Trish sensed a shift in Christina's mood the moment they entered the domed, air-conditioned building, which smelled of both chlorine and salt. This irritable change in Christina's temperament bothered her and she wondered what the trigger was.

"Hey, Christina, Trish," Adam called out, "good timing. We need a few extra to make the game exciting. Come join."

Trish held up a hand, signaling her greeting to a group of three teenagers tossing around a volleyball in the far end of the pool. She'd met them at a function the city held the previous week to welcome Aralyn's group. Adam, the nineteen-year-old, born in Missouri, was the leader of this miniature gaggle of friends, and Trish liked his personality the moment they met. The other two were Brian, who she'd met the night the bus was attacked, and Gab, Adam's closest friend.

"Yes, Christina bought the PX480 two weeks ago when she took me shopping." Trish sat on the bench by Christina and pulled off her shoes.

"I heard you technically bought it, but whatever," Stephanie said, sitting down between her and Christina, water dripping onto the bench from what little suit she wore. She wrapped her arms around Trish's forearm and playfully pouted. "It's said to be the best virtual gaming system on the planet. The movement station, the graphics, it all sounds so fascinating. I've always wanted to try it."

Christina stood and tossed her towel over her shoulder. "Doesn't your boyfriend have one?"

Trish glimpsed over, seeing the instant transformation of Stephanie's anger flash to amusement. Stephanie took her eyes off Christina and threw her gaze to Trish and laughed. "Brian and I broke up last week. He was too egotistical. Unfortunately, he never let me play on his system, but I've always wanted to."

Christina said, "Trish, are we joining the others or not?"

Stephanie leapt swiftly to her feet and clasped Trish's hand. "Yes, let's. It'll be fun." Her smile faded when the door opened, and a group of excited children rushed inside, followed by a swift, "*No running,*" from Mrs. Johnson.

"Damn," Stephanie groused, "I guess we'll be moving to the deep end. Why don't the orphans use the smaller pool at the community center? It's closer to the shelter."

Christina glared, her fist encircling her towel in what looked like a death grip. "You're all heart, Stephanie."

"What's *your* problem?" Stephanie retorted.

The girl named Jennifer who had taken a shine to Trish during the Gramite attack saw her and squealed with glee. Ignoring the animosity continuing between the two women, Trish brightened as Jennifer headed her way. She stood and grabbed the child up in her arms.

"Do you like the bathing suit you and Christina got me?" Jennifer asked, pushing out her belly so Trish could see a colorful mermaid.

"Oh my, you look so grown up. If I didn't know any better, I'd say you were six, maybe even seven."

Jennifer flashed a full set of teeth, blushed, then buried her face in Trish's hair.

Christina turned away from Stephanie and rubbed Jennifer's arm. "Did all the clothes fit?" The girl nodded, then giggled and squirmed when Christina tickled her side. "Did you know, Trish picked out the jewelry box all by herself?"

Jennifer leaned back. "You did? I think it's beautiful. It plays music." Jennifer whispered the last part.

Trish feigned surprise. "No, does it? Are you pulling my leg?"

Jennifer laughed out her response. "No."

Mrs. Johnson told the sulking teens to take the volleyball and vacate the shallow end so the children could play there. Christina hopped into the water. Trish followed to the edge and bent to pass her Jennifer before turning away and nearly bumped into Stephanie.

"Where are you going?" Christina asked.

"I forgot to put my hair up."

"No, please don't. I like it down."

"You have yours up," Trish said to Christina.

"She's right, Trish," Stephanie said, "you're so beautiful with it down." She climbed in the pool and elbowed her way between the splashing kids, then hovered next to Christina.

With a renewed scowl of agitation, Christina whirled through the water. She held Jennifer at arm's length, so the child could practice floating. Stephanie batted her lashes and waited for Trish to climb in. Trish turned, went to her pile of clothes, and searched for her hairband. She fastened a simple ponytail, and decided before movie night, she would stop putting off her decision and go see Sergeant Givens to deal with the mop on her head.

Trish rerouted to the other side of the pool to climb in the shallow end beside Mrs. Johnson. Keeping her voice low so Jennifer couldn't hear, Trish asked the older woman, who was bouncing an infant boy on her knee, if tonight was still on. Thankfully it was. Nearby, Gabe loudly insisted to Stephanie that swimming was over and they needed to get ready for guard detail. Mrs. Johnson gave the complaining teenager the eye, and even though Stephanie continued to protest, she reluctantly climbed out of the water.

Breathing a sigh of relief at seeing Stephanie go, Trish thanked Mrs. Johnson. She dove under the water and swam to Christina who was still assisting Jennifer with floating. The second Trish resurfaced, she noticed how Christina's gaze followed Stephanie from the building. Was she relieved at seeing her go, or was she upset the self-confident woman was leaving? Trish couldn't tell. When Stephanie was no longer in sight, Christina's mood did seem to improve.

Trish gave a thumbs up and Christina returned it, then pulled Jennifer to her and held her close to whisper in her ear. "Guess what. How would you like to come over tonight to my house, and watch movies with Trish and me?"

Jennifer eyes widened. "Really!" she squealed.

"Really. My mom's gonna make us some pizza, chocolate cupcakes, and we'll stay up all night if you want."

Jennifer bobbed excitedly in Christina's arms, visibly on the verge of exploding with delight. "Can I sleep with you guys, too?"

Trish blushed. "Oh, well, we don't—"

"Of course." Christina touched Trish's arm. "We'll make a pallet on the floor, and we'll all pass out together. How's that sound?"

When Jennifer clapped her excitement, Trish didn't know if the fluttering in her stomach was from the little girl's bouts of enthusiasm, or for the idea of sleeping so close to Christina. Even with their late movie nights and evening conversations in Trish's renovated apartment, Christina always went home to her own bed, and Trish never tried to stop her. If she had Stephanie's cocky assertiveness, life would be so much easier.

Christina dropped Trish off at the old hotel to get a few things together while she went to help Jennifer pack an overnight bag. When Trish went inside, she found Givens in the basement with Susan, both organizing the recent haul from a supply bunker. The second she asked for one of his renowned haircuts, he jumped at the chance, and swiftly ushered her into a chair before she had a chance to change her mind.

"You know, Aralyn won't be happy with this length," Susan said, as his electric shears made the first pass.

"No," he said, "but I'll shave the sides and back to about a half-inch and taper it up to a few inches on top. It'll fit beautifully with her facial features. Trust me, I've tried to talk Trish into this style for the last two years. It will emphasize her high cheekbones."

As if on cue, Aralyn and Phillips walked in. Trish saw her godmother's eyes widen momentarily before she spun on her heel and tramped away.

"Damn," Givens said, staring worriedly at Susan. "Should I stop?"

"It's a bit late for that, don't you think?" Susan answered. "A big chunk of her hair is already on the floor. What are you going to do, glue it on?"

Phillips leaned in. "This will look amazing, and your helmet will be more comfortable without all that girly-hair getting in the way." He whacked Trish on the arm. "I say to stand your ground. If you don't like the length, it's hair. It'll grow." He winked at her—as if she needed his affirmation to make her own decisions. She wanted to roll her eyes at Phillips, before he followed Aralyn upstairs, but managed to restrain herself.

"Givens, I really don't care what you do. I'm ready for something different. Phillips is right. It's hair, it'll grow." Trish's tone was casual, encouraging, yet, at seeing the years of growth lying on the floor, she inwardly shuddered. Maybe this short cut *was* a bad idea. She had left her hair long because that was how her mother had worn her own hair. But now, Trish felt ready to let this part of her past go, to be her own woman, and not live life from the memory of another.

Givens flipped the shears on. Between Givens and Susan tossing out ideas to one another, the entire cut took way longer than Trish had anticipated. If they didn't hurry, Christina and Jennifer would return before she had a chance to pack.

When the scissors stopped cutting along the top, and both were inspecting all angles, Givens suddenly legged it out of the room.

"Is it bad?" Trish asked, rubbing her hands through the short thick hairs at the base of her scalp.

"Honey," Susan said, all attitude, "you're one of those people who would look beautiful with no hair."

"Oh my god, it's bad." Trish leaped from the chair.

"Believe me, your hair's amazing," Givens said upon reentering the room. He pointed to the seat and flicked the lid on a pale blue bottle he held and squeezed out a tiny amount of clear gel. After briefly rubbing his hands together, he worked his fingers through the hair along the top of Trish's head.

When he finished, he fetched a mirror from a nearby bench. "Okay, here you go."

Holding her breath, Trish examined her reflection. "Wow, I love it."

Givens beamed. "See, everyone needs to trust me, I know what I'm doing." He gave her the blue bottle. "Use a miniscule amount for this windblown style. If you're going for messy, then use a bit more."

Trish scooped out the tiny hairs from her ears as Susan brushed away any other pieces she could find. Trish kissed them both on the cheek before running upstairs to pack.

Christina opened the door to Trish's revamped apartment and stepped inside. "Are you not ready yet?" At hearing the movement from the other room, she went to the king-sized bed and plopped down. "Hurry up, woman, Jennifer's being entertained by Phillips and your first sergeant. If you take too long, no telling what they'll have her do. Either pushups or run her around the building until she pukes."

From the other room, she heard Trish's laughter and grinned. Trish was the one person who consistently found her jokes amusing. Even when Christina's dry sense of humor made others cringe, Trish was able to see beyond the obstacles of normalcy and laugh. "Look, Mom will be pissed if we eat her pizza cold."

When Trish entered the room, Christina's mouth went dry.

Trish flipped off the lights to the adjacent hotel room, which now served as her living room. She slung her overnight bag over her shoulder. "Okay, I'm ready." She stopped and touched her hair. "You don't like it?"

Christina stood beside the bed, unable to speak. This short, stylish haircut was a complete transformation, which both thrilled and scared Christina. She stepped forward, reached up, and rubbed the thick, soft bristles at the back of Trish's head. She swallowed. Her mouth still felt dry, even though her body was producing vast amounts of moisture. Everywhere.

Alarmed, Christina jerked her hand away and managed to find the words. "No, I like it a lot." She inhaled slowly and blinked a few times. Focus, you idiot, her mind screamed.

"Okay," Trish said, "let's go save Jennifer from a fate worse than puke, so we can have our evening."

She pivoted briskly away from Trish's snickering. God, even Trish's tone sounded deeper, sexier. Christina left the room, trying hard not to trip over her own feet. Careful, she warned herself as she headed downstairs. The evening would likely be a long one.

Once they were loaded into the truck with seatbelts fastened, Christina headed toward her house. Thankfully, when they pulled into the drive, Jennifer stopped talking about how pretty Trish's hair was. As they made it into the house, her mother yelled out that the last pizza was out of the oven.

"It smells amazing in here, Mom," Christina shouted toward the kitchen.

She placed the keys in the drawer by the entryway stand and sent Jennifer upstairs to the bathroom to change for bed. She'd decided on the drive that her emotions were too raw to host movie night downstairs in her secluded living space as she had originally planned. The front room would be safer. Christina had Trish help her shift some furniture around and arrange the bedding on the floor in front of the wall screen.

Once the Jennifer came downstairs, she was entertained by Eva so Trish could change in the upstairs bathroom. Christina hustled downstairs to do the same. She tried on three different sleeping outfits, feeling nervous and a little aroused. On her fourth set of nightclothes, her airy silk shorts and matching pink blouse, she stared at her reflection in the mirror and finally came to her senses. She dropped onto the edge of her bed, dismayed at how nervous she felt.

Today was July ninth. She did the math. She refused to be swept off her feet by a woman she met less than a month ago, who wasn't even sure what her preference in relationships were. No, not happening.

Short, sexy hair be damned. All she needed was to fall head-over-heels in love, just to walk in on Trish having sex with Brian . . . or Gabe, or whoever. She had no intention of being someone else's experiment. They were friends, and nothing more.

She stood, stripped to her undies for the last time, put on a pair of sweatpants and a long T-shirt, and went upstairs. Jennifer and Trish had pizza on their plates and were sitting on the pallet ready to go. Christina rolled her eyes at the colorful swim trunks Trish had on but fought to keep her gaze away from Trish's sexily chiseled arms, which were exposed by the sleeveless shirt.

She stopped mid-stride and did a double-take at the shirt. "You—you didn't . . . really, Trish? You ripped the sleeves off a Terri Michaels? That was a designer shirt. People paid top dollar before the virus for any one of her pieces."

Trish cocked her lips and grinned. "I can see why. This thing is so comfortable to sleep in. Say the word, and I can rip the other shirt just for you. You need but ask."

God, that ridiculous outfit somehow made Trish's roguish grin sexier. Christina looked to her mother for support, but Eva was sitting on the couch holding out a pre-made plate of goodies, clearly not willing to engage in the fashion disagreement. She patted the seat beside her once Christina took the offering. When everyone was settled, her mother started the first movie.

Halfway through the animated musical, Christina's father came home after a long day in the lab. Christina moved to the other side of Jennifer, so her parents could snuggle up together, as they always did during movie nights. Before the end of the second movie, her parents had gone upstairs to bed, and Trish was passed out on the pallet, where Jennifer lay asleep, snuggled in her arms.

Christina's chest felt light as she gazed at the pair of them. Both had faint chocolate rings encircling their lips from the numerous cupcakes they'd eaten. Christina turned off the movie, switched to her side, and cuddled with Jennifer, while trying to decide which of the two were snoring the loudest. When Trish's body shifted, she put her hand on

Christina's arm. Christina stiffened, holding her breath. After several seconds, Trish's airy snoring fell into rhythm with Jennifer's. Christina relaxed and breathed slowly. While listening to the duo exhale out a nightly tune, Christina welcomed the warmth Trish's hand offered.

She tried puckering her lips to resist the urge to grin, but the endeavor was useless. The edges of her mouth continued to snap upward after each failed attempt. Eventually, she gave up and closed her eyes, drifting off into the best dream she'd had in years.

CHAPTER THIRTEEN

Captain Rebecca Thomas motioned behind her, waving her lieutenant forward as she peered down the sight of her weapon. She shot off a round, dropping an infected to the weeded gravel on the other side of the gate. Grumbling, she saw the creature's leg twitch, and its filthy body rolled, preparing to rise.

"Lieutenant, I want you, Staff Sergeant Young, and Corporal Davis to finish loading these people into the bunker and seal the door. Don't open until I give you the all-clear."

The lieutenant headed off. Captain Thomas raised her rifle and fired, ending the creature's life. She took a position behind a supply vehicle as rapid fire from her troops shot through the trees surrounding the compound. If they could manage to get the gate closed, they could get closer for better shots. Until then, with the infected randomly breaking cover and rushing through the fence line, the risk of contamination was too great.

"Private, have you been able to reach Command yet?" she called out to a soldier on her right.

"No ma'am, the signal's still not going through."

"Okay, keep trying."

Thirty minutes later, the last infected fell. All eyes scanned the terrain. Captain Thomas and her troops crept closer to the gate. The day had been long, emotional, and physically draining. Her soldiers were tired and in need of a rest. She herself couldn't wait to kick her feet up and try a shot or two of the aged whisky from the stash they found hidden at the gas station in Idaho Falls.

Keeping her focus, she lined up her four soldiers several feet away from the fence line where they readied themselves just in case a contingent of infected came out of nowhere and descended upon the gate.

Once everyone was in position, she motioned to the private to go secure the gate. The second his hand touched metal, a loud pop echoed and the soldier fell. The private squirmed on the gravel, hands clasping his leg. She opened her mouth to give an order to her other soldiers, but before she could tell them to fall back, another pop sounded, and another soldier dropped.

"Captain, those were warning shots," a deep voice intoned. "If you or any of your troops try to take cover, grenade rounds will follow."

Captain Thomas couldn't see the man's face, but she grasped the steadfast manner of his voice. He meant what he said. She twisted her head in the direction of the bunker's camera, and gave a minor shake, signaling no. She hoped those inside were watching and understood the meaning. She had been too focused on the infected and had forgotten about the other threat high on the list, NORAD. She'd led these soldiers into harm's way, but the ones in the bunker, they still had a chance for survival.

Colonel, we could really use your help right about now, she silently prayed. When she dropped her weapon, the last two standing soldiers followed suit.

A stiff wind blew at Trish as she stood guard atop a moving train. With her rifle in hand, she watched the landscape slide by on one side while Christina stood facing the opposite direction. Trish had to admit she rather enjoyed this assignment. She got to see different kinds of terrain as the miles sped by, and nobody was perched over her shoulder telling her what to do.

The train averaged sixty miles an hour on the track, with section after section of cars packed full of trash and debris in front and behind their guard platform located midway down the train. The platform was the top section of the train car, which those who worked security called the double-decker bus. The long steel railcar had been reconverted into work and sleeping quarters for the guards. Below the ladder heading down from the access hatch, were two toilets, a tiny galley, a storage area, fold-down bunkbeds to sleep eight, and a locked cabinet housing additional weapons and ammo. If the train needed emergency maintenance, had to stop overnight in an area to be loaded with rubbish, or made the long trip straight to Salt Lake, the guards had someplace safe to go.

The garbage the train carried came from various overflowing landfills and towns throughout South Dakota. They filled the train during the week, then ran it on Sundays to the reclamation center in Casper, Wyoming, four hours away. Once there, the rubbish was fed into machines located underground to be broken down and divided to its most elemental form. Additional unmanned machinery later processed the reclaimed material into wall panels, construction material, hand tools, whatever the cities needed, the machines provided.

These reclamation centers were the only actual gift the United World Task Force contributed to the planet while they surreptitiously planned out the mass genocide the world suffered from now. Trish knew the contribution had been purely selfish, the UWTF's way of removing as much of the overflowing waste from the populated areas before and after their chosen citizens resettled the planet. Fusion-powered rail lines to each reclamation center throughout North and South America were added at the same time, most of which were constructed where old train tracks once stood.

This particular reclamation center was its own fortress jointly shared by another walled-in community located in Salt Lake City, Utah. Each community provided staff and security to keep the process running and safe from the infected. Once a month, someone from the two cities met at the reclamation center to switch out workers and to trade needed goods with one another.

The hard wind let up for a minute, and Trish raised her visor, recoiling from the moldy smell of garbage. Over her shoulder, she called out to Christina. "I'm worried. The other three teams have returned, but not the California group, and last night, Aralyn still couldn't reach them when they missed their second call-in."

Trish, I'm sure they're fine," Christina yelled over the bustling wind rising again around the swiftly moving train. "When and where was their last call-in?"

"Idaho Falls on July nineteenth, two days ago. They found a few groups of survivors."

"How many?" Christina shouted.

"Thirty-eight," Trish hollered over the wind. "They were scattered around Boise. That's why the team was behind schedule."

"There you go, they probably have their hands full."

Trish wasn't convinced. Captain Thomas wasn't one to sluff off orders. The salty woman was a stickler for schedules. If she hadn't called in, something was wrong.

When the mildew odor of garbage amplified into the putrid stench of rot, Trish closed her visor and glanced up to a desolate hillside. Her insides prickled with danger, the alarming warning she got any time the creatures were nearby.

She squinted down into the access panel and nodded to Adam. He leaned over the desk, found the location on the map, and marked the spot where she'd sensed the infected were. Later, the city would send a team out to deal with the Gramites.

When she looked up from the access panel, Christina was staring over at her. Trish's left brow raised with her visor. "What?"

Christina shrugged and came closer. "I don't know. I guess, like the rest of the idiots here, I find you to be a remarkable woman."

"What?" Trish shouted and met her in the center of the train.

"I said you're a remarkable woman." At the amused grin forming on Trish's face, Christina pushed Trish on the shoulder. "You suck."

Trish laughed. "Are we going to the party tonight?"

Christina's eyes flinched and her smile receded. "If you want to."

"Not if you don't. You're the one who suggested it last week, but we can skip it."

Christina didn't respond. Instead she stepped back to retake her guard post, but was tossed slightly off balance by the squealing pitch of brakes. The train was nearing its destination.

Beyond a long stretch of burnt fields, the grass was overgrown. Out there, Trish detected an intense threat. Though she couldn't see the dangerous creatures, she felt them. She nodded the direction to Christina, bent low to the access plate, and pointed so Adam could mark the location.

When she stood, she spotted the solid concrete wall of the reclamation center spanning out for about a mile on either side of the tracks. A gate located across the tracks raised, seconds before the front of the train reached the opening. The guards in the front scanned the entrance, then disappeared inside the concrete structure. Trish and Christina continued to safeguard the area surrounding the tracks, on the other side of the burnt fields, until they too were swallowed by the enclosure.

Once the train stopped and the gate shut, Christina stepped down onto a concrete platform with an elevation a few inches below the top of the train. She said, "I can't believe the Gramites are so close."

"I take it the fields are intentionally burnt?" Trish asked, following her onto the platform.

Christina nodded, "It's done twice a year to keep the Gramites from hiding so close to the train's entrance."

Adam soon joined them on the concrete platform. When a platform guard approached, Adam handed her a stack of papers. "Here's what we need loaded once this rubbish is dumped."

The guard skimmed over the pages. "I don't think we have eight hundred feet of wall sections ready, but I'll check."

Adam was as polite as ever. "Do what you can. If you guys need any help, holler. Oh, wait a second." He pivoted and reentered the security car. When he emerged, he was carrying the long-range radio setup Aralyn had given the group. "This communicator is for Salt Lake City's crew. Can you make sure they send it to the city? Tell them we're making more, but with locating the parts, it'll take some time."

Cradling the device as if it were a carton of eggs, the station guard drew closer to Trish. "Since you guys have shown up, life has greatly improved. Tell your commander thanks."

Trish removed her helmet. "I'll let her know."

Trish fidgeted uncomfortably with the buttons on her helmet as the guard continued to stare her way. She wanted to check her teeth, see if maybe she had missed a spot from her after breakfast brushing. A speck of pepper, a wedged-in fleck of spinach, something.

"Let's wait inside the reclamation center's breakroom. The smell's better in there," Christina said, louder than she needed with the noise of the engine dwindling next to nothing.

Once they were settled at a table with their lunches out, Trish eyed Christina. "We still haven't finished the movie from last night. Wanna do that later instead of the party?"

"Oh, no you don't," Adam broke in. "Trish has been here for a month, and you've monopolized most of her evenings. You promised us last week you'd both go. Christina, is it because of Stephanie? I take it you guys are no longer seeing each other. Whatever happened between the two of you, you need to kiss and make up. This tension's so thick, it's interfering with our weekend get-togethers."

Trish's insides felt queasy, and her throat tightened. She had to force down the mouthful of meatloaf sandwich Eva Burgos had made for her. She opened her water and took a long drink. Other than a pulsating in her ears, everything around her sounded like a staticky reverberation. She knew she and Christina were friends, but the image of Christina kissing Stephanie made her stomach tense.

Keeping her eyes off Christina, Trish slowly rose and asked Adam where the restrooms were. He pointed toward the back. She thanked him and left, trying to act as casual as possible. Once the door was closed, she went to the sink and splashed cold water on her face. Gripping the edge of the porcelain, she lowered her head and observed the gush of water and tiny air bubbles smack against the chrome stopper.

Throughout their long, late-night talks where personal past experiences were shared in secret, why hadn't Christina mentioned a relationship with Stephanie? She talked about her first kiss with the kid who had the cute little dimples and about the two awkward months she and Adam had dated when she was fourteen, but Christina had never brought up Stephanie. Did she still have feelings for her? Maybe this was why Christina had warned Trish not to get too close to the woman with chestnut-blond hair, who apparently had slept with everyone in their graduating class.

If Christina still held a torch for Stephanie, why didn't she just say so? It wasn't like Trish was interested. The first time they met, she didn't care for Stephanie's self-obsessed personality. Maybe Christina didn't say anything because Stephanie had been showing Trish a lot of unwanted attention. That's why Christina became upset every time Stephanie was around. Why didn't Trish see it before? Christina was jealous.

She knew Christina could do better, but if Stephanie was who Christina wanted, Trish needed to approach this in a careful way so no one got hurt. When they returned to Rapid City, she'd ask Susan how to tell Stephanie politely to leave her alone. She should probably even mention to Stephanie to stop being so flirty with everyone when Christina was around, since her open advances were obviously hurting Christina. She might even talk with Adam. Maybe he could help with this.

Trish splashed more water on her face and glanced in the mirror, then rotated away from her reflection. Who was she kidding? Of course, Christina wasn't interested in her? Why would she be? Hell, even her father couldn't stand to be around her for more than a few minutes, and she was his own daughter. Trish closed her eyes. Stop acting so pitiful, she thought.

When the door opened, sending Christina in, Trish shut off the water and quickly dried her hands and face. She turned, displaying her best cheerful mood.

"Train's loaded, and we're ready to leave."

"Sounds good. When we get home, can you tell your father I need to skip the lesson tonight? There's a few things I have to do before the party."

Christina stepped forward, seemingly worried. "Look Trish, we should talk about Stephanie."

Trish's heart plummeted. She dug deep to find the hearty tone. "Hey, not a big deal, you don't have to tell me *everything* about your life. I think it's cool, and I'm here for you however you need." Trish blinked a few times, knowing her eyes were on the verge of dampening.

From the other side of the door, Adam said, "Come on guys we've got to get this train to Rapid City, so they can unload it before dark."

"Look, Trish—"

Trish nudged Christina on the shoulder. "Woman, stop acting so glum. Let's get this job done so we can have some fun tonight. I might even try my very first drink." Trish held her smile, stepped around Christina, and headed out to throw away her trash and retrieved her gear. No matter how much it hurt, she would do all she could to see Christina was happy.

"Here, I had her make it twice as strong as last time." Adam raised his voice above the beat of the music. He passed Trish a plastic cup with caramel-colored liquor inside.

"Where's the ice?" Trish asked loudly, inspecting the drink.

"You said you wanted to get drunk, but not even feeling buzzed after already having two, I left out the soda and ice, hoping this would help."

He pointed toward the main door on the other side of the room. They both watched as Christina entered, greeted a few people as she skirted beside the dancefloor, and headed to the bar to wait in line.

Adam nudged her shoulder with his. "Are you sure you want to do this? I mean, this will be your first kiss. Don't you want it to be with someone you're actually dating?"

"If it'll get Stephanie off me and onto Christina, then kissing you will be worth it."

"Ouch. You know," Adam said taking a drink, "I'm not a half-bad kisser."

Trish seized his arm with such speed, he almost dropped his cup. "I didn't mean it like that. You're the only one here I trust. You respect our friendship and adore Christina as much as I do and want the best for her." She lowered her eyes. "Adam, if you don't want to do this, I'll understand."

He sighed, flicking spilled droplets off his hand. "No, I do. It's simply a bruised ego. Even though I've come to terms with your one-sided attractions, being placed in the friendship category by a desirable woman is never pleasant."

Trish sipped on the hellacious booze as she observed Christina pay for her order. "Believe me, I know the feeling."

Christina took her drink and weaved her way through the growing crowed. Everything about Christina was captivating. Her looks, personality, and good lord that stubborn streak. The very definition of desirable in Trish's eyes. Feeling miserable for blowing her one chance when they first met, Trish drained her cup in several bitter gulps. "It's my turn to get the next round."

He stopped her from moving. "If we want to really sell this, I'll buy your drinks."

"You've bought my last three."

"Everyone knows me. I'd never take a woman on a date and have her pay."

"That's ridiculous," she said, but he was already on his way to the bar.

Christina approached, looking a bit hurt. "I went to pick you up, but Phillips told me you'd already left. What's the deal?"

"I didn't realize we were coming here together. We never talked about it."

"We would have if you hadn't left the train so fast. Seriously, what's up with you? Does this have to do with what Adam said earlier about me and Stephanie? If so, believe me there's nothing—"

"Sorry, I'm late," Stephanie said.

"Speak of the devil," Christina muttered before lifting the drink to her lips.

"I see you guys have already started. I guess I'll go stand in line." Stephanie stared at Trish but didn't move. After a lengthy stretch, she reeled toward the bar.

"I think she likes you," Christina said flatly.

Trish crushed her cup and tossed it in the trashcan. "Too bad, my heart's already spoken for."

"Oh, you don't say?" Christina's voice shifted, sounding lighter.

Naturally, she was in a better mood. Trish wouldn't be getting in the way of the woman Christina clearly wanted, and their friendship could remain intact. After she kissed Adam, Trish was planning to leave the club and head straight to her apartment in the remodeled hotel. Her feelings were growing too difficult to withstand.

"Do I know who this lucky someone is?" Christina's eyes literally gleamed over the rim of her cup. Could Christina not at least hold her excitement in a little longer, maybe until after Trish left, or vomited, whichever came first?

Adam returned with Trish's refill. When his arm went around her waist, Trish averted her eyes from Christina. By the time Stephanie reappeared, Trish was finding it hard to breathe. The arm that held her wasn't tight, but she still felt an odd sense of claustrophobia. Fighting the urge to break free of the restraint, she took another drink and shifted her weight to her other foot.

With no one speaking, Adam lowered his cup and leaned in closer. "Wanna dance?" he asked, but instead of waiting for Trish to reply, he grabbed her cup and set both drinks on the nearby counter. He led her to the circular area where colorful lights were rotating, and couples were grinding.

"Trish," he said, loud enough for her to hear. "Don't get me wrong, but your matchmaking sensor's broken. If it's all the same to you, I believe your first kiss will need to be left for another day."

She frowned, "What do you mean?" She tried to sway her body to the beat, but feeling completely off rhythm, she stopped and waited.

"Christina doesn't want to get with Stephanie."

"What makes you say that?"

"Because, by the look on her face before she ran outside, it's you she likes."

Confused, Trish spun around. Adam was right, Christina was gone.

Christina put her head down and moved through the groups of people heading into the club. Some called her name, others asked if she was all right. She didn't respond. She was too upset to acknowledge anybody. She had known from the beginning if she opened her heart, exposed it to Trish, she would get hurt. She didn't listen. Somewhere along the line she left it vulnerable, and now she was suffering through the heartache from her poor choices. What an understatement. This agony was worse than any pain she'd ever experienced before. Clearly, Trish wasn't interested in her.

Christina felt through her pockets, fumbling with the keys. She pulled them free, climbed into the truck and slammed the door. Her hands were shaking, her mind playing out the scene in the club over and over until she thought her head would explode. She smacked the steering wheel several times, then dropped her head and trembled as her tears fell.

When her crying subsided, she started the truck and pulled from the parking lot. She turned the opposite direction from her house, not ready to go home. Pressing play on the stereo system, she cranked the volume and picked a street to drive down. She stayed on it until reaching the wall. She deviated onto another street, shouting out the words on her favorite playlist through watery eyes. She continued driving until the pain numbed enough to propel the image of Trish and Adam from her mind. Over an hour later, she headed home.

Christina stomped into the kitchen and opened the refrigerator door. She exhaled loudly and closed it. She went to the cabinet and searched through her mom's canned goods, but nothing jumped out, to tempt her irritable early-morning appetite. Deciding on a cup of black coffee to go with her bitter mood, she prepared a steaming cup, and crossed to the table where her mother was poring over her recipe tablet.

Her mother glanced up. "Did you not sleep well?"

"I slept okay. Where's dad?"

Eva frowned. "He and Phillips took Trish out to those Gramite locations you guys spotted yesterday, to work on her training. They said these smaller hordes were a perfect opportunity to sharpen her senses. Smell, sight, and threat perception. If you ask me, it all sounds too dangerous."

The last person Christina wanted to discuss was Trish, so she didn't say anything.

"Did you know your father and Phillips have her running twenty-five miles around the city every other day? They've also set up a training yard at the old construction site off Maple. Your father said the weights in the gym weren't heavy enough. So now, she's lifting sheets of concrete up to fourteen hundred pounds. I told him they were pushing the poor child too hard, but your father argued"—Eva deepened her voice to the same tone she always used when mimicking Christina's father—"'The weight isn't even half as much as a gorilla can lift, and she's just getting started.' I told them both they were crazy. She's too young, and their training methods are treacherous, but he said, 'She's not like you and me, she's special, rare. Keeping her abilities corralled would be like asking a prized thoroughbred not to race, or a bloodhound not to hunt.'"

Christina remained quiet, with her lips pressed firmly together.

"Since they've combined their teaching program, the dangerous exercises and combat drills they're coming up with seems to be getting worse. Maybe you could say something."

Christina grunted and took a sip.

Eva tapped on her tablet and said, "Aralyn went out with a team this morning to locate their missing group members. I believe they're heading to Idaho Falls. With their vehicles, they should be arriving here by noon tomorrow."

After a lengthy pause, she continued. "You're awfully quiet, did something happen last night? You didn't touch the dinner I left for you. Was Stephanie hanging all over Trish again? Christina, you told me Trish didn't act like she was interested in her. Has this changed? I swear, you need to stop letting Stephanie get to you."

Lowering her cup, Christina sulked. "No, that's not it. Apparently, Trish and Adam are now an item. Really, those two . . . all cozying up together. And she let him take her onto the dance floor. The first time she met everyone I tried to get her to dance with a group of us. She told me she wouldn't ever be caught dead dancing with others watching."

Eva reached her arm across the table and cupped her daughter's hand. "Honey, I thought you wanted to be Trish's friend and nothing more. You said Trish was developing socially and wouldn't be able to offer you the deep-level of relationship you needed."

"I did, I do, yes. Trish and I are only friends."

"Yet, since the others have shown interest in Trish, you've turned into a jealous monster, which is totally out of character."

"I'm not jealous. She can date anyone she wants. Like I said, we're friends." Christina lowered her cup, feeling restless. Short-tempered. "I can't go through this again."

"Christina, Trish isn't Stephanie."

Christina felt her bottom lip quiver. She glanced at the clock. "I've gotta go make the supply run to the hydro-plant." She stood, gave her mother a quick peck on the forehead, and left.

CHAPTER FOURTEEN

Sergeant Phillips and Doctor Burgos hovered above Trish as she lay prone on a roof and sighted into the distance through her rifle scope. They were situated on the tallest roof in the paltry town, basking fully in the summer sun, though Trish's suit mitigated a lot of the heat.

Despite the suit shield, because of her thoughts, Trish's body was warm all over. She continued to stare through the rifle scope, but her mind strayed to the events of yesterday evening at the bar. They were friends. Christina clarified it over a month ago on the night they arrived in Rapid City, and Trish had reined in her emotions since. Had she miscalculated Christina's feelings? Misread the situation? Or maybe Adam's perceptions were off.

Christina was an extraordinary woman. Trish knew it at the supply bunker when they first met but brushed off her own instant attraction as ordinary sexual desire, less spectacular than what it truly was. Her feelings for Christina ran so much deeper than desire. Everything about Christina was dazzling: her mannerisms, her personality, even the flare of her stubbornness pulled Trish in. What really sealed the deal was how, whenever Christina was near, Trish felt a strong sense of belonging. But by her own actions, she unwittingly shattered her chance at building something together. Or did she?

Was all hope lost at having more than a friendship with Christina? Should she risk speaking up, and pray her heart didn't suffer for it? The feelings she had the day they left the bunker were painful, but she knew, after getting to know Christina, if she screwed up, the outcome could be devastating. What if she lost the cherished friendship as well?

"Got anything?" Doctor Burgos asked, wiping sweat from his neck.

"Nothing yet." Trish peered into the scope and tried to put Christina out of her mind to focus on the job at hand.

"Did you intentionally pick the hottest roof, Phillips?" Doctor Burgos snorted. "I literally smell scorched tar."

Phillips handed him a bottled water. "We have a perfect vantage point. Maybe a mile is too far away. Should we get closer?"

Doctor Burgos sighed while removing an additional collection of perspiration. "No, let's give it a little more time. With the first group she killed, my rangefinder pinged them at over three-quarters of a mile. She needs to push harder. Trish, relax your body, take in your surroundings, focus your instincts, don't use your eyes. Definitely no utilizing the scope on your rifle to locate them until you sense something."

What the hell did that even mean? How was she supposed to "focus" her instincts?

"I don't understand," she muttered. She didn't want to focus. She didn't want to train today. She wanted to buck up, go find Christina, and talk to her.

Doctor Burgos knelt beside her prone body and pointed to the tall fields stretching away from the rundown buildings of the ghost town. "See how the wind sways along, and it makes a ripple of yellow waves emerge? Reach out with your mind and feel the wheat blowing against the blue of the horizon. Inhale the breeze, absorb the sun."

He stood and in a completely different tone of voice said, "I can actually see waves of heat coming off the roof. We'll all probably get skin cancer up here."

"Damn! Stop complaining and let's change locations," Phillips grumbled. "Or better yet, why don't you go wait in the air-conditioned vehicle?"

"No, I'll stay and observe. You'll probably screw up her lesson if I leave."

"You should've worn a bodysuit. We gave the city ten." Phillips sounded more agitated than ever. "Trish, stop playing with the pistol holster before you shoot your own ass."

Doctor Burgos said, "No, I couldn't take any of the suits. They need to be used by the people doing the runs, and can't you see? The holster's digging into her lower back. I told you to switch it to the side of her getup, over her hip."

"Absolutely not," Phillips insisted. "It'd be more noticeable on the side. There's several advantages leaving the firearm where it is."

"Does she really need this added equipment? With her strength, the boot knife is more than enough in a tight space. All this other gear is only hindering her movements."

"It's the way she's laying there. Her knee needs to be up more."

Trish was tired of their commentary and not amused by their tendency to talk about her as if she weren't there. She was doing her best to accept training from two men who had no clue how to teach someone to use powers that neither they nor anyone else possessed.

"Wait, straight ahead." Trish pointed to a massive tree standing against the skyline. She searched the area through the scope as the other two stopped their bickering long enough to scan the area with their binoculars.

Doctor Burgos said, "Yep, I see it. There's one over a mile away. Great job, Trish. No, we have two—wait, another popped its head up. Make that three. Are they coming up from a hole in the ground? I wonder if they construct underground dens. This would explain why my late colleague and I had such a hard time tracking them. We could've swept right over them and not known."

Trish adjusted the scope. "Do you want me to start?"

Phillips tapped her shoulder. "What are you waiting for kiddo. Fire away."

Christina opened a bottle of water as muggy wind poured in the rear van window, tossing her hair about. Even with the setting sun, the heat was unbearable. Gabe, who was driving, blocked some of the rays coming in through the front windshield, but the vehicle was becoming increasingly warm.

The drive to and from Oahe Dam felt longer than normal on this supply run, but she didn't mind. Those working inside the power plant needed to eat and she appreciated the time away to think.

Groups of four did three-month rotations to perform maintenance and daily inspections of the power plant. This preserved the machines supplying the city with electricity. Because of their dedication, folks in Rapid City organized weekly runs to the plant to keep the fortified post well stocked of food and any necessities they asked for. This week's collection included extra fruit and homemade ice cream, cravings from a woman there who was three months pregnant. Last month, when the city offered to replace her and her husband due to her "delicate" condition, both had refused. They were looking to buy one of the limited vehicles the city had for sale, and the double hazard pay helped.

Since the cost was twenty-five thousand credits for a vehicle, transportation around the city was normally accomplished by walking, riding a bike, or the electric trains. If anyone wanted to fork over ten credits a day and pay for and go through the driving courses for an operator's license, they could rent a solar-powered golf cart from a rental booth. Yet, if something happened to the miniature vehicle, the cost for replacement was astronomical.

The governors of the city decided on this transportation system at the beginning. To them, the expense ensured the personal vehicles were purchased by those in the city who had contributed for several years toward everyone's welfare. Not to young adults who were usually careless with their newfound freedoms, or to someone who hadn't grown deep roots within the community.

The abundant supply of houses inside the city were free for the survivors who arrived. One deed per family, or groups of two people or more, and they could choose any unoccupied home. If they didn't want to take over the required lawn care, then townhomes were also available. Once a young adult graduated from school, they added their name to the work details, were issued their first five hundred credits, and allowed to pick their own condo or apartment. Christina wasn't ready to select her residence yet. Like several in her graduating class, she enjoyed living with her parents. She tried contributing some of her pay toward household expenses, but her parents insisted she save up for when she had her own place.

"Damn, it's sure hot," she said.

"You're right. Let's turn the AC on," Adam replied from the front passenger seat. He flashed Christina a sideways glance, but promptly turned away.

Good, let him worry. After what he and Trish pulled last night, he should be concerned. At the power plant, when Adam told her how he and Trish were simply trying to steer her and Stephanie together, she had been livid. The idea of them believing she needed to be hooked up, and with Stephanie of all people, was infuriating. Now, though, the more she stewed over the entire conversation, the more her mind raced and the pieces fell into place. Trish had strong feelings for her. Enough to put her own desires aside so Christina could be happy—even if Trish's assessment of what would make her happy was completely cracked.

With cold air blowing through the vent, Christina latched her window and stared at the black shine of Adam's helmet. Did Trish confess to him how she felt, or did Adam merely assume? Christina had been too upset at the time to ask. As soon as they return to the city, and Gabe isn't around, she would speak with Adam. The second Adam told her Trish almost lost her virgin lips, something sparked inside. The more Christina thought, the more she knew she wanted to be Trish's first kiss.

"Damn," Gabe said under his breath. "Hey guys, something's up?"

Adam must have been dozing because he jerked and leaned toward the windshield.

Christina shifted to the side to peer around Gabe. Far ahead, the entire stretch of highway was blocked by a line of rusted vehicles and busted household appliances. Refrigerators with no doors. Washing machines rusted through. Where did all this stuff come from? A strong sense of fear gripped her as Gabe slowed.

Gabe said, "How the hell could someone move this crap to completely block the highway in a matter of hours?"

Adam pointed to the upcoming off ramp before the blockade. "Get off here, and we'll bypass it."

Placing her helmet on her head, Christina gripped the headrest of the driver's seat and leaned as far forward as the lap belt allowed. The road heading north was also blocked. She reached over and secured her rifle. "Pull off the road and drive around."

Gabe braked slightly but didn't stop. "Not in this van. The ground's too wet from the rain last night. We'll get stuck. We can drive into New Underwood and go to the next on-ramp. We're right at twenty miles from the gate."

Christina narrowed her eyes to the lowering sun. If they didn't make it by dark, the gate would be closed until morning. The city strictly enforced that one rule. "Maybe we should turn around and drive to the power plant and call the city. Have them send someone out tomorrow to meet us."

Adam nodded. "I agree with Christina. Whoever blocked the roads is funneling us to New Underwood. Let's flip around and drive to the plant while we still have light."

Without warning, something hard struck the van on the right side. The rear of the van spun into a skid, shifting the front end toward impact. The right front bumper of the van smacked into the guardrail. The steering wheel yanked to the left, and Gabe hit the brakes while mumbling, "No, no, no . . ."

A moment of silence and then a frenzied shriek rang in Christina's ear. Golden-orange eyes glowered directly at her through the closed window.

She screamed and slid away from the slavering face. "Get us out of here!" Nothing happened.

"Gabe, back up!" Adam shouted, bringing Gabe out of his shock.

Gabe threw the transmission in reverse and floored the accelerator. Christina watched in horror as the Gramite jumped straight up and landed with a metal crunch on the roof. She let out another scream when the Gramite punched its long, thick claws several inches into the dented hood.

Gabe slammed on the brakes and in a swift motion yanked on the gearshift. He pounded the pedal. The van lurched forward toward a stop sign at the bottom of the offramp. He accelerated into a wide turn, then jerked the wheel, and the Gramite went flying onto the pavement.

When Christina squinted through the rear window, she saw twelve, maybe fifteen, creatures dashing toward them, all yelling out their rage as they raced on all fours. She'd never seen a group of this size before. "There's so many. Gabe go faster!"

"I'm trying!" he shouted, whipping the wheel, and sending the van on a road to the right, running alongside the highway.

With the speed at which they were moving, the creatures weren't gaining, but the gap separating them wasn't increasing either.

"Speed up!"

"I'm trying!"

She unbuckled her seatbelt, turned about face, opened the side window and poked her rifle out. Sighting into the mass, she pulled the trigger multiple times, trying to slow their advance. Only two of the creatures dropped out of the pack.

A loud bang blasted out. The van swerved, threatening to flip over. Christina's heart quivered when her weapon almost slipped from her hands with the vehicle's violent jerking. She regained control and fired again. A repeated thumping followed, and the vehicle dropped in speed.

"We lost a tire," Gabe yelled. "What the fuck are we supposed to do now?"

Adam said, "Head over to the gas station, the east side by the ladder there. We have to make it onto the roof. Christina, as soon as we stop, jump out and climb. We'll cover you. Gabe, you'll go next, and I'll follow. The second you reach the top, lay down a shit-ton of fire."

Slinging her rifle, Christina slid to the other side of the lengthy seat and braced herself. She racked open the van door. With the crunching of gravel and a cloud of white dust, the van skidded to a stop. She leapt out and ran toward the red ladder. Keeping one hand working ahead of the other, she climbed as fast as she could. Bullets vibrated behind her and she choked in the musky, putrid air. The creatures were close.

Reaching the top, she slung her leg over the edge. Sharp sounds of screaming pierced the air. Her foot touched tiny pebbles. Animalistic thundering followed from below.

She spun as she unslung her weapon, and her throat released a sorrowful moan at seeing blond, blood-streaked hair, and Gabe's face twisted in terror. He disappeared into the overwhelming sea of Gramites before she could fire a shot.

Adam reached the ladder and climbed as she opened fire. When his hand was a few rungs away from the top, a Gramite jumped with incredible strength, and soared, latching its grip onto his left foot. Adam's hands slipped, but he caught the next bar down.

Christina aimed and fired, striking the Gramite in the stomach. It didn't let go. Instead, it bared its teeth and snarled directly at her, its features flaring with hatred.

She tried to fire again, but Adam was in the way.

"I can't hold on, Christina!"

"No," she cried. She seized his arm and pulled with all the strength she had. No matter how hard she tried, her effort was useless against the creature tugging fiercely on the other end.

Adam's eyes glistened and he gave her a weak smile. "Tell my mom I love her."

Another creature lunged into the air and smacked against Adam. His hands ripped from the ladder, and his arm slipped from her grasp. She watched in horror as he fell into a swarm of frenzied creatures, his high-pitched voice yelping in agony. She closed her eyes in anguish, but barely for a moment.

With tears streaming down her cheeks, her body shaking with uncontrollable sobs, she pointed her weapon and fired.

Trish trotted to Phillips's Gladiator and grabbed the remainder of the ammunition. She heard a commotion at the gate and frowned when she saw Eva scolding a guard. Should she go see what the problem was?

Eva was clearly upset. She would hate to have that anger directed at her. When the Burgos women were pissed, the best thing to do was to not get in the way.

She turned to head inside the old hotel, as the solar lights out front clicked on. She veered around the splashing of the soldiers enjoying the indoor pool and made her way down the steps to the newly reinforced basement. At the armory she deposited the remaining rounds.

Her spirits plummeted when she first walked into the old hotel and found her apartment empty. On days they didn't do runs together, Christina was usually there, waiting to hang out when Trish arrived later than her, like tonight. She wondered if she should go track down Christina and talk. Or maybe Adam was wrong, and she and Stephanie *were* together. If Christina didn't come and find her by tomorrow evening, she would go to Christina's house. Insist on talking. Beg if needed.

She headed upstairs and saw Susan. "What's going on?" Trish asked, worried by Susan's anxious approach.

"Trish, the Oahe Dam supply run hasn't made it in yet. They're refusing to open the gates so we can send a vehicle out to look for them."

Her body went rigid. "Christina was on that run."

Susan nodded. "Eva tried to get them to open, but the governors aren't allowing it. Even Doctor Burgos said no."

Trish remembered Doctor Burgos telling her about the time the gates were opened in the evening and the Gramites almost got in. Before the city could get the gates closed, four of their guards were savagely slaughtered.

"They won't open up," Trish said. "What time did they leave the Dam?"

"Over three hours ago. They're in a civilian van, so we have no way to contact them."

"Doesn't anyone have a wrist processor? We have plenty to spare."

"No, with the security codes and documents they contain, Aralyn said they're too dangerous to hand out to anyone not in our group."

Trish winced, then raced back downstairs to the supply wing. She maneuvered around the loaded pallets of rations, passing several locked doors, then rushed to a far shelf and retrieved a bundle of thick rope. Trish hurried upstairs, but instead of going over to Susan, she continued up to the second level to her apartment. She threw open the door and went to the locked closet she kept her equipment in and got her gear. She stared at the crossbow. No, until Givens was able to come up with different bolts, this wouldn't do enough damage against a creature, and its awkwardness, combined with the rifle, would only slow her down.

Susan entered the room. "What do you think you can do? Scale the wall and go after them on foot? It's over a hundred and fifty miles to the outpost. Just thinking of going is absurd!"

Trish sheathed her boot knife and loaded her utility belt with extra ammo clips until she had no more room left in her pouches. "I'm hoping to find a working vehicle along the way, maybe a town or a rest stop. We're not even sure what happened. They could be close, maybe broke down a few miles from here. Either way, I've gotta go."

"No, you're not leaving. I'm in command while Aralyn's gone, and I won't let you."

Trish spun with a venom triggered by her increasing concern. She closed her eyes and inhaled slowly. "Susan, Christina's in danger. I don't care how you try, or how many soldiers it takes, you won't be able to stop me."

Trish shifted around Susan and out the door. When she heard Susan call out to several soldiers, Trish quickened her pace and exited the building.

A gathering of people, including Adam's mother, were arguing with another crowd beside the gate. Doctor Burgos was off in the corner holding his sobbing wife in his arms.

When Eva spotted Trish, she broke free from her husband and ran toward her. "Christina's out there, and they won't open the gate. Maybe they'll listen to you. You can sense danger. Please tell them it's safe to open."

Doctor Burgos said, "Eva, it doesn't matter—"

"Trish!" Susan's commanding voice bellowed out. "I said you're *not* leaving."

The entire commotion quieted. Trish slung her rifle strap over her head and onto her other shoulder. She put on her helmet, pressed the button, and dropped the rope. Gently, she pushed Eva toward her husband and turned to address Susan and the three soldiers standing behind her, all of whom Trish knew would give their lives to protect her, and she them.

Trish held up her hands. "I don't want to hurt any of you. It would kill me. But I'm heading out to go find the others. Please, don't try to stop me."

Susan said, "Trish, go inside the hotel now. That's an order. As soon as the gates open tomorrow, we'll find them."

Trish glared at Susan, picked up the rope, and pivoted to the gate. She heard shuffling movements behind her, spun, and brought the rope up to catch an arm in the loop. She swung her butt to Corporal Leonard and used the rope to flip him over her body and hard onto his stomach.

"Damnit Trish," Corporal Leonard said, wiping at blood falling from his nose. "I was simply going to touch you on the shoulder,"

She glared at the other two soldiers. They both held up their hands in surrender. She went to Leonard and helped him stand and tilted his head forward while he pinched his nose closed.

Phillips strolled over, a pack and rifle slung over each shoulder. "Nice takedown, Trish, but you need to be faster if you continue fighting the creatures hand-to-hand."

"What are you doing?" she asked.

"I'm going with you, what do you think?" He put on his helmet.

"No, you can't come. I'm running, and you'll slow me down."

"Trish, I'll keep up."

She shook her head. "I really appreciate it, but you can't and you know it." Trish handed him the rope. "If you want to help, pull this up once I'm clear."

Eva rushed forward and gave her a hug. "Trish, be safe and please, bring our children home."

Trish nodded. She saw the fear and heartbreak in Susan's eyes. She walked over and held her. "I love you," she said.

Before Susan could respond, Trish sprinted toward the tower. Once she and Phillips were up top, he secured the rope. When Trish was on the other side of the wall, she waved, then turned and ran.

CHAPTER FIFTEEN

Corporal Davis clutched the arms of his chair each time he heard a grunt or groan from Captain Rebecca Thomas during a lengthy beating he watched on a video screen. As a guy sent another backhand to her battered face, he looked away in anger. Davis stood, picked up his rifle, and moved to leave the room. Two sets of hands stopped him.

"This is bullshit," Davis sneered, struggling to break their grips. "He's going to kill her!"

They held on tighter. One reached out and pried the weapon from his hands. The other swiveled a chair over and shoved Davis into it. He heard another *smack*, followed by his captain's fleeting cry of pain, and Davis averted his eyes to the ground. His built-up rage and feeling of hopelessness clashed, and he kicked his foot out hard, sending a wastebasket flying. It struck the wall beside a couch with a loud crash. His commotion propelled a new wave of whimpers from children who were hunched on the floor in the sleeping bay.

Davis's lieutenant pointed to the group of frightened eyes behind her. "If you go out there to try to save her, you place all of them in danger." She directed his watery gaze to the screen. "She knew this, and that's why she ordered us *not* to unlock the supply bunker."

Raising a trembling hand, he wiped his perspiring face. "I owe her everything. I can't sit here and watch her die like the others." Pleading, he said, "You have to do something. See if you can reach the colonel again."

"We've tried. The invaders are still blocking our signal."

Staff Sergeant Young's tone was sympathetic but firm, "Look, Davis, this crap is hard on everyone, but you've gotta pull your shit together, or all this"—he steered Davis's beseeching pout toward the monitor—"it'll be for nothing if we open the bunker."

"Okay," the voice on the screen said, "apparently you guys don't care about your captain either. I guess she's useless to me then."

They all scowled at the man who peered up at them from the outside camera. "Play time's over. You've got five minutes to open the door and send out Doctor Webber's daughter, or, well, you know what'll happen. Guys, get the straps ready."

Corporal Davis brought his shaking hands up and covered his face. "I can't watch any more of this," he whispered. A second later he was weeping.

Sergeant Givens and Lieutenant Strong scurried forward, keeping low but moving with urgency. They dove behind the earthy terrain where Aralyn and a few others were observing their movements. The sound of rushing water echoed from the Snake River running alongside their position, which was brighter than expected, due to the moon reflecting its light off the watery surface. They were less than a quarter mile from the supply bunker outside Idaho Falls, at the location where Captain Thomas had missed her scheduled call-in.

Lieutenant Strong took a swig from her canteen and wiped her mouth on the arm of her bodysuit. "We count twelve, Colonel, all spread out along both sides of the fence. We didn't see any guards posted in back, only the front."

"And our troops? The civilians? Are any still alive?"

Lieutenant Strong shared a troubled glance with Sergeant Givens before continuing. "We counted four of our troops dead. Their limbs were pulled from their bodies. The supply bunker's closed. The soldiers from NORAD have Captain Thomas beside the door. It seems like they're using her to try to get whoever's inside to open the bunker. Colonel, Captain Thomas is in a bad way. To save her, we need to move now."

Aralyn nodded. "Did you see what's interfering with comms?"

Givens said, "They have a jamming system planted on top of the hill above the bunker door. Nothing's fortifying it, so won't be hard to take out."

Aralyn kept the plan simple, knowing the soldiers she brough with her had enough training and skill to improvise as needed. "Lieutenant O'Brian, take your group of three along the west side. Sergeant Perez, move your team along the south end. Stay low, get your shots lined up, and wait until Sergeant Givens takes out the jammer. The moment it's down, strike. Hit them hard and fast but leave their commander alive."

She viewed the eight faces staring at her, their fate resting on her shoulders. "We won't lose anyone else tonight, understand?"

With eager determination, they silently signaled their agreement.

"Givens, Strong, you're both with me. Now move out," she ordered.

Saying a silent prayer for her troops to whomever was watching over them, Aralyn pressed the button to seal her helmet, then flipped the night vision to auto. Crouching, she ran low, keeping herself in line with the other two soldiers. When they drew closer to the jammer, she let Givens take the lead, hoping he had an idea where to set up position for the shot.

As if able to sense her thoughts, Givens pointed to the wild shrubs lining the road heading toward the gate. Once situated, Aralyn signaled for him to wait, to give their troops time to get into position. She scanned the area. From where they hid, she saw a band of four invaders clustered together, conversing. Two had their helmets off as they laughed, and the others were smoking cigarettes with visors raised. Whoever oversaw this gaggle of misfits had done these soldiers an ill service, from both a lack of leadership and training.

She peered to Lieutenant Strong and pointed to the unprepared group, signaling for a one-shot kill. Lieutenant Strong nodded and switched her weapon rounds to grenade. Aralyn drew closer to Givens and focused on the commotion by the door.

In full view of the video-camera outside the bunker, Captain Thomas slumped against the grill on the front of a Gladiator. Her hands were bound to the frame's pulley apparatus.

"That's it. Strap her in good and tight," said a man inches away from where Captain Thomas's head hung to her chest.

The man said, "You saw what we did with the others. Now come on, Captain, save yourself the agony. Order those inside to open the door. We want Patricia Webber. Everyone else can go."

Captain Thomas's head shot up, and she leaned in, biting firmly onto the man's cheek. He shrieked in pain. She yanked off a chunk of flesh and spit it at him in one fluid movement.

"Fuck you!" she shouted through the blood and gave a bitter laugh.

"Now, that's a soldier," Aralyn whispered to Givens.

Panting in pain, the man sent three heated jabs to the captain's face. To a man beside him, he said, "Hook the bitch up."

The second man scurried to Captain Thomas and secured straps from her feet to the bumper of a second vehicle. Before he climbed in behind the wheel, Aralyn tapped Givens's shoulder.

Givens fired, shattering the jammer.

Lifting her rifle, an explosion went off, and Aralyn took aim. She pulled the trigger and the subordinate by the open vehicle dropped to the ground.

Weapon fire erupted from all sides, raining bullets down into the area surrounding the bunker. The battle didn't last long. Even though her group was outnumbered, they were well trained, with a solid foundation in leadership and unit camaraderie. She motioned to Givens and Strong, and they advanced to the gate, opened it, and finished sealing the fate of any enemy who still drew breath.

All the invaders perished but one, the leader in charge of the failed band of soldiers. Aralyn found him cowering under the vehicle to which the captain's feet were tied.

"Lieutenant Strong, get the bunker open and check on whoever's inside." Aralyn motioned to Givens, and he yanked the protesting man out from under the vehicle. "Sergeant, secure him."

The man violently objected, shouting so crazily she could barely understand him.

"Shut up, you imbecile," she said. "The irony here is that Trish Webber isn't even at this location."

Ignoring the man's continued, under-the-breath rant, Aralyn hurried over to the still-trussed Thomas.

"You sure took your sweet ass time, Colonel." Captain Thomas choked out as Aralyn cut her bindings and helped her to her feet.

"Damn, Captain!" Aralyn pointed to the man she'd shot, lying dead on the ground. "How could you let this gaggle of morons get the drop on you? Most weren't even wearing their helmets when we showed."

Captain Thomas glared at her for a moment. Her face was swollen, bloody, and bruised. "Colonel, you try hauling one-hundred and sixty-eight people around, protecting them from these assholes and blood-thirsty creatures, and we'll see how you fare."

"One-hundred and sixty-eight? How the hell—"

"No!" Captain Thomas spotted the pile of her soldiers' severed remains. She dropped to her knees, shaking. "It's my fault, Aralyn," she bellowed. "I failed them."

Stunned, Aralyn noticed how her troops were now watching the unexpected actions of her second-in-command, all equally as surprised by Captain Thomas's sudden outburst. She hoisted up Rebecca and guided her away from the others.

"Rebecca," she whispered, "you and I both know you did nothing of the sort." Aralyn gestured to a group of civilians exiting the bunker. "All those people are alive because of you. I'm sorry for making light of the situation. I was being hatefully callous, as usual. Now, get yourself under control, and have the medic look over your wounds. These assholes did a real number on you. I'll make sure your troops are properly buried."

Once the captain was taken inside the bunker, Aralyn had Givens forcefully interrogated the sole survivor, while her soldiers gathered up the enemy troops, stripped them of supplies and equipment, and stacked them to be burned.

As soon as Givens had the information Aralyn needed, he loaded a video clip onto the prisoner's wristband. She connected the feed to her helmet and used it to call Trish's father, Doctor Frank Webber. She focused on the mangled bodies of Captain Thomas's team and her heart wept. She wanted to glance away, but she needed her painful fury to grow for this to work.

When Frank finally answered, he was clearly alarmed at seeing her face instead of his own man's. His surprise swiftly transformed to rage. "Where's my daughter, Aralyn?" he said through clenched teeth. "I want her back. Now! Do you understand?"

"Your daughter, you cold-blooded bastard!" she screamed out as her tears fell. "Like Julie, *you* killed her, sending these ill-trained thugs after us. One of them shot her. You bastard, you've taken everything from me! Do you hear? Both the people I've ever cared about are gone because of you!"

She waved a hand and Givens sent the video clip of Susan holding Trish's lifeless body, the day she was injured by the creature in the tunnel.

Once the video played for Frank, Givens shut it off. Aralyn used the voice-activated display to show the current, real-time image from her own viewpoint. She signaled, and the pile of Frank's soldiers burst into flames. After a minute of having him watch the burning inferno, she directed the video to her own face.

"I'm coming for you, Frank. I don't care how long it takes. I'll kill you for Julie's and Trish's murders." She ended the connection and removed her helmet. "Guess that scared him. Hopefully, he'll be too busy hiding to send out more troops." She tossed the prisoner's wristband to Lieutenant Strong. "Reformat this and add it with the rest of the gear. I want the trackers disabled and every vehicle loaded by sunup. We're not leaving anything behind."

"What about him?" Lieutenant Strong nodded across the way at the only remaining marauder.

"Give him a shovel and let him dig the graves for our dead. When he's done, shoot him."

Captain Thomas, half bandaged, emerged from the bunker. She wandered up to Strong and pulled the pistol from the Lieutenant's holster. She sidestepped, raised it, and shot the man in the forehead. "He's not touching our soldiers."

Stepping closer, she spat on the body when it dropped. She tossed Strong her pistol and reached for the shovel in Corporal Davis's hand. "Throw this bastard in the fire, I'll dig the holes myself."

Aralyn nodded at Davis's bewildered expression, then turned and went inside.

Christina used this last break between attacks to check her dwindling ammo and finish off the few drops of water she had left. She kept a constant watch on the area surrounding the ladder, trying to avoid looking at what little remained of Adam and Gabe. She knew she was exhausted, dehydrated, and possibly in shock, and she didn't know what to do once she ran out of ammunition. She had killed some of the monsters, but close to a dozen were left, and she didn't see herself making it through the night.

She had suffered through the gnawing, crunching, and sucking disturbance as the creatures feasted on the corpses of her lost friends. They devoured every bit of flesh, organ, and bone marrow, as if understanding the traumatic suffering it caused her. Each time she gagged, her eyes watered, but she couldn't take her gaze away. They would use any lack of focus to scurry up the ladder and add her head beside the other two.

Bits and pieces of the black bodysuits lay scattered below. The creatures either managed to shred the material from flesh or to vomit it up once consumed.

The creatures displayed Adam and Gabe's heads in the center of the bloody mess, as if to torture her even more.

The entire commotion had pulled in three other Gramites, apparently not belonging to this horde. One of the original horde who towered above the rest beat the two hairless males to death, but left the female with only a few scrapes and bruises. Christina watched how the female was hissed and screamed at by the other circling Gramites. After a lengthy time keeping her head low, letting out an occasional murmur, and taking on a new wave of beatings, the leader eventually let the female Gramite have a few bites of what was left.

Christina removed her magazine for the fourth time, recounted the bullets, and inserted it in the rifle. Eight rounds left. Definitely not enough to keep her alive through the night. Most of her ammunition was spent in the initial fray when the Gramites rushed for the ladder and dove out of the way before the bullets made contact. They almost behaved as if they wanted her to waste her ammo, but how would they know she would run out? They surely couldn't tell these weapons didn't come with an endless supply.

And not a single one of them picked up Adam's or Gabe's rifles which lay nearby in puddles of blood. She didn't understand how their minds worked.

Now, they were staying hidden behind obstacles blocking her view. They would dart out briefly, before diving behind cover when she took aim. Were they getting a feel for how well she could see in the moonlight? Where her blind spots were? This logic was absurd. She was tired, they were creatures, her mind was running wild, it was as simple as that.

She pressed the buttons on her helmet, lifted it, and wiped at her sweat. She gagged at the rotten stench. Probably from the pile of dead Gramites they'd left at the base of the ladder. They didn't remove them to bury, or mourn over their corpses, as she had mourned over Adam and Gabe for the last several hours.

She heard rustling below and threw her helmet on, frantically searching for the sealing buttons. She activated both, raised her rifle, and fired two shots. The Gramite, whose head poked up from the top of the ladder, plummeted to the ground. She peered over the edge and saw two more scurrying away. Her gaze dropped to the pile of dead carcasses. The Gramite lying on the putrid mound got to his feet. She sent two more rounds through the top of its filthy head. It fell.

Damn, four rounds left. Would she save the last one for herself? She sure as hell didn't want to be conscious and go through what Gabe and Adam had.

She tried pushing the building anxiety from her mind in case they could read her thoughts or sense her fears. She didn't want them to know how terrified she felt. And after watching them for the past four hours, she understood her father was right. These creatures *were* intelligent. How intelligent, she didn't know, and she probably wouldn't be alive much longer to find out.

She looked down at where Adam's rifle had dropped, now half-buried underneath one of the dead creature's legs. His utility belt was also within reach of the ladder, and it held a canteen and several clips of ammo. Should she try for it? Did she have much of a choice? She stood and leaned over the edge. She saw some movement over by a shed and knew their leader was there. God, why did these things have to move so freakin' fast?

Throwing a leg over, testing the waters, she waited. Sitting on her hind-end, she swung the other foot over, and pointed her rifle out, trying to come off as threatening. She spun her lower body around, finding the ladder's rungs. She swallowed hard, and her heart quickened so fast she thought she might have an attack. She dropped one foot down, then the other.

An animalistic scream echoed in her ears.

She sprang up the ladder, firing two rounds at the moving creature, but she missed. Another scream came from the direction of the shed. The creature abruptly stopped advancing and hurried behind the tree it had emerged from.

She froze, one leg on each side of the ledge. The leader had called it off. It wanted her to get farther down before they attacked. It knew they'd have a stronger advantage.

Shit, two damn rounds left.

She wondered if the leader would have them turn her or eat her? What a tough decision it must be to make. She sat for a moment before bursting into uncontrollable laughter. She couldn't stop it, didn't understand it, and had to do everything in her power to keep her eyes open as her body released it. Struggling, not sure why she was laughing maniacally, she finally got her emotions under control.

She flung her leg over and thought, screw it. She descended rapidly and pushed off the ladder several feet from the ground to try to throw off the creatures' timing. She landed next to the belt, jerking it upward hard. A creature shrieked. She flung the belt over her shoulder and hopped onto the ladder, climbing as fast as possible.

Something smacked her leg. When she glanced downward, the leader had its mouth open and bit with force onto her calf. She kicked her leg wildly trying to shake it off. Gripping on tight with her upper body, she struck out with the other foot, smacking it hard enough on the nose so that it let go. She climbed. When she got to the top, she jumped over, and spun.

Too late. The leader lunged.

Trish stood panting and wiped at her mouth. She thought about taking a drink of water but was afraid she'd vomit again. Activating the map on her wrist processor, Trish searched for her location. She had run eighteen miles in a little over an hour. She flipped off the device, with Doctor Burgos's voice ringing through her mind. *"Not as fast as a cheetah can run, so you need to push harder."*

She still had two miles left before reaching New Underwood. She hoped to find a working vehicle there. But she doubted it. She continued along the old highway, pumping her legs mechanically, boots contacting the pavement in a steady slap-slap-slap. The moon was bright, offering her a cloudless view. This allowed her to keep her visor raised and relish the minimal coolness the breeze offered. She passed a few recreational signs and an advertisement board shot through with holes.

Skin crawling, she picked up danger off to the right. She unslung her weapon, lowered her visor, and activated the buttons. Keeping a steady pace, she pushed forward, scanning the grassy terrain. When she drew closer to the town, she heard shots ring out in the same direction. She stopped, raised her rifle, and squinted through the scope. She adjusted the focus. She spotted a few scattered buildings in the distance, but she saw no movement. She needed to get closer.

She hurried on until she reached the silhouette of a motel where a few more buildings stood. She loped off the highway, cutting through weeds and rocky terrain toward a grouping of darkened structures in the distance. The prickling sensation intensified. She hurried to the top of a nearby grassy mound and paused long enough to take aim.

Her heart raced when she saw a dark figure covered in a bodysuit hurrying up a ladder with an infected close behind. She steadied her rapid breath and aimed. When the individual jumped over the ledge, the creature also made it up, stood on the edge of the building, and leapt.

Trish pulled the trigger, sending a bullet straight into the creature's temple. The head jerked to the side, and the body fell. She dropped her sight to the ladder, then the area around it. Two more were rushing to the ladder. She squeezed the trigger and sent a bullet out for each.

Still sensing danger, she lowered her weapon and sprinted forward as fast as her legs would take her. Between two abandoned houses she slowed and moved carefully across the street. A creature, crouching behind a weathered sign, was staring at the old gas station ladder. It spotted her right before the butt of her weapon smashed into its face. It dropped and she dropped with it. Pulling her knife, she plunged it in before it could rise. She covered its moans with her gloved hand and waited till the jerking stopped.

She scanned the area. Creatures moved in the shadows, all circling the side of the gas station. She counted four. Her pulse quickened and the tightening of her chest constricted even more. God, she hoped all three of her friends had made it.

Staying low, she slipped ahead, toward the two hidden infected crouched behind abandoned fuel pumps. She pulled out one of her throwing knives and flipped it in her hand. The weight was too light, too small to penetrate hardened bone. Replacing it, now she wished she had brought her crossbow after all. At this close range, it probably would have been adequate. Quieter than her rifle, anyway. The built-in suppressor on the rifle was a joke. Unless you were fighting a band of deaf assailants, or shooting enemies farther than a hundred yards away, the gun's stealth was worthless. The suppression was more to protect the shooter's eardrums than to keep the kills silent.

She pondered for a moment to decide her mode of attack. She knew two were dead, and two were in front of her. There couldn't be many more left, could there? Probably one or two over by the vehicle charging ports. Six was a sizeable number for a band of creatures. Well, compared to the five groups she had already encountered since leaving NORAD.

Pulling out her boot knife, Trish slung her rifle and inched closer. She sprang at the closest Gramite, driving her knife into its skull. The creature slumped to the ground taking her knife with it. The second whipped around, and she unslung her rifle. When it opened its mouth to scream, she fired three times, cutting off the sound with the first bullet.

She reached for the knife sticking out of the first kill, but the area around her was suddenly filled with four infected. She backed up, took aim, and fired, dropping two.

Without warning, a powerful impact jolted her from the side, bringing her off her feet, spiraling sideways. She slammed hard into the nearby gas pump. The blow brought a swift pain to her right side and her rifle flew from her grasp.

Before she could stand, the infected who sideswiped her picked her up and raised her over its head. It pulled back to throw her, to the sounds of frantic screams around. All were awaiting their turn.

She grasped tight onto its arm with both hands. The creature threw her with ferocious force, while letting loose its grip . . . and stumbled when its prey didn't detach.

Stunned, golden-orange eyes glanced up. She jerked her head forward, smashing her helmet into the creature's forehead. She dropped to her feet and dove under its powerful swing. Standing, she kicked its knee and pivoted away from another creature's blow. She punched an advancing creature in the face, and sidestepped the third, who lunged for her waistline. Either these creatures were slower than the others had been, or her ridiculous training was paying off. Whichever the case, she knew her foes would be her downfall if they gained the advantage. She needed to stay focused, use her surroundings.

She whirled, rushed toward a shed, with her enemies closing in. She faked a move to jump onto the roof but dove sideways instead. With a loud crash, she spun to see two creatures on the ground in a heap, the third pivoting straight for her. She reached to the back of her utility belt, flipped a metal snap, and drew out her pistol.

She sent all ten rounds into its head.

Pulling another mag from her pouch, she rushed to the abandoned gas pumps. She inserted the magazine right as a creature lunged. Without having time to think, she slid on her butt in the gravel. It flew over her and she rocketed onto her knees and took aim. Before she could pull the trigger, she was tackled from behind. She and the infected collided into the body of one of its dead companions. The Gramite raised its arms and pounded furiously against her sides and legs. She swung around and struck hard, but not enough to stop the attack, only to slow it briefly. Stretching out her arm, she yanked her knife from the corpse and hurled it backwards into the creature's throat. The last creature shrieked when the female fell.

Trish twisted out from underneath, reaching for her pistol. She snatched it, aimed, and fired until the last one was down.

She climbed to her feet to no other movement, but her sense of danger still flared. After wiping the bloody goo from her knife on the torn pantleg of a dead mutant, she sheathed it. While watching for movement, she reloaded her pistol and replaced it in the holster.

Grabbing her rifle from the weedy gravel, she crept forward, searching. When she drew near the backside of the shed, she heard deep, panicked breathing. Raising her weapon to fire, she swiveled around the paint-chipped building.

Golden-orange eyes locked onto hers, and the infected barked out a weary cry. Trish pulled the slack out of the trigger, and the creature swung its head away, as if waiting. By the bulging under her torn shirt, Trish could tell this one was female. It had also been in a recent fight.

Not from bullets or stab wounds, but a beating along its chest and face. A numbness coursed through Trish, and her finger slightly relaxed.

Why was she not pulling the trigger? This creature was an infected who could easily kill or injure someone she loved. Today, tomorrow, next year. Their world would be safer if she put the creature out of its misery here and now.

She eased her squinted eye and lowered her rifle slightly. The creature's head moved, and they stared at each other. Its face held the force of rage, but its sad eyes didn't match the hatred. The creature looked so, well, so human.

Trish gave a nod.

The creature's eyes widened, then it whirled and dashed off into the thickets of the fields encircling the town. Trish waited until her sense of it grew weaker, the prickling sensation dulled, then vanished.

She moved toward the rusty ladder, unsure why the others hadn't climbed down or attempted to assist her. Near the ladder, she pulled up short.

She saw two battered heads lying in the center of a wide circle of blood and vomit. With shaking hands, she dropped her rifle and landed on her knees. Screaming out, she crawled forward through the chaos, her tears and anger coming in waves. Gabe's eyes were gone, his mouth hung open. Adam, dear sweet Adam, eyes closed, had a flat look of frightening peace.

Her throat constricted, her chest tightened, and she reached out her gloved hand, hysterically bawling as she touched Adam's blood-caked hair. Her hands pounded hard on the gravel, her fury building. She seized her rifle and rose, firing in the direction the female had run. When the magazine was empty, she released the trigger and sank onto the gravel to scream.

Completely unaware of the situation around her, she stayed there frozen in a state of shock until at long last, additional neurons fired. She visually raked the area, looking for remnants of a third body. What about Christina? Where was she?

"Christina!" she shouted, gripping her weapon tight. She flipped over, struggling to regain her footing. Stumbling forward, she slung her rifle, and climbed the ladder, scared of what she would find. When she managed to reach the top, she pulled herself over, and her entire body shook. Her worst fears were realized. There, on the roof, clawing at the helmet, was not the Christina she had fallen in love with. Now, a deranged creature took her place, whimpering and fighting with the device covering its head.

Trish dropped to her butt and leaned against the miniature wall. Her cries shook her body, and she brought a hand up, releasing her helmet's grip. She removed it and threw it at the infected, cursing herself for not being fast enough.

The creature spun, looked at her, and backed away. "No, Trish. I've been bit. Stay away."

"Christina?" Heart racing, Trish left her weapon on the ground and dodged forward. Avoiding the dead lump she'd shot earlier, she slipped on pebbles but climbed to her feet.

Christina's helmet shook. She darted toward the closest ledge, and Trish ran after her, tackling her before she could throw herself over. Trish bear-hugged Christina. The pleading cries from the woman she loved pierced her heart.

"I'm infected. Let me die."

Trish reached over and pressed the buttons on Christina's helmet. She yanked it off, seeing the frightened, red-streaked face beneath it.

She sobbed. "Trish, I'm going to change, and I don't want to hurt you. Please, let me go."

"Where, where were you bit?" Trish shouted, removing her flashlight.

"My leg. It bit my leg."

Trish's shook the device and turned it on. She released her grip and inspected Christina's eyes, then her leg.

"No, the other one, right here."

Trish ran her hands over the material. The armor was still intact. "It didn't go through," she said, shaking the crying woman. "Christina, listen to me! The teeth *didn't pierce your flesh.*"

Wide eyed, Christina's gaze shot downward and her hand stretched along the hardened fabric. "But it hurts, Trish, I can feel it."

Christina's hands went up and she pulled, fumbling with the suit's fasteners.

Trying to calm her, Trish whispered, "You're okay, it's okay, you're fine . . ." When Christina's trembling fingers failed to open the suit, Trish took over undoing the clasp. She helped Christina wiggle the suit free, until her calf was exposed. Trish shined the light to reveal only a dark, blueish-black bruise on the smooth skin.

"Thank God," Christina cried out before collapsing in Trish's arms. Trish held her tight, rocking her as they both sobbed out their relief and heartache.

CHAPTER SIXTEEN

Doctor Frank Webber shifted in his seat, waiting for the low-ranking officer to announce his presence to the eight members of the committee. When the captain returned, Frank stood. As the officer passed him and headed to the coffee machine, Frank Webber tightened his neck muscles. The nerve of this man to completely ignore me, he thought, retaking his seat.

Thirty minutes later, the buzzer on the officer's desk sounded. "They're ready for you."

Frank glared at the man as he slowly climbed to his feet. The captain hadn't even bothered to give him the courtesy of looking up from his work to relay the information. Instead, the captain kept his head down and busied himself with whatever he thought was more important than showing respect to the scientist who made his way of life possible.

Grunting to himself, Frank moved down the long hallway, toward the mahogany double doors. Before he reached the end, he wondered to himself if he should knock or not. His distaste for the captain grew for placing him in this awkward predicament. He figured he'd earned the right to walk in. After all, he had already been announced, almost a freaking hour ago.

The members of the committee greeted him with silence. The lone woman who secured the honor to have a place at the highly-polished table pointed to an empty, leather chair across from where they sat. "We reviewed the video you sent, along with other information we collected."

She motioned around the table to each member. "We would like to know why you took it upon yourself to send a team after Patricia."

Surprised by the question, Frank replied, "Because I was in charge of studying her medical . . . uniqueness."

"You mean the one responsible for allowing her to get way," snapped General Princeton, the Director of Military Forces.

"That was not my fault!"

The woman, who had once been called Madam President, held up a hand, demanding silence. "We are here for the facts, gentlemen."

"Trish is also my daughter. As her father—"

Princeton snickered under his breath, sending a wave of anger through Frank. "Noble father, keeping his beloved daughter sedated. We read the reports."

"I did what I had to for the sake of this government—"

"Funny," the general said, interrupting Frank again. "Those were the same words he used the day he shot his own wife."

Frank shifted in his seat, feeling uncertain. None of the other committee members were coming to his aid. Not even the man overseeing scientifical advancement, the one who lobbied for using Frank's virus in the first place. "I did what I had to do—"

"What you *had* to do was make sure Julie never found out we released a virus onto the populace." General Princeton gritted his teeth. "But since *that* was apparently too *hard* for you to do, and she managed to break into *your* processor, you killed her. The one person who could have ensured our greatness on this planet."

He could ensure greatness. His wife was not as brilliant as he. She got lucky, that was all. "She destroyed her own research, all the data gone, her creation over." Why could they not see how his decisions had always been for the good of this government?

"Yes, research that came from her brilliant mind, which could have been recreated until you ended her life. Without our permission, I might add. Like your careless management of Patricia. Because of you, she's lost to us." The general slammed his fist down on the table, and Frank jumped. "You have a way of overstepping yourself Doctor Webber."

The Head of the Committee held up her hand. Frank could see the reserve in her eyes. They needed him, and she knew it. "Doctor Webber, you will, from here on out, run any further decisions through this committee, not pertaining to your urgent task at hand."

Demonstrating to him this preposterous meeting was over, she waved him from the table. As he left the room she called out, "Find an inoculation from these creatures, Doctor Webber. Soon."

Trish awoke to Christina's screams. She shook in Trish's arms, crying out for Adam and Gabe. Feeling powerless, unable to battle the demons running rampant through Christina's mind, Trish could only hold her tight until the remnants of the nightmare passed. When Christina was under control, she pleaded with Trish to take her somewhere else. She wanted to be anywhere but this hellish gas station.

At the roof's edge, she scoped out the strip of abandoned buildings running through the meager town. Trish spotted the police department across a doublewide street covered in weeds and flowery vines. She returned to Christina's side to assist her shaking hands with her wardrobe. Trish collected the rest of their gear and they got down off the roof. At seeing Adam and Gabe's weapons beneath filthy corpses and shrouded in human and Gramite blood, Trish decided to get Christina settled somewhere safe and come collect the weapons later.

She did a brief search of the van for anything of use but came up empty. No rations, no emergency equipment, nothing but two half-empty bottles of water.

Aralyn wasn't taking over security until her troops finished emptying the two remaining supply bunkers in North Dakota and her last team was safely in Rapid City. Still a good week away. Something needed to be done until then to instruct the people doing the runs on how to better prepare.

When Trish took Christina across the street, they walked around the entire building. Every window of the police department was boarded, secured by bolted on sheets of metal, and the doors were heavily reinforced steel. She used her boot knife to jimmy the front lock. After several minutes of under-the-breath swearing, it opened. She had to jiggle the door to free the chair propped on the other side of the latch. Once inside she tried the light switch. They heard the sound of a click and no light followed.

"Damn."

"They won't work," Christina said, shining her flashlight around. "The city shut off all the other feeds not being utilized on the power grid."

"They must have something here—a generator, maybe?—in case they lost power. Do you want to wait by the door while I do a walkthrough?"

Christina scraped her teeth over her bottom lip. "Oh, no. I'll be all right coming with you. I'd rather keep busy. If not, I'm afraid my mind will get the best of me, and I'll be frightened by my own shadow." She grabbed Trish by the hand and squeezed. "Thank you again for saving me. Coming to my rescue is becoming a habit for you."

Not losing a beat, Trish faced her in the dim light. "I would march through Hell itself and pull you from the burning flames if I had to."

Trish held her breath and gaped, thinking her own face probably matched Christina's surprised expression. Did she really say that out loud?

Trish dropped her gaze, released Christina's hand, and moved away to comb through the room. Desks, chairs, coffee cups, framed photos— all were coated in a thick layer of dust, cobwebs, and flashlight-scattering insects hustling back into the darkness. Yet nothing appeared disordered. No strewn papers lined the floor, no furniture lay overturned. No hurried chaos or planned packing of keepsakes. As if everyone who worked here departed in an instant, and fragments of nature took over.

She found three windup lanterns in a corner office. A plate engraved *Capt. McMichael* sat on the desk. Powdered filth hid family photos on every dusty surface, including the framed certificates and wooden plaques which remained hanging level on the far wall.

Christina helped Trish wind up and place the handheld lamps throughout the main office area before picking an empty jail cell to wait out the night. Christina shook out the mattress and hunted for pillows and bedding while Trish continued her search of the place.

A gush of malodorous brown liquid flowed when Trish turned a sink faucet in the bathroom. She scrunched her nose before twisting the handle to off. Thankfully, they had water left in Trish's and Adam's canteens, but they needed food. Between her long run and the conflict with the creatures, Trish felt as if her body had burned every last calorie she had at her disposal. Her muscles and mind were both spent and slowing because of it.

Locating the staff breakroom, Trish's excitement faded. Everything was gone. The vending machines, the cabinets, even the powerless refrigerator sat open and bare. When she checked the back door, she frowned. The deadbolt and slider bar were both engaged. She spun, shining her flashlight to the last remaining unopened door.

"What's wrong?" Christina asked behind her, her voice edgy.

"This place was locked up tight from the inside. So, where's the person or corpse of the individual who was here?"

"Father said the virus decomposed the bodies at an elevated rate. With the bulk of humanity, they probably disintegrated. The Gramites and scavenging animals eat the remains of everyone else who dies."

"Not with the doors locked and the building sealed they don't. If the virus killed anyone here, what about their clothes? Shoes, jewelry? Even in the hotel where I found you, I spotted those kinds of articles scattered about. Yet here, there's nothing."

Trish reached for the doorknob. Christina's hand stopped her. "Trish, you're scaring me. Look, I found the keys for the jail cell, let's go wait inside until morning."

"If there was something dangerous on the other side, I would have sensed it. Why don't you go to the cell, while I do a sweep of the last room? I'd feel more comfortable if I knew this building was thoroughly inspected."

Christina forcefully shook her head. "Not without you. I can't."

Trish offered her a reassuring smile. "Okay, we'll stay together."

Trish rotated the handle, but instead of the door opening to a room, the floor dropped into a long set of stairs. Trish shined her light down and spotted a metal door at the bottom.

"Crap," Christina whispered.

"On second thought, you wait here, I won't be long."

Christina gripped her arm. "No, if you must go, I'm coming with you. I'm not ready to be alone."

Understanding what Christina was feeling, Trish headed down the stairs cautiously, her hand close to her pistol. When she reached the door, she shined her light around the frame. The brick wall surrounding the door didn't match with the wooden panels of the enclosed stairway. Someone installed the bricks after the building went up. When or why, she had no idea. What she did know from reviewing the locking mechanism, if this door was latched from the inside, she wouldn't be able to open it. Holding her breath, she tried the handle.

"Dang," she said, when it refused to budge.

Christina held out a ring of keys. "Here, I used these for the cells. Maybe one will work."

Trish tried the first five keys on the ring. When she inserted the sixth, the lock clicked, and the door opened. The moment her light pierced the darkness, she saw the partially covered remains of two skeletons curled together near the foot of the stairs.

She reeled against Christina, blocking the view. "You wait here. I'll be right back."

"No, I'm fine. I can take whatever we find, more than I can handle being alone. I tried it setting up the bed, but the solitude caused the shadows around me come to life." She peered down. "I don't like this place, Trish. The town, this building, any of it. It's shrouded by ghosts, and I feel they're all watching me. Please. Don't leave me alone."

Seeing Christina in so much distress tore at Trish's heart. She wanted to pull her close, to hold her, but she stopped herself. She nodded and headed into the basement. Shining her light around, Trish noticed how all the windows and vents were covered.

They found five more partially-clothed skeletons, and on further inspection, Trish saw miniature teeth marks notched into many of the bones. After these people died, tiny rodents were the obvious theory for how the bodies were so thoroughly stripped of flesh. Where the rodents were now or how they got out, she didn't have a clue. These questions, and this part of her examination she kept to herself.

She found another set of keys and a note off to the side, next to a corner stacked full of supplies, including weapons, ammo, and two full pallets of unused rations. Picking up the slip of paper, she quickly read it.

> *To whoever finds this . . .*
>
> *We tried outlasting this last viral epidemic, only to discover our water is tainted. By what, we haven't a clue. As of last night, everyone else is gone and I'm the last survivor. I was the one who ordered the deputy to dump out and fill the unmarked barrels from the fire station, so I claim complete responsibility. The pain in my gut, is nothing compared to the guilt in my heart.*
>
> > *Captain Brandon McMichael*
> > *May God forgive me*

Trish passed the letter to Christina who read through it twice. "What a terrible way to die."

Trish agreed. She went to the four plastic drums to see if she could figure out what they had consumed, but each of the valves had been left opened and nothing remained inside. She snatched the keys left behind by the captain and a box of the rations, before doing a last sweep of the area. "When they come get us tomorrow, they can decide what to do with the rest."

Once they were upstairs and settled on the cot in the cell, Trish devoured three of the ration kits by herself, while Christina struggled with a few bites of her first. Trish had left her testing equipment and water purification crystals in her room, stored safely and uselessly inside her rucksack with the rest of her emergency gear. She drank a few sips of water from her canteen but made Christina down the rest to rehydrate. After seeing the brown liquid coming from the tap, and reading the note they found downstairs, she wasn't about to chance ingesting any water from this town.

When they finished eating, Trish cleaned up their mess and locked the cell. She went to the cot and sat down, leaning against the wall. Christina put her head in Trish's lap and fell asleep. Trish listened to Christina's light breathing, feeling a pang of guilt at knowing what she had to do. The idea of Christina waking alone in the cell was upsetting, but Christina needed to sleep, and she knew Christina wouldn't let Trish go by herself. She would need to hurry.

Scootching out from under the sleeping woman, Trish reloaded Christina's weapon and left it leaning by the cot. She donned her helmet, activated the buttons, and slung her weapon. She wrote out a short message in the dust by the lights, left the cell closed, and locked it with the second set of keys, then grabbed some unused bedding. At the front door, she made sure the latch wasn't damaged when she jimmied the door open, then exited the building and engaged the lock.

She ran across the street and gently wrapped the remains of Adam and Gabe in a blanket. The blanket went into the back of the van along with the two rifles and their other gear. She wanted to change the tire and clean the blood from the gear, but she didn't want to be away from Christina any longer than necessary.

Carrying three wadded-up sheets, she sprinted to the highway and tied the first sheet to a tree where the others would see it in the morning. She continued the trail along the road heading toward the police department. She secured the second sheet to a stop sign, and the last she fastened out front before inspecting the area one last time.

Entering the police station, she heard the heartbreaking sounds of Christina's recurring nightmare. She locked the main door and entered the cell. Once she had secured the cage, she removed her helmet and stuck her rifle and gear beside the rest of the stuff on the floor. She squirmed her way onto the cot next to Christina and wrapped her securely in her arms. At once, Christina's frightened muttering ceased. Closing her eyes, Trish gently rocked Christina until she herself fell asleep.

The sounds of heavy banging jolted both women awake.

"Trish, are you in there?" a woman's voice hollered.

Trish reluctantly removed her arms from around Christina and extricated herself from the cot. Once she found the keys under the blankets, she unlocked the cell and rushed to the door.

Susan hugged her the moment the door opened. "I swear child, you will be the death of me."

Trish held her tight. Before she broke free, she whispered about the heads and weapons hidden in the van and asked Susan not to open it with Christina around. Susan murmured her understanding.

"Adam and Gabe's parents are in the lead vehicle," Susan said. "I'll talk to them while the guys help you with your gear." She moved to go comfort Christina but added, "I'm so proud of who you are. No matter what you face, Trish, never let it change you."

Trish watched Susan hug Christina, then lead her to the center Gladiator where the Burgos were anxiously waiting.

Once the van's tire was switched out with the spare, and the gear was loaded, Trish showed First Sergeant Stevens the location of the supplies in the basement, for later pickup once the families were safely in Rapid City, and Stevens had a few extra soldiers to help.

Soon, the convoy departed. Trish rode with Susan and First Sergeant Stevens to give Christina and her family some space to grieve. Susan delivered Trish the information concerning the California team, and how Aralyn and the survivors should arrive a little past noon.

The news about the lost lives of their group was heartbreaking. She was infuriated by her father's role in their tragic deaths, simply because he wanted her, his lab rat, returned. Combined with Adam and Gabe's horrific slaughter, and how close she had come to losing Christina, Trish wanted to jump from the vehicle and run. She didn't care where, but far enough away until she could no longer feel the painful splitting in her chest.

She stared out of the window listlessly, even when they stopped and waited for the gate to open. Once inside, the vehicle with Adam and Gabe's parents retreated to the right. Christina's vehicle rolled forward, and Stevens pulled their vehicle into the circle drive in front of the reconstructed hotel. Without a word, she got out, grabbed her gear, and went up to her room.

She had always left her door unlocked so the guys could access her living room to play on her gaming system or watch a movie from her growing collection on her wall display. Today, as she stepped inside and closed the door, her apartment was unnaturally quiet. She dropped everything she was holding and slowly slid down against the door until her butt rested on the softness of the dark-brown carpet. She slumped onto her side, closed her eyes, and cried.

She wasn't sure how much time passed before her tears finally stopped. Or if her eyes were still red when a knock resonated from behind her. She didn't care. She slowly climbed to her feet and rotated the knob counterclockwise.

First Sergeant Stevens stood in the doorway twisting his military cap nervously in his hands. He cleared his throat. "Hey, Trish. I wanted you to know, if you needed to talk about anything, we're here for you. Me, the others, most of us have been through shit—er, stuff, I mean, that's hard to put into words, much less process. The experiences—sometimes they can be tragic. Knowing that others understand, who've gone into the mouth of the beast themselves, well . . . sometimes talking helps."

"Thank you, First Sergeant. Right now, I just want to be alone."

Stevens waved his cap around. "Of course, Trish, of course. I'll make sure the guys use the outside pool tonight, to give you some peace and quiet."

"There's really no need. I'll be fine."

His smile was warm, fatherly. He gave her an awkward hug and left.

Trish closed the door and locked it. She leaned against its cool surface for a moment, thinking about Christina. She wished she knew

Christina was physically and mentally all right. Peering down, she noticed spots of dried blood splashed on her suit. A flash of Adam's blood-caked hair popped up. In a frenzy, she tugged at her outfit, feeling a sickening need to remove it from her body.

Naked, she rushed into the bathroom and flipped on the water. In the shower she scrubbed as hard as she could, working up a lather and washing it away. Then again, working up a lather, and washing with water so hot, it teetered to the point of scalding. By the time she turned off the valve, dense steam covered the room, and every part of her skin looked sunburnt.

She toweled off, not bothering to glance at her reflection in the mirror above the double-sink. Hanging the damp towel on the hook behind the bathroom door, she crossed to her dresser, threw on shorts, sports bra, and the first tank top her fingers touched. She picked up her suit and utility belt from the floor and slipped into flipflops before leaving the room. This time, she locked it when she left.

Ignoring the inquisitive eyes of those around her, she went to the basement, snatched a bucket, added some warm water and cleaning soap, and selected a soft-bristle scrub brush. When she was outside, she paused for a moment to feel the hot breeze on her face. She breathed in the summer aroma of cut grass and the blended floral fragrance of roses and lavender. She examined the group of kids playing with a barking puppy across the street.

She tilted her head and squinted as she surveyed the neighborhood, silently absorbing in the daily rituals. Outside the wall, life was vicious, chaotic. Inside the wall, people waved to each other, children laughed, and swimmers basked in the sun and worked on perfecting their tan. Cats chased mice in a secured environment, grateful to be the hunters and not the prey.

The laidback atmosphere of this community wasn't life lived in fantasy, but the reach for a reason to keep on going. People in here knew what life outside the wall was like. They'd lived in it, lost loved ones from it, and built a wall to defend themselves and others against it. None were slouching through the streets, hanging their heads in defeat for the horrors they had faced. Instead, they mentally pushed back.

Drawing emotional strength from those around them, the city's occupants ventured out past the wall, risking their own lives to bring others in. To share this bit of sanity and safety with them, while still finding the enjoyment in each day they drew breath. This was a reason to live.

She sat on a stone bench, picked up her suit and the soapy brush, and scrubbed. She would do everything she could to see this way of life continued. Whatever it took. Like Adam and Gabe, if she had to, she would give her own life for this community.

Trish sighed, clutching tight onto this very reason to keep on going.

Trish rose from her bed. She assumed the knock had been Aralyn returning to her room to check on her again. When the door opened, she was surprised to see Doctor Burgos standing in the hallway. She ushered him inside.

"I don't mean to bother you. I know you've been through a lot, and I could never begin to express Eva's and my gratitude for what you did for our daughter."

Feeling uncontrolled suspense, Trish blurted out, "Is Christina okay?"

Doctor Burgos's shoulders slumped and he shook his head. "No, that's why I'm here."

The heart beneath Trish's ribs beat rapidly, threatening to break free from her aching chest. "What happened? Is she safe?"

He held up his hands. "No, she's fine physically. She's, well, she's scared. Traumatized, and she's refusing a sedative to help her sleep." He shifted, sat on her bed, and slouched his shoulders even further. "Trish, I know what you've already been through, and I hate asking you this."

Trish knelt beside the exhausted and mournful man and gripped his arm. "Doctor Burgos, anything you need, I'll do it."

"The wife and I were wondering if you wouldn't mind coming over for dinner?"

Trish was surprised by the simplicity of his request. "Of course, I will. I haven't eaten yet, so you'll be the ones doing me a favor."

"We're also hoping you would stay over. I know you have your own life to live, but it shouldn't be longer than a few days. You see, Christina keeps asking for you, and Eva hopes by having you there, our daughter will relax a little. Feel safer."

Without hesitating, Trish went to her closet and found an empty duffel bag. Quickly, she tossed a variety of clothes inside, not bothering with what matched with what. She went through her apartment, packing anything else she might need.

When she met Doctor Burgos at the door, he touched her arm gently. "You're a wonderful woman, Trish. Thank you."

The drive to the house didn't take long. When they got out, she wanted to rush past him to check on Christina, but she forced herself to wait. The moment she stepped inside, Eva was there to greet her with a tender hug. She took Trish's bag and nodded silently toward the living room.

Christina sat on the couch, hair wet, in her nightclothes, her arms wrapped around her legs with her knees to her chest. She didn't seem to be gazing at anything of interest but stared off past the view of the open window. The thousand-yard stare. Trish sat down beside her and touched her. The moment Trish's hand made contact, Christina jumped to the side, frightened. When her eyes focused onto Trish, she gasped, throwing herself into Trish's arms.

"I keep hearing the sounds Trish," she cried, burying her head in Trish's chest. "When they ate Adam and Gabe, I had to keep watch. I heard and saw everything."

Christina's body shook and Trish rubbed her back. "If I didn't watch I would've died, and all this would be over. I should've looked away."

At hearing the painful declaration, Trish's eyes welled. She didn't say a word, only whispered soothing sounds in Christina's ear. Eventually, Christina fell asleep in her arms. Trish continued to stroke Christina's hair and listen to the gentle moans escaping from Christina's parted lips. She needed to find a way to ease this woman's pain.

CHAPTER SEVENTEEN
AUGUST 5, 2088

Trish opened her eyes and stretched out the stiffness in her right leg. Her back was twisted at an odd angle, bringing her head to hang off the edge of the sofa-bed. She was surprised to find Christina had remained curled in her arms throughout the night and hadn't moved to her own bed.

Trish wiggled her foot tucked between Christina's warm calves. She flexed her neck, then rearranged herself so that her head was on the pillow. Christina squirmed in even closer, and Trish held her a little tighter.

Trish smiled. Christina had kicked all but a small corner of the blankets off during the night, a feat Trish had found not uncommon over the last few weeks of sleeping together. Not that Trish had planned to wake up holding Christina. As always, they fell asleep watching movies, and this is what happened in the night.

She buried her face into the full thickness of Christina's hair. The aroma of citrus shampoo made Trish's stomach flutter.

"Breakfast is ready," Christina's mother bellowed from the kitchen down the stairs.

When Eva closed the basement door, Christina began to stir. Trish's heart sank. She wasn't ready to release her grip. She wanted to savor this last night of *accidentally* sleeping together. Trish knew she was being selfish. These last few weeks had been a sorrowful blessing, but the excuses for her continuing to stay were stretching thin. After the first week, Christina no longer woke with nightmares. This week, Trish managed to get Christina out of the house to socialize with Trish's group and others in the community. With Christina being cleared to work the supply run tomorrow, there really wasn't a good reason Trish needed to be here.

Christina rolled over and pressed her face into Trish's chest, her arm draped over Trish's waist and their legs were intertwined. Trish closed her eyes and swallowed. This closeness was growing more difficult each night. She wanted, more than anything, to pull Christina up and kiss her, to part the fullness of Christina's lips with her tongue and see what flavors she offered. She'd almost done it last night when they were sprawled together watching movies, but as usual, Trish chickened out. What if Christina didn't like the way she kissed, or worse, what if she found Trish's morning breath repulsive. Trish rolled her tongue around in her mouth and smacked her lips together. She released her grip around Christina's waist, blew her breath into her hand, and sniffed.

Christina's laugh startled her. "What are you doing?"

Trish fumbled with her words. "Umm, I . . . a fly buzzing," she said, laboring to materialize any excuse. "There was a fly, I got rid of it."

With fading giggles, Christina balled tighter into Trish's chest. "Once again, you're my hero."

Mentally, Trish scolded herself for sounding like a nitwit but she couldn't help herself. Physically, her body continued to surge with burning enthusiasm. Her hormones were reaching new heights every day they were together. Trish had to do all she could to beat them back into their crate and nail the lid shut tight.

The basement door opened, and Eva yelled down, "Trish, your first sergeant radioed again. He said if you guys are late, he'll personally smoke you two with the rest. I'm not sure what he means, but it didn't sound good. Breakfast is getting cold."

Christina jumped from the pullout bed. "I get the first shower. Yesterday, you left me lukewarm water," she playfully whined, tossing a smirk at Trish. Gathering up her outfit, Christina rushed toward the basement bathroom.

Trish sighed and rolled her face into a soft pillow. Christina's scent lingered in her nose when she inhaled. Sleeping alone tonight would be quite difficult. She kicked off what little covers remained and swung her legs over onto the fluffy, crimson-carpeted floor. Trish knew one thing: she wouldn't miss the vivacious decor of the room. From the pale-pink furniture and splashy colorful knickknacks, half the time Trish felt the need to wear shades in the basement. Christina's flamboyant clutter edged on the side of messy, compared to the order Trish was used to. So maybe being in her own room tonight was a good thing.

Grumbling, Trish snatched up her duffel bag and roughly shoved her items inside. She scanned the mounting number of photos Christina had tacked to the wall of their various moments together. Trish turned to her duffel, feeling a sudden jolt of depression. Who was she kidding? She would take the colorful mess with outstretched arms if it meant she could wake up each day holding Christina.

"What are you doing?"

Christina stood in the bathroom doorway fully dressed and toweling her hair. Confused, Trish asked, "What do you mean? I'm waiting for my turn in the shower."

Christina removed the towel from her wet, wavy hair and pointed to the bag. "You're packing. Are you staying at your place tonight?"

Trish shrugged. "I figured, seeing as how you're scheduled to do a run tomorrow." She placed her flipflops on top of the pile and closed the bag. "If I stayed much longer, people would talk."

Christina gazed at her evenly. "Since when has the opinion of others bothered you?"

Trish watched Christina drop the towel, head to her dresser, and rip a brush through her hair. Was she upset?

"I don't care. I was only joking."

"Yet, you're leaving." Christina wrapped her hair in a ponytail. "What would they say, Trish? That we're together?" She turned, staring at Trish, and waving the brush at her. "What exactly are we? We've *never* actually talked about it."

The ferocity of Christina's words struck Trish speechless. Why was Christina so upset? What was happening? Trish tried replaying the last few moments in her mind.

An impatient voice floated down from above. "Come on you two! Food's getting cold."

This time, Trish didn't hear Eva close the door.

Christina stared a bit longer, then groaned. "Just forget it. Hurry up and shower. We've got to go." She picked up Trish's duffel bag and headed for the stairs.

"That's just great," Trish muttered.

By the time Trish had showered and gone upstairs, her mood was off kilter. She sat at her usual spot at the table where a plate containing scrambled eggs and a couple pieces of bacon with toast was waiting.

Eva eyed her curiously over the rim of her coffee-cup then dipped her head to where Christina had dropped the duffle bag. "Are you leaving us?"

"Yes," Christina said in a scathing tone of voice, "she's staying at *her* place tonight. I guess she's growing tired of our long walks and late-night movies." Christina stood and went to the counter to fill a to-go cup with coffee.

Christina drank her coffee black when she was upset. Maybe she was too irritated to bother with additions? Trish wasn't sure, but today, Christina left the sugar and milk untouched and grabbed a lid.

Trish exchanged a look with Eva expecting sympathy, but received an entertained shrug instead, followed by the outline of a grin sneaking past the top of Eva's cup.

"We've got to go. Take the food with you. *I'll* put your bag in the truck."

Trish watched Christina pick up the duffel and head to the front door. She let loose a lengthy chorus of heated Spanish as she left the house.

Trish exhaled, dropped the bacon onto her toast and folded it together. "I really need to learn Spanish. Thank you for your hospitality, Mrs. Burgos." Gripping her meager breakfast, she left the table.

"Good luck with her," Eva called out.

On the freshly-mowed hill overlooking the golf course parking lot, Trish accepted a cold beer from Susan, leaned back in an unfolded chaise longue, and listened to Lieutenant Strong and Susan shout and heckle the newly-enlisted privates. The young recruits were lined up with their recently-issued gear spread out on the pavement in front of them. When they had arrived, Trish sat next to Christina, but before taking her seat, Christina had slid her own trifold longue chair toward Strong. Trish still didn't know what she had done, but Christina's attitude was bordering on the point of childish.

"Come on First Sergeant," Strong yelled. "You're gonna make the little boy cry. Lighten up, ya big brute."

When the nineteen-year-old trainee turned his freckled face to Strong on the hillside, First Sergeant Stevens lunged, his nose stopping inches from the frightened kid's face. "Who are you eyeballing, boy!" he barked. "Does your lieutenant give you a wee-boner?" First Sergeant Stevens gawped left, then right, then to the teenager. "What's your name, son?"

"Excuse me, sir."

"What'd you call me?"

"Sergeant . . . First Sergeant," the youth muttered, then shouted, "sorry, First Sergeant."

"So, you think I'm a *sorry* first sergeant?" Stevens yelled, then followed it with a wide variety of colorful sentences containing mostly swear words Trish had never heard before. He glowered angrier than normal, which made Trish cringe. The young man worked hard at keeping his eyes forward and face expressionless.

Trish was temporarily relieved when First Sergeant Stevens moved away from the kid. Unexpectedly, First Sergeant spun and shouted out a new round of cusswords. The recruit's bottom lip quivered, and Susan and Strong clanked their bottles together.

Phillips strolled toward them dressed in swim trunks, flipflops, and a straw hat. His pale chest contrasted with his sunburnt face.

Christina pointed at the group of twenty newbies standing at attention for in-processing. "You do this to all the new soldiers?"

222 | MICHELE L. COFFMAN

"Yep," Phillips said, pulling a cold beer from a cooler. He took the open chair on the other side of Trish. "We have to break them, before we shape them. It's a painful yet proven fact. Painful for them, fun for us. I can guarantee all those sergeants down there have side-bets going on who can make the most cry."

Since Aralyn's group had taken over security, the city offered an unlimited supply of construction material and a hefty yearly budget for individual pay and troop rations. Three of the unused apartment buildings closest to the panels at the north, south, and west exit doors had been reconstructed into barracks. Major Thomas's team, monitoring the gate and east side wall, remained with headquarters at the old hotel. Watchtowers were being erected above the inside roadway to keep an eye on every direction along the wall.

Aralyn kept the original teams together, to be assigned to the newly constructed barracks. The teams would monitor and be responsible for their sections of the wall and grid area of the city, while Aralyn's team focused on management and training.

Once the recruits completed their ten-week boot camp at the old golf course, these new troops, and future soldiers to follow, would be reassigned to a team. A female recruit with a tight body and long, red hair pulled in a ponytail was the only one Trish didn't like. Everyone else she was eager to work with.

Major Rebecca Thomas was the next to arrive. "Sorry I'm late. Colonel had me up doing reports all night. You'd think during an apocalypse she would ease up on certain things."

"Congrats on the promotion, ma'am," Phillips said, passing her a cold beer. "Sorry we missed the ceremony. Doctor Burgos wouldn't let Trish out of training."

She waved him off. "Not at all, Phillips." She gawked with enthusiasm at the crowded parking lot, then hollered, "Come on, you pansy. Quit your crying." She took the seat beside Phillips. "Who's winning?"

Strong said, "Of course First Sergeant, who do you think? Sour old goat walks by any one of them and they start bawling." Again, she and Susan tapped their bottles together.

Major Thomas sat forward in her longue chair. "Congratulations to you, too, Trish. Battlefield promotion to officer, not bad." She gulped down the rest of her beer in one swig.

Phillips gave her another. "Chug it, ma'am, and you'll be caught up." The major obliged. Phillips rummaged in the cooler to pull out another beer.

"What do you mean?" Trish asked, once Major Thomas was settled with her third beer.

The Major directed her question to Phillips. "You didn't tell her?"

"Tell me what?"

Susan said, "Aralyn promoted you to second lieutenant yesterday."

Phillips grunted. "It's a butter bar, and the colonel said I'm still in charge while you're in training, so don't get cocky."

"Wait, what? I never signed up for the military."

Major Thomas kicked off her flipflops and wiggled her toes. "You didn't have to. You were raised in it, unlike this lot." She motioned toward the new recruits. "With your training and educational background, most of us thought captain would've been appropriate, but you know your godmother."

Trish sat up straight. "Wait a minute. Nobody asked me if I was even interested."

"Are you not a part of us?" Susan asked, almost demanding.

"Yes, of course. That's not what I mean. You guys are my family. All of you, you're blood."

"Exactly," Major Thomas said, "now shut up and let me watch the show in peace. Phillips, give me another beer."

Trish wasn't about to challenge Rebecca Thomas. The woman's face was still healing from the damage done to her by the marauders from NORAD who'd come to kidnap Trish. She already felt bad enough about that, and she had no desire to rile up the newly-minted major.

Trish had felt lucky to escape most of Aralyn's wrath. If she were an official member of the military, Aralyn could have confined her to quarters for insubordination when she went to rescue Christina. Both times. But now Aralyn had gone and given her a military rank, and dammit all if she wasn't trapped by her new designation. If this so-called promotion was their attempt at keeping her in line, they were in for a rude awakening. She'd never be able to blindly follow orders.

The Major, sounding a little inebriated from her rapid intake of alcohol, pointed the top of her beer bottle toward the female recruit with red hair. "She just winked up here. How the hell did all those sergeants miss that?"

Lieutenant Strong said, "She's been doing it since they started. I think she has a thing for Christina."

"She definitely does," Susan said, sounding somewhat amused. "After all, Christina's a wonderful catch. She's young, beautiful, and on the market. Any woman would be a fool not to flirt."

Shifting uncomfortably, Trish didn't like the humor in either of their voices. She downed the last dregs in her bottle and wondered where to put the empty. Before she could ask for another beer, Christina leaned over and slid her hand down Trish's arm. Trish froze.

"Well? Am I?" Christina asked with a sensual undertone.

Trish swallowed. "Are you," she cleared her throat, "are you what?"

Christina let out a frustrated sigh. In a smooth motion she rose and was straddling Trish's lap before Trish could even blink. Christina leaned forward and kissed her. Trish felt every eye was on them. Her lips stiffened and she couldn't breathe what with the way her heart raced. Christina tilted away, her emerald eyes holding the appearance of an emotional plea.

Trish dropped the bottle in the grass beside the chair and pulled Christina in. This time, she didn't care who was watching. The moment their lips connected, Trish allowed her desires to run free. The bittersweet taste of beer mixed with Christina's soft lips, and Trish was aroused in ways she never would have believed possible. She felt Christina's heartbeat against her chest, the pounding matching her own.

When they broke free, Christina lowered her head and Trish held her. "Even better than how you kiss me in my dreams," Christina whispered. "Does this mean we're *both* unavailable?"

"I don't want anyone but you." Trish was surprised by how husky her own voice sounded.

"Neither do I, and everyone here already knows it."

Someone's chair creaked and someone else was giggling. Trish heard Phillips humming, but she ignored it all. She touched Christina's chin and leaned in, but Christina brought a hand to Trish's chest, stopping the next kiss. She spoke seductively in Spanish, then translated. "For someone so brave at fighting monsters, you really are a coward when it comes to taking what you want."

Trish lowered her eyes. "I was afraid of losing you completely if I tried."

Christina leaned in, her lips less than an inch away from Trish's. "Coward," she murmured, seconds before their lips touched.

Trish heard beer bottles clinking together from both sides.

Trish quickly lit the last of a dozen candles and visually inspected her room. Satisfied with her preparations, she double-checked her sleeping attire. The butterflies in her stomach were growing anxious, to the point of aggressive. She pushed play on her stereo system and expected to wait for quite a while longer.

A sharp rap at the door belied her expectations. Astounded by the speed Christina had packed an overnight bag and returned, she crossed the room and threw open the door. Her grin faded to surprise.

Aralyn smiled. "Is this a bad time?" Instead of waiting for a reply, she crossed into the dimly lit apartment and glanced around. "Planning a romantic evening? Or have you become an arsonist without us noticing?"

Trish threw up her hand and flipped on the lights. "Organizing a séance. You interested?" Trish blew out a few of the candles. She went to the stereo and flipped off Christina's favorite song by Shakira.

Aralyn laughed with delight. "You know, you're so much like your mother. A bit more infuriating than her, but I guess this adds to your uniqueness." She gaped around the room again, inspecting Trish's organized bedroom more closely. "Speaking of your mother, I've noticed how you've stopped asking me about her. You also don't wear the locket I gave you. Is there something you want to talk about?"

Trish peered away and blew out the last candle. "No, not really. I keep it in her jewelry box. I don't want to lose it during training or doing runs."

The way Aralyn nodded, Trish knew her godmother wasn't buying it. Aralyn moved into the living room. Reluctantly, Trish followed. Aralyn's gaze skimmed swiftly over the furniture as if she were searching for something.

"Her jewelry box isn't out. It's in my closet."

Aralyn wheeled around to face her. "Trish, your mother loved you. I know you have so many questions, but unfortunately, I don't have the answers. What I do know is she would have given her life to keep you safe."

Trish felt a headache form with her rising resentment. She bit back the bitterness and spoke evenly. "I wanted so much to be like her. To follow in her footsteps and do something remarkable. Yet, the more I've learned about the type of research she dabbled in, the more I understand that what she was doing wasn't amazing. Her precious invention was dangerous, and she used me as her test subject."

"Trish—"

"No. How does a mother do that to her child? Eva wouldn't dream of risking Christina's life so blatantly. And Jennifer—I would die before seeing anything bad happen to that little girl. I don't think my mother loved me. I believe she was like my father, selfish and more concerned with her serum than what it could do to others, even her own daughter."

"Trish, stop and think," Aralyn said reasonably. She wasn't angered by her words. Her voice held only concern. "You were injected the night she was killed. We don't know what happened or why, but she wasn't using you to advance her serum. That night she was trying to get you out of the bunker where you'd be safe. Your mother loved you, very much."

Pressing her palm into the ache on her forehead, Trish reeled away, trying to manage all the questions scrambling around in her head. She closed her eyes to the throbbing between her ears, wishing for quiet. "Why are you here?" she finally asked, staring at the bathroom door.

"You wanted to be kept informed about what our plans are. Has this changed?"

"No, it hasn't."

A brief pause lingered before Aralyn spoke. "We've gathered enough proof to show those in the bunkers they've been lied to. No nuclear war happened. The planet was safe from hazardous pollutants this entire time. We have credible witnesses to show a virus was released intentionally to kill off the remaining populace, but not by whom. The others think we should go ahead and use this information now and hope it's enough evidence for an uprising in the bunkers."

Trish wrinkled her brow. "But you don't believe it will be?"

Aralyn sighed. "I don't think the facts hold enough strength without some missing pieces. People in the bunkers have been brainwashed for so long. They may have difficulty believing our testimony. I also believe these revelations will give those in charge too much room to leverage an excuse for their crimes. However, we really have no other choice. If we put enough doubt in people's minds, it might work."

"I'm in," Trish said, without hesitation. "What's the plan?"

"Lieutenant Strong's working on that now. I'll let you know when and how we'll proceed."

Trish walked Aralyn to the door. Before she left, she said, "You know, I've never been very motherly to you."

Trish's eyes widened. "That's not true! You've been the one person—"

Aralyn raised a hand. "I don't mean I haven't loved you. In my heart, you've always been my child. I simply meant, I protected you and kept you safe, as your father should have done. I left this motherly nonsense to Susan." She motioned toward Trish's burgundy boxer-briefs.

With a wave of embarrassment, Trish lowered her head. She fiddled with the handle on her door, wondering if Aralyn was gearing up for the sex talk. She was seventeen; why was she feeling like a ten-year-old again?

Aralyn placed a hand on Trish's shoulder and Trish met her gaze. "You're a grown woman now. If you're ready for this next phase in a relationship, that's fine. Just remember, you don't need to jump so fast into things. Let them unfold on their own. Either way, you treat that woman with respect. If I find out you've hurt her, physically or mentally, I'll kick your ass."

Trish smiled. "I love you."

Aralyn gave her a hug. "If she hurts you, I'll let Susan handle it. I don't hit girls."

Trish laughed and returned the embrace. Once the door closed, Trish stared over at her closet. Feeling a tug of uncertainty, she opened the closet door and peered up to the shelf running above her hanging clothes. She removed the stack of microbiology and genetics books she had borrowed from Christina's father. She shifted aside the mounds of her own personal biochemistry and science textbooks purchased through the city's shopping center. When her fingers touched a wooden box, she grabbed the side and pulled it down.

The mahogany-stained carvings on the four sides of the box portrayed views of a farmland with deer, an old watermill, a farmhouse, and a mountain setting all wrapped together. Trish wiped away a minute collection of dust from the top and side edges. She sat on the recliner by the closet and twisted the music box mechanism on the bottom, but as always, the windup lever held no resistance. She lifted the lid and no sound emerged.

When the apartment door cracked open, Christina stuck her head inside. "I wasn't sure if I should knock or not?"

Trish waved her in. "Don't worry. My new girlfriend's already left. You're safe."

Christina rolled her eyes. "Thank God for that. I heard she was a real witch." She closed the door behind her.

Trish shrugged. "She's an amazing kisser. It makes up for her moody disposition."

Christina dropped her bag by the bed. "Don't push it."

Trish grinned. "The spare key is on the dresser, there's plenty of room in the closet, and the dressers in the living room are still empty."

"Hang on now," Christina playfully opened her eyes wide, exaggerating her hand movements. "Rushing kinda fast, aren't we?"

Trish chuckled "What I'm saying is, if you want to leave some things over, help yourself. There's room."

"That, or we need to go shopping for more clothes."

Trish's lungs caught on an inhale. "Please don't make me."

Christina laughed. "Fine, from now on, I'll buy your clothes. I promise nothing girly, but no more ripping up designer shirts." Christina bent forward and kissed her. When their lips separated, Christina's eyelashes fluttered, and she exhaled slowly. "I'll never get tired of that."

Christina straightened and went to the dresser. She retrieved the key and held it up. "I will keep this, not because I'm moving in, but to make sure you don't try to hide any of your bimbos under the bed. I'll be doing surprise inspections whenever I feel like it. Expect several when I'm on my monthly cycle. I become overly emotional then."

"Oh, I already know."

Christina gently shoved Trish on the shoulder. "I was kidding. Don't be an ass."

Astonished by how Christina made her feel more alive and loved than she had ever felt in her entire life, Trish put the box on the arm of the chair beside her and pulled Christina onto her lap. She kissed her with a fierce passion that surprised even herself. Christina's lips held a sliver of the salty taste of summer, which grew sweeter the further inside her tongue moved. Her breathing quickened. The skin on her neck tingled to Christina's gentle touch. Christina's breaths turned husky, and Trish moved her hands down, gripping onto Christina's waistline. When Christina broke the connection, Trish lowered her forehead on Christina's chest. She took longer breaths to work to calm her building lust. Christina's chin leaned against Trish's head, her nails lightly scraping through the hairs on Trish's scalp.

"Do you realize how much power you have?" Christina squeezed Trish's bicep. "I'm not talking about your physical strength." She placed her hand above Trish's heart. "I mean here." Her hand slid to Trish's head, and then her fingers brushed along Trish's lips. "Your intelligence, your body, your compassion. Trish, you move me in ways that . . . terrify me."

"I terrify you?"

"Not *you* personally, but the thought of losing you."

Trish looked into the sea of green filling Christina's eyes, which fueled the ignited fire deep within. "You will never find any bimbos under my bed, in my closet, or stealing my heart. I'm completely taken by you."

Christina ran her fingers through the top part of Trish's hair and snatched a handful of the short locks. She didn't pull, but used the grip to bring their foreheads together. "I'm not worried about other women. I know I have your heart. I'm talking about the dangers past the wall. If you died, I'd never recover." Christina whispered something in Spanish, then nibbled lightly on Trish's earlobe. The sensation was overpowering.

Trish brought her hands upward, clasping onto Christina's hands, which were working slowly up the front of her shirt. Stopping the momentum of her rising need was harder than she realized. Trish had to bite her bottom lip and focus to keep the room from spinning.

"Are we not ready yet?" Christina asked.

Trish reluctantly shook her head. Before she could give her reasons why, Christina kissed her neck. She gently pulled herself off Trish's lap, climbed to her feet, and took Trish's jewelry box to the dresser. Trish followed her over to the head of the bed. Christina folded back the covers and motioned for Trish to climb in. Christina pulled the bedding up and sat beside her on the bed.

Trish opened her mouth to speak, but Christina put a finger lightly on Trish's lips. "We'll wait as long as we need, but we sleep together, understand?"

"You'll receive no complaints here."

"Good. Now you get comfortable, and I'll go shower and change. I should take a moment longer to calm myself before I crawl in beside you."

Trish brought a hand up, interrupting Christina's movements. "Can I ask you something?"

"Of course, anything."

Trish scrunched her lips sideways, uncertain if her question was one she should be asking. She knew what Christina did or didn't do with others wasn't her business, but for some irrational reason, she couldn't get the query to vacate her thoughts. "If you don't want to tell me, I'll more than understand."

Christina tilted her head. "Stephanie?" she asked. When Trish nodded, Christina sighed. "No, we never had sex. We didn't get past second base. Even as hard as she tried, or made me feel guilty for saying no, I wasn't ready."

"Second base?"

Christina smiled. She ran her tongue slowly across Trish's lips. "First base." She gently slid her hand over the nipple protruding beneath Trish's shirt. "Second base." Kissing her finger, she slid her hand down the blankets to Trish's parted legs. "Third base." Christina's voice was growing rough and her breathing deepened. She brought her hand up, made a circle, and inserted two fingers from her other hand deep inside. "Homerun."

Trish closed her eyes against the vision of her mouth between Christina's legs.

"I know," Christina said with a sudden breath out. "I'll go take a cold shower before I unpack."

She winked as if joking, but Trish didn't detect any humor in her eyes, only a matching desire.

"Anyhow, the way Stephanie constantly pouted, saying I was *holding out on her*, as she put it, I was starting to feel our relationship was nothing more than an experimental venture for her. When I found her and Brian in the locker-room at the pool having sex, I was hurt, but relieved at the same time.

"I'm sorry, I didn't mean to bring it up."

"Oh, Trish." Christina murmured, kissing Trish gently and with such emotion. "You have nothing to worry about. My feelings for her were trivial and short-lived. Now you rest. I'll be to bed soon."

With Christina gone, Trish stared at the jewelry box until her eyes grew heavy. Part of her wished the heirloom was still in the closet, out of sight. Another part longed for her mother's guidance for everything Trish had gone through these last few months. What would she say? Would she be proud of who Trish was? Would she help her daughter walk through the multiple paths she was on?

Eventually she became too drowsy for her mind to entertain further questions. Before Christina returned, she fell restlessly to sleep.

CHAPTER EIGHTEEN

Watching her mother move at a rushed pace throughout the room, Trish eyed a toy gun her mother discarded on the desk. It looked like the gun one boy had played with on her recent visit to the room full of kids and colorful toys. But this gun was shiny. Her father had said, girls didn't play with guns, only dolls, and he refused to let her have one. Oh, how she hated dolls.

She scooted off the seat and pushed her mother's box farther on the cushion so it wouldn't fall. The closer she drew to the desk, the more her excitement grew. She struggled to move the swivel chair under it. She climbed up, seized the gun, and hurried to the corner of the room before her mother noticed. She wanted to play with it for a moment, then she would put the heavy toy back.

The door beeped and Trish's hand trembled, afraid her father would see her with the forbidden toy. Someone on the other side of the door spoke, but the strange, squeaky voice didn't belong to her father. She quickly spun, grabbing tight, keeping the weighty item from slipping. When the excruciating sting struck the front of her thigh, she closed her eyes, trying hard not to scream.

"Trish?" her mother called, but Trish was too busy stifling her cries to respond. "Patricia, answer me!"

Trish dropped the gun and covered her leg. "Mommy, it hurts."

Her mother rushed forward. "It's okay honey. Mommy's got you." Her mother lifted her pantleg. She pulled her close and her eyes watered.

Was her mommy mad or sad? "Are we going to see the trees now?"

Her mother didn't answer. She rushed to the chair, sat Trish down, and took the music box which she flipped over. She opened a tiny panel and inserted something inside, closed the bottom of the box, and put it in the bag.

"You cannot tell anyone about your leg. Do you understand? Not even daddy."

Trish nodded. She watched her mother take off toward the far side of the room. She wanted to run after her, but when her father rushed in, she froze. Her heart sank. She knew they were no longer going to see the trees.

"Julie, stop or I'll shoot."

Trish was suddenly, without any explanation, beside her mother. Julie Webber's eyes were overflowing with tears. This scene was all wrong. The red liquid wasn't seeping out from her mother's shirt, but something inside told her it should have been. Instead, when her mother opened her mouth, crimson-blood poured out and pooled on the floor.

With red-stained teeth, her mother coughed out her last words. "Hush my sweet girl. Can you hear the music?"

"Trish, wake up. Trish."

Trish's eyes flew open to Christina's worried expression. She bolted up in bed, her shirt drenched with sweat. Christina was in the center sitting on her knees. "The music," she said, trying to think of the words her brain was forming.

"Yes, you kept saying *can you hear the music.* What does it mean?"

Trish threw off the covers and sprang from the bed. Searching the recliner, then the floor, she got down and peered under the bed. When her eyes and hands came back empty, she glared at the closet, and shambled to her feet.

Christina followed. "Trish what's wrong? What're you looking for?"

"My mother's jewelry box." She answered, frantically dumping the heavy books onto the ground in repetitive *thuds*, scarcely missing her own feet. She fought with such fierceness to get to the item in the corner.

"Here, remember? I put it on the dresser before bed."

Taking the wooden box from Christina, she flipped it over. The lid opened and the locket fell out. "I need my knife."

Christina picked up the locket and went to the closet housing Trish's gear. "What's going on?" she asked as soon as she returned.

"I'm not sure, but I think my mother put something in the box right before she died. It could have been a dream, but it felt so real."

"Here, let me do it. As desperately as you're moving, you'll cut yourself."

Trish handed Christina the box and waited anxiously as Christina gently pried open the bottom panel. When the bottom parted, Trish's brow pulled together at the void inside. Christina tilted it around. "There's nothing in it. I'm sorry, Trish, but it's empty."

Trish's sense of excitement faded completely. "I don't understand. It felt so real." She kept her eyes glued to the opening where the music box gears were located until Christina led her to bed.

She sat atop the rumpled sheets, not understanding why her mind would create such an authentic dream. "It's a broken heirloom, from a woman I scarcely remember."

Christina sat beside her and rubbed a hand around Trish's back. "It's beautiful, Trish. I'm sorry about your mother. I'm sure she was an amazing woman."

Trish was about to say she wasn't sure if she agreed with the last part, when a gear caught her eye. She leaned in closer and lifted the jagged wheel. When she did, a little component shifted to the side, then dropped onto the wooden surface. The object was roughly an inch in length and width, with metal lines along the edges. She picked it up and flipped it over to find three letters embossed upon it: CDC.

"It's a computer drive. My father sometimes uses those." Christina's eyes widened. "Trish, this drive was what your mother put in the box. What do you suppose is on it?"

Trish jumped from the bed. "We need to show Aralyn right away," she shouted, rushing to unlock the door. She heard Christina saying something, but her heart was beating so loud, everything else faded away. She sprinted up to the third floor, seeing Major Thomas stepping out of her room down the hall. She whipped past without slowing.

"Trish," the major called out. "Why are you running through the hall with no bra and in briefs?"

She didn't care. Her boxer-briefs were like shorts, and she had more pressing matters than worrying about jiggling breasts. She made it to Aralyn's suite, pounded, and was momentarily surprised when Susan opened the door. She hurried in, too focused on finding Aralyn to inquire about any personal issues.

"Trish, what's wrong?" Aralyn asked, walking from the bedroom fastening her robe.

Trish held out the chip. "My mom, she hid this in her jewelry box right before she died."

Aralyn glanced at Trish, then the chip. She picked it out of Trish's palm and flipped it over. "They used these at the CDC in Fort Collins. For security reasons, it's designed to work only on their systems. To protect her research, your mother took a computer with her when she went to the bunker."

Breathing heavily, Christina entered, her face red and her hair disarranged. She handed Trish her shorts and bathrobe. Trish thanked her and dressed while asking, "What do we do? Go to Fort Collins?"

"You both get fully dressed. We'll meet in five minutes and head to Christina's to see if Doctor Burgos brought a system with him. If not, we'll have to go."

Upstairs in the office of Doctor Burgos's lab, Aralyn, Susan, Trish, Christina, and Major Thomas silently waited for the doctor to remove the old computer system from his storage closet and connect the processor to his updated workstation.

In his night-robe, Doctor Burgos plugged in the last cable and activated his hand over a black panel. The system powered on.

A blue holographic image formed directly above a circular light. "Good evening Doctor Burgos," a pleasant female voice said. "It's been a long time."

"Yes, it has." He greeted the hologram as if addressing an old friend. "I have a CDC drive I need you to read."

"Of course, Doctor."

Aralyn placed the chip in his hand, and he inserted it into a slot on the side of the computer. Trish shifted, waiting impatiently. Those gathered around the desk in Doctor Burgos's lab were silent, also anxious.

"The drive contains several documents and videos, all but one originating from Doctor Frank Webber's system."

"Are the files coded or secured?"

"No, Doctor."

Doctor Burgos looked to Aralyn. Focusing on the files, she leaned over his shoulder. "Have her pull up the video there, the one created the night Julie died."

Without waiting to be ordered from Doctor Burgos, the wall screen above the desk filled with a picture of Trish's mother. Trish straightened, stepped around the desk, and moved closer to the wall.

"Adjust the volume to seven and play the video," Doctor Burgos told his personalized processor.

"Yes, Doctor."

An image of her mother came to life. She sat in a low-lit room, surrounded by shadowy pictures hanging on the wall directly behind her. Darkness shrouded both sides of a leather couch. Trish thought the location might be her parents' living quarters, but she wasn't sure. Her father hadn't allowed her into his lodgings after her mother died.

"To whomever's watching this footage, my name is Doctor Julie Webber. I'm filming from inside NORAD, a United States bunker located in Colorado. I discovered the leaders of the United World Task Force have lied to everyone living inside the bunkers. No nuclear attack occurred. Instead, the governments sponsoring the UWTF released a virus to kill every man, woman, and child left topside. My husband, Doctor Frank Webber, created this virus.

"With the attached documents and videos I've downloaded from my husband's processor, you'll see how their way of saving humanity was by killing off the population and starting over with those of us they considered worthy. All your friends, families, everyone you've ever loved is gone. They wasted the ten years that could have been used finding a solution to our global crisis, by building long-sustaining bunkers like this one and a biological weapon to do the unthinkable. Over ten billion lives lost.

"My husband's virus decomposes the dead at an elevated rate. Once the numerous bodies no longer remain, teams are to be sent topside to recover key cities throughout the world, through reclamation and reconstruction. After this, the bunkers will open, and civilization, crafted and controlled by them, will be in business again. We will have no democracy, no rights, but live in a world where those in power will rule over those of us who remain.

"Each of the thirty-two countries in the UWTF are involved. Each country constructed multiple bunkers, holding populations of fifty thousand each." She swiveled around in her chair and whispered something behind her, but Trish couldn't hear what her mother was saying or see who she was talking to. Her mother faced the screen. "That's mere millions saved from a population of almost eleven billion. As you will see in the attached file marked Second Phase, you'll read top-secret correspondence and watch documented videos of how the United States, along with nineteen other countries, built hidden bunkers throughout various parts of the world, housing even more people. They have instructed the twelve remaining countries to administer a 'five-year booster' against my husband's virus, to its citizens in the bunkers. That's May of this next year. I implore you not to use this injection. The evidence shows this dose was created to kill anyone receiving it."

Her mother glared at the camera. "We need to stop these needless deaths and hold those in charge responsible for what they've done." She glanced away momentarily. "It pains me to say this, but I'm partially responsible for a new threat we now face. Due to my own arrogance, through my exploration of genetic-bridging and artificial intelligence, I've constructed a genetic-altering serum, which would change humanity into stronger, more advanced beings. I've discovered my government is looking to use my serum for themselves, to become a superior race against the nations remaining.

"Unfortunately, after going through my husband's research, I realized he somehow stole part of my serum's original framework. He used this to construct and administer his antibody to those of us who went inside the bunkers. It prevents a virus from penetrating the host's cells. What he took from this framework was my initial design. I didn't use it because when the serum is introduced to a hemorrhagic virus, like the one my husband created, the artificial compound becomes unstable and mutates."

"Mommy, can we go see the trees now?"

Trish froze. That was her own voice. She was *there* with her mother. This video had to have been created the same night she was carelessly injected. The memories struck her, and now she understood the truth. Her mother wasn't at fault for the serum being inside her. Her curious four-year-old self had caused it. She'd remembered this in her earlier dream, but the reality of her past hadn't registered until now.

Julie pulled her daughter onto her lap. As her mother kissed her forehead, Trish's eyes swelled with tears. She was overcome by waves of loss and emotion.

Someone touched Trish's shoulder, gripped onto her waistline, but she didn't turn around. She kept her gaze on the video, fiercely wiping at her blurry eyes, wanting to see her mother for every single brief moment.

"I'm planning on destroying my life's work and heading topside to procure my old research. I will try to come up with a way to reverse the unstable vaccines we were all given. I hope everyone remains safe in the bunkers until I'm able to achieve my task. I also leave you with the undertaking of removing those in charge. These were criminal acts against so many innocent human beings. They must not get away with this. May God watch over us all." Her mother flipped off the camera, and the video ended.

Trish reached a hand outward. She wanted to scream for her mother, to yell at her to stop, warn her she was about to die, murdered by her own husband, but no words came out. People around her were talking, but Trish kept her eyes fixated on the blank wall screen. Her mother had been right there, almost as if in the flesh.

Trish felt like she had stepped back in time and experienced her life from a completely different viewpoint. Yet she knew, no matter how many times she replayed the footage and shouted out any warnings, her mother couldn't hear her. She had long since perished.

It wasn't until Christina and Susan led her, shaking and confused, from the room, that Trish drifted out of her emotional haze enough to grasp what her father had taken from her. Her mother, her childhood, her innocence, her memories.

He'd put those she loved in unforeseen danger and killed the one person who loved her unconditionally. Her mother was unarmed, and he shot her in cold blood.

And that creature on the bed in her father's lab, its mutation was what her mother was referring to. Her father had made that happen. The poor infected person could have just as easily been Aralyn or Susan, any of those she loved more than her own life.

Her father had done this. He was to blame.

When Trish left the lab, she told Susan and Christina she needed some time alone. She lurched down the sidewalk, feeling lightheaded, and directed her shuffling feet toward the barracks.

Let Aralyn and the others deal with the world leaders and those in the bunkers. The moment had come for Trish to find and confront her father.

Trish threw a second bodysuit on top of the items in her backpack and closed it. She left it on the bed with the rest of her gear, then went to the dresser and searched inside the jewelry box. The heirloom was empty. She combed through the bed and poked around under the scattered books on the floor of her closet.

"Are you looking for this?" Christina held out the locket, dangling it off her fingers.

Trish rose and met Christina by the edge of the bed. Christina motioned for Trish to lower her head.

"You understand, I've got to go."

"No, I don't understand," Christina said, clasping the chain behind Trish's neck. She wrapped her arms around Trish's waist. "Your team is leaving in a few days once Carlen is finished prepping and analyzing the recordings. If you're leaving with them, then yes, I do understand, but it seems like you're planning on going out alone. If you are, then no, I definitely do not."

"I need to find him. Aralyn and the others will be heading to the bunker to send the broadcast through the network. I don't see how else they can connect with the UWTF satellite. The man Aralyn captured, he said my father went to Colorado Springs early, with most of the people in NORAD. I plan to hunt down my father there."

"So, you can kill him?"

"He murdered my mother, took everything from me. He needs to answer for it."

Christina cupped Trish's cheek. "Not like this, Trish. You're letting your hatred get the better of you."

Trish tucked the locket inside her shirt and kissed Christina on the forehead. She reached for her backpack, but Christina stepped between Trish and the bed. "No, you're making this about him and vengeance. Trish, I know you. You're better than this. Think about everyone still alive. Help Aralyn and the others stop those your father works for."

Trish frowned. "What, and let him walk away? You don't realize the danger. I can't allow that to happen. He has to answer for his actions."

"No, not walk away, but give it time. Aralyn even said he'll come looking for you one day. Just let him. We'll be ready when he does."

Trish shook her head. "I won't permit him the opportunity to hurt you or the others I love. When he's dead, our world's safer. Trust me." Trish reached around and snatched her bag. She flung a strap over her shoulder. Christina grabbed her weapon and helmet from the bed before Trish had a chance.

Trish forcefully growled. "Woman, do you have to be so difficult?" She reached for her rifle.

"*I'm* difficult?" Christina shouted, then rattled something in Spanish. Trish sighed. Christina switched to English, but her voice was twice as loud. "I'm not the one running off, half-cocked, to get myself killed!" Christina pointed a finger. "*You* are the difficult one. You're being selfish!"

Trish gulped and tried to settle her rising temper. She didn't look at Christina for long moments.

"Don't you care about me?" Christina eventually asked, her voice calmer, but unsteady. "About us?"

"How can you ask me that?" Trish exclaimed, locking eyes with Christina. "I'm doing this because I don't want to lose you. My father hates me. He would go out of his way to make sure I lost everything I ever cared about, especially you. I would rather die than see him come anywhere near you, or this city."

Christina stood unmoving, mouth open, gawking as if she had suddenly lost the power of speech. Trish dropped the backpack on the floor and shifted closer. "Christina, I don't know why, but my father has never seen me as a daughter. I'm nothing more than an annoying burden, and I have something inside me he wants badly. Hurting those closest to me in the process of getting it, he would see that as a gift."

"Oh Trish, I'm so sorry." Christina dumped the rifle and helmet on the bed and reached for her.

Trish didn't resist, but no tears formed. The topic regarding her father was one she no longer needed to be consoled over.

Behind them, someone cleared her throat. "I'm afraid Trish is right. Frank is many things, none of which are moral." Aralyn stepped in and motioned to the bag. "Put the gear in my vehicle, Lieutenant Webber. We're leaving at first light. We're taking Doctor Burgos to the Fort Collins CDC branch to locate the old research your mother mentioned, then we'll head to NORAD once Lieutenant Strong's finished with the data. After we're done, *we'll* find and capture your father, convict him of his treasonous acts, and have him put to death. I agree with you, Trish. Our world isn't safe for anyone if he remains alive."

Christina let go of Trish. "Okay, I'll pack my things."

"No," Aralyn said. "This mission is a military matter and you're a civilian, Christina. You'll stay behind and help the others fortify the city."

"You're right, Aralyn. I'm not in the military, but I can come and go as I please."

"No, that's not true. I already spoke with your father and he agrees. I need Trish and my team focused. Worrying about you in addition to your father will be a larger distraction."

Christina looked to Trish for help, but Trish only shook her head. The last thing she wanted was to take the woman she loved on a mission closer to her father. Christina's eyes pleaded, glistening as she continued to stare Trish down. Finally, Christina threw up her arms and stormed into the living room, shutting the bedroom door forcefully as she went.

Trish went to the door and touched the cool surface. She lowered her head, feeling ashamed for what she had done.

There was nothing she could do. She nodded to Aralyn, picked up her gear, and headed to the vehicle to load up.

When she returned, her stomach cramped, and her heart grew heavier. She wouldn't be able to say goodbye. Christina was gone.

Three Gladiators were lined up outside Headquarters and being readied for the half-day drive to the Fort Collins branch of the Centers for Disease Control. Trish took her usual seat in the lead vehicle behind Sergeant Givens. She closed the door, nudged her weapon over, and fastened her seatbelt. Leaning against the headrest, she bore the guilt pulling at her chest.

Givens eyed her from the rearview mirror. "Why does it seem like you're always depressed when we're in a vehicle together? What is it, Trish? Girl problems?"

Trish straightened up and sighed loudly. She fiddled with her helmet, then dropped it to the floorboard. "It's nothing," she mumbled.

Aralyn and Susan entered, and Trish sighed again.

Aralyn said, "Child, if you need to pee, you best do it now."

"She's fine," Susan said as she hooked into her seatbelt. "I think it's woman issues."

"Already?" Aralyn was surprised. "You both started dating yesterday. I'm sure you couldn't have screwed this up in one day. Could you?"

"Thank you, Colonel, I've got this," Susan sounded a bit perturbed. She leaned closer to Trish. "Come on, spill it. What'd you do?"

"Why do you both always assume *I* did something wrong?"

"Did you?" Aralyn asked, as the vehicle rolled forward.

Such a simple question, but Trish struggled to answer. "Yes, I did. I didn't support her like I should've when she wanted to come with us."

"No, you followed your gut," Aralyn said. "This will be dangerous, and she'd get in the way."

Trish squinted at Aralyn, a wave of defensiveness setting in. "Christina's a capable woman. She handles herself well on the runs."

"I'm not saying she isn't, but she doesn't have the proper training for what we're about to undertake. Don't forget, she also experienced a traumatic incident recently. Trish, you made the right call."

"No, I made a selfish call. I figured by keeping her locked up inside the city she'd be safe, but now I feel like a controlling idiot. She's so upset she didn't even say goodbye."

Trish rubbed at a piece of lint on the seat. Her heart hurt in several different ways. The loss of her mother felt painfully renewed, her father was her bitter enemy, and the woman she loved had probably left her for good. She slumped her shoulders. "Christina deserves better than this."

"Just so you're aware," Susan said, "things have a way of becoming more powerful after sex. Maybe you're both experiencing the rush of all these unfamiliar emotions, and it's making this dilemma seem more intense than it really is."

Trish glanced over. "We didn't make love last night. We're both still . . . you know . . ."

Givens slapped the wheel. "There you go. You and Christina are sexually frustrated. Give it time. Once you've had a chance to release all those built-up passions, everything will fall into place." Aralyn shot him an unpleasant glare and his amusement faded. He turned his eyes to the road.

Aralyn wouldn't let it rest. "Like I said last night, just because you're together, it doesn't mean you need to rush into things. Take it slow. Don't throw sex into your relationship too fast."

Susan mumbled, "Says the woman who made me wait ten years."

"What was that?" Aralyn asked.

"Nothing, Colonel. I'm merely confirming what you said."

Trish and Susan shared a grin. Trish whispered, "I'm sorry it took her so long,"

Susan squeezed Trish's hand. "Believe me, the wait was worth it." She let go and pointed to Aralyn who was punching in some commands on her wrist processor. Her voice soft, she asked, "Is she the reason behind your lack of intimacy or was this yours and Christina's decision?"

"No, I asked Christina if we could wait, and not because of Aralyn."

"How did she take it?"

Trish raised her head proudly. "Like a loving partner." Trish hunched over and slapped her forehead. "God, I'm such an idiot. I probably lost her for good."

"I don't believe you did. My daughter is completely taken by you."

Trish jumped, realizing for the first time Christina's father and one of Aralyn's soldiers were riding in the last row of seating behind some netting. Burgos slid the netting to the side and leaned around to peer into her face.

"Doctor Burgos! I—I—didn't know you were—" She let out a groan. Could things get any worse? "Sir, I'm very sorry if I said anything inappropriate."

"On the contrary, you've behaved quite admirably. Like my Eva, Christina is a lucky woman." He laughed, giving her a wink. "Unfortunately, my daughter has my family's notorious Hispanic temper coursing through her veins. I'm not sure how it skipped me and passed to my wife, who isn't related to me in any way in case you were all wondering."

Trish smiled awkwardly, then faced forward. What an embarrassing way to start the morning. She turned her focus to the other side of the tinted window, seeing the sun coming up over the hillside. She knew the next couple of days would be long. She was tired, but the thoughts and images and emotions in her brain were running rampant.

Closing her eyes, she sagged against the door hoping to sleep through the five-hour drive.

CHAPTER NINETEEN

The three-vehicle convoy came to a stop alongside the main parking lot of the CDC complex at Fort Collins, Colorado. The newer addition to the left was a massive, state-of-the-art building dominating the remaining brick and glass structures in both height and width. The white, stone foundation was overlapped by black, sectional panels appearing both modern and impenetrable. Embedded throughout the top three floors of this five-story building were a number of rectangular windows, too narrow to offer much light, let alone see out of.

Surrounding most of the complex stood an unfinished, beautifully patterned concrete wall, close to twelve-feet high. Next to the uncompleted section Trish saw piles of various construction materials, some rusted, and some generously covered by overgrown Colorado weeds and wildflowers, remnants of a time when elegant craftsmanship mattered.

Doctor Burgos said, "This state-of-the-art building is where the biosafety-level-four contaminants are stored."

Even through the tinted windows, Trish squinted from the glare of the sun's brightness magnified off the glass building to the right. "How dangerous was my mother's research?" she asked, focusing her gaze on the secured entrance they were parked beside.

"The research itself wasn't dangerous. It was the application of it. Her office isn't in this section, but this entrance is the safest way to head to the adjoining building. This facility is where we all stayed before we traveled to Rapid City. When we left, I made sure to activate the security system so nothing could get in. I've come back twice for supplies and equipment since then and to verify the electrical systems are operational."

Aralyn said, "Trish, when we go inside, you'll move with Doctor Burgos and help his guard keep him safe. Susan, Givens, and I will head in first with a squad of four to clear the area, and you'll follow close behind with the doc. The rest of our patrol will cover your rear. Got it?"

Trish nodded, threw on her helmet, and grabbed her weapon. Once outside, she raised the visor and stood next to Doctor Burgos and the soldier guarding him. Everyone in the group wore a suit and helmet. Aralyn wasn't taking any chances.

Aralyn posted Lieutenant Strong and Sergeant Phillips outside to guard the vehicles while the rest followed Doctor Burgos up the stone steps to a receptacle containing an electrical security monitor. Doctor Burgos scanned his hand and punched in a list of codes. The door slid open.

Aralyn motioned for the first group of four to enter with First Sergeant Stevens leading the way. Aralyn and her team followed, and when she motioned, Trish and the rest filed in.

Once the main area was deemed secure, Aralyn asked Doctor Burgos which direction they should take, the tunnel or the catwalk. When he suggested the catwalk, she signaled the teams up the wide flight of stairs to the next level. They exited a set of double doors and moved away from the reinforced structure to a windowed, enclosed walkway. On the other side stood the less secure office building.

As they negotiated various corridors through the building, Trish tried picturing her mother walking the same partitioned halls. She could imagine her mother's long-legged strides and her dark hair swaying over a white lab coat, her hazel eyes shimmering from the sun pouring in through lightly-tinted windows. Did she smile often and greet others as she carried disposable cups of hot coffee to her work area? Did everyone like her?

Aralyn and Doctor Burgos had already answered this last question. From how they spoke about her mother, Julie Webber was a hard woman not to adore. An 'instant attraction' seemed to be the response of those who met her. What was her favorite food? Had she had one color she was fond of, or were there many? Maybe her choice of color was the same as her daughter's, green. The deep, rich color of vegetational growth, mimicking the shade of Christina's eyes.

Trish stopped with Aralyn's hand movement, and the others did the same. Despite her musings, she was attentive to the sounds, smells, and visuals around them. She wasn't getting any prickling of her Spidey senses, and with so many guards escorting the doctor, she actually felt confident.

When they returned to the city, she needed to figure out some way to tell Christina how sorry she was. She wished she could rewind the last few hours and rectify her mistake, but she'd been in a Catch-22. Since she couldn't change the circumstances, she would have to openly face the consequences and try to make things right. Maybe she could find something in Colorado Springs to bring home to her. Trish rolled her eyes, picturing the exchange. "Hey Christina, sorry I was an unsupportive ass. Here's an 'I-heart-the-Springs' T-shirt. Hope you like it."

Trish lost the ridiculous image when Doctor Burgos loudly cleared his throat. She glanced around. The others had continued further down the hall before coming to another stop. Susan made her way over, heading straight to Trish.

"Hey, what's up," Susan asked. "Why are you guys moving so slow? Are you sensing something in the building?"

Trish blushed and shook her head. "No, nothing. Sorry, I wasn't focused on rapid forward progress."

Givens hustled to them, taking a knee beside Susan. "What's up? Colonel wants to know if you're sensing any danger."

"No danger at all. I was thinking about how to apologize to Christina. I'll stay focused from now on."

"What'd you come up with?" Givens asked, switching his weight to his other knee.

"I thought about a T-shirt or something from Colorado Springs."

"What, like a souvenir shirt?" Givens sounded skeptical.

"Really, you two?" Susan snapped.

"Actually," Doctor Burgos said, "I think that's a great idea. My daughter loves clothes."

Trish silently wondered if her head looked as awkward as his in the helmet. She hoped it didn't. She certainly *felt* awkward. Again.

Susan sighed and pointed a sideways I'm-pissed-and-you-better-listen-up hand at Givens. "Sergeant, go tell Aralyn everything's fine and that Trish thought she picked up on something, but it passed." She eyeballed Trish. "I'll hang back here with you three." In a much quieter voice, she said, "Trish, pull yourself together."

Once the group was moving again, Trish, the guard, and Doctor Burgos faithfully followed Susan through the remainder of the building. At the far end, they scrambled down a stairway to a door marked, *Basement-Level-One.* From there, they went by a winding set of dividing passageways. Aralyn positioned the team around a white door across from a glass-enclosed lab room.

Trish's mother's name was stenciled on the glass next to the lab's entrance, but Aralyn and Doctor Burgos didn't head inside. Instead they went through the white metal door. When Trish drew closer, she spotted a plaque with her mother's name and title fixed to the wall beside it.

Standing near Susan and Burgos's guard, Trish stared at the door, her hand hovering inches from the handle. She forced her lungs to release the air they were holding. Slowly she turned the knob.

The office light cast a glow throughout the space. Several drawers in the five filing cabinets against the far wall were pulled out, and scatters of papers and folders littered the desk, couch, and floor.

"Sorry about the mess," Doctor Burgos said. "We thoroughly searched through all the offices of everyone who disappeared to see if we could find out any information." He waved his arm around. "I was actually gentle with your mother's office. You should see your father's."

Trish removed her helmet and set it on a leather chair in front of the desk. Behind the desk she removed a plaque hanging on a nail beside a hinged picture, exposing a safe with a keypad. Trish wiped off the glass and traced her finger over the slick surface, displaying her mother's Biochemistry degree. Her eyes went upward to the next plaque, which she also confiscated. Instead of reading it, she stacked it on the desk with the first one. She snatched other wall-hangings, including a photo she believed was of her mother and grandmother sitting on a porch swing together, smiling. After depositing the mementos on the desk, she searched around the room for something to carry it all in.

Doctor Burgos's guard came closer and handed her an empty tote with a lid. She thanked the soldier, then filled the plastic container with the items on the desk and with some other photos she located in the desk drawers. When she was finished and popped the lid on top, she looked up to find four people staring at her. Avoiding their eyes, she donned her helmet and tucked the box under an arm.

Doctor Burgos cleared his throat. "I believe your mother's old research may be in this safe, but we didn't know the combination. After three attempts, the locking mechanism freezes and headquarters would have to send someone out to work on it. Since we lost contact with the main branch, I didn't want to chance it. I was afraid Julie would return and not be able to access whatever was inside."

Trish was amazed by those lives her mother had touched. Why had her father not been influenced by her mother in the same way as Aralyn and the rest? Did Trish take after her father or mother? One parent she lost too young to remember, the other was never around long enough nor was he open enough for her to get to know. She hoped she not only resembled her mother physically but had inherited her other traits as well.

Aralyn said, "We have three chances, so I say we give it a shot. How many numbers does it take?"

"Six," Burgos said. "The light will turn green if the correct combination is entered. Try her birthday."

Aralyn tapped in the six numbers, but nothing happened. "Do you think she would have used Frank's birthday or their anniversary?"

"Something tells me no, but it could be my distaste for the man. You knew her better than anyone, try whichever you believe she would've used." Doctor Burgos turned to Trish. "Why is your face scrunched like that?"

Trish didn't respond. Instead, she opened the box to go through the photos. She heard Aralyn say "Damn," after hitting the second set of numbers and getting a red light.

For the final try, Aralyn was poised to punch in the first number, but Trish rushed over and grabbed her hand. She gave Aralyn a handful of photos and stared at the keypad.

"What?" Aralyn asked. She thumbed through the photos.

Trish flexed her fingers through the gloves, and leaned in. She pressed the numbers for the month, day, and year of Aralyn's birthday.

The light turned green.

Trish tossed a meaningful look toward Aralyn but blinked and turned away when she saw a tear slide down her godmother's cheek.

Aralyn handed Trish the pictures and opened the safe.

"What was it?" Doctor Burgos asked.

Trish kept her eyes off Susan, feeling guilty for not answering. She wasn't sure how Susan would have taken it, but the last thing she wanted to do was cause her any discomfort.

Trish returned the numerous pictures of her mother and Aralyn to the box. Her mom's lighter complexion pressed against Aralyn's shiny ebony skin in many of the poses. The intimate scenes didn't capture evidence of an affair, but the close love both women had for one another was unmistakable. Their happy faces, gentle touches, and fond expressions in each picture revealed that Julie and Aralyn's strong connection was overpowering. Her mother had loved Aralyn, but for reasons unknown, she had married Frank.

Trish froze, her stomach suddenly cramping. She locked eyes with Aralyn. "We've got to move. Now."

In a hurry, Aralyn tossed the items from the safe into Trish's box, secured the lid, and handed the container to Doctor Burgos. She whirled to face the others in the room. "Helmets on, visors down. Let's head to the Gladiators the same way we came in. Trish and I will lead. Aralyn pointed to Doctor Burgos's guard. "You keep him moving in the center of the group. Don't be a hero. If anything happens, you focus on keeping Doctor Burgos safe. Got it?"

The soldier nodded. Aralyn moved through the group giving curt instructions and orders. Before long, the entire group had made it upstairs, through the low-access building, and over the catwalk heading to the high-level area.

At the security sensor, Trish gestured to Aralyn who motioned for Doctor Burgos. He hustled forward, unfastened the latch on his glove, scanned his hand, and entered the code. Once the doors unlocked, Aralyn pointed for him to return to his guard at the center of the formation.

By the time Trish reached the main door, her prickles-of-warning had amplified into daggers-of-danger. She held up a hand and whispered, "They're right outside."

Aralyn signaled for the armed contingent to be ready. The moment Trish opened the door, her body went rigid, and she felt she might throw up.

Close to thirty crazed infected were fanned out in a wide circle around Lieutenant Strong and Sergeant Phillips who were on the ground. The creatures bellowed out their war cries and pounded the ground around the two soldiers, who looked as if they had lived through an overnight battle.

Phillips's visor was raised and his head and shoulders rested in Strong's lap. A piece of rebar stuck all the way through the side of his armor, poking out several inches behind him.

Strong, with her pistol held out at arm's length, also had her visor up and was screaming out her own battle cries. One of their rifles lay smashed next to a pig pile of dead creatures. The other rifle was nowhere in sight.

Were the creatures toying with their soon-to-be meal, or were they assessing if the two they surrounded were worthy enough to be turned and added to their overflowing numbers?

As the others behind her poured out of the building, the area swiftly exploded with gunfire.

Golden-orange eyes of the creatures swung in their direction. A few bodies dropped, but most scurried toward the overgrown brush along the edge of the walkway. That's when Trish saw who—or what—Strong was pointing her weapon at: a scaly creature like the one she'd awakened next to in her father's lab all those weeks ago. The grotesque malformation was massive in both height and muscle-mass compared to the original Gramites.

The monster's exposed flesh, bulging from its tattered clothes, was covered in inflamed pustules. Its teeth had grown longer, like the claws protruding from each digit, and Trish noticed how the bright-orange eyes sharply surveyed the scene.

With incredible speed, the massive mutation leapt over Strong. In one easy movement, it snapped her arm back at the elbow joint. She cried out against the pain and dropped the pistol. It bellowed out a roar and the creatures around it stopped as if in awe.

Some of the infected dropped to more gunfire, but others moved behind the vehicles or the two fallen soldiers and the beast in command.

Aralyn raised her arm and yelled out, "Cease fire." Instantly, the soldiers' weapons fell silent.

Clasping her rifle, Susan said, "What the hell is that thing doing? Holding them hostage?" She, like the rest of the team, watched helplessly, obviously anxious to rush forward and save the two wounded lying on the weedy earth.

Doctor Burgos said, "No, the thing's trying to bide some time to figure out its next move. See how its eyes are studying us and the terrain?"

Keeping a watchful eye on the infected, Trish directed a question to Doctor Burgos. "Christina said when they were attacked in New Underwood, there was a creature in the horde who controlled the rest."

"Yes, like a silverback gorilla, the strongest watching over and directing the others. A harsh but effective form of leadership. The Gramites are driven by primitive instincts. They respect brute strength and follow the one who they believe can keep their band, or clan, strong and together." He waved toward the creatures. "They reminded my late colleague and I of a gorilla family, but shrewder in their actions."

"What do you suggest we do then?" asked Aralyn. "How do we retrieve our soldiers without getting them or us killed?"

Trish analyzed the two on the ground. Phillips had lost quite a bit of blood, even with Strong's good hand trying to cover the front section of the entry site around the metal rod. Lieutenant Strong herself seemed to be wearing down from her own pain.

"I have an idea," Trish said, "but I'm not sure if it'll work."

"Go on," said Aralyn, hopeful.

"Will you trust me?"

Her godmother stared at her for a moment. When she agreed, Trish handed over her weapon. "I'll try to direct them away from Phillips and Strong. If this works, take the wounded inside, then come save my ass." She unclipped her utility belt and inspected the creature towering over Strong.

"What the hell?" Susan said. "You have to stop her."

"No," Doctor Burgos replied. "Give her a minute. Believe me, you need to have a little faith. Trish can handle herself."

"Then I'm going with her," Givens insisted

In unison, Trish and Doctor Burgos both said, "No!"

"You'll only get in her way," Doctor Burgos said. "You all need to trust Trish. She can do this."

Without waiting, Trish headed down the stone steps. The creature fixed its scowl on her, looking enraged. She kept her eyes and muscles relaxed, and wouldn't allow anxiety to work itself in. The leader let out a threatening growl, its eyes growing angrier by the second. Maybe it didn't like her calm movements or her absence of fear at witnessing his mighty form. The way the creature deepened its glare, she knew her lack of intimidation outraged him. Did her absence of fear make him appear weak to the Gramites around him? Her body certainly wasn't offering the same level of alarm they held.

The second her foot touched the concrete sidewalk at the bottom, the monster jerked a hand at the base of Strong's helmet, standing as if getting ready to rip her helmeted head straight off her shoulders. Trish stopped and waited, assessing the situation, feeling the pounding movements of those behind the beast. She undid her helmet and dropped it to the ground. The mutation released its hand from Strong's head, changing his glower of hatred to an angry interest.

"I'm right here," Trish shouted, slowly moving in the direction of the parking lot, away from Aralyn and the others.

The creature barked out commands. She watched golden-orange eyes gazing at one another in panic, but none moved.

The leader growled directly at his flock of followers, and the line of Gramites shifted reluctantly toward the humans with the killing weapons. They stopped once they were blocking the two soldiers on the ground from those by the building.

"Crap," Trish whispered, coming to a standstill. This monstrosity was smart, no matter how repulsive it looked.

Once the Gramites were lined up, again pounding the earth around Strong and Phillips, their leader released his prisoner. He beat on his chest and advanced to Trish on all fours. Trish shouted at the beast, while holding her stance. It stopped twenty feet from her and raised to its full height. This time, it bent over, smacking the ground with powerful swings. Trish's heart skipped a beat, but she remained calm and ready.

The beast moved to circle here. Trish took a few steps farther away from the swarm of Gramites. A few pushed closer, fueled on by anticipation for the coming show. Maybe if she moved nearer to the last completed section of the concrete wall, the vehicles would block their view enough, and the horde would shift closer to the fight and away from Strong and Phillips. The concept was worth a try.

Trish spotted a flash from the creature's eyes a split second before it charged at her. She ducked under a massive swing and pushed her hands into the mutant's suppurating side, increasing his momentum, and throwing off his footing.

He stumbled slightly, regained his balance on all fours, and took out his rage on the ground. Panting and shrieking, it gradually settled down, its eyes squinting at her with hate.

He came at her, three hundred pounds of pure rage. She went airborne and flipped over the lunge. Her hands bounced forcefully off its upper body, driving it downward. He stumbled and fell. His face went into a skid onto the cracked pavement. She landed on her feet and sprinted toward the wall.

An arm's length away from the patterned surface, she stopped to study the Gramites who were now less interested in circling their prey. Most of them wanted a view of the fight. They shuffled away from Strong and Phillips, moving closer to the parked Gladiators. Aralyn mouthed something to Givens, and he went inside the building with a handful of troops and Doctor Burgos. First Sergeant Stevens and the rest ventured closer to the two injured on the ground, with the exception of Doctor Burgos's guard, who remained by the building with his weapon raised, pointing the muzzle at the leader advancing on Trish. If the idiot shot a round off, Strong and Phillips would surely be killed by the closest Gramites. Trish wanted to shout out to the guard to lower his weapon, but she didn't want to attract the attention to what the team was trying to do.

Instead, she refocused on the massive creature. Its wickedness was seconds away from reaching her. Part of the flesh on its face and neck was stripped and bleeding, dangling from the abrasive faceplant. Bloody mucus seeped from both its new and old open wounds. Trish sidestepped to the right. Her attacker adjusted to her position, then dove forward, reaching with his claws. She jumped to the left and it flew straight, crashing headfirst into the lower section of the fractured wall. It might have started out the day huge and powerful, but now its movements were labored, and it was slow to rise.

Trish turned her attention away, spotting the team helping Strong to her feet and carrying Phillips toward the building.

In that brief lapse of focus, a powerful blow smacked her across her unprotected head. She went flying, landing in a roll several feet from her attacker and coming back to her feet. She fought against the *ringing* in her ears, the stinging on her neck, and her vision spinning. Her legs wobbled, and she adjusted her weight as she fought for balance.

The creature advanced and seized her. The grip of the monster was intense. A blur of the blue sky streaked by as it flipped her over its giant body. She smashed headfirst to the ground with a *crunch*. Extreme pain exploded through her skull.

Lying dazed, she heard a cry. A hail of bullets smacked into the monster. The mutant bellowed at the guard running for Trish's position.

"Stupid fool." Trish spat out a mouthful of blood, tasting the copper warmth coating her tongue. "He'll get himself killed."

As the beast swung, the guard tried ducking, but not fast enough. The impact sent the short man flying into the wall. As the other Gramites drew closer, the leader shouted out a thunderous noise, as if claiming the additional kill for itself.

Trish rose to her feet.

The beast loomed above the guard who lay half senseless against the base of the wall. The creature grabbed hold of the top section of the weakening barrier, yanking on the slab, intending to crush the guard beneath the solid weight.

The guard shook the sluggishness from his head and tried unsuccessfully to rise.

Vision blurry, Trish reached him just in time, allowing her body to take the heavy impact of the toppling wall onto her back and left shoulder. She struggled with her footing and pressed her hands against the coarse stone, pushing up while shouting for the guard to move.

As if reality set in, the guard rolled out of the way, peering from Trish to the heavy slab.

A giant fist pounded against her side, and her hands slipped. Weapons fired from behind, and Trish heard a multitude of Gramites screaming. She needed to move out of the way so her team would have a clear shot. Furious, the monster pounded her several more times, each strike weakening her hold on the wall.

"Trish, I'm free."

Trish spun toward the familiar voice.

The creature bit her arm.

The massive jaw crushed her forearm with such strength, Trish wasn't sure if its sharp teeth went through the armor or not. She pushed up on the wall hard and dove backwards, barely clearing the collapsing slab. The creature tried to jump out of the way but wasn't fast enough. The mutant's body toppled with the wall, its legs trapped underneath. It let out a roar of rage so loud that she thought her eardrums might burst.

She removed her boot knife and plunged it into its skull twice before it stopped moving. She dropped onto her knees, landed on her stomach, and took in quick gulps of air. Every part of her hurt, but her arm and her head down to her lower spine were on fire.

Trish raised her head when Susan reached them.

The guard had her helmet off and was making her way toward Trish.

Her vision was still blurry, but Trish could swear the guard who'd been following Doctor Burgos around all day looked just like Christina. But of course, that wasn't possible. Christina was in Rapid City and pissed as hell. What the hell? she thought. That disgusting creature must have hit me harder in the head that I realized.

"Don't touch her," she heard Susan scream.

"Why not?" The guard's voice sounded just like Christina's. She was demanding to know why and struggling to break Susan's grip.

"Look at where that thing struck you, Christina, and the bodysuit Trish is wearing. We don't know if those sores on the creature are a way in which the virus can be transmitted or not, but whatever this fluid is, it's eating through the armor."

Trish closed her eyes and tried to shake the cobwebs from her head. She opened her eyes and surveyed across the area, still sensing danger and smelling the filth in the air. The lifeless bodies of Gramites lay scattered around the vehicles. She figured by the numbers, at least ten remained at large.

She sat up and spotted Givens and the soldiers posted on the roof, and her worry eased some.

Doctor Burgos rushed forward with three armed soldiers. "Both of you! Bodysuits off *now*. Be careful not to touch your skin to the outside of the suit."

Trish was still swooning in her own little world and allowed hands to unfasten clasps and start removing her suit.

"Damn, do you see the sores on Trish's neck?" Susan asked Doctor Burgos, her voice sick with worry.

"I see them. My guess is acid burns. Look here. Some of the acid went through her suit as well. We need to keep her outside and away from others until we see how her body reacts." He bent down and carefully collected a sample of the goo dripping from an open sore on the dead creature. He then scraped a bit off Trish's and Christina's suits.

Trish mumbled, "You guys need to get inside. I can feel the other Gramites close by."

Trish smiled into Christina's worried eyes. She knew this was just a dream and that the love of her life wasn't really here, but she planned to enjoy it all the same.

Someone removed her boots and finished pulling off her suit, then got her to her feet where she teetered slightly before achieving a sense of balance. At this point, she didn't care if she was standing in front of the team in a sports bra and boxer-briefs. All she wanted was to lie down and continue this dream of Christina being with her.

"Trish has claw marks on her neck," Doctor Burgos said, on a closer inspection. "And several acid burns. I don't see any on Christina."

Trish's head cleared. "Wait a minute. You—you're really here."

"I am."

Trish and Christina stared at one another. "I thought I was dreaming, but you're really truly here."

Christina reached out, but her father slapped her hand away. "No, don't touch. Trish could be infected."

With a bit of a pout, Christina said, "I don't care what anyone says! I want to help Trish inside to safety."

"I'll be fine," Trish said, "You, however, need to head in."

"No, I'm staying with you."

Doctor Burgos leveled his gaze at his daughter. "You will go inside and disinfect, then thoroughly shower. Susan will follow you in, then she'll treat Trish out here. Leave your suits. We'll burn them with these bodies later."

"But—"

"Stop arguing! I have to get samples off this monstrosity, and you and Trish need medical care stat!"

Trish bent down and picked up Christina's weapon. When she did, she heard Christina suck in a lungful of air. Trish quickly glanced around. "Trish, your entire backside is covered in bruises."

Trish waved it off and directed Christina toward the building. "This will heal pretty fast. I'm worried about you. Your right side, where you hit the wall, looks red and angry. I would ask what the hell were you thinking running out there like that, but I might be dead if you hadn't. Probably not, but you never know," she said with a playful grin. "I'll say thank you instead."

"I'm waiting out here until you go in."

"No, you're not," Susan cut in. "Listen to your father and get cleaned up. You shouldn't even *be* on this mission."

Trish agreed. "The sooner they treat that sexy body of yours, the happier I'll be. Nice undies by the way."

"Okay, once I scrub down, I'll come wait with you." Christina tried to move closer, but Susan stopped her.

"I swear," Susan said, "you two are really annoying me. You're both stubborn and reckless. Christina, if you try to kiss her, so help me god, I'll drag you into the building kicking and screaming. Now move."

With once last attempt to look behind her, Susan pulled Christina toward the building, and Trish watched every step. The moment the door finally closed, Trish gently lowered her battered body down against the building. The sores on her neck were switching from a burning pain to an itch, and she fought hard against aggressively scratching.

"Doctor Burgos, how's Phillips and Strong?" Trish asked.

"Stable. Don't worry, they'll live."

"That's good." Weariness passed through her, and pain as well. She wanted to sleep wrapped in Christina's arms for the next week.

"Can you get up, Trish? Come on, follow me. Let's get you near the building. You can wait by the door, and once we're sure you won't mutate into one of these freaks, which I'm sure you won't, you can come in and shower as well."

Susan came out close to twenty minutes later, inspected her eyes, and body. Her forearm hadn't been pierced, so that was good news. Next, Susan dumped a burning solution all over her. When Susan used a scrub brush, it felt like every inch of her skin was on fire. Before Susan left, she upended what remained in the bottle onto Trish's raw flesh. Trish grunted against the pain.

Once Doctor Burgos judged it safe for Trish to enter the building, he informed her the pustules didn't contain the virus, but they were filled with an acidic substance he'd never seen before, some sort of defensive mechanism produced by the creature. Trish's body was already repairing itself, but if his daughter hadn't been wearing the body armor, the potent acidic fluid from the ruptured pustules could have eaten Christina's fragile flesh down to the bone.

After locating one of his old kits, he had gone out and collected additional tissue and blood samples off the dead creatures. He said he was taking them to Rapid City to run extensive tests in his own lab.

Trish devoured a ration kit and drank two bottles of water before Susan escorted her to a private bedroom. On the way, Susan gave her a motherly lecture on her willingness to run blindly into danger. Trish silently took the criticism. She knew if the roles were reversed, she would have been just as terrified for Susan.

Susan also told her this part of the complex was in the same wing Christina and her parents' group had lived in for several years after the viral epidemic. The room Trish was staying in tonight had two sets of bunkbeds, two dressers, a desk, and a bathroom.

Trish flipped on the water in the shower and leaned her head against the cool tiled wall. When she heard the bathroom door open, she shouted, "Occupied." Thankfully, the door closed again.

Her body felt better, but she was physically and mentally drained. She was ready to enjoy the rest of her shower, have her second ration tray, and go straight to sleep.

Dumping an entire tiny bottle of shampoo onto her palm, she rubbed her hands through her hair and scrubbed at her scalp. She felt a warm touch on her back and jumped, barely managing to suppress a girlish shriek. Her swift movement caused her elbow to bang against the tile.

"I'm sorry," Christina said. Her voice was soft, stimulating. "I didn't mean to scare you."

"Thank goodness. I was afraid one of my bimbos followed us from Rapid City." Trish heard the nervousness in her own tone. Her attempt at humor wasn't fooling anyone. She rinsed the soap from her hair.

"Want me to leave in case any of them show?"

Trish was aware Christina was climbing into the shower behind her. She knew what she would find if she turned—the most beautiful woman in the world standing against her, wet, and completely naked. Her mouth moistened and she swallowed. Head bowed, she clenched her fist against the tile. Her breathing rolled out heavier with each exhale. Christina reached around her, one arm gliding against Trish's breast while she grabbed a washrag and body soap from the rack.

One touch, and Trish's nipples hardened.

"If you want me to go, I will," Christina said in her inimitable sexy voice.

The water poured from the showerhead, repetitively tapping down on Trish's head. She swallowed again, trying to focus on the sound it made and not her rapidly pounding heart. She couldn't speak. No words formed in her mind or on her lips. If she moved even a fraction of an inch, Trish was sure she would drop dead on the spot. Coroner's Report: Cause of Death: massive heart attack from her overwhelming desire.

What a stern lecture Mother Susan would give Christina in the morning.

"Trish, you're shaking. Is it me? Am I making you uncomfortable? I really can go." Christina's words held concern, maybe a pinch of sadness. Trish couldn't tell which. All she knew for sure is that she needed to say something, or risk hurting Christina again.

"I can't turn around. If I do, I know what'll happen. I have a hard-enough time controlling myself when you're clothed. Seeing you naked, that would be it for me."

This time when Christina spoke, the pitch of her words held a shade of jauntiness. "I see. You're afraid you'll steal my precious virginity away. Fine, I'll scrub your back, and let you finish up. Then I'll go to the other room and finish up myself."

Trish's head came up, and she stared at the pale-blue tile in front of her. Did Christina mean she was going to touch herself, or get ready for bed? Trish closed her eyes tight as she pictured Christina under the covers, naked, her hand between her legs. She could vividly see her bringing herself to climax, body shaking, hand gripping frantically at a pillow.

Trish let out a slight moan. The rag slid down her back. She bit her lip and cursed herself for allowing her mind to build a vision stimulating her own ache. Christina ran the soapy washcloth along her shoulders and down her side, and Trish slowly exhaled.

"This is so incredible. Your bruises are getting better, and your sores have already closed over."

Christina glided the rag around Trish's neck. When she touched her lips to Trish's back, Trish suppressed a moan with an unconvincing cough. She covered Christina's hand holding the washcloth. "I need a moment," Trish mumbled, her voice rough, her muscles tensing.

"Why? I can tell you want me as bad as I want you. Why are you putting up barriers and not allowing yourself to let go?"

Trish cleared her throat, keeping her voice as even as her body would allow. "Do you remember what you said to me in my bedroom? How you couldn't go on if I died?"

"Yes, but what does that have to do with this?"

"I've known since before we met I would one day be facing my father. I have no problems going toe-to-toe with a horde of creatures, but him . . ." Trish struggled to get the words out. "He frightens me."

"Trish—"

"No, please let me finish." Trish took a deep breath and continued. "I have no idea what'll happen, but I won't lie. I'm worried. If we made love, that would only make it harder for you to move on."

"Stop. I'm serious. Enough with this morbid talk," Christina insisted. "You'll be fine. He's not stronger or smarter than you. Do you hear me? Dammit Trish, turn around and talk to me."

Wiping the water off her face, Trish slowly turned, keeping her eye level a few inches above Christina's forehead.

"I guess that's kind of better." Christina dropped the washcloth, placed her hands on each side of Trish's head, and tilted it downward until their eyes met. "He's bullied you your entire life, and it's left you believing you're somehow inferior to him. You're miles above what that man could ever dream to be. Do you understand me?"

Trish didn't nod. She didn't verbally or physically offer her response. Instead, she looked directly at Christina and decided to remove every obstacle in her path. She bent closer and said what she had been wanting to tell her for weeks now. "I'm in love with you."

Christina put a hand behind Trish's neck and pulled her closer. "I love you even more," she murmured.

Trish smiled. "Do you always have to win?"

Christina's eyes sparkled. She whispered, "Always."

Their kiss was soft, passionate. Christina grasped Trish's hands and directed them to each side of her waist. Touching the smooth curves above Christina's hips melted every muscle in Trish's body. Her mind became blurry, with one thought taking shape; she wanted to experience a lifetime to explore this woman. Track down the delicate locations which would push Christina to unimaginable heights. Taste every inch offered and find where all her secrets lay waiting. To worship her completely, and have Christina do the same.

Determined to begin that exploration, Trish fought against Christina's hunger and pulled her lips away. Christina started to protest, until Trish worked her mouth downward, along Christina's jaw, then neck. When Christina let out a moan, Trish slowly returned to the spot below Christina's ear. This triggered another vocal release. She pulled Christina's nakedness against her own. By the third moan, Trish felt her burning excitement mounting. The sound was warm honey dripping in her ears, and she wanted more.

She worked her mouth around, nibbling, sucking, gliding her tongue all over, to see which method worked best. Christina liked a mixture of all three, but the further back Trish's mouth moved, Christina's moans grew deeper, rougher. Trish turned Christina toward the tile, lifted her wet, wavy hair, and nibbled. Gripping her hands over Christina's thighs and lower stomach at the same time intensified the moans into slow bodily sways. Christina brought her hand up, latching onto Trish's hair, and she arched her shoulders backwards against Trish's breasts.

Trish felt a deep craving to bring her hand downward and glide her fingers between Christina's legs. Instead, she clenched her jaw and mentally screamed at herself to take it slow, not to rush it. When Christina grabbed hold and directed Trish's hand to her breast, Trish whispered in her ear, "Do you have to be so sexy?" She nudged Christina to turn around, and she pinned Christina's hands over her head against the tile. She moved her mouth down, exploring both shoulders, the curves on her collarbone, then the soft areas around the toughening rings encircling each nipple.

Christina uttered something in Spanish, then blurted out, "Please Trish, you're driving me crazy."

"I won't make you wait long, but we're not rushing this," Trish said, feeling a growing throb form between her own legs.

Trish released her hold, and Christina brought Trish's hand once again to her breast. Trish held Christina tight against her and slid her hand gently over the firm nipple. Christina muttered seductively, rubbing her hand along the nape of Trish's neck and through her hair.

Trish felt the heartbeat in Christina's chest match the strength of her own. This time when their lips found each other, the contact was an instant explosion of desire. Both tongues searched deeply, sliding against the other as if they were one and the same. When Trish gripped her hand a little tighter around the softness of Christina's breast, a moan escaped between their kiss.

Trish relinquished the embrace and stood a few inches away to watch the water flow over Christina's nipples, stomach, and the curly hairs between her thighs. Her head spun as her feeling of desire soared. She lowered her mouth to cover the dark area encircling a nipple, suckled it gently and rolled her tongue over, feeling the center's firmness grow. Then she tasted the other. The Spanish that flowed out above her was thick with lust. Christina pushed her chest against Trish's mouth and released a shaking moan.

"Trish, please. I need to feel you in me." Christina's words dragged out, her tone pleading and bringing the hunger inside Trish to a ravenous state. But Trish knew if she did, it wouldn't take long for Christina to find her release. Trish wasn't ready to end this so soon after they'd just started. She shook her head and continued moving her mouth downward, water flowing around her as she explored. Her tongue slid, her teeth gently bit, and her mouth sucked in the dampness of the honey-tan skin.

Lowering to her knees. Trish traced the curve along the hip, lower stomach, and the soft vale between. Christina's body trembled and her legs parted. Trish investigated the taste and touch of both thighs against her lips. When Christina's hips shifted to direct Trish's mouth to what lay between, Trish lifted Christina's legs onto her shoulders, Christina's head resting against the tile. Trish moved in, parting the seam of the lips with her tongue. The dampness that lay inside was invigorating. Its salty sweetness drove Trish further in to enjoy every inch. The swollen mound was so soft, and her tongue glided over it so easily. She explored along the sides, then returned to the center.

When Christina's body exploded into a wave of fierce shaking, Trish held on, not stopping her pursuit until Christina's quivering hand finally pushed her away.

Christina climbed off, her legs still trembling. She slid herself slowly down the tile, coming to a rest in Trish's encircled arms. The water rained down on them both, and Trish rocked her gently until Christina's muscles stopped twitching. Her emerald eyes came up, and she kissed Trish, her lips fuller than normal.

When she pulled away, she stared at Trish. Her features grew concerned. "What's wrong? Did you not like it?"

Trish bent down and nibbled her ear. "Are you kidding, I've never enjoyed anything so much in my life," she said, averting her gaze.

Christina's gentle fingers turned Trish's face until their eyes connected. "Then what is it? Something's wrong."

Trish shrugged. "We were just getting started. I didn't realize you were so close. I should've backed off."

Christina laughed, her voice full of love and longing. "My dear Trish, our night is far from over."

CHAPTER TWENTY

Trish crept into the darkened room, closed the door, and moved toward the bed where Christina lay sleeping. A sliver of light spilled in from the slightly cracked bathroom door, enough to allow her a fair amount of clarity. She lowered the items she carried to the floor, kicked off her flipflops, and crawled into bed. Situating herself on the springy mattress, she pressed her body firmly against her stark-naked lover.

Her muscles were sore, particularly her arm where the creature's voracious maw had exerted so much pressure. She was lucky it hadn't broken the bone. She was also lucky that her body healed so quickly and that the intense headache had passed. She might not have much left from her mother, but as it turned out, the accidental injection of her mother's serum was a healing gift that kept on giving.

Christina shifted, moaned, and settled. Trish held her breath until she was sure Christina was asleep. She stared at Christina for a long while, until her desires grew too ravenous not to have a small taste. She first ran her finger then her moistened tongue softly down the length of Christina's spine. Christina gently muttered but remained still. Trish worked her mouth along the far side of Christina's waist.

Christina lurched up and onto her side. "Ouch, tender."

"Sorry. I was just seeing what you like and what you don't. No nibbling around the waist—got it."

Christina guided Trish into her arms and kissed her deeply. When she broke the connection, her voice was low, seductive. "I never said I didn't like it. My body is completely yours, no limitations. But I'm still feeling some tenderness from the bruises."

"I'll be extra gentle then." Trish took Christina's nipple in her mouth and sucked.

Christina jerked slightly and pressed her hand to Trish's chest.

Alarmed, Trish said, "Are you okay?"

"Yes, fine. This is something entirely different from the bruises. Some body parts need longer to bounce back after being overworked all night long."

"Oh, God. Was I too rough? Last night when you told me to bite, I was afraid I might have hurt you."

Christina squirmed under the blankets. "No, beautiful, everything was beyond perfect." Her voice sounded hoarse. "They only need a little time to recover." She laughed. "Stop your worrying. Last night was amazing. I love how well you read my body. It's mind-blowing." She stared longingly at Trish. "What about you, did you enjoy it?"

Trish closed her eyes, thinking about fingers thrusting magically inside. Christina's mouth covering her dampness as she was hit with waves of ecstatic explosions. She swallowed, wishing the faucet in her mouth would subside. "Enjoy is such an understatement. Woman, you have skills beyond belief."

Christina pulled her in for a new wave of kisses. She brought a hand down between Trish's legs, then halted. "Why are you dressed? What happened to our new, no-clothes-in-bed rule?"

Trish couldn't help but laugh as Christina grabbed at her shorts and shirt, divesting her of them in short order. "Hey, sleepyhead, I went to check on Strong and Phillips, and I could hardly do that buck-naked. Then I got us some food. Found out we're staying for a few days. Strong's working at her computer between intermittent doses of pain meds. Phillips is sleeping."

Trish leaned away to toss clothes to the floor and reached off the bed for two ration trays.

Christina said, "What are you doing now?"

"Getting the food, what does it look like?"

"Oh, no you don't." She pulled Trish to her, bit Trish's bottom lip, and sucked it gently into her mouth. She purred her next words. "Your healthy appetite can wait until you've finished what you've started." Without waiting, she guided Trish's hand down to the damp mound between her legs.

"Gladly," Trish breathed, kissing her lips softly. She slowly worked her hand through the wetness, enjoying the warm feel it offered. When she finally plunged inside, their eyes remained lovingly fixed on one another until Christina's body quivered with her release.

After three days of rest and healing, Aralyn summoned her troops for departure. Packing up took little time, but parting with Christina was proving to be difficult.

Trish and Christina stood close together, touching hands, near a vehicle outside the bunker while Aralyn confronted them. "No, Miss Burgos, you're going to Rapid City with your father and Phillips. End of discussion." Aralyn climbed into the lead Gladiator. Out of the open window she shouted, "Lieutenant Webber, come on. We've got to go."

When Trish didn't move, Aralyn fixed her with a glare that said this drawn-out evening was strumming on her last nerve. "I gave you an order, Lieutenant. Say your goodbyes and get in the vehicle. You have one minute."

"Are you sure you don't want to go with your dad?" Trish asked, ignoring her godmother's piercing eyes.

"Yes." The way Christina lowered her head onto Trish's chest, Trish knew Christina was worried for her safety and about the hazards Trish might face. "Unless you can come with us."

"I wish I could be your escort."

"Going there will be dangerous." Christina gestured toward the direction of NORAD, Colorado Springs and Trish's father. "We should stay together to deal with it. I can help."

"I'll be careful."

Christina's green eyes came up. "I know. But I still wish I could stay with you. Please don't make me go home alone."

Trish executed a feeble attempt at a smile. If she asked Christina to head to Rapid City with her father, Christina would go. She'd be hurt, but she would understand the fear which drove Trish to keep her safe. Christina would likely forgive her for this outcome, but Trish didn't want to micromanage the choices Christina made simply to ease her own worries. What kind of relationship would that be? One doomed for future failure?

Trish made up her mind. "If going with us is what you want, then I'll support your decision. For the record, if your mother finds out I said yes, she'll probably kill me."

"Trish, my mother knows I'm old enough to live my own life. It's your godmother I'm worried about."

Trish leaned closer. "I've got this."

"Trish! Now," Aralyn grumbled from the passenger seat.

Trish locked eyes with her godmother. She didn't say a word, only stared. The busy movements of those around them, who were adding the last of the supplies into the vehicles, stopped. What was her godmother going to do? Write her up, demote her, kick her from the position she didn't sign up for?

To Trish's surprise, Aralyn broke the silence first. In a voice even deeper than normal, she said, "All right then. When we get to NORAD, Christina will remain beside the vehicles with Sergeant Givens. She will do nothing stupid like try to save your ass again. Now hurry up and get in."

Knowing now was a good time to make as little noise as possible, Trish pointed toward the Gladiator, and they climbed into the second row. Had she made the wrong call? Technically, the decision wasn't hers to make. She understood where Aralyn was coming from, but she also knew Christina could handle herself. She possessed a rare strength—an internal courage—which triggered when a dangerous situation put loved ones in harm's way. The normal instinct to flee was overshadowed by a fighting mechanism, pushing past logic. This fearlessness made

Christina powerful, yet also placed her in danger, especially since she wasn't trained like Trish and her fellow soldiers.

Trish squeezed Christina's hand tighter and gave her a slight wink. Christina lowered her head onto Trish's arm and closed her tired eyes. Even though they'd had several days of downtime to give Lieutenant Strong time to work on computer calculations, she and Christina didn't get much sleep. Trish stifled a giggle, thinking of the broken bunkbed in the room they had left. Not completely their fault, though. The frame appeared cheaply made.

Christina slept holding Trish's hand during the short drive to NORAD. When the vehicle drew close, Trish woke Christina from her nap and watched her stretch and yawn. "Can you do me a favor?"

Christina abruptly ended her stretching. She softly kissed Trish's lips. "You know I will. What do you need?"

Trish made sure her eyes expressed the seriousness of her question. "Will you go wait at the supply bunker with Lieutenant Strong and Corporal Leonard once we leave the NORAD site?"

Christina's posture sagged. "You don't want me to go to Colorado Springs with you?"

"No, but if you're adamant about going, then I'll support your choice."

Christina focused on her a bit longer, then took Trish's gloved hand. She held the black material against her cheek. "I'll go to the bunker, but you need to promise to be careful. Don't take any of your outlandish risks. I want to grow old with you, understand?"

Trish threw an arm around Christina. She never would have imagined such a love was possible. "I promise to do everything I can to stay safe."

Their vehicle braked hard, swerved, and ground to a bone-jarring halt. Corporal Leonard got out of the second vehicle and ran up to Aralyn's window, slightly breathless. "Something's up, Colonel. Lieutenant Strong said she's not picking up any radio waves on the receiver she constructed. We're still two miles away. What do you want to do? Pull off and hide out until dark, or get closer?"

Aralyn reached for the dash console. She opened the display and flipped through the menu. "Surely NORAD is still in operation. We're two-point-two miles away and there's no signal. Something's wrong." Aralyn glanced to Trish. At the enquiring look, Trish shook her head. She wasn't sensing any Gramite danger.

"Let's take it slow," Aralyn said. "Go another mile and let's see what we find. Even with NORAD being down to a skeletal crew, they'll still keep the facility guarded."

When Leonard returned to his vehicle, Christina squeezed Trish's hand. "What's wrong?"

Trish shrugged. "It's a bad sign if the comms are down. We won't know what we're walking into. Don't worry, we've got a strong team. We need to figure a way to sneak inside, make it to the elevator, and head to the sixth-level. Once Lieutenant Strong hacks into NORAD's mainframe, she'll upload her program. Every system connected to the UWTF satellite will broadcast what my mother discovered and more."

"Then the people will fight against those who started all of this?"

"That's what we're hoping for," Trish said. "Anyone who stays with the UWTF will be just as guilty as those who committed mass genocide."

"You're all sure this will work?"

"It's got to," Trish replied.

Doctor Frank Webber was surprised to see the Director of Military Forces contacting him personally and not someone from the General's staff. He activated his processor to materialize the stern features embodying a hologram. "General Princeton, what can I do for you?"

"You can pray I don't find out you intentionally lied to us. If I do, I'll kill you myself—do you understand me, Webber?"

Stunned, Doctor Webber rose slowly from his desk. "Sir, I can honestly say, I don't know what you mean. If someone has told you anything about me—"

"Your daughter, Frank. Informing this committee she was dead. The video link you sent us. Having it staged for our benefit. Were you planning on capturing her for your own personal advancement? Are you really this stupid?"

Frank's head was spinning. "My daughter? What do you mean, General? I don't understand."

The General's holographic image blinked out and switched to a video display of the area surrounding the main tunnel of NORAD. Two armored vehicles were positioned at the mouth of the tunnel with seven troops in armored bodysuits moving in a tactical formation through the passageway toward NORAD's reinforced doors. When the camera focused in, he spotted Trish leading the group with Colonel Aralyn Williams right beside her.

"Aralyn! You fucking dyke!" he shouted, feeling his entire face growing hot with fever. He grabbed the closest thing he could find and with force threw a priceless statue against the wall where it shattered. He seized another statue.

"Frank," Princeton's disembodied voice barked out, "get ahold of yourself."

Frank Webber smacked the controls to deactivate the connection. Screw all of them. He owed them nothing. Sucking up to a committee full of ungrateful buffoons was not at the forefront of his mind. He was consumed by the thought of his daughter and Aralyn's images, both of them alive and kicking.

He opened a private display and contacted the one individual he could trust. When he connected, his orders were curt: "Major Porter, I need you and your team to meet me at the helipad in thirty minutes. Make sure you're all heavily armed and ready for action. I guarantee your adversaries are going to be well-skilled in combat."

Inside the NORAD building, Aralyn's team moved with care, Trish following on alert. They'd already looked over the grounds and found nothing unusual, but there was plenty of dried blood smeared on the walls and floor of the entrance tunnel.

"Trish," Aralyn muttered, "are you sure you're not sensing anything dangerous?"

"No, nothing." She glanced through the two wide-open reinforced doors. The lit corridor of the first level revealed bloody remnants of a tragic killing spree.

Lieutenant Strong and First Sergeant Stevens emerged from an enclosed room where the entrance guard usually sat. Lieutenant Strong shook her head, looking glum. "Sorry, Colonel. Nothing in there is salvageable, and all the video monitors have been smashed. We'll be going in blind."

Trish looked over her shoulder and down the tunnel. Christina and Givens were out of sight, guarding the entrance by the vehicles. Was it more dangerous for them to be outside or inside NORAD? She turned back and Susan gave her a look of reassurance.

"Okay, plan's still the same. Trish, Sergeant Perez, and I will lead. First Sergeant, you and Corporal Leonard will take up the rear. Lieutenant Strong, Lieutenant Travis, you make sure to stay tight on each other. With her injury, we're down a rifle." Aralyn switched her weapon to full auto. "Trish, if you detect any sort of threat, signal us to stop. And hey, everybody, when we head below, our links and comms may not work with those outside, so pay attention to our flank."

Aralyn pointed to Trish's wrist processor and Trish swiped it on. She sealed her helmet and pulled up the display, connected to the active link, and minimized the screen. She was as ready as she'd ever be.

Aralyn moved in through the bunker doors. Trish stayed on her right and Perez was on her left. With each opening Trish passed, she scanned the rooms, searching and feeling for any signs of movement or danger. She kept her mind focused on the task at hand and off the two people they'd left by the vehicles. She wasn't about to miss anything that would exit the bunker behind them for Christina and Givens to deal with.

With the first-level clear, the team filed into the double-wide elevator and Strong activated the button. The main elevator went to the fifth-level. To gain access to the sixth-level, a high-security elevator was located beside a guard post on the fifth-level, a few hundred feet down the corridor from the main elevator shaft.

THE PURIFICATION | 277

The second the doors closed, Trish spotted a red flashing display on the lower left side of her screen. Christina and Givens were no longer sharing the comms. Damn, Aralyn was right. Trish waited, hopeful that when they emerged from the elevator they could reconnect.

The elevator panel beeped and the steel door slid open. For a split second no one moved. The entire visual stretch of corridor was encased in darkness. The only light was pouring out from the elevator, and a soft glow flickered far ahead where the pathway curved close to the entrance to the swimming pool. Trish and those around her activated their night vision.

Aralyn took a moment to try to reconnect the comm link to the outside vehicles, but their signal was indeed lost. The team was probably too far inside to merge with the others, which made Trish feel more nervous.

They moved on. When Trish passed her father's office and then his lab, she fought down the urge to send a grenade round into each.

Before hitting the alcove that housed the elevator to the sixth-level, Trish and Perez each dropped to a knee. Trish raised her hand to the sound of hollow pings. She moved closer to Perez. "We've got some movement close by," she whispered loud enough so the others connected to comms could hear.

Perez said, "I think it's coming from inside the canteen on the right."

After a short pause, Aralyn said, "I don't want to divide us. Let's carry out our mission. Once the transmission's sent, we'll come check it out."

Trish and Perez advanced to the elevator. He typed in the code Aralyn gave him, but the door remained closed. Lieutenant Strong came forward and removed a device from her bag. Perez helped her attach cables to the console.

Peeking her head inside the guard booth, Trish spotted a mangled arm sitting in a dried accumulation of blood near the booth entrance. Her stomach clenched. She visually explored the compacted workspace which was almost completely covered in a bodily grime. It looked like whoever was attacked here had exploded upon death. Even the ceiling was splattered with dried splotches of darkened red. She squinted toward the corner. A rifle with a bent muzzle lay on its side, claw marks splintered into its base.

Trish felt a chill spread through her body. She leaned her upper body out and scanned the corridor. Lieutenant Strong and Sergeant Perez succeeded in activating the elevator and it beeped, allowing the team to load in.

"What is it?" Aralyn asked from behind.

Trish backed out and pointed into the bloodied booth. "Whatever happened there, I'm betting the creatures were responsible. I don't know how they got in, but I still don't sense any danger." She was about to turn until she remembered the infected soldier her father had in his lab. "Or maybe they didn't get in but escaped."

"I'm not following."

"My father had a mutant in his lab, remember? What if he brought down more and one got loose? Started attacking people, turning them."

Aralyn pondered the question. "It's a good possibility. Trish. With this mutated strand, are we even sure you can pick up on their presence?"

"No, I—I guess I *can't* be entirely sure." In her father's lab, when she woke up next to a recently turned creature, she didn't experience any unusual sensations. Then again, she had also been coming out of sedation.

If she couldn't rely on her senses after all, she'd feel eerily blind, not to mention useless.

They squeezed into the elevator. On the way down, Aralyn said, "Okay, listen up everyone. We need to be extra careful here on out. Trish might not detect the mutated creatures. They could very well be in here with us. We all know how resourceful they are, so watch each other's backs."

When the doors opened at the sixth-level, the lights inside the massive entryway were on and the area quiet. As they made their way toward the mainframe, past the rows of cubicles and offices, Trish noted how unique the craftsmanship in this level was, compared with the rest of NORAD. From the arched, sky-painted ceilings to the marble floors, colorfully decorated walls, and expensive furniture, the UWTF had spared no expense. Trees, blooming with a wide variety of fruit, were elegantly arranged throughout the level. Underneath each, Trish saw sizable patches of grass and benches for the residents to rest upon.

The cafeteria resembled two five-star restaurants positioned back-to-back. Running beside the eateries was an expansion containing a two-story movie house. The sign outside announced the live production of *Fiddler on the Roof* would be presented soon.

Perez let out a string of curses, then said, "They've lived like this while the rest of us ate ration trays and stared at white and gray walls for eighteen years."

Trish more than understood his distaste.

"You should see their living quarters," Aralyn said. "Makes this appear dull in comparison."

They reached a room between an empty armory and security headquarters where Aralyn said the mainframe was housed. Trish, Perez, and the First Sergeant performed a full sweep of each of the long server rows filled with black, floor-to-ceiling processors. Deeming the cool room secure, they returned to help guard the corridors while Aralyn, Susan, and Lieutenant Strong went inside to breach the UWTF satellite and send out their pre-recorded broadcast.

During the thirty minutes it took to hack the system and transmit the information, Susan kept the team abreast of the minute-to-minute details. Despite dealing with one arm in a cast, Lieutenant Strong was able to work her magic. The broadcast upload took seconds. What ate most of the time away was the uploads of many other programs and downloads of various files off the mainframe.

Trish was surprised when Aralyn announced the deed was done and they were coming out. Lieutenant Strong was definitely a wizard when it came to her electronics and programming skills.

They filed into their assigned formation and headed out the same way they came. Reaching the fifth-level, their night vision kicked on and Trish and Perez stopped again at the intersection to listen for movement.

They heard nothing. She and Perez exchanged a lengthy stare and kept listening.

Trish was ready to rise and signal for the team to move, but then a distinct metallic rattling echoed close by.

"Okay," Perez whispered, "we have movement in the cafeteria. Want us to go have a look-see?"

"Yes," Aralyn said. "You two head in. We'll cover you. Be careful."

"Aralyn . . . I mean, Colonel," Susan corrected, "I—

Aralyn's and Susan's comms muted, and Aralyn raised a hand to still the group.

Trish and Perez waited. Trish had a feeling Susan was protesting the decision to allow Trish to head into possible danger. Her godmother more than likely gave her lover, yet subordinate, *the look* or *the talk*. Trish loved Susan for her worry and Aralyn for her confidence in her ability to handle herself. Life was falling into place the way it always should have been.

"Move out," Aralyn said, once their mics came online. Without a doubt, she'd won their disagreement.

Trish headed along the left side as Perez took the right. At the cafeteria door, she crossed the corridor and checked to make sure the others were in position. He glanced at her and she signaled for him to go. He scanned his hand over the entry-pad, and the door buzzed. But it didn't open. Someone had engaged the lock from the inside.

"Colonel, door's locked. Wanna send over Lieutenant Strong?"

Strong dug through her tools as Perez helped her one-handed maneuvers go faster. Once Strong had the device set and ready, Trish and Perez trained their rifles on the solid barrier. Strong entered a code and the door slid to the side.

The main lights in the dining area were off, but several glowing lanterns were scattered about. Every muscle in Trish's body tightened, but her stomach and heart melted to the sight. At least fifty sets of uncontaminated eyes, both young and old, were spread around the room, staring panic-stricken in their direction.

Trish held up her hand and rifle, displaying an unthreatening stance. Multiple tables had been either broken down or moved to the side, and scattered food trays lay half eaten on the floor by makeshift pallets. She squinted to the only electrical device operating, a wall screen with her mother's face giving the message they had just uploaded. Lieutenant Strong was right; the recording would tap into every device on the UWTF network.

"Major Reilly?" Perez called out to someone staring at them in fear.

"Sergeant Perez, oh thank goodness." A soldier rushed forward in a raggedy uniform not characteristic of how such a high-ranking officer normally appeared. Reilly's face was covered in hair, but his scalp remained bald.

"We were afraid you were sent by the assholes who left us here to die." He exchanged a handshake with Perez, then turned to the screen. "I take it this broadcast is your handy work."

"Sort of." Perez held up a finger and called out to Aralyn, still covering them from the hallway. "Colonel, we have a roomful of survivors."

Major Reilly's eyes widened to see Aralyn. "I'll be damned, I guess the traitors have returned. However, I can see now who the *real* traitors are." He pointed to the screen. "Looks like you were right all along, Colonel. I'm sorry I doubted you."

Aralyn nodded. "Do you have any wounded?"

He gestured to his group. "Our severely injured we had to put down when this mess started, to keep them from infecting the rest of us. We've been through a lot, but we're far from licked. There's one civilian who has a limp, but he's still self-sufficient and mobile enough. You get us out of here, and we'll do whatever you need."

Someone screamed from the hall.

Trish heard a mighty roar and the sounds of a scuffle. The First Sergeant shouted for Corporal Leonard, his voice garbled.

She raced out with the others, but not fast enough. When the door opened, both men were gone.

First Sergeant Stevens sprinted through the corridor after two creatures who had a hold on his young corporal. One wore shredded black scrubs, the other was in a red-stained, off-white lab coat. He raised his weapon a few times, but each time, Leonard's body was moved in the way, blocking a clear shot. These ugly sonsofbitches were clever, no doubt about it.

Entering the swimming pool area, First Sergeant Stevens trained his weapon and fired multiple times at the departing figures, finally taking down the foe in the lab coat. The creature with his claws around Leonard smacked the struggling corporal several more times until he fell still. He tossed Leonard easily onto his burly shoulder and continued toward the locker-room. The door burst open, sending three other disfigured beasts out, all in ripped and filthy custodial uniforms. The one holding Leonard dropped him to the ground like a rag-doll and whirled to face Stevens.

Stevens's pulse raced. He shifted his footing and ran along the edge of the pool. He hoped the hideous monsters couldn't swim. Three creatures circled around the far end of the pool, away from where Leonard lay. Raising his rifle, he flipped the ammo to grenade function and pulled the trigger, hitting one dead center with a massive explosion. The impact scattered chunks of flesh, bone, and bloody bits of innards, with the head and some limbs splashing into the water.

The two others were both knocked off their feet, smashed sideways into a robust tree inside a planter box. The impact snapped the fifteen-foot growth like a twig, and a creature rolled to the ground behind it while the other beast landed a few feet away.

First Sergeant Stevens sent two more grenade rounds at them before the mutants had a chance to climb to their feet. A bellow came from the right, a loud roar that echoed off the high ceiling. He spun to take aim as the creature in the shredded scrubs pushed off on all fours, soaring the width of the pool directly at him. He switched to rounds and fired.

Three blows to the creature's chest weren't enough to slow its momentum. It struck the First Sergeant's head and upper body with such force that his helmet was ripped from his suit.

Stevens went flying and crashed into an arrangement of pool furniture. He was unable to take a breath. Blood filled his nose and mouth, and the creature wasn't dead. It landed on his torso and swiped away a chunk of his left ear.

When Stevens looked up, the monster's scream revealed a mouth full of sharp, fierce teeth, ready to bite.

Trish shouted out a cry and pushed herself across the pool deck as fast as her legs could go. Before vicious teeth sank into Steven's flesh she smashed into the creature's chest with brutal impact. Both tumbled away from Stevens and made a giant splash when they hit the water.

Intertwined, they plummeted to the bottom. The creature's arms and legs flailed wildly about, its orange eyes fixed on the surface it couldn't reach.

Wearing the body armor, Trish's movements were restricted, and she struggled. As long as her helmet wasn't pierced, she'd briefly have some air, but how long would that last?

She remembered the very first improvised swimming technique Aralyn had taught her: Don't panic. Apparently, the similarly dense-boned beast hadn't received the same lessons. It sucked in mouthfuls of chlorinated water. Despite being submerged, Trish could hear its vocal outcries as it flailed about.

She shifted and felt for her boot knife. With a tight grip on the shiny weapon, she pressed the tip to the base of the mutant's neck, pushed it in and twisted. The creature convulsed through the water for a few seconds, then fell still, dying with its head raised and eyes open as if drifting into the afterlife in search of air. Blood bloomed around the wound.

Trish yanked out her knife and sheathed it, backing up fast. She knew she would need both hands free, and she wanted to get away from the creature's disgusting body and blood. She pressed her feet firmly on the pool's bottom and kicked off. When her hand broke the surface, then her head, her helmet took in more air. She used her arms, but after a few fatigued strokes, her dense body combined with the body armor caused her to sink like an anchor. She kicked off the bottom again, angling more toward the pool's edge. She reached for the side, and Aralyn clasped her arm firmly and pulled at her. Perez assisted until Trish was completely on the deck, then he rushed over to help First Sergeant Stevens.

Trish took in gulps of air while Aralyn rubbed her back. "You okay?" Trish nodded.

"Jesus Christ, Trish. Are you trying to give me a heart attack?"

Trish was too weary to answer. She wished she could remove her helmet, but she left it on for the moment. Aralyn helped her to her feet and over to the First Sergeant's side.

Stevens smiled wearily up at her. Seeing the yellowing of his eyes, Trish cried out, "No," and dropped to her knees beside him.

He squeezed her arm. "You did good, kid. I was the one who wasn't fast enough. Ugly brute got my ear before you guys showed." He averted his eyes to meet Aralyn's gaze. Trish saw how fast they were turning orange. "Is the boy all right?" he asked. "Leonard got hit pretty hard."

Aralyn waved across the pool to Susan, who was examining Corporal Leonard as Strong clasped the kid's limp hand in hers. Susan's eyes were full of tears. She shook her head and turned mournfully away.

Aralyn became all business. In a command voice, she said, "He's fine, First Sergeant. It'd take more than an ugly beast to bring that boy down. You've taught him well."

Stevens eyes showed relief, and he gave a weak salute. "It's been an honor serving under you, Colonel. You're the best—"

His words ended with a low-vocal rumbling. His eyes widened in fear, then narrowed. He glared at the colonel, as if she were an enemy he was seeing for the first time.

Before Stevens could transform and react, Sergeant Perez slammed a blade through his ear.

Trish went numb, shock setting in so fast that it felt like physical pain. She closed her eyes and fought the anguish slashing at her heart.

This mission had cost them dearly. Maybe going to Colorado Springs tomorrow wasn't the best idea after all.

Aralyn gave her team the time they needed to recover from the horrors they'd just experienced. Since First Sergeant was infected, Trish handled placing Stevens in the body bag, as Perez and Susan unfurled a bag for Leonard, and they packed the corporal inside. After a while, they formed up and tried to summon enough energy to lead out the fifty or so refugees they'd just picked up.

Trish remained in a defensive position beside Perez, as Major Reilly lead out the last of the survivors from the elevators with the body bags in tow. Aralyn nodded once they were lined up and the children settled. Trish took the lead, not wanting to see the plastic shapes of their two lifeless fallen any longer than she had too. The view was painful. She noticed how Perez kept his gaze off as well.

Before reaching the first of the reinforced exit doors, Trish felt her insides spark with warning. She stopped, dropped to a knee, and removed her helmet.

Perez moved up beside her. "What's wrong? Is it the creatures?"

Trish lifted her head slightly, trying to gain a better understanding of this new sensation. "No, it's something else." She peeked over her shoulder to see Aralyn approaching. She waited until Aralyn drew closer. "I'm not sure what I'm picking up, but it isn't good," Trish said.

Aralyn opened her comms. "Lieutenant Strong, Lieutenant Travis, take these people to the garage and search for any remaining vehicles. We'll make sure the tunnel's clear."

Christina closed her eyes tight to the sound of Givens's grunting. If she'd listened to him when the soldiers first repelled down from the helicopter, and gone into NORAD to warn the others, they might not have been captured in the first place. Givens had already killed two before a soldier snuck up behind Christina's position and grabbed her, forcing Givens to drop his weapon to save her life. Now, he was paying the price for her obstinacy.

A soldier sent a right cross, then a jab into Givens's battered face.

"Damnit leave him alone," Christina shouted, struggling a few feet away.

The soldier directly in front of her brought a second backhand across her cheek. If it hadn't been for the captor holding her shoulders, Christina would have gone from a kneeling position, straight to the ground.

She spat a mouthful of metallic-tasting blood onto the pavement by the guard's feet. "You're a coward. You all are." She struggled against the restraints binding her hands together behind her. She rattled out a list of Spanish cusswords, her mind fuming with anger.

The guard beside her laughed. "You've got a filthy mouth on you, girly. A pretty one at that," he said. He brought a hand up and stroked her cheek. He screamed when Christina bit down on his index finger.

He reared back to slap her again, but the hand of a superior officer stopped him. "Rodriguez, go check on the camera. You guys, that's enough for now. Doctor Webber still needs to ask them some questions before you beat 'em unconscious."

Rodriguez sketched a brief salute. "Yes, Major." He hurried away.

The major—Porter according to his uniform name tag—signaled to an idling helicopter across the empty parking lot.

Christina turned her head, trying to see past their vehicles. When a towering gentleman in an expensive suit emerged from the chopper, she knew at once he was Trish's father. They had the same sharp, blue eyes, the same broad build and height, yet he was less muscular considering he was male.

He carried himself with a boastful type of confidence, which suggested he wasn't a man to tangle with. When he examined her, she saw an unmistakable difference between him and his daughter. His blue eyes held no kindness like Trish's did. Not one speck of empathy. They were dark, with a distinguished degree of animosity.

Trish's father came to a stop in front of Givens, who lay bleeding on the ground and held there by a soldier. Frank Webber fixed his icy stare on the good eye not yet swollen shut. "Sergeant, why did Aralyn return to NORAD? What exactly are you searching for, and why would she risk bringing my daughter with her?"

With a sigh of boredom, Givens angled his head away.

Trish's father exchanged a look with the soldier holding Givens, and the full force of the soldier's hardened fist crashed into Givens's jaw.

Christina jerked against the hands holding her and screamed, "Stop, you'll kill him! Stop, please stop!"

Trish's father held up a hand, halting the next blow. He took a step toward her and studied her to the point Christina grew uncomfortable. As difficult as it was to stare into eyes holding such malice, she refused to avert her glare.

"Sir, I wouldn't get too close to this one," said the soldier restraining her. "She's got some fight to her."

Frank didn't take his eyes away. He continued to analyze her, tilting his head in the process. "I don't believe she'll do anything. She appears quite intelligent, can't you see. She knows if she displeases me in any way, her friend here will be killed."

Fighting against her own defiance, Christina lowered her eyes.

"Now you see, we're making progress." He gripped Christina's shoulder. "You tell me what I need to know, and I'll let you live. Hell, I'll let your entire group stroll out of here. Except not Aralyn. She must die. But you, your bleeding friend here, those inside, you can all go. I only want my daughter."

Christina's gaze shot upward. "You'll never touch her again, do you understand? Never." She pulled hard against her captor, with an anger growing inside unlike anything she had ever experienced before.

Frank's sudden scowl slowly softened. "Interesting," he said, rising to his feet and stepping away. "How exactly do you know my daughter?" His voice was low, his back facing her. When he wheeled around, his glare was probing. She diverted her eyes for fear of what he would see. She did not want him to know of the love she held for his daughter. Trish was right, this man would use this against Trish, and Christina wasn't about to let him.

Frank's hands seized the front of her bodysuit, and he lifted her off her feet. His cold eyes were so close, inches from her own, and she could hardly bear to look into them.

"It seems Aralyn's influence has tainted my daughter in more ways than one. So, you're her *lover*. Tell me, sweet child, does my daughter care deeply for you?"

Rodriguez rushed forward, out of breath and holding a tablet. "Sir, three people are moving through the tunnel, heading in our direction. One is a tall, black woman, just like you described."

"Aralyn," Frank growled. He released Christina and she stumbled but held her ground as the captor behind her grabbed her again. Frank spun toward the dimly-lit entryway.

"Sir, another intruder resembles your daughter, Patricia."

Frank's grin widened, but it wasn't with the pleasure of a loving father about to be reunited with a daughter he hadn't seen in months and whom he thought had died. No, his excitement was evil, disturbing. Christina's fear increased. The thought of Trish being this man's prisoner was more than she could bear. She kicked a foot backwards, striking the man behind her in the knee. He cried out in pain and his hold on her vanished.

She jerked forward and took in a lungful of air. "Trish, run! It's your father—run!"

An impact to her cheek felt like a broad-swinging hammer-blow. Her head snapped and her knees buckled. She dropped to the asphalt, tasting fresh blood in her mouth. She knew she was injured badly now since every part of her from the neck up was ablaze with pain. Seeing the movement farther in the tunnel, she blinked rapidly, trying to clear her blurry vision.

"Trish, no," she heard Aralyn shout. Christina's eyesight wasn't improving fast enough.

"Get away from her!"

Christina's heart raced at the sound of Trish's voice. She fought to get to her knees, shaking her head for clarity. Her eyes widened in horror as Major Porter and the other four of Frank's men advanced, weapons pointed at Trish.

"No," Christina screamed in panic. She struggled to get to her feet. Maybe she could rush forward and knock a few off-guard, distract the others, to give Trish a fighting chance. Screw her own life—what mattered was saving Trish.

A hand grasped a fist full of her hair and yanked her onto her butt. The shooting pain on her tailbone was great, but not as painful as the look of fear on Trish's face. She smelled the cloying cologne Frank Webber wore and tried to break free of him, but Frank's grip was so strong she couldn't. Cold metal pressed into her temple, and she knew Frank held a gun to her head. Her tears fell, knowing her time was over. Would she see Trish again in the next life? Was there even something better after this?

"You love her, don't you?" Frank Webber said to his daughter. Trish froze, her face drenched with fury. Why wasn't Trish wearing her helmet?

Seeing Trish so close to harm nearly broke Christina's heart. She had to do something, anything. She closed her eyes and prayed to whomever was listening to keep her mother and father safe. To watch over Trish and allow her to find happiness in this world full of grief and danger. When she opened her eyes, Trish stared at her, her face white, eyes searching as if she was trying to decide what to do.

Christina mouthed, "I'm sorry. I love you." She planted a foot, preparing to push away from Frank's grasp. She knew the movement would end with a bullet in her head, but she was ready.

"No," Trish cried out, taking a step forward.

Suddenly, Trish's eyes closed, and her body jerked. The way she moved, almost lifeless, but with purpose, as if she were a puppet on invisible strings, frightened Christina. Trish's entire body seemed to almost ripple. Christina stopped straining, unsure of what she was seeing, like someone or something had entered Trish, controlling her every move.

The strange spectacle changed, and Christina saw red lines slide down Trish's jawline. Her heart skipped a beat. Blood. Had she been shot? But Christina hadn't heard any weapons go off.

Trish raised a hand, and the amount of blood trickling out from each ear steadily increased.

The gun was no longer against her skin, and Frank had loosened his grip. Desperate, she wiggled to get free. "Trish, stop whatever you're doing. It's killing you."

More blood formed around Trish's nose, and Christina was almost certain a line of redness was developing under Trish's squinted eyelids. Her heart raced. She needed to stop this. Aralyn, where was Aralyn?

Before she could get free, everything happened all at once. The men dropped their weapons and fell to their knees, hands over their ears, as if hearing a high-pitched noise Christina herself could not hear. An invisible force knocked her onto her back, an energy force like a flash of lightning, which sucked the air from her chest. She rolled to the side, blinking and dizzy, and tried and failed get up. In amazement, she realized the binding around her wrists was gone.

Nearby, Givens rolled onto his side, as if in a daze. Trish's father was nowhere in sight. A puddle of blood was on the ground where he'd been standing, but he himself had disappeared.

When she sat up, she saw the soldiers lying on the ground, their weapons melted. Every orifice in their heads spilled blood, their heads were distended, and their eyes bulged out. They hardly looked human. She scrunched up her nose with the sudden urge to vomit and she averted her gaze.

Their vehicles were still parked nearby, but the helicopter was gone like it had disappeared into thin air. She hadn't heard it leave.

Swaying, she climbed to her feet and stood, off balance, shifting her feet to keep from falling.

From the mouth of the tunnel, a voice shouted, "Trish!" and a body tore into a sprint drawing closer.

The desperation of Aralyn's scream turned the warm blood in Christina's veins to ice. When she saw Trish lying motionless on the asphalt, a lump in her throat turned solid, preventing any air from leaving.

She staggered forward, trying to shout out Trish's name, but no sound emerged. Aralyn skidded to a stop beside the still body and checked for a pulse. She began applying chest compressions.

Christina fell to her hands and knees next to Aralyn. Tears spilled down her cheeks, and she touched Trish's red-stained throat. Where was her pulse? So much blood covered Trish's hair, face, neck, and pooled onto the pavement beneath her.

Christina shook the lifeless body but to no avail.

Their ending was not supposed to happen this way. Christina closed her eyes, dropped her head back, and finally her throat allowed the release of a built-up scream that ended in hopelessness.

CHAPTER TWENTY-ONE

Trish opened her eyes and tried to focus past the blur. Each time she blinked, her eyelids felt pasty as they pulled apart. She brought a weak hand up and wiped at each eye, feeling a gel beneath her fingertips, an ointment of some kind, and the more she removed, the better she could see.

The room was dark, yet her eyes adjusted enough to reveal various medical supplies lining the shelves and equipment hanging from the walls.

Her hands brushed a plastic item coming from her left nostril. Confused, she explored the thin line. Tape secured it in place before it continued around her ear and down toward her chest. Her stomach clenched and her breathing quickened. She was fairly sure she knew the item was a feeding tube.

Where was she? Despite the medical supplies, this place didn't feel like a hospital. Was she in her father's lab? She wracked her brain, searching for a memory to give clarity to her spinning mind.

A vision flooded in of Christina clutched in her father's arms with a pistol pressed to her head. Her father? Where had he come from? She glanced from one end of the room to the other, but he was nowhere in sight.

She tried to move, but her body wouldn't cooperate. Instead, she opened her mouth to speak, to call for the woman she loved, but a croaking noise emerged. Her throat was tight, rough. Like someone had

THE PURIFICATION | 293

cleaned out her esophagus with coarse sandpaper before depositing her in the darkened room.

Frantically, she dug a fingernail under the tape on her face, peeling the stickiness away. Her nails were longer than normal, and they cut into her lip as she worked at removing the foreign item from her body. Once freed, she tossed the long snakish tube away from her and tried to sit up. She couldn't move her legs or torso.

Surveying her body, she thought she lay under a sheet and a single blanket. The air was warm. She felt a little sweaty.

Some sort of clasp secured her in place on an unusual bed. Not a normal hospital bed or a hard lab table her father used. Her body was sunken into a soft blue vibrating foam. In her shoulders, legs, back, and neck she felt a minor throbbing, almost as if the bed were caressing her body.

She reached down and fumbled for a moment until the clasp broke free and dangled over the side. Something released slightly, and she was able to throw off the bedding and wrest one leg out of the pulsing foam. She dropped a leg over the edge, then the other, and used the momentum of her lower body to tumble from the bed.

Her knees struck tiled ground first, shooting a pain up both thighs to her hips. Landing on her stomach, she cried out, but only a wisp of a sound left her throat. She lay shaking on the ground for what felt like an hour, but then she thought she might have passed out for a while. She pressed her forehead against the cold floor and steadied her raspy breathing.

When she felt clear-headed again, she realized her feet were bare and all she wore was a hospital gown with the back open. She also noticed a clear tube sticking out of her arm and yanked on the taped section of the setup to remove it from her body. Blood followed, but not enough for concern.

She didn't pick up on the sporadic beeping above her until it was too late. The door behind her flew open, sending in additional light. Someone flipped on the switch, and the room flooded with brightness, stinging her eyes. She clenched her fists tight and wormed her body under the bed.

"My god, you're awake," someone said in wonderment. The raspy voice came from a woman who was either a smoker or in her later years of life. Or both. Trish felt movement behind her, and when the person touched her, Trish jerked away. Her throat released a croak, and she searched the floor for anything she could use as a weapon.

"Honey, I'm not going to hurt you. You're safe here."

A slight pause followed. Soon after, a soft material, maybe the same blanket, covered her. Trish gripped the edge of it and shielded her eyes.

The lights turned off, but the door remained open. Trish blinked against the reduced glow. A woman came into view and squatted down next to her. She was aged, with gray hair and a caring face. She smiled, revealing an added gentleness. Trish found it hard not to let her guard down with the kindness in the woman's eyes.

The woman frowned and pointed at Trish's arm. "Dear, you're bleeding. Would you mind if I dress that? I promise not to hurt you."

Trish stared at her for a moment, then nodded. The woman rose and moved over to a counter.

Trish watched her and shifted around, trying to figure out how to get her feet under her. Finding the slightest movement difficult, she slowly made it onto her side, still partially under the bed-like contraption. She felt exhausted and out of breath.

Holding some gauze and tape, the woman turned and clicked her tongue to the roof of her mouth. "You need to take things slow. You really shouldn't be out of bed yet. With long-term comas, your muscles are in a weakened state. I don't know how I'll get you off the floor."

Trish's eyes widened. Long-term comas? She's been in a coma? For how long exactly? She opened her mouth to speak, but a slight croak sounded.

"Let me put some disinfectant there, and after I bandage you up, then I'll give you something for your throat. Once I manage to get you in bed that is. I'll also need to call Doctor Burgos to let him know you're awake."

Trish's pulse settled at the name. She must be in Rapid City, but where exactly? This didn't look like Doctor Burgos's lab or a hospital room. Trish's eyes squinted past the crouched woman patiently cleaning her arm. She spotted a banister heading down to a lower level, and a memory clicked. She was in the house Doctor Burgos used for his lab but across the hall from where he usually worked. She was sure of it. She took a deep breath and relaxed even more.

She wanted to ask about Christina. Was she safe? Was she in her parent's house next door? What about the others? Her voice wouldn't cooperate, so she waited.

"There you go. Now, let's stand you up, and I'll fix you something to sip on after you're safely in bed."

Trish shook her head forcefully. She was not about to be trapped in that bed for one more second. She pointed to a chair sitting against the wall by the door.

The woman sighed. "Fine, for a little bit. At least until I reach Doctor Burgos, okay? Let's see if we can manage this without help . . ."

Thankful, Trish signaled her agreement. She knew Doctor Burgos wouldn't force her to get into bed. Christina might, and to see her face, just to know she was safe, Trish would do anything.

The struggle to get to her feet wasn't as hard as remaining upright. She shuffled with the help of the woman, whom she assumed by her scrubs and the way she cared for Trish, was either a nurse or an aide. Trish halted when she was a few feet away from the chair. Her hand came down to her waistline and she scrunched her nose. She squeezed on material under her gown and smelled the pungent odor of urine.

"Almost there, dear. A few more steps and you'll be able to rest."

Trish tapped the nurse on the arm and pointed to her abdomen.

"Did you have an accident? Don't worry, perfectly natural. That's what the briefs are for, dear."

Trish shook her head again, and this time she rolled her eyes. She made a motion signaling for a pen. The woman's understanding was etched in her upbeat manner. "What a great idea. Let's get you seated, and I'll find something for you to write on."

Trish shook her head and pointed to the ground.

"You want to wait here?"

Trish nodded.

The woman wasn't pleased with the plan. "You're not stable enough—"

This time, Trish scowled when she pointed to the ground.

The nurse shrugged. "Okay, hold on to the bed, and I'll be super quick. For the record, if nobody has ever told you, you're a stubborn woman."

Trish smiled. Her caregiver left the room but returned in less than a minute. She handed over a pad and pen, and Trish wrote out a list of names with the word *safe* followed by a question mark. She handed the list over and, curious, watched her helper scan it. With the slow way the woman's head shook, Trish's stomach convulsed. She tasted bile at the back of her throat.

"I'm sorry, dear. I'm not sure of these names except for Colonel Williams, and she's fine. She was here earlier with some other people." She gave the notepad to Trish. "I arrived in the city a month ago with a group of friends, so everyone's new to me. We were living in a bunker close to Grand Forks, North Dakota."

Feeling a great sense of relief, Trish took the pen and added Burgos after Christina's name. She held her breath and waited.

"Oh, yes, that's Doctor Burgos's daughter. Beautiful woman. She was here, too. She was going to a party with her parents and Colonel Williams."

Trish released her breath. She knew she was on the verge of tears. She then scribbled some more and passed it over. The nurse read the note and laughed. She put the pad and pen on the bed and again, she left the room. When she returned, she held a dark blue sweat outfit and a pair of ugly yellow socks. "You don't strike me as the type to wear gowns, hospital or otherwise." She helped Trish remove the gown and adult briefs, before putting on the baggy sweat outfit.

"You're already moving much better." She helped Trish into the chair and assisted Trish with slipping on her socks, then fetched the pad and pen. "Now, is there anything else you need before I go call Doctor Burgos?"

Trish ran a hand over her throat.

"Silly me, of course." She went to a mini fridge and removed a clear bottle containing a thick, pink liquid. While the nurse filled a cup, Trish set the pad against the arm of the chair and made some circles on the page around the word party with several question marks. When the woman handed her the drink, Trish gave her the notepad.

Trish slowly sipped the sweetened beverage. The chilled thickness coated her throat as it went down, soothing the dry scratchiness. She cleared her throat before taking in some more.

"Party? Oh, I get it. You're asking what party they were going to. I believe it was Doctor Burgos's granddaughter's birthday party."

Trish almost choked on the drink. The nurse patted her gently and continued. "Christina's daughter—it's her birthday today."

Trish snatched the pad with trembling hands. The woman grabbed the drink before it fell to the floor. She wrote as quickly as her hand would allow and rotated the pad so the woman could read it. "Christina has a daughter? How long have I been in a coma? Is she married?"

The woman read each question carefully. "Yes, she has a daughter. I'm not sure if she's married. Like I said before, I haven't been here long, but from how it sounded earlier, she is most definitely living with someone. As far as your coma, several years have gone by, I believe, but I'm not exactly sure about how many. I usually work in the hospital. I'm filling in here for the night nurse. She had a cold and Doctor Burgos said his daughter wouldn't let her come near you with a fever."

When the pad hit the floor, the nurse jumped slightly. Trish covered her eyes and allowed tears to fall.

"Oh, my." The nurse patted her arm. "Listen, I'm calling Doctor Burgos to let him know you're awake. He can answer any questions you might have. I should've called the moment you woke, he was adamant about this before they left."

While she was gone, Trish's body shook with a mixture of different emotions. All were raw, painful, making it harder and harder for her to breathe. The room was stifling, claustrophobic, and she needed fresh air. She used her trembling arms to raise herself to her feet. Guiding herself along the wall for support, she left the room and headed to the stairs. She wiped at the tears stinging her swollen eyes, but her effort was futile. More tears fell in their place.

Carefully, she shifted her weight to the railing, and made her way down, taking one step at a time. Reaching the bottom step, sweat rolled from her brow, mixing with her tears. She felt the dampened sweatshirt cling to her chest and neck, making it harder to breath. She fumbled with a deadbolt. As soon as the door opened, she tumbled out onto a wooden porch in the darkness. She dropped to her hands and knees, feeling bitter cold engulf her body.

Snow mounds were piled up between the shoveled walkway and blanketed the street in drifts over a foot deep. She glanced up to a streetlight. Clusters of flakes were falling.

This was it, her first sight and touch of actual snow. All the Christmases she'd experienced, living the long years inside the bunker, she had pictured what this encounter would be like. A broken heart was never a part of it. She realized this first experience would ruin every winter she would ever live through, from here on out. She climbed to her feet and closed the door behind her. She needed to go, to leave this place before Christina returned, with or without the person who now had her heart. She wasn't ready to add to the razor-sharp ache she was feeling. Their reunion would surely kill her.

Doctor Burgos inserted an earpiece and activated the handheld. Christina watched his expression change from excited grandpa to all business. He moved away from the partygoers, either to hear better or to keep from being heard. Frowning, she removed the knife from the cake and handed it to her mother.

"Christina, what's the matter?" Aralyn asked, removing a party hat from her own head.

Christina didn't respond, ignoring those around her. Something was wrong. She knew it, could feel it. Her father's upset appearance had to do with Trish, but it couldn't be . . . no, anything but *that*. Trish had held on for so long, she was a fighter, and her life couldn't end like this, especially not at a birthday party with everyone she knew, soldiers and civilians alike, in attendance.

Christina sidestepped around a group of children on the floor and rushed into the living room. When her father saw her, he turned away.

With damp eyes, she stopped and braced herself for the news. She felt arms around her from behind. Susan whispered softly, "I'm sure everything's fine."

Christina could tell Susan also knew what was coming, and that knowledge made her hands shake.

Her father ended the call and faced them. "Trish is awake."

She gasped, unsure how she managed to stay on her feet. *Trish is awake. Trish is awake.* She kept hearing her father's voice over and over as if the three simple words were a foreign language and she was trying hard to decipher their meaning.

Susan and those around her cheered and shouted out their prayers of happiness, and Christina broke down, crying and laughing at the same time.

"Trish is awake." The words she spoke now had meaning. She ran to the closet by the stairwell and grabbed her winter coat. She didn't bother to button it. Her eyes found her mother.

Eva came to her and fiddled with the coat's buttons. "Don't worry. I'll wait here and hold down the fort. If you end up staying the night, tell your father to pack us an overnight bag. We'll sleep here at your place as long as you need."

She gave her mother a hug, but everything came to a screeching halt when her father said, "Hang on. Trish is missing. The nurse is searching each floor for her now, but she thinks maybe Trish left the lab altogether."

Christina spun, facing her father. "Missing? How? Dad, it's fourteen degrees outside and freezing ice is on the way." Christina rushed to the door. "She only had to watch her for a few hours."

Aralyn called out, "Christina, wait! You can ride with us—"

But Christina opened the door and hurried outside and never heard the rest.

She was two blocks away and stumbling around in the snow when Givens pulled up beside her. With several more blocks left to go, Susan didn't have to tell her twice to get her foolish butt in the vehicle. Two more Gladiators were following, carrying several members of Major Thomas's and Lieutenant O'Brian's teams.

At her parents' house, Christina jumped out before the vehicle came to a full stop. She ran through the walkway to her father's lab, hunting for any signs of footprints. With the heavy snowfall, no tracks were visible.

At the top of the steps to her father's lab the door opened. The nurse looked ragged and on edge. "I've searched all throughout the house, but I couldn't find her anywhere."

Moving past the woman, Christina clenched her jaw and ran up to the next level. She entered the room where Trish should have been, and found the compression bed left empty, with the sheet crumpled on the ground. Her heart sank.

Her foot kicked something, sending it to roll against the chair beside the door. She peered down to see a pen, then spotted a notepad which she picked up and read. She took in the list of names by the word *safe* and a question mark. Her hand covered her mouth. Trish woke up worried about everyone's safety, yet no one was here to greet her.

She read how Trish asked for something to wear other than "a dress and a diaper." Christina's eyes watered but she also laughed. This sounded so very much like Trish.

She traced the word *party* with her finger. Trish's next three questions made her heart race and her palms sweat. *Christina has a daughter? How long have I been in a coma? Is she married?*

Clutching the notepad, Christina rushed downstairs, taking two steps at a time. She held out the pad to the woman. "How did you answer these questions?"

The nurse stared at the notepad and then at Christina. She opened her mouth but didn't speak. Fuming with worry, Christina shouted, "What did you say to her?"

"Christina." Her father's tone was filled with an unspoken warning.

"No, father. She needs to answer my question."

"Um, I told her you had a daughter, and today was her birthday. I wasn't sure if you were married, but I thought you were living with someone, and—" she glimpsed at the pad "—and I told her she was in a coma for several years, but I wasn't sure exactly how long, since I'm new to this city."

Christina frowned to Aralyn and Susan. "Trish left because she thinks I'm with someone else." She turned to the woman. "Did you tell her my daughter's name or age?"

The woman's head shook. "She didn't ask, and I wouldn't know either of those questions if she had."

"But you told her I was in a relationship."

"Yes, but because she asked. You and your father were talking earlier about how you were waiting for your partner to come home. Naturally, I assumed you were with someone, and with a child, that added to it. Did I say something wrong?"

Christina threw the pad on the ground and made her way out the door. At this moment, the thought of forgiving herself for not being here was miles away.

"Where are you going?" Susan hollered after her.

"To find Trish before she tries to climb over the damn wall."

With a shaking hand, Trish twisted the door handle. Her entire body was drenched in a frozen wetness from slipping around in the snow to make it here. Her feet, clad only in socks, felt like chunks of ice. Damn, the door was locked. She tried it again, but still it refused to turn. She wasn't sure where her keys were, but everything else she owned was behind this door. She needed to get in. If she busted it down, would Aralyn be mad? Did she have enough strength left to even breach the barrier?

When the door swung open, she took a few steps backwards. The eyes that met hers were tired and annoyed. "I have guard duty in less than four hours. What the hell do you want?"

Trish glanced around, worried she had the wrong room.

"You've got to be shitting me. It's you." The man rubbed at his eyes and took a step forward. Trish squinted, studying his face closer. "Do you know how much trouble we got into because of you?" The clean-shaven man marched from his room and went to the next apartment over. He pounded forcefully on the door.

Trish's eyes widened at the recollection of who he was. Scruffy-beard from NORAD. No facial hair, no smirk above his square chin, just an angry man in boxers and a T-shirt. Trish rubbed the spot on her forehead where the gash had once stood. John, that was his name. He was with a woman and another guy at the pool when she was injured.

Trish rushed inside her room as the man called out for his neighbor. She stopped right at the opening. Everything was different, messy, and nothing belonged to her. What was happening? Had she been erased from existence? She bolted to the closet and searched along the top shelf.

"Hey, what are you doing! Get out of my room!"

Trish turned, seeing John and his buddy from the pool standing in the doorway staring at her. Crap, she was trapped. "Move out of the way, and I'll leave," Trish croaked.

John squared his shoulders. "What are you doing here, this building is for soldiers."

"This is my room, or it used to be." Her head spun. Where was her mother's jewelry box, the locket, all her things? Did no one, Aralyn, Christina, Susan, anticipate she would wake? Why had they kept her on a feeding tube and fluids for so long if they didn't expect her to pull through? She was forgotten. The woman she loved, the family she had, everything was gone. Taken from her during the years she spent in a coma. Yes, she wanted Christina to be happy, for everyone to move on, but not until she died. And she hadn't died.

Exactly how many years had she been asleep in that godforsaken bed?

Her breaths became short and raspy. She put her hands on her knees and closed her eyes. When someone forcefully grabbed her arm, she balled up a fist and sent a jab straight into John's nose. He cried out, and Trish tackled his friend guarding the door. They both stumbled out onto the hallway. Their commotion sent additional sets of eyes and shouts their way.

Without waiting, Trish took off, heading to the stairs, wishing to be as far away from this building, these people, this city as she could get. The entire place was closing in on her, driving her to the point where she couldn't cope. Her thoughts, emotions, her life was suffocating her, preventing her from thinking about anything, yet spilling over to the point of drowning her sanity. Maybe she could make it to New Underwood before freezing to death or losing her fingers and toes to frostbite. Either way, she was sure going to try.

"Hey, someone stop her!" The shout came from behind. She hurriedly crossed the threshold of the old hotel, heading out into the bitter cold. She slid a few inches, correcting her balance right before hitting the circle drive.

She broke into a shambling run, a stitch in her side screaming as her lungs took in gulps of the frigid air. Saying she was out of shape would have been an understatement. Her entire body felt as if every part had physically wasted away, leaving nothing more than bones and skin keeping her upright. Every muscle burned. Her stomach cramped against her brisk movements, but she couldn't stop. If she did, she would perish from the pain of losing the life she'd had.

Trish saw a guard standing on the walkway between the two towers, and another entering the tower base on the left side. She pushed hard, aiming straight for the right tower. When she was but a few feet away, something, or someone, struck her hard. She fell face first into the snow. The impact was more pain than her body could handle. She let out a cry, trying hard to get her bearings. The same person that collided into her pulled her up onto her knees, uncontested. She was too weak to struggle.

"What the hell are you guys doing?" The female guard from the walkway shouted down, but Trish didn't look up. Her head was too heavy to lift that high. The one holding her upright jerked her around, toward the figure approaching. John wore his camouflaged uniform, his pants left untucked, and his boots unlaced. He had his coat on, but it wasn't fastened, as if he hurriedly threw on what he could before running out after her.

Streaks of blood covered his chin and most of his mouth, but his nose was no longer bleeding. Trish saw just how pissed off he was.

"You punched me," he said, drawing closer.

"Karma's a bitch, isn't it," Trish replied, managing a weak smile.

"Wanna see Karma? I'll show you Karma." John reared back and punched her in the face.

Trish's head snapped and she grunted against the blow. He sent another fist to her other side and was gearing up for a third. At the sound of a gun cocking, he stopped. Trish was scarcely able to lift her head, but when she did, the view of the person with the gun surprised her. Red hair pulled in a bun behind her cap, rifle raised, pointing right at John. She was the same woman Trish saw the day Christina first kissed her, the one who kept winking at Christina on the hillside. She wanted to laugh at Karma herself but didn't have the strength. Instead, she spit out a mouthful of blood.

"What the hell are you doing, Corporal? I outrank you," John angrily announced.

"Yes Sergeant, you do. But she outranks us both. You and your friend happen to be assaulting one of our officers."

Before John could say another word, headlights flashed to Trish's right, and she heard the sound of tires crunching to a stop against the snow.

A voice shouted, "Get away from her!"

Christina. That voice came from Christina.

Trish tried to bring her head up, but her body refused to cooperate. It had already given her everything it had at its disposal and then some. When the hands clutching her shoulders released her, she dropped straight to the snow.

"Corporal, lower your weapon," Aralyn said in her most commanding tone. "I want everyone to back away now. Sergeant Givens, let go of his throat."

Trish's tears mixed with her blood in the snow. She didn't want to see them, all these people from her past, but she was so happy they were here. She was beyond weary, but the cold feel of the snow seemed to help. She needed to close her eyelids for just a moment, if only to ease how heavy they were. She heard others around her speaking, until finally, her world went dark.

CHAPTER TWENTY-TWO

Trish opened her eyes to the sun's rays poking in past curtains hanging over two casement windows. The king-sized bed was soft, and a pale blue, down comforter covered her body up to her neck. The walls were also a pale blue with a bright white trim around the baseboards, matching cheerfully with each door. She was in a real bedroom, not a hospital bed.

The spot in the bed beside her had been slept in by someone recently, with indentations still left on the pillow. Rolling over renewed the ache she felt throughout her body. She inhaled deeply the fragrance of the one who had left her bed. *Christina.* Confused, Trish breathed in again, trying to confirm what her mind was telling her.

"Pillows are nice, but I can guarantee smelling the real woman is so much better."

Startled, Trish's face felt a wave of heat. Spotting Christina standing in the doorway smiling, Trish's bottom lip quivered. She averted her watering eyes, closed them, and tried to force down the uncomfortable lump forming in her throat.

"Listen, my beautiful woman, this is not a morning for crying." Christina moved to the bed and crawled under the blankets. She held Trish in her arms as more tears fell. "My love, please stop. There's no reason for you to hurt like this. Everything you were told has been nothing more than mistaken information."

The sound of tiny feet running through the room caught in her ears. An intruder jumped onto the bed, and one of Christina's arms broke free. "Jennifer, what did we talk about last night? You need to be careful around Trish for a while until she gets her strength back."

A hand touched her cheek, and Trish opened her eyes. Jennifer's big round eyes held worry. "Did I hurt you?" she asked, her eyes glistening as she waited for a response.

Seeing the girl's face brought so many pleasant memories, but the child didn't look exactly the same as sweet little Jennifer. This girl was bigger. More solid. Her hair was longer, and her face had changed from its lost, waifish appearance to filled out and healthy.

Trish said, "I'm okay," and raised the covers so the child could crawl under, between her and Christina. She held Jennifer in her arms as Christina held on to them both. When their eyes met, Christina kissed Trish's forehead.

Trish had to swallow a few times before she was able to speak. "I don't understand," she whispered, feeling Christina's hand on her cheek. She opened her mouth to continue, but no words came out.

"First off, it's November the second, 2089. You've been in a coma for fifteen months, and since then, a lot has happened."

Trish tried to take this in. Fifteen months. Wow. No wonder Jennifer looked different. She'd grown.

Christina said, "Jennifer, you know the breakfast you made me yesterday? Do you think you could go make Trish the same thing?"

"Sure!" Excited, Jennifer climbed out of the covers and kissed Trish on the cheek.

When she'd left the room, Christina continued. "Before I go on, I want you to know that if there's anything you don't like about these arrangements, you're not obligated to any of this."

Trish frowned. "What do you mean? If I'm staying with you and someone else, then no. I'm sorry, but I can't do it."

"Even if the other person is Jennifer?"

Trish looked from the door to Christina, still not understanding. "Exactly how many people live here?"

Christina sat against the backboard. "Umm, there's Jennifer, you, and me. Whatever the nurse told you last night, she worked off assumptions. I'd never even met her until she showed up to relieve us for Jennifer's birthday party."

"So, you don't have another child?"

Christina smiled. "I'm not sure how that would be possible. No matter how many times I wanted to climb on the bed and ravish you, you were in a coma. I'm confident you wouldn't have objected, but I'm almost positive, if I'd abandoned my moral judgment and jumped your bones, our ability to reproduce with one another would still be damn near impossible."

Christina was making light of the situation, but Trish still fought the urge to cry. Christina loved her. She hadn't lost her. Christina had been here waiting for her to wake this entire time.

Christina moved closer and wrapped her arms around Trish. "Since the day we first met, there's only been you. No matter how our lives play out, I will never love another."

Trish felt exactly the same way, but she couldn't speak. All she could do was grip Christina more tightly and try not to cry.

"So, on with the next piece of news. After your mother's broadcast aired, those inside many of the bunkers fought their way out and came here, or to Salt Lake City. With the numbers growing, both cities have worked together on cleaning up a city in Missouri and stabilizing the rail-line for travel. When it's complete, many of the newer residents inside both cities will relocate there. Until then, we are standing at over forty-five thousand here, and close to double that in Salt Lake.

"When people started to come in, I found this house for us and had your things moved from the old hotel. FYI, Aralyn and Susan are our neighbors. When adoptions were finally put in place, I hurried to adopt Jennifer, knowing she belonged with us and not strangers. Mom and I opened a restaurant. With you in a coma and Jennifer needing a stable environment, I thought it best not to go out on runs anymore. To be honest, I've never seen Mom happier."

She peered into Trish's eyes. "I understand how overwhelming this must be for you. Like I said before, if you're not comfortable with any of it, or need time to adjust, everyone's on standby to help move you to the old hotel—or to wherever you want to go."

Trish shook her head. "I have the family I've always prayed for. I'm not going anywhere else." Her words were hardly louder than a whisper with her throat tightening at how real and complete life felt. "I love you, Christina."

Christina wiped at her own eyes, then she cleared the dampness from Trish's. Her crying laughter blended with their kisses, making the taste saltier, and sweeter than what Trish remembered.

"I'm finished," said a voice by the door. Trish rubbed her eyes and peered over to Jennifer and the tray swaying in her outstretched arms. Sitting on a folded napkin were two pieces of burnt toast, and beside it a jar of homemade preserves, a saucer of butter, and a glass half full of milk, with the rest of the white liquid sloshing around on the swaying tray.

Christina laughed harder and jumped from the bed to help. "It looks wonderful."

Trish sat up higher against the headboard as they climbed in bed. Jennifer prepared the first slice and passed the smeared jelly, butter, and black toast to her. Trish took a huge bite, savoring the burnt-strawberry flavor. This breakfast was by far the best meal she had ever had.

Christina watched Jennifer throw a snowball at Trish. On impact, Trish fell to the ground and remained still. She knew Trish was performing for her young audience, but she still brought the dishcloth to her chest and held her breath. When Jennifer reached out to touch Trish, the unmoving woman came to life, grabbed the giggling girl in her arms, and rolled around in the snow. Trish made growling noises that sent Jennifer into a fit of struggles and laughter. From inside the house, Christina laughed right along with them.

Twisting off the water, she wrung out the rag and hung it up to dry. She stirred the pot containing her mother's famous homemade chicken and dumpling recipe and inhaled the simmering aroma, knowing this batch was the closest to her mother's masterpiece by far. She opened the stove and inspected the homemade bread. Less than twenty minutes and dinner would be finished.

From the fridge she removed a covered bowl and set it on the counter. Peering out the window, she gave a hearty giggle at the perfect snow angels both her girls were creating. She touched the windowpane. With a lightness in her heart, she turned, heading into the front room, where Adele's, "Someone Like You" followed Shakira's "Hips Don't Lie" on the stereo system. She shook her head with amusement at Trish's odd order on her oldies' playlist.

She took a moment to visually savor the colorful lights on the Christmas tree. She added a few logs to the fireplace and retrieved the box of matches. A knock on the front door rang out before she struck the match. She set the box on the mantel and opened the door, surprised to see Phillips, Aralyn, and her father standing on the enclosed porch.

"Is this a bad time?" Aralyn asked glancing to Christina's apron.

She waved them all inside. "Of course not. The girls are out gathering firewood mixed with snowball fights. With a backyard full of white canvas still to be covered in snow-angels, they might be a while. Would you all like something to drink? I've made more than enough for dinner. I can add some place settings if you want to join us."

With the grave look on each of their faces, Christina's smile receded.

"Actually," her father said, "we've come to talk to Trish. We need to see if she's ready to start training again. With what I've discovered about the creatures, we're hopeful that with her skillset, we'll have a better understanding of what we're facing beyond the walls. Maybe even find a cure or a way to stop the spread."

Christina was beside herself with anger for what her father was suggesting. The three of them, who loved Trish, wanted the best for her, how could they show up like this, asking for what exactly? That Trish continue where she left off before the coma?

She glared at Aralyn. "You're her godmother. Of all the people . . . Is this why Susan isn't here with you? She doesn't agree with this absurd idea, does she?" Christina threw up her hands. "No, Trish is done with it all. After everything she's been through, risking her own life for the people she loves, no. She's earned a retirement from your training, the fighting, all of it."

Phillips said, "Did you tell her about her father? How they never found his body. He may still be alive."

Christina narrowed her eyes. "I want you to leave, now."

"Christina, Trish can decide for herself," Aralyn said, but Christina spun away before she could continue.

She went to the door and threw it open. "She's been awake for six weeks, only six weeks after over a year in bed, and you come here with this. Two weeks before Christmas? No, I'm sorry, but you all need to leave. I'll tell her about her father, but not until after the holidays. This other stuff you want her to do, forget it. She can do runs for the city if she gets bored—" Gasping, Christina broke off speaking at seeing Trish and Jennifer standing beside the dining table with logs filling their arms.

Trish moved to the fireplace and deposited her armful neatly into the holder. She relieved Jennifer of the two small pieces she carried. "Jennifer, go tell everyone goodbye, then get washed up for dinner." Trish went along behind Jennifer and hugged each one as well. When she came to Aralyn she said, "Can you let Susan know we'll be over tomorrow afternoon to help decorate the tree? She asked me last night to pass it along to Christina and I forgot."

Christina waited until the three left and the door was shut before she latched the deadbolt and turned to Trish. "How much did you hear?"

"Enough." Trish wrapped Christina in her arms. "I agree with you. Let's enjoy the holidays and leave this discussion until after New Year's."

Christina's heart felt heavy. She didn't want to discuss anything. In her eyes, they had nothing to discuss. She needed to keep Trish here, safe, and as far away from Frank Webber and the creatures on the other side of the wall as she could.

Trish said, "Hey, no tears. We have an amazing life, an amazing daughter, and each other. Whatever happens, we're in this together." She bent her head forward and kissed her.

Together, Christina thought. Yes, being together was all that mattered.

For now.

TO BE CONTINUED IN
THE UNDERSTANDING
BOOK TWO OF THE ALPHA EVOLUTION SERIES

ACKNOWLEDGMENTS

A big thanks to my editors Rob Bignell, Kay Grey, and Jane Cuthbertson for the hard work and dedication you put into this manuscript.

Many thanks to my publisher Lori L. Lake. Because of the confidence and devotion you've given to me and my writing, I'm able to do what I love and share my stories with others.

ABOUT THE AUTHOR

Michele Coffman is an author who also moonlights as a Journeyman Plumber in the Kansas City, Missouri, area. She's an Army Veteran with fifteen years of service where she froze in Germany, sweated in Kuwait, unknowingly bedded down with a tarantula in Nicaragua, almost got bit by a poisonous snake in Ecuador, and even sought shelter from the noon rainstorms of Panama.

Michele has two wonderful children and is a proud grandmother of one incredible granddaughter. She is a passionate writer, has an untamable imagination, and enjoys writing sci-fi, conspiracy thrillers and – well, just about anything that strikes her fancy. You can find out more about Michele's work at her website: www.michelecoffman.com.

CPSIA information can be obtained
at www.ICGtesting.com
Printed in the USA
BVHW041251100222
628586BV00011B/756